DESTINY'S PATH

GOVANNON OF THE WOOD

ALLAN FREWIN JONES

Hodder
Children's
Books

A division of Hachette Children's Books

Copyright © 2009 Working Partners Limited

First published in the US in 2009 by HarperTeen,
an imprint of HarperCollins Publishers

First published in Great Britain in 2011
by Hodder Children's Books

1

A Catalogue record for this book is available from the British Library

ISBN 978 0 340 99939 4

Typeset in Caslon by Avon DataSet ltd,
Bidford on Avon, Warwickshire

Printed and bound in Great Britain by
CPI Bookmarque Ltd, Croydon, Surrey

The paper and board used in this paperback by Hodder Children's Books
are natural recyclable products made from wood grown in
sustainable forests. The manufacturing processes conform to the
environmental regulations of the country of origin.

Hodder Children's Books
a division of Hachette Children's Books
338 Euston Road, London NW1 3BH
An Hachette UK Company
www.hachette.co.uk

For Sydney Jatter

CHAPTER ONE

Branwen ap Griffith pulled back on the reins and her weary horse gradually came to a halt, snorting softly and shaking its mane. She swayed in the saddle, her long black hair cascading down the sides of her face. Her limbs trembled with fatigue, her whole body ached. Rhodri's horse went clopping on for another few paces through the trees before it, too, halted. The half-Saxon runaway looked back at her, his bright brown eyes sunken in his ashen face, his brow furrowed.

They had travelled far together, following the magical path of glittering light that had drawn Branwen from her home and from all that she held dear, leading her towards the High Destiny prophesied for her by Rhiannon of the Spring, the ancient Earth Spirit of the Land.

Rhiannon of the Shining Ones.

Branwen had fought long and fiercely against the ominous visions of the woman in white, struggling to free herself of the destiny that gaped like a dragon's maw in front of her, a destiny that threatened to swallow her entire life.

But the foretelling would not be denied. What was it the bard had sung to Branwen in Prince Llew's Great Hall? Sung to her alone:

> *The Old Gods are sleepless this night*
> *They watch and they wait*
> *For the land is in peril once more*
> *And the Shining Ones gather*
> *To choose a weapon, to save the land*
> *The Warrior*
> *The Sword of Destiny*
> *A worthy human to be their tool*
> *Child of the far-seeing eye*
> *Child of the strong limb*
> *Child of the fleet foot*
> *Child of the keen ear*

Such a weight to carry for a young girl who had seen only fifteen summers. To be the saviour of her land and of her people. To drive back the rising tide of bloodied Saxon iron. To be a warrior – a leader.

But Branwen had taken up the fearful burden and had followed Rhiannon's path. And for friendship's sake, Rhodri had come with her.

She was clad in the chain-mail jerkin and the dark-green cloak once worn by her brother Geraint. He no longer needed them – murdered by Saxons, his ashes blown away on the wind. His sword was at her hip, and his round wooden shield hung from the saddle, white with a rampant red dragon. The jerkin and cloak were flecked and stained with dried blood, the shield notched and dented from the blows of swords and axes. Marks that were the result of Branwen's fighting, not Geraint's. Dead too young, her brother had never met the Saxons in battle – had never grown to be the warrior he should have been.

Branwen and Rhodri had ridden through the starless gulf of the night, following the flickering silver path through dense forests and over ridge and bluff, spine and spur of the high hills. But with the passing of time, the mystical moonshine path had waned and its light had bled away into the ground, and Branwen's hope and faith had faded with it, replaced by frustration and growing anger.

She turned and gazed back the way they had come.

The distant ridges of the hills were now showing sharp and black against a streak of dreary grey light.

Dawn was coming.

A dawn empty of all magic.

Where was Rhiannon?

Branwen gritted her teeth, a cold fire burning in her heart at the capricious nature of the Old Gods. If the Shining Ones offered her no guidance – no clear path to her destiny – then why should she not simply turn back and fight the Saxons in her own way, on the familiar ground of Cyffin Tir?

Back there, her home was burning. Her father lay dead on the battlefield. The image of the battle-weary, grieving face of her mother, Lady Alis, forced its way into Branwen's mind. She could almost hear the words she had spoken as Rhiannon's path had unreeled itself into the night.

This is the Old Magic, Branwen. It is wild and pitiless. Do not follow this path, Branwen. It will devour you!

And she remembered her own reply.

It won't, because I'm part of it. The Shining Ones have chosen me. They brought me here. They helped save us. Let me go to them, Mama. I'm doing this of my own free will.

A fresh wave of anger and disillusionment broke over Branwen as she thought of all she had left behind. Rhodri had dismounted and was leading his horse back to Branwen.

'Who am I, Rhodri?' she demanded. 'Who do the Shining Ones think I am?'

'You are Princess Branwen, daughter of Prince

Griffith and Lady Alis of Cyffin Tir,' he replied, his face full of compassion as he gazed up at her. 'And you're exhausted and ready to drop. We should rest now. For a while at least.' He gave a faded smile. 'Can your destiny wait a little while longer, Branwen?'

'What destiny?' hissed Branwen, her head swimming. '*Whose* destiny?' She struggled to remain upright in the saddle as she threw her head back, using the last of her energy to shout into the night. 'Rhiannon! Where are you? What do you want of me?'

But the rugged hills and the shadowed forests made no reply.

'I will not go purposelessly into the west,' said Branwen. 'The shining path has vanished and Rhiannon hides herself from me!' Red anger flooded her mind. 'Even her winged messenger, Fain, has left us. I will not follow blindly,' she said bitterly. 'If this is all the Shining Ones offer, then I will turn my back on them!' A wave of absolute exhaustion struck her, making her lurch in the saddle. 'I'm going back, Rhodri,' she murmured. 'Back to my own people. That way lies hope for the future. That is the true path to my destiny . . .' A black fist closed around her mind and Branwen felt herself falling.

She was vaguely aware of strong arms around her and Rhodri's friendly voice in her ear.

'Let destiny go for now,' he said. 'You need rest and

you need food inside you. Just put your arm around my neck. Let's find you a soft spot to lie down on.'

She allowed herself to be carried, one muscular arm under her knees and another behind her back. Her head lolled on Rhodri's shoulder. She could hear his rasping breath as he lowered her to the ground.

She opened her eyes and found herself half lying under a massive old oak tree, its gnarled and twisted roots rising on either side of her like knuckled fingers. Her nostrils were filled with the smell of damp earth and rich mould.

'You wait here,' Rhodri said. 'I have something we both need.' Branwen watched him walk to where the two horses were standing. He led them to a tree and tethered their reins loosely to a low branch. He ungirdled the horses' saddles and drew them off, laying one on top of the other under the tree, then unwound a small sack from his saddle and came back with it hanging from his fist.

'What is it?' Branwen asked tiredly as he crouched at her side.

'Not much, but hopefully enough for our present needs,' said Rhodri. 'A hunk of bread and some cheese and a small flask of milk that I managed to purloin from the stores before the battle started. A wise precaution against hunger, if I do say so myself. Providing for an empty belly was a lesson hard-learned on the lean and hungry roads of Brython.'

Branwen smiled grimly. 'This is more than Rhiannon has given us,' she said.

'Ahh, well . . . *Rhiannon*,' murmured Rhodri, sitting cross-legged at her side and handing her a chunk of bread and a piece of ripe yellow cheese. He looked sideways at her. 'You aren't really turning back, are you?'

She shook her head. 'I don't know,' she said. 'But this is not what I expected when we followed the shining path. I imagined it would take us . . . I'm not sure . . . somewhere . . . *special*. A place where everything would be explained.' She narrowed her eyes. 'I should have known better. Rhiannon seems to delight in confusing me. Tormenting me with her riddles—' She dug the heels of her hands into her eyes, trying to shake off the lethargy that dragged at her limbs and clouded her mind.

She looked at Rhodri sitting quietly at her side, chewing bread, his tawny hair hanging in his eyes.

'What would you do?' she asked. 'If you were me?'

'I would eat and drink and sleep,' Rhodri replied. 'Maybe things will seem clearer then? Who knows?' He looked at her with deep sympathy in his eyes. 'I've never met anyone with a destiny before, Branwen. What do you think Rhiannon is playing at? Is this some kind of test?'

'Haven't I passed enough tests?' Branwen asked.

Surely she *had* done enough? She had heeded Rhiannon's terrible warning.

Your enemy comes creeping over the eastern hills even as we speak, cloaked in deception. Speed is your only ally now, Branwen. Fly as fast as you can, and you may still save many lives.

She had galloped her horse down the mountain like the west wind, desperate to thwart the Saxon plans to kill her mother and father and to burn the hill fort of Garth Milain. She had taken part in the battle that raged at the foot of the ancient mound. She had killed men. And then, despite her efforts, she had seen her father cut down and her home burning. The battle had been won – but at what cost!

Heed me, child. When the battle is done, for good or ill you must make your choice: to follow your destiny, or to turn for ever from it. But choose wisely – for your decision will seal the fate of thousands. This is my final foretelling.

And she had made that decision – leaving her grieving warrior mother standing proud but haggard on the charnel house of the battlefield; leaving her home, Garth Milain, in flames.

'Sleep,' Rhodri said gently, his hand on her shoulder.

She slid sideways and rested her head in his lap, feeling the soft touch of his hand on her hair as the dead weight of her fatigue finally dragged her into slumber.

CHAPTER TWO

Blood. Flames. Darkness. Screaming chaos.

Savage voices shouting in an unknown tongue.

Hel! Gastcwalu Hel!

Hetende Wotan!

Gehata! Tiw! Tiw!

Branwen's sword clashed against a thrusting spearpoint, knocking it aside. The whirl and *thunk* of axes rang in her ears. Around her, arrows fell, thudding into flesh. There was the hideous tearing crack of iron cleaving bone. A sword slashed down towards her neck, the agonizing impact knocking her to the ground as her blood spurted hot and high.

Branwen awoke with a jolt into a pale dawn. She knew she could not have been asleep for very long. It was that mysterious time halfway between night and day, the sun still hidden under the horizon.

She sat up, unwilling to fall back into her gruesome

dreams. Rhodri was leaning against the trunk of the old tree, his head drooping, his eyes closed. She hoped his dreams were sweeter than hers. She looked fondly at him, remembering their first meeting. She had been lost and alone in the fog-bound mountains. She had thought him a Saxon marauder and clouted him with a stick, only learning her mistake afterwards. He wasn't an enemy, but he had spent most of his life in Saxon captivity.

Branwen learned much later that Rhiannon of the Spring had engineered their meeting, and they met again, in the forest outside Doeth Palas, the fortress village of Prince Llew of Bras Mynydd. For some unexplained reason their fates were intertwined.

By all the saints, that seemed a whole lifetime away! But it was not – she and Rhodri had fled Doeth Palas only two nights past.

She rested back against the tree, gazing up into the branches, watching the shifting patterns of the leaves in the breeze, oil-black against the cloudy sky.

A small, almost inaudible scuttering caught her attention. Then she felt the kiss of a tiny motion on her hand, which was lying in the brown leaf-mould that gathered in heaps and drifts under the tree. Something had pattered with soft feet over her fingers. She tilted her head a little trying to see.

It was a mouse – a small grey mouse. Branwen smiled,

her heart lifted by the sight of the little beast as it nosed and ploughed its way through the rot and debris between her hand and her leg, its whiskers twitching, its eyes bright and black and shining.

The mouse scampered around her hand and dived under a gnarled root, vanishing with a whisk of its tail. Branwen lifted her hand, slowly, slowly – and took a piece of bread, crumbling it in her palm. She rested her hand, palm upwards close to the root.

'Come on, little one,' she whispered. 'Come and feed.'

She waited, listening to Rhodri's slow, deep breathing, her eyes on the dark gap under the root.

A grey nose appeared. Whiskers quivered. The mouse emerged, rising on to its haunches, sniffing the air. Could it smell the bread?

It moved closer, its body trembling. It lifted its forepaws up on to her hand, sniffing the breadcrumbs.

That's it. Eat your fill, my friend. Have no fear.

But to her disappointment the mouse turned and slipped away under the root again without eating.

You can trust me, little one. I won't harm you.

She heard furtive movements from beneath the root. More movement than could be explained by a single mouse. A family of mice perhaps?

She smiled with joy to see the mouse appear again. And, to her delight, the mouse was followed by five others, perfect little children, scuttling and tumbling over the rotting leaves as they followed their mother's lead.

Biting her lip, Branwen hardly dared breathe as the mother sprang on to her hand, leading the children to the food. Their feet tickled Branwen's skin as they gathered and fed in her bounteous palm.

Suddenly a shape came sweeping down from the sky, startling Branwen and making her heart jump. A browny-grey shape, gliding phantom-soft on widespread wings. She gasped and jerked her head back as it pounced. Then it was gone again – a mouse clutched in either claw.

The other mice fled.

'*No!*' Branwen howled in distress, her whole body contracting in a spasm of horror, her hands beating the ground as the owl glided away into the trees.

Rhodri woke with a start. 'Branwen? What?'

Branwen scrambled to her feet, running in pursuit of the grey predator.

She heard Rhodri chasing after her. He caught her arm and brought her to a halt.

'Branwen? What is it?' he asked.

'An owl took the baby mice,' Branwen cried. 'I gave them bread. They were on my hand.'

Rhodri stared at her. His voice was low and calm. 'Owls eat mice, Branwen,' he told her. 'It's what they do.'

She turned on him, angry for a moment. 'I know that,' she said. 'I'm not a fool!'

He paused before speaking. 'So why has it upset you so much?'

She held her palm out towards his face. 'They came because I offered them bread,' she said. 'They trusted me and the owl took them. It was my *fault*.'

His brows knitted. 'It's your fault that owls eat mice?' he said.

She glowered at him. 'No. But I tempted the mice into the open,' she said slowly. 'If I hadn't been there, they would still be alive.' She walked back to the tree, but couldn't bring herself to sit again beside that root.

She pointed down to where it lifted from the leaf-mould. 'Keep away from me if you wish to live,' she called.

'Branwen, stop,' said Rhodri. 'Try to sleep some more. Things will seem less bleak when the sun is up, I promise you.'

'I can't sleep,' said Branwen. She looked solemnly at him. 'Rhiannon told me I was the sword of destiny – the bright blade who would save the people of Brython from the Saxons.' Her voice rose. 'And yet I cannot keep even a handful of mice safe!'

Rhodri bit his lip, looking anxiously at her, but not speaking.

13

Branwen's shoulders slumped. 'Rhiannon was wrong,' she said. 'The Shining Ones chose badly.' She took a deep breath. 'Do you hear me, Rhiannon? You chose the wrong person! Choose again. Choose better next time!'

She turned and walked towards the horses. Rhodri snatched up the bag that still held the remnants of their food and drink.

'You want to ride on?' he asked. 'Without any real rest?'

'Ride, yes,' said Branwen. 'On? No!' She picked up her saddle and threw it over the horse's broad back.

Rhodri frowned at her. 'You're going back?'

'I am.' She stooped and fastened the saddle girth. 'Back home where I belong.' She stood up. 'I'm not the great leader the Shining Ones need,' she said. She pointed into the east. 'We took the Saxons unawares and threw them back for a time,' she said. 'But you know the truth better than I do. You were Ironfist's servant – how big is the Saxon army that is encamped outside Chester?'

'At least ten times the number that came against Garth Milain,' Rhodri said, his voice subdued. 'Maybe more.'

General Herewulf Ironfist was the King of Northumbria's strong right hand – the hammer with which the Saxons intended to smash Brython. Rhodri had learned of his plan to take Garth Milain by treachery shortly before he had escaped his long captivity. It was

Rhodri's warning that had prevented a massacre. But even forewarned, the battle had been close-fought, and dearly won.

'And what will be your ex-master's response to the defeat of the host he sent against us?' Branwen asked.

'He will be angry,' Rhodri said. 'He may decide to send five times the number against Cyffin Tir to make sure of a swift and complete victory.'

Branwen nodded as she climbed into the saddle. Her weariness was gone now – she felt renewed energy flowing through her, a new certainty. 'And if he comes, I will be where I *should* be – at my mother's side. Shoulder to shoulder. Blade by blade. Let Rhiannon find someone else to be saviour of Brython.'

Rhodri picked up his own saddle. 'Then I will come with you,' he said. 'Let the wrath of the Shining Ones fall upon both our heads, if it must be so.'

'No,' said Branwen. 'Your home lies in the west. You have no mission in the east and I won't let you put yourself in danger because of me.'

'You rescued me from torture and certain death in Doeth Palas,' said Rhodri. 'And I should repay you by scurrying off into the west while you ride eastwards? I think not!'

'You're a fool then.'

'Perhaps,' said Rhodri. 'But a grateful and faithful fool,

I hope, and one who will never desert you.' He bent to tie the saddle girth under his horse. 'And I ride with you knowing that we will probably be killed at journey's end. Killed quickly if I'm lucky, because if Ironfist captures me alive . . .' The sentence was not finished. His face appeared over his horse's back. 'Escaped servants are dealt with most harshly if recaptured,' he said. 'I have seen it once and have no wish to see it again – especially not with myself as the victim. The Saxons have cruel and slow ways of punishing those who seek to defy them.'

'Then you're twice the fool,' Branwen said with a wry smile. 'Come then – saddle up. I'd be home again as soon as possible.' She looked around, feeling as though inhuman eyes might be watching her from the shadows under the trees.

Had Rhiannon really departed, or was she merely standing back, watching with those terrible ice-blue eyes, waiting cat-like for Branwen to make a wrong move?

Rhodri had once said: *How do you run away from a goddess? Where can you hide?* Branwen had no answer to those questions, but the sooner she was down off the mountains and out of the forest, the safer she would feel. And the thought of being once more with her mother was like a bright guiding light in the front of her mind. To the east then – to Garth Milain and whatever else fate and the Saxon menace had in store for her.

Branwen watched as Rhodri clambered awkwardly into the saddle, then they both turned towards the brightening dawn. The light was grey and grainy still, but it was slowly climbing the sky and snuffing out the stars, and a hint of dusky green was colouring the forested hills that tumbled before them.

Branwen clicked her tongue and nudged her heels into her horse's flanks. Rhodri followed dutifully behind as they rode into a wide clearing.

They had not gone more than a few paces across the open ground when a sudden gust of wind came swirling out of the west, lifting Branwen's hair and whipping it about her face.

She turned, eyes narrowed against the wind. It came hissing through the trees, fluttering the leaves, bending the branches.

'It seems the very air is intent on helping us on our way,' said Rhodri, his hair flying, his clothes flapping. 'A good omen perhaps?'

'But do you feel it?' Branwen called to him. 'It's strange. It isn't cold.'

It was not. It came dashing through the trees, as warm as blood and as relentless as a racing tide. The wind grew in intensity, filling the forest with creaking and rustling and groaning as the boughs of the trees were twisted and wrenched, their leaves quivering with a shrill sound like the swarming of bees.

It flung itself in among the rusted leaves of past autumns, sending the litter of the forest floor whirling into the air so that Branwen and Rhodri had to cover their faces with their arms for fear of being blinded by the flying debris.

The horses snorted and whickered, their manes and tails torn by the wind, their eyes rolling in fear. It was all Branwen could do to keep her seat as the wind – scorching now – buffeted her and slapped her face with its hot hands. Her shield was torn from the saddle, and went bowling across the forest floor.

Above her, shredded clouds running across the sky; below her the ground seethed in racing turmoil. And then, suddenly, the forest vibrated to a deep, reverberating howl.

Branwen clung on grimly as the wind sought to tear her from her horse's back. She knew now that this was nothing natural. This was no wind of the world – this was something *other*. A warning, a lesson – a punishment! Beside her, Rhodri was hunched over in his saddle, his horse staggering.

Blindly, Branwen reached for her sword, drawing it and brandishing it defiantly in the air.

'I . . . do . . . not . . . fear . . . you!' she shouted, the wind throwing her words back into her throat. 'Do your ... worst! I *will* ... go ... home ...!' The maniacal wind dropped as suddenly as it had risen. The swirl and storm of dead leaves ebbed and fell away around them and all became suddenly silent.

It was as if the forest and the mountains and the sky and the very ground beneath her feet were suddenly poised and listening.

Waiting.

Rhodri lifted his head, his mouth open, gasping.

'Is that all you have?' shouted Branwen, turning in the saddle, staring defiantly into the west and waving her sword above her head. 'Is this what I should fear?'

'*Branwen!*' Rhodri's voice was urgent, ringing with alarm.

She turned to follow the line of his eyes.

The rushing air was thronged with attacking owls.

CHAPTER THREE

Before Branwen could react, the leading bird struck her, its brown wings wider than the span of her arms, its golden eyes circular and luminous and deadly. A tawny wing hit her hard in the face. Claws raked at her sword hand, drawing blood. She snatched her arm away, her sword falling from her fingers.

She reeled in the saddle, aware of Rhodri shouting behind her. A second owl came at her, its sharp beak open, its claws stretching forward.

The other owls descended on them, twenty or more in number, almost overwhelming them. Great owls were all around Branwen, circling, swooping, floating on the air, silent as ghosts. Wings struck her from all sides. Claws tore at her clothes and tangled in her hair.

Her horse reared up, neighing in fear and pawing the air. She tumbled backwards out of the saddle, striking the ground with bone-jarring force, the breath beaten out of her.

As she struggled to rise, she saw Rhodri vanish in a maelstrom of battering wings. Still the owls came plunging and plummeting down upon her, claws grabbing her clothes, ripping her hair, giving her no chance to get to her feet.

'Stop! Stop!' she cried, striking out with her fists. But there were too many of them for her to fight. She huddled on the ground, her arms up to protect her face. The world was all owls. Silent and terrible and huge.

She was completely blinded by the bodies and wings of the mobbing birds. Through the clamour of their attack, she heard hoofbeats fading rapidly away. Her horse – fleeing in fear. Next she heard Rhodri's horse – also galloping away! Was Rhodri leaving her? Escaping from the talons and the ripping beaks? If only she could see! If only the birds would give her a moment's respite!

She was startled by the feel of a hand on her arm. Rhodri! He was down on hands and knees, his head down to protect his eyes from the chaos of the wheeling birds.

And then, quite suddenly, the owls drew off, leaving Branwen and Rhodri huddled together on the ground, gasping for breath.

The owls rose into the sky, their eyes glowing as they circled the small clearing, as though they were confident in the weakness of their prey and content now simply to patrol – to keep Branwen and Rhodri pinned down in a deadly ring of claws and knife-sharp beaks and pummelling wings.

Gathering her wits, Branwen moved her hand cautiously towards her slingshot. Her sword had fallen out of reach, and she was sure the birds would not allow her to make a grab for it. Perhaps if she flung to show she was capable of fighting back, they might hold off long enough for her and Rhodri to run for shelter under the trees.

She ducked as an owl swept close over her head.

Branwen loosened the pouch from her belt and picked out a stone. She kept low, bent over to hide her movements, bobbing her head every time one of the birds plunged towards her.

'Are you hurt?' Rhodri gasped, crouching low to the ground.

'No. Just a scratch on my hand.'

'I'm not hurt either, but they could have caused much harm. Branwen – why are they doing this to us?'

'I don't know. I'm going to sling a stone at the largest one – I think it may be their leader. When I hit it, run to the trees if you can.'

'Aim well, Branwen,' warned Rhodri. 'If you fight back and anger them, you had better prove you can hurt them, otherwise I don't hold out much hope for our survival!'

'I won't miss!' Branwen said confidently. She was ready. The knuckle of stone was nestling in the fold of the slingshot.

A wing grazed her shoulder.

Now!

She rose, whirling the slingshot around her head. An owl flew at her face. She flipped her fingers open and the stone sped straight and true at the owl that had first attacked her.

The stone struck the bird high on the wing. It gave a fearsome screech as it faltered in the air, then spiralled downwards. Branwen dived to the ground as several owls came for her. Through the cage of her fingers, she saw the wounded owl tumble heavily down under the trees into a dense pile of leaf-litter. Its wings flapped, then the bird became still.

Branwen lay face down on the ground, hoping she had given Rhodri time to escape. She was certain the owls would not let her go – not after she had injured their leader.

It was strange – there was the flurry of wings all around her, but still she felt no claw or beak. Why were the owls not ripping at her?

And then, only moments after the fallen owl stopped moving, the rest of the flock drew off, rising into the air and speeding away over the trees. Branwen heard their faint, eerie hooting as they departed.

Gasping, she pulled herself on to her knees and dragged a hank of hair off her face, staring all around. The owls were gone.

She got to her feet. Rhodri had stopped halfway to the trees. He walked back to her, gazing uncomprehendingly around.

'You did it,' he said, his eyes wide. 'You drove them off.'

'I think I killed their leader,' said Branwen, pointing to the heap of leaves that lay at the foot of an ancient wrinkled oak tree. 'I wish I had not needed to do that. It was a magnificent creature and it did me little harm.'

'Magnificent, maybe,' Rhodri pointed out. 'But did you see the size of its claws?'

'I did,' said Branwen, sucking at her bloodied hand. The wounds were not deep or painful – she had suffered worse injury in her childhood adventures in the forests. 'I was only cut once – to force me to drop my sword. It is very strange. I don't understand it.' She looked into the sky. 'And why did the others fly away like that?'

'I have no idea,' said Rhodri. 'And there is something else I do not understand.' He pointed under the trees. Their two horses were standing in the shadows, calmly waiting as though the owl attack had never happened.

'This is not natural,' Branwen said. 'None of this is natural – but I do not know what it means.' A movement caught her attention – the slightest of tremors in the pile of leaves where the owl lay hidden.

Could it be alive?

'Rhodri, you have some healing powers,' Branwen said. 'I think the owl may not be dead.'

They ran across the clearing.

Rhodri reached the mound of dead leaves first. He stooped, carefully sifting through the leaves with his fingers.

'It must be buried deeply,' he murmured, raking more leaves aside.

'Be careful!'

A sudden burst of movement erupted from beneath the leaves, as though the injured bird was thrashing about in agony. Rhodri jerked back, startled.

'I cannot see it!' he gasped. He reached down again.

A slender arm shot up out of the leaves and a narrow, long-nailed hand caught his wrist in a fierce grip. Rhodri gave a shout of shock and alarm as he struggled to get free of the hand, digging in with his heels and heaving backwards.

A form rose out of the leaf-mound. Not a bird – but a slim-bodied girl of about Branwen's age.

With a yell, Rhodri finally managed to get his arm free. He fell backwards, hands and feet scrabbling on the ground to get away.

Branwen too took a step back, her fingers groping for a stone to fit into her slingshot, her eyes fixed on the girl.

She was shorter than Branwen by a full head, her thin body clad in a dappled brown garment that left her arms and legs bare. Her skin was the colour of toasted wheat, and the long curved nails of her hands were as white as stone.

But it was her face that held Branwen's attention. It was round and wide-cheeked, framed by a feathered fall of dark-brown hair and centred by huge amber eyes, lustrous and deep under sweeping brows. A beautiful face, but one filled with fury and pain.

One hand came up to a small wound on her upper arm.

An impossible suspicion dawned in Branwen's mind. The owl that she had hit with the stone was nowhere to be seen – and in its place was this strange girl – a girl with an injury on her arm! 'Could it be . . . ?'

The girl's blood threaded down, dark as pitch. Her wide mouth opened and she let out an inhuman, high-pitched scream.

Rhodri scrambled to his feet, keeping well away from

the strange girl, moving to be close to Branwen.

The girl's mouth snapped closed. She lowered her head and stared balefully at them, her eyes burning like molten gold, her whole body trembling.

Branwen's mouth was dry. She swallowed hard. There was something frightful about the glaring girl – something feral. But she had confronted the supernatural before, and she was resolved to show no fear to this uncanny stranger.

'I am Branwen ap Griffiths,' she said. 'My companion's name is Rhodri. Will you give us your name?'

The girl's throat moved and she opened her mouth as if she was trying to speak. But for a few moments only harsh, croaking sounds came from her.

'Don't be afraid,' said Branwen. 'We mean you no harm.'

The girl coughed, her hand to her throat.

'You're hurt,' Rhodri said. 'I can tend your wound if you will let me.'

He took a tentative step towards the girl. She fixed her huge owl eyes on him, her lips drawing back in a snarl, one hand still at her wounded shoulder, but the other hand lifting like a claw.

Branwen watched her closely, seeing the blood that spun down from her injury, seeing the dangerous, predatory shine of her golden eyes.

'Rhodri, be wary,' she said quietly. 'Don't you see what she is?'

Rhodri glanced back at her. 'What do you mean?'

'She is the owl I hit with my slingshot,' said Branwen, hardly able to believe what she was saying – but knowing that it was true.

Rhodri halted in his tracks, staring at Branwen. 'What do you mean? She can't be. Look at her – she's human.'

The girl finally found her voice. 'Not . . . human . . .' she croaked in a weird, throaty tone. 'Not human . . . but cursed to appear so.' She coughed again. 'My name . . . is Blodwedd.' Her uncanny gaze switched to Branwen. 'You have injured me,' she cried, stepping forwards with the claw of her hand lifted towards Branwen's face. 'You shall pay dearly for causing harm to the messenger of the Shining Ones! You shall pay with your eyes!'

CHAPTER FOUR

'Stop that now!' shouted Rhodri, stepping between Branwen and the enraged girl. 'Enough violence!'

Blodwedd halted, trembling and glowering. She was so small – the top of her head hardly came as high as Rhodri's shoulder, but Branwen sensed a strength in her.

'Were you sent by Rhiannon?' asked Branwen, moving to one side, her slingshot ready.

'Not *her*,' said Blodwedd, her voice less ragged now, its tone lower and deeper. 'Brother to *her* – brother of the woods. My Lord Govannon.'

Govannon of the Wood. Branwen remembered the bard's song:

I sing of Rhiannon of the Spring
The ageless water goddess, earth-mother, storm-calmer
Of Govannon of the Wood

He of the twelve-points
Stag-man of the deep forest, wise and deadly
Of Merion of the Stones
Mountain crone, cave-dweller, oracle and deceiver
And of Caradoc of the North Wind
Wild and free and dangerous and full of treachery

Branwen's eyes narrowed. 'What do you want of me?' she asked.

'I was sent to be your eyes and ears on your long journey,' said the girl.

'But . . . were you one of the owls that attacked us?' Branwen asked. 'Are you a sorceress – able to change at will into the form of an owl?'

Loss and grief and pain filled Blodwedd's face. 'Govannon called me to him,' she said, almost as if speaking to herself. 'He said, I have a great duty for you to perform, Blodwedd of the Far-seeing Eye. You must find the Warrior Child, you must speak with her, guide her – she is lost and wandering in mind, spirit and body.' She flashed Branwen an angry look. 'She will not understand your speech, he said to me – she has not the skill. You must shed your coat of downy feathers. You must forfeit the wide fields of the evening sky. You must become . . . like *her*.'

'You were a bird,' gasped Rhodri. 'Govannon

made you into a human?'

The golden eyes fixed on him. 'No,' she said. 'Lord Govannon gave me the ugly, spindly, naked body of a human to wear for a *time* – he did not make me human. It is but a cage.' She gazed up over the treetops. 'When my duty is done my wings will be returned to me.'

Branwen eyed her uneasily. 'So I didn't . . . when I shot you – *I* didn't turn you human somehow?'

'Dullard!' hissed Blodwedd. 'What power do you have over such things?' She winced and clutched her arm. 'I am in pain.'

'You attacked us!' said Branwen. 'I was defending myself.'

'You were riding east,' said Blodwedd. 'You have no business in the east. I gathered my brothers and my sisters to stop you.' She looked past Branwen to where the sword still lay on the ground. 'I tore your skin to rid you of your weapon,' she said. 'What other injury did I do you that you should set sharp stone to my flesh?'

'I thought you were going to kill us,' said Branwen.

'No, not kill. Awaken!' said Blodwedd. 'Lord Govannon said to me, the Warrior Child is wilful and wayward – stubborn as tree roots, fickle as thistledown on the wind. She must be taught to follow the straight path and to heed the call of her destiny.'

Branwen trembled with anger, her fists clenching, the muscles tightening in her chest. 'Go back to your master and tell him he can send all the winds of the world down on me – he can set wolves on me if he wishes – I will not do what he wants me to do. Let him kill me if he can – but I will die on the homeward path.'

Blodwedd frowned. 'Stubborn as tree roots indeed!' she said. 'You do not listen! I cannot give your message to Lord Govannon. I cannot return to the Great One until my duty is done, Warrior Child. Until your destiny is fulfilled. That is *my* doom!'

'Then I pity you,' said Branwen. 'You had best learn to love your human shape, Blodwedd – because your master has given you a task that you will never fulfil.' She turned and walked away, stooping to pick up her sword. She would retrieve the two horses and continue her journey east.

'Rhodri?' she called back. 'Are you coming?'

'Wait,' called Rhodri.

Branwen paused, turning to look at him.

'She's hurt,' Rhodri said mildly. 'Let me tend her wound. It could fester and go bad. It won't take long.'

'As you please,' Branwen said grudgingly.

Rhodri turned to Blodwedd. 'Will you let me help you?' he asked. 'I can take the pain away.'

Blodwedd stared at him for a long while, her unhuman

eyes round and full of light. She nodded.

'Stay there, please,' Rhodri urged her. 'I won't be long.'

He walked quickly to where Branwen was standing. He stood in front of her, looking unspeakingly into her face.

'What?' she snapped, irked by his silence.

'It seems to be *my* destiny to be for ever tending the wounds that you cause,' he said without reproach.

He didn't need to explain further. She knew what he meant. First his own leg, cut open in the fall she had caused by hitting him with a tree branch. Then the falcon Fain, injured by a stone in the forest outside Doeth Palas. And now this owl-girl.

'Will you fetch herbs for me to make a poultice?' Rhodri asked.

'I will,' Branwen said. 'Watch the horses while I am gone.' She glanced at Blodwedd. 'Don't let her scare them away. And don't trust her.'

'Look for comfrey and wormwood,' said Rhodri. 'Lobelia is also good, if you can find it. Oh, and mullein. Do you know it?'

Branwen nodded. 'A tall-stemmed herb with leaves covered in hairs,' she said. 'It has yellow flowers with five petals.'

Rhodri smiled. 'You make a fine herbalist's assistant,' he said.

'My brother taught me much woodcraft before ...'
She set her jaw. 'I will not be long,' she said. 'Watch her!'

She headed into the trees. The sooner she returned with the things Rhodri needed, the sooner he could deal with Govannon's messenger and the sooner they could be on their way again.

It took Branwen longer than she wanted to gather the plants Rhodri had asked for, and the sun was two hand's-breadths above the eastern horizon when she finally came running back to the clearing with her hands full of leaves and flowers.

She had half feared finding Rhodri sprawled on the ground with his face raked by claws, the owl-girl and the horses gone.

Instead, Blodwedd sat cross-legged in the middle of the clearing, gazing up wide-eyed and smiling at Rhodri, who was leaping around in front of her, waving his arms and clearly telling an exciting tale.

'A Saxon warrior was coming at us, bellowing like an angry bear,' Rhodri was saying with high animation. '"*Gehata! Bana Hel!*" he shouted, which more or less means "You're my enemy and I will kill you and send you to the kingdom of the dead!" He had a sword as long as a roof beam, and I didn't have so much as a stick to defend myself with! "Get behind me," Branwen shouted and, I

34

can tell you, I did just that! Then Branwen and Lady Alis stood side by side on the hill. And Lady Alis called out, "Death to the Saxons! Let us strike as one, my daughter!" ' Rhodri slapped his hands together. 'And in the blink of an eye, that Saxon devil's head was rolling down the hillside like an apple from the branch!'

Blodwedd laughed. 'Ha! That is a good tale! And did you feast on his flesh thereafter?'

For a moment, Rhodri stared at her with his mouth half open. Then he blinked at her, swallowing hard. 'Uh . . . *no* . . .' he replied, his forehead wrinkling in distaste. 'We don't do that.'

'The Saxon had an axe, not a sword,' said Branwen flatly, finding herself rather disturbed by Rhodri's friendly behaviour towards the owl-girl. She walked up to him and thrust the leaves and flowers into his hands. 'And my mother said, "Strike as one! The throat! Strike as one!" ' She glanced at Blodwedd, whose smile had vanished. 'The rest is as Rhodri told you.' She looked at him. 'Where are the horses?'

'Perfectly safe and very close by,' said Rhodri, his face a little red, although Branwen could not tell whether the colouring was from the exertions of his recent playacting or from embarrassment at being caught entertaining the weird owl-girl. 'I found a small stream with fresh grass growing beside it. They will be comfortable there . . . till we are ready to leave.'

'And how soon will that be?' Branwen asked.

'Soon,' said Rhodri, giving her a slightly uneasy smile. 'You did well,' he said, looking at the spoils of her long search. 'You even found lobelia. Splendid. All I need now is water and a couple of flat pounding stones.' He looked at Branwen. 'I have been telling Blodwedd about the battle at Garth Milain.'

'So I heard,' Branwen said drily. She pointed at Blodwedd, keenly aware of the poisonous looks the owl-girl was giving her. 'You know what she is!' she said, not caring that the girl could hear her. 'You know why she was sent here! Tend her wound, by all means – but then we're going to leave her here and go to my mother, whether her *master* likes it or not.'

Blodwedd got to her feet. 'You must not go east,' she said. 'Your destiny lies elsewhere – in the place where the Saxon hawks circle above the house of the singing gulls.'

'My destiny lies where I choose,' said Branwen. 'Come, Rhodri. Lead me to the stream. Work your skills on her – then we two shall return to Cyffin Tir.' She looked at Blodwedd. 'And you will not follow us!'

'I must,' said Blodwedd.

'Try, and you will regret it,' said Branwen, her hand moving to the hilt of her sword.

'What will you do?' Rhodri asked gently. 'Kill her?

This is not her fault, Branwen – you heard what she said. Blame Govannon if you need to blame anyone.'

'Where is the stream?' Branwen asked dismissively.

'This way,' Rhodri said, his voice subdued. 'Blodwedd, come with us. I want to wash the wound first.'

The stream was not far away. It ran through a narrow stony gully, splashing cold over stones and mossy ridges. And as Rhodri had said, the two horses were close by, their reins held under a large stone, their heads down as they grazed.

Rhodri got the owl-girl to squat at the side of the tumbling stream while he wetted some of the broad comfrey leaves and gently dabbed with them at the small wound in her shoulder.

'Good, good,' he murmured, wiping the dried blood off her dark skin. 'It's not as bad as I feared – and the wound is clean.' He began to shred the plants, wetting them in the stream and laying them on a flat grey stone. 'This is wormwood,' he told her, holding up the fern-like leaves with their haze of fine white hair. 'It will prevent the wound from becoming inflamed. And this,' he showed her the spiral leaves on the long stem, 'this is mullein for the pain.'

Branwen stood behind him, prepared to help if asked, but unwilling to volunteer. A strange anger grew like a fist tightening in her stomach as she listened to Rhodri explaining the uses of the herbs to the owl-girl.

Why was Rhodri speaking to her as if she was a chance companion met upon the way? She was no such thing. She was a creature of the Old Gods. She wasn't even human!

I have half a mind to draw my sword and swipe her head off as a warning to the Shining Ones to leave me be!

She eyed Blodwedd uncertainly. The owl-girl looked smaller than ever now, her slim legs folded up under her as she watched Rhodri pound the herbs and grind them to paste.

She looks more like a frog than an owl! A scrawny little frog squatting on a rock. Why is Rhodri taking so long?

'I need something to bind the poultice to your arm,' Rhodri said. 'I would rip a length of cloth from my clothes, but they're so ragged I'd be concerned they'd fall to pieces.'

Branwen felt a pang – he had said something very similar to her on their first meeting. She had torn the hem of her riding gown for him to bind the wound in his leg.

Not this time. Not for her!

Rhodri's head turned towards her. 'Branwen? Do we have anything that we could use as a bandage?'

You're not getting a piece of my clothing!

'The bag you brought the food in perhaps,' she said.

'Do you want me to tear a length off?'

'Please.'

She stepped over the stones to the grassy place where the horses were grazing and retrieved the bag. Ripping a length from the mouth of the bag, she brought it back.

'Perfect,' said Rhodri, taking it from her. He smiled at Blodwedd, his voice soft and coaxing. 'It will feel cold and a little strange, but the pain will soon fade. I shall try not to bind it too tightly. You must tell me if it feels uncomfortable. Hold your arm out now.'

Looking straight into his face, Blodwedd stretched out her arm. He leaned close to her. Scooping up the green paste in his fingers, he began very gently to press it against the wound. Spirals of green water ran down under her arm.

'It is cold,' she murmured.

'I told you it would be. Now I'll tie the cloth around it. Say if it's too tight.'

A hot anger erupted in Branwen.

'Are you finished?' she asked. 'I'm leaving now – the day is wasting away while we linger here.'

'Almost done,' Rhodri answered.

Blodwedd turned her uncanny eyes on to Branwen. 'You must continue west. Your home is safe, Warrior Child.'

39

'How do you know that?' Branwen spat.

'Lord Govannon has seen it,' Blodwedd replied. 'The Saxons will not ride upon the hill of fierce warriors – their wrath will fall elsewhere.'

'I do not believe you,' Branwen said. 'You would say anything to make me do what you wish.'

'I have no wishes,' said Blodwedd. 'And I cannot speak falsehoods. Lord Govannon sent me to tell only truths.'

'And I am to trust these *truths* you tell?' asked Branwen. 'No! Say nothing more to me – I will not listen. Rhodri – I'm going to ready the horses.' She looked hard at Blodwedd. 'Can you run as fast as you once flew?' she asked. 'Because if not, you will have a hard time keeping up with us.'

She turned and walked up the rocky hill, heading back towards the horses. 'Do as you please – follow or not. I do not care. I am done with you!'

There was a soft sound behind her – or rather, two sounds: a thud followed closely by a dull groan.

Branwen spun around. Blodwedd was running fast up the hill towards her, a rock clasped in one hand, her face ferocious, her eyes ablaze. Behind her, Rhodri was slumped on his side by the stream.

Branwen's fingers went instinctively to her slingshot, but Blodwedd was too swift for her. The owl-girl pounced on Branwen, the rock raised in her fist ready to beat down on her head. Stumbling backwards over the uneven terrain, Branwen grabbed at Blodwedd's raised arm, gripping her wrist.

But she was so strong! It was all Branwen could do to hold her off.

They fell, Blodwedd on top, her lips drawn back in a fierce snarl, her teeth sharp and white.

Using all her strength, Branwen forced Blodwedd's arm sideways, jerking it down so that the back of her hand cracked against a rock.

Blodwedd hissed with pain as the stone was knocked from her fingers. Branwen lurched, trying to throw her off. But Blodwedd wrested her arm free, forcing her legs up so that she was sitting astride Branwen's chest, her knees pinning Branwen's arms with a strength that seemed almost impossible in so slight a frame.

Blodwedd's claw-thin hands grasped either side of Branwen's head, holding her in an unbreakable grip. The owl-girl reared up over her, bringing her head down, their faces so close that their noses almost touched.

'Stubborn and wilful!' Blodwedd hissed. 'But you will listen! You will look!'

Branwen fought desperately to get free, wrenching her head from side to side in the vice-like grip of the owl-girl's hands. But she could not get free.

'Look into my eyes!' shouted Blodwedd, her breath

hot on Branwen's face. 'See! See what is to come!'

And against her will, Branwen found herself staring into those two radiant eyes, and as she looked, the unearthly eyes grew and deepened until the whole world was drawn into them and Branwen lost herself in a blazing golden light.

CHAPTER FIVE

Branwen was flying. Above her the wide sky went on for ever. Below her, dark forested mountains wheeled slowly away, cut by canyons and chasms, threaded by racing rivers and falls, punctuated by jutting peaks and crests and pinnacles of stone.

She turned toward the rising sun. Instinctively, she tried to draw her gaze away from that shimmering white light, but could not. Then she found she could look into the sun – into its very burning heart and be neither dazzled nor blinded.

The mountains fell away beneath her, descending into foothills cloaked in oak and ash and elm. She swooped down, following the plunge of the land. Ahead, a rugged, wild countryside stretched away in heaths and moorlands into a distant landscape of cliffs and bluffs and hazy blue distances.

She knew what she was seeing. She was flying over her

homeland – over the long, narrow cantref of Cyffin Tir. There, in the east where the horizon blurred, lay the Saxon stronghold of Chester – no more than a dark smudge on the very edge of sight.

Herewulf Ironfist was camped there with his army; a Saxon serpent preparing to uncoil and fall upon the ancient kingdom of Powys, iron fangs filled with venom.

The ground rushed up. Smoke was rising, thin and pale in the morning light. A tumulus thrust up out of the flat grasslands – the lone hump of a hill with a blackened crown burning on its brow.

Centuries upon centuries ago – so long ago that Branwen could not hold the span of years in her mind – ancient peoples had laboured to build that lonely mound. The ground occasionally offered up curious treasures. Flints cut into arrowheads, delicate as dragonfly-wings, sharp as thorns. Rounded stones etched with strange markings. Beads of green or blue or yellow. Puzzling glimpses of a people who had lived once on this land, who had built the hill that became the fortified village of Garth Milain.

But the lofty citadel was no more – its tall fence of wooden stakes burned and broken, its huts and houses destroyed. Even the Great Hall with its high walls of seasoned timber and its long, thatched roof was now no more than a smouldering, broken-backed hulk.

People were coming and going along the steep ramp that led to the hilltop. Salvaging what goods they could from the ruin, bringing down the bodies of the dead. And even from such a height, Branwen could see her mother, striding through the mayhem of the battle's aftermath, striving to bring order to the chaos, marshalling her warriors, organizing the burial of the dead. Preparing what defences she could against further attack.

Tears fell from Branwen's eyes, spinning down, shining like jewels in the treacherous sunlight.

But she was not allowed to linger over her heartbreak. She flew onwards into the east, passing beyond the bounds of her homeland, winging into the dark land of Mercia where the Saxons held sway. And now she saw wonders and horrors!

The town of Chester sprawled beneath her, teeming with people. Far more people than lived in Garth Milain, more even than dwelt in the great hill fort of Doeth Palas, largest of the fortified villages in the Kingdom of Powys. The people swarmed like ants among the houses, forging iron for swords and axes, training horses for battle, baking bread to fill the bellies of their savage warriors.

There, like a black stain on the land, she saw the great encampment of Horsa Herewulf Ironfist, the bane of Brython, the hammer of the east.

She dreaded seeing Saxon warriors pouring westwards

from the palisaded camp – new forces sent to annihilate what was left of the army of Cyffin Tir. But the way west was clear of movement. Branwen gave a gasp of relief – Ironfist was not sending a second force to crush her homeland. Instead, a long line of soldiers and horsemen were wending their way north-west, their spearheads and axes and helmets glinting cold in the morning light.

You see? A low, husky voice whispered close to her ear. The owl-girl's voice. *They come not to grind Garth Milain under their heel. They have other purposes. And see now what they intend! See what fate awaits those upon whom you would turn your back.*

The world spun like a golden wheel and Branwen found herself standing on a rocky seashore, a shrill north wind smarting in her eyes, a sickly, horrible smell in her nostrils. She stood among a host of fallen warriors. She winced at the sight of bloodied faces and hewn limbs, of butchered men and horses, of cracked shields and dented helmets and shattered swords. A young man, eyes wide and empty, stared into the sky, blood matted thick in his hair.

A slaughter had taken place here. And she could see from the emblems on the shields and from the tattered remnants of once-proud banners, that these were – that they *had been* – men of Powys.

She smelled smoke, and turned. A fortress lay on a

cliff overlooking the pounding sea. There was a high wall of dry-laid stone, ash-grey in the pitiless sunlight. Its gates were broken apart. Fire raged in the open heart of the fortress, consuming the thatched roofs of hut and hall, blackening the timbers, flooding the sky with thick dark smoke. Saxon pennants flew in the wind. Saxon ships clove the sea.

A black-bearded Saxon chieftain sat in the saddle of a great black stallion, his arm raised, a grisly trophy hanging from his fingers.

A severed head.

Branwen tried to look away, wanting rid of this abominable vision! But against her will she was drawn closer and she found her eyes would not close.

The Saxon fist clutched the head by its light brown hair, clotted with blood.

Branwen's mind fought to deny what she was seeing – to break the dreadful power of the images searing her mind.

She knew that face – the blank dead eyes that had once flashed with wit and intelligence. The slender, handsome face, now bruised and beaten, the hanging jaw where a knowing smile had once played.

It was Iwan ap Madoc, from the court of Prince Llew. A charming, intriguing but untrustworthy young man Branwen had met in Doeth Palas.

Iwan's lifeless eyes turned to her and an eerie light came into them.

The dead lips moved. 'So here you are at last, Branwen.' The voice was Iwan's, but it was toneless, hollow, dead. 'You have arrived too late, as you can see – the west is lost. You cheated your destiny well, my friend – the war is played out and the Saxons are in the ascendancy. All is done.' The voice sighed like the sea. 'All . . . is . . . done . . .'

'No!' Branwen shouted. 'I never wanted this! I didn't know! Forgive me, Iwan – I didn't know!'

But Iwan's face was lost in a vortex of golden light.

CHAPTER SIX

The wheel of burning light divided and pulled back and suddenly Branwen was staring up into Blodwedd's two golden eyes. She felt the owl-girl's weight on her chest, stifling her breathing – the sharp points of her knees on her arms and the cruel grip of her hands on either side of her face.

'Get off me!' Branwen heaved and Blodwedd sprang away, bounding feather-light up on to a boulder. She crouched there, watching Branwen through the curtain of her hair, her fingers gripping the boulder's edge like claws.

Branwen struggled to stand. She manged to get to her knees, but a wave of dizziness pinned her there. She knelt, panting, waiting for her head to stop spinning.

'What did you do to me?' she shouted as the world slithered and writhed around her.

'I showed you the future that will be forged if you

forswear your true calling,' said Blodwedd. She angled her mouth in a sharp grin. 'Did you like what you saw?'

'Lies!' shouted Branwen, pulling herself upright again. 'It was all lies!'

A look of disdain crossed Blodwedd's face. 'I do not lie,' she said. 'I fly. I hunt. I eat. I watch. I sleep. I do not lie.'

Suddenly Branwen remembered Rhodri. She stared down towards the stream. He was sitting up, leaning heavily on one arm, rubbing his head with his other hand.

'Why did you hit him?' raged Branwen. 'He was trying to *help* you!'

'I like him, he has an open and kindly heart,' Blodwedd said, looking down at Rhodri. 'That is why I only hit him gently.'

'You didn't need to hit him at all!'

'He would have tried to stop me,' Blodwedd said with a shrug of her thin shoulders. 'You needed to see what a threadbare cloth your selfishness would weave. Warp and weft – blood and death.' She cocked her head, her eyes on Branwen again. 'If you go to the east, you will shape for yourself a necklace of corpses that will bow your head down to the bowels of Annwn!'

'Be silent!' Branwen shouted. 'I won't listen to you any more.' She ran unsteadily down the hill. 'Rhodri? Rhodri, are you all right?'

He was on his feet now, grimacing and holding his head. 'She hit me!' he gasped. 'I turned away for a moment and she hit me.'

Blodwedd came racing down the hill, her feet as light as a breeze as she leaped from rock to rock. 'Rhodri, forgive me,' she called. 'I did not mean you harm. I had business with the Warrior Child. I could not let you stop me with your great heart and your strong muscles.'

Rhodri winced and frowned at her.

'I shall make amends,' said Blodwedd. 'I shall gather wildflowers and roots and herbs for you to make a soothing mash as you did for my arm. Tell me what you need to ease your pain.'

'There's no need,' said Rhodri, the anger draining from his voice. 'It's not that bad. The skin's not even broken. But please don't do it again!' He looked at Branwen. 'What business did she have with you?'

'She wanted to show me phantoms,' said Branwen. 'Ghosts of the pretended future to make me change my mind about going home.'

'Ghosts, you say? What kind of ghosts?'

'A Saxon army heading north-away,' Branwen said sullenly. 'A battlefield strewn with the dead of Brython. A citadel broken and burning.' She narrowed her eyes, the memory still too fresh in her mind. 'Iwan ap Madoc's severed head – speaking to me from beyond death.'

'And what did he have to say?' Rhodri asked quietly.

'Yes,' murmured Blodwedd, her eyes filled with a knowing light. 'Tell him the words of the dead.'

'He told me his death was my fault,' said Branwen. 'But what does it matter what he said? It was not Iwan – it was just a trick.'

'Are you sure?' murmured Rhodri. 'In your heart, are you sure it was a trick?'

'Yes!' Branwen glared at him. '*Yes!*'

His eyes were troubled. 'But what if . . .'

'No!' Branwen shouted, uncertainty and anger boiling up in her. 'Leave me alone. Just leave me alone! It's too much. I cannot bear it!'

She turned and ran frantically off into the trees, desperate to escape the confusion that was threatening to overwhelm her.

She had not gone far when she heard behind her a flutter of wings and a familiar '*caw!*'

She stumbled to a halt, holding her breath, her heart thumping, her ears straining.

'Caw!'

She turned. 'Fain!'

The falcon was perched on a rock among the trees, watching her intently, his clever eyes bright and black. Something shone between his claws, flashing with reflected sunlight.

'Caw!'

'Why did you leave me?' Branwen asked. 'I thought you would guide me, but you flew away and the shining path disappeared and I was lost in the forest. *Why?*'

She walked slowly towards him.

The thing at the falcon's feet was a knife. A hunting knife with a riveted handle of brown bone, worn smooth by generations of use.

It was the knife Branwen had held when she had stood vigil over Geraint's dead body in Bevan's field. The knife she had taken from among his belongings when she left Garth Milain. The knife that she had thrown in her anger and frustration at Rhiannon of the Spring. The knife the Shining One had turned to a hail of silver drops. But how . . . ?

Fain bobbed his head and stepped aside. Branwen picked up the knife. Oh, but the worn handle felt so familiar in her hand. Geraint's knife, made whole again and returned to her.

She took a deep breath. 'Rhiannon!' she shouted.

The ghost of a voice was carried to her like a scent on the breeze.

My part is done, Warrior Child, let others now light your path. Have faith. The stronger the tree, the fiercer the storm it can withstand. The brighter the flame, the darker the night. The truer the sword, the stronger the foe. Fare you well, child of the far-seeing eye, child of the strong limb, child of the fleet foot, child of the keen ear . . . fare you well . . .

Branwen stood still for a long time, her arms hanging heavy at her sides, Geraint's knife held in her loose fingers. Her heart ached and her throat was so tight that she could hardly swallow.

'Caw!'

Fain's voice was sharp and insistent.

She looked down at the bird. He was watching her with an impatient glint in his eye. 'The vision was true,' she said. 'If I go home, terrible things will happen in Powys. The Saxons will come and spread death and destruction among my people.' She frowned at the bird. 'I must fight my doubt as though it were a Saxon enemy. In many ways, it is . . .'

Her destiny towered ahead of her like an unclimbable mountain, its lofty peak soaring far beyond the extent of her vision. She thought what she dare not speak aloud:

I shall follow their path, although I cannot see what end it leads towards. I shall follow, even if I arrive at this end only to discover that I am Destiny's fool.

She slipped Geraint's knife into her belt and began to walk back to where Rhodri and the owl-girl would be waiting for her.

CHAPTER SEVEN

Branwen found Rhodri and Blodwedd together by the stream, he kneeling while the owl-girl dabbed at his bowed head with wetted mullein leaves. Making amends for hitting him, Branwen thought. And knowing Rhodri's good heart, it would probably be enough.

As she approached them, Fain cut through the air and swooped down in a long curve, his wings cupping as he came to rest into the grass slightly behind her. He stared hard at Blodwedd, moving uneasily from foot to foot and ruffling his feathers.

'Where would you have me go?' Branwen asked, her eyes on Blodwedd.

They looked up at her as she spoke.

Rhodri glanced from Branwen to the falcon. He smiled but did not speak.

Blodwedd glowered at her. 'The Saxon hawks circle above the place of singing gulls,' she said. 'There you must go, and there you must tear them from the sky before their feasting begins.'

'I don't know what you mean,' said Branwen. 'Where is the place of singing gulls?' She recalled the burning fortress of her vision. 'Is it on the coast? North of here?'

'Singing gulls,' said Rhodri. 'That would be Gwylan Canu in the old language.' He looked at Branwen. 'Do you know of such a place?'

'I do,' said Branwen in surprise. 'It is upon the north coast of Powys – it is the citadel of the House of Puw. Its lord is Madoc ap Rhain – Iwan's father.'

Rhodri gave a low whistle. 'Well now, that would explain why Iwan spoke to you in your vision – it was *his* home that you saw in flames, and his people who were slaughtered.'

'It would be a tempting prize for the Saxons,' said Branwen. 'Gwylan Canu stands in the gap between the mountains and the sea. If the citadel of the House of Puw could be taken, there would be nothing to stop the Saxons sweeping west into the cantref of Prince Llew. And if that happened what hope would there be for Powys or Gwynedd or all the north of Brython?'

'And once the Saxon cock sits crowing his triumph in the north, what will prevent him gathering his armies and strutting southwards,' said Rhodri. 'Ironfist has an insatiable appetite for war, Branwen, and King

Oswald will not sleep easy until all of Brython is under his thumb.'

Branwen glared at Blodwedd. 'You said Govannon sent you to be my eyes and ears. So do what you were sent to do – show me the way and tell me what I should do when I get there.'

Blodwedd seemed puzzled, her large eyes blinking as she looked into Branwen's face. 'I have told you where to go and what you must do,' she said. 'I do not know *how* you are to travel to meet your destiny, nor how to fulfil it when you reach journey's end.'

'Then go back to your master and tell him to send me a guide who *does* know,' Branwen snapped. She turned about, staring into the trees. 'Govannon? Do you hear me? I will do as you ask – but I don't know *how*!'

She waited, peering in under the branches, listening for a voice from the forest gloaming. None came. The wind sighed. The stream chimed and sang. The sun rose in a clear blue sky.

'I think he has sent you all the help you are going to get, Branwen,' Rhodri said. 'The rest is up to you.' He gazed northwards. 'How far is it to the sea?'

As though in response, Fain let out a series of shrill, carping calls.

Blodwedd watched him with her head cocked to one side. 'Not far, as the falcon's wing makes it,' she said. 'But there are no roads northwards over the mountains. You must make your way down to the western lowlands and follow clearer paths.'

'Did you understand his speech?' Rhodri asked.

'Indeed,' Blodwed replied.

Branwen turned to Rhodri. 'So? We should go down into Bras Mynydd and then head north.' She frowned. 'A curious troop we'll look, too. You in your beggar's rags, I in my brother's battle-gear.' She glanced at Blodwedd. 'And *her*.'

'What if we meet the prince's search parties on the road?' asked Rhodri. 'They will not have stopped looking for us yet, and I've no wish to be dragged bound and gagged back to a certain death in Doeth Palas.'

'We will be wary,' said Branwen.

But he had good cause for his fear. It was only a brief time since he had been captured in the woods outside Prince Llew's citadel and condemned as a Saxon spy. Had Branwen not rescued him, his broken body would be hanging from the gallows by now. But Branwen's actions had made them fugitives, and capture by Prince Llew's soldiers would be the end of them both.

Branwen mounted up and flicked the reins to get her horse moving. Rhodri's horse followed, Rhodri as awkward as ever in the saddle, the owl-girl seated at his back, her arms around his waist, her eyes uneasy.

Rhodri's words ran through Branwen's mind as they rode, sounding more and more ominous as they moved through the mountain forest and drew ever nearer to the Cantref of Brys Mynydd.

What if we meet the prince's search parties on the road?

Rhiannon's sparkling path had led them into the mountains and left them in the wilds, deep in unknown forests, far from hearth and home and the well-trodden roadways of man. Even if she could have found it, Branwen knew she could not risk taking the usual route down into the west. If Prince Llew's soldiers came over the mountains, they would surely choose High Saddle Way, and at all costs she wanted to avoid meeting armed men on the high passes. She knew of no other safe pathways through the rearing peaks, but a way off the mountains had to be found, perilous as that venture might prove to be.

The whole day was spent seeking a safe corridor between crags and pinnacles of naked rock. Fain flew on ahead, never straying far out of sight and often returning to guide them away from precipitous falls or from crumbling slopes where a single misplaced hoof could set the whole hillside moving in a deadly river of rubble and scree.

But at last they came over the highmost ridges and, as

the afternoon bled away, they began to make their way down the forested slopes to the less perilous foothills and valleys.

They made camp in a narrow defile cut by a racing river of white water. Alder trees reached out overhead and the air was filled with the soft drone of bees. With tinder and flint, Branwen kindled a small fire; it was midsummer and the evening was not cold, but the dancing flames were cheering in the wilderness, and the crackling and leaping fire would warn predatory animals to stay clear. The mountains were full of wolves, and although they seldom attacked people in the food-rich summer months, it was wise to take precautions.

Fain perched on a low branch close by. He sat silently, a shadow among the leaves, only half seen, his head tucked into his feathers, his black eyes unblinking. Branwen was oddly comforted by his presence – although he too was a messenger from the Shining Ones, he did not disturb her half so much as did the owl-girl.

There she was, Blodwedd the owl-girl, squatting huddled at the fire by Rhodri's side as he went through their meagre provisions. Her arms were wrapped around her shins, her chin on her pointed knees, the flames reflecting in her wary eyes. There was something unnatural in her pose, Branwen thought, as though she did not entirely know how to use her human body.

'Not much to fill our bellies after such a hard day,' Rhodri observed with a sigh, laying out a small remnant of cheese and a piece of bread no bigger than a clenched fist. He upended the earthenware flask. 'No milk either.'

'We have water enough to hand,' said Branwen, nodding towards the gushing stream. 'Give me a few moments to rest and then I will see if I can bring down something for us to eat.' She had in mind hunting with her slingshot for a hare or a small wild boar – or even a young deer if luck was with her.

'There is no need,' said Blodwedd. 'I will find food for us.' Her eyes shone in the firelight. 'Fresh meat. A shrew perhaps, or a plump mole.' Her lips curled in a pointed smile. 'They make good eating while the blood runs warm.'

Branwen looked at her in revulsion.

'We can't eat raw meat, Blodwedd,' Rhodri said gently. 'And I'm not sure we'd like the taste of moles and shrews even if we could.'

Blodwedd's eyebrows knitted. 'Would a young hare be to your liking?' she asked him.

She follows him around like a newborn puppy. Things were better when it was just the two of us. Look at those big eyes of hers, gazing up at him as if the sun rose in his face!

'A young hare would suit us very well,' said Rhodri.

'The last hot meal we ate was roast hare. Branwen killed it with her slingshot.'

'The Warrior Child hunts with stones and leather,' Blodwedd said, getting to her feet. 'I need only my hands and my teeth. I shall not be long.'

'Be careful,' Rhodri said. 'Your wound is still fresh.'

'Have no fear,' said Blodwedd, resting her hand for a moment on the bandage. 'We heal swiftly or not at all.' So saying, she bounded off into the trees, her footfalls silent as the night wind.

Rhodri glanced sideways at Branwen. 'Roast hare, eh?' he said. 'I can almost taste the juice on my fingers already.'

Branwen turned away from him and stared into the fire without speaking.

'Why do you dislike her so much?' Rhodri asked.

'I don't want to talk about her,' Branwen replied. 'We need to discuss what we are to do next. Go north and tear the Saxon hawks out of the sky.'

'If the lord of Gwylan Canu is given warning of the Saxon attack, he will be able to close the gates and defend his citadel,' said Rhodri. 'Perhaps that is all Govannon wants you to do – warn them of the coming danger.'

'I have already learned how little weight people give to my words,' said Branwen. 'When I tried to tell Prince Llew about the attack that was coming to Garth

Milain, he ignored me.' Bitterness laced her voice. She looked at Rhodri as a new thought came to her. 'And what if Prince Llew's soldiers have already been to Gwylan Canu to warn them about *us*?' she continued. 'What if we are thrown into chains the moment we show ourselves? What if their only response is to send us to Doeth Palas to be hanged?'

Rhodri raised an eyebrow. 'Do you think it is your ultimate destiny to swing alongside me on Prince Llew's gallows pole?' he asked. 'I doubt that very much! But you may be right, the straight road to Gwylan Canu may not be our best hope.' He shot her a sudden glance. 'What was the last thing that Iwan ap Madoc said to you before you gagged him?'

'I don't remember exactly – he asked me to leave his sword. He said it had been passed down from his great-grandfather, or something of that sort. What does that matter?'

'I heard something else that he said,' Rhodri murmured. 'He said, "You are going to have an interesting life, Branwen. I wish I could have shared it." Do you remember that?'

'Yes. I remember.'

'I think perhaps you have still one friend in Doeth Palas.'

Branwen gave a harsh laugh. 'Iwan ap Madoc was

never my friend. If I had a friend at all, it was Gavan ap Huw – but he will think I betrayed him as I betrayed everyone else when I set you free.' She narrowed her eyes as she thought of the grizzled old warrior who had briefly been her confederate and her tutor in the ways of warfare. It pained her to know that he must hate her now, but there was nothing to be done about it.

'I disagree. I think we should not go to Gwylan Canu,' Rhodri replied. 'I think we should make our way with all the stealth we can across Bras Mynydd and tell our tale to Iwan ap Madoc.'

'Go to Doeth Palas?' exclaimed Branwen. 'Are you moonstruck?'

'If Iwan can be convinced that you're telling the truth, he will surely go to Prince Llew and have him send reinforcements to Gwylan Canu,' said Rhodri. 'A fast rider could be sent on ahead to warn the lord of the citadel to bolt his gates and hold fast till the Prince's warriors arrive. Ironfist will be thwarted: where he hoped to fall upon an unprepared foe, he will find all in readiness for his coming. The citadel will be saved and you will have fulfilled the task Govannon has given you.'

Branwen looked at him. 'And if the saints watched over us and we made our way to Doeth Palas without being hunted down, what then?' she asked. 'Our faces are known there, Rhodri. We would not get past the gates without being recognized. We'll need disguises.'

'Yes! Good thinking,' said Rhodri. 'A dress and wimple for you so that your hunting leathers are hidden and you can cover your head. And a cloak and cowl for me – and perhaps mud rubbed into my hair to darken it. That way we could slip in among the everyday market crowd and go unnoticed.'

'And your new friend?' asked Branwen. 'Have you looked closely into her eyes, Rhodri? Govannon may have given her a human shape, but there are no *whites* to her eyes. She will be spotted immediately.' She shook her head. 'And even if I agreed with your plan, where are we to find these clothes? We have nothing to trade for them, even if we dared show ourselves.'

Rhodri stared pensively into the flames but did not reply.

Branwen sighed. 'I am not even convinced that Iwan would—'

Her words were broken into by the sudden sound of choking and retching. A slender figure came stumbling out into the firelight. It was Blodwedd, her face red, her eyes bulging. She took a few staggering steps forward then fell to her knees, her hands clutching at her throat.

CHAPTER EIGHT

Blodwedd tumbled on to her side, her knees up to her chest, her hands clawing at her neck. Hideous strangulated noises came from her throat. It sounded as if she were choking to death.

Rhodri sprang up and ran to her side.

'What is it?' gasped Branwen, scrambling up in Rhodri's wake. 'What's happening to her?'

'I don't know!'

Rhodri dropped to his knees, leaning close over the stricken owl-girl, trying to hold her steady as her bare feet kicked in the dirt.

'Does she need water?' cried Branwen.

'Wait!' he said. 'I think I have it!'

Branwen saw his hand move to Blodwedd's mouth, but his shoulder covered what he did next. After a moment or two, Rhodri pulled his hand away and Branwen saw him throw something small and dark off into the grass.

Blodwedd let out a scream then sat up, coughing and retching, gasping for breath.

'It's all right,' Rhodri said gently, holding her shaking shoulders between his hands. 'You're safe now.'

Blodwedd looked up at him, her face still ruddy, her eyes streaming tears.

'I could not . . . swallow . . .' she panted, '. . . could not . . . breathe . . .'

'What did you do?' Branwen asked Rhodri. 'What was that thing you took out of her mouth?'

'I'm not sure,' said Rhodri. 'A small animal of some kind. A vole maybe.'

Branwen stared at him in disgust. '*What?*'

Rhodri looked up at her. 'She was trying to swallow it whole,' he said. 'Her throat wasn't wide enough. It got stuck. She's fine now.'

'Swallow it whole?' she asked, revolted.

'Up until today she was an owl!' he snapped. 'Owls swallow their food whole then cough up the parts they don't want later as pellets. Skin and fur and bones. She doesn't know how else to eat.'

Blodwedd began to breathe more easily, her cheeks returning to their usual colour, her brittle body relaxing a little.

'I shall starve!' she gasped, pulling away from Rhodri. She turned her face to the sky, her voice rising to a howl.

'Lord Govannon! Release me from this bondage! I cannot eat! I cannot fly! It is too cruel!'

She began to sob, her hands over her eyes, her shoulders jerking. Rhodri put an arm around her and held her against him.

'It will be all right,' he said to her. 'I will teach you to eat like humans do. You won't starve. I won't let you starve.'

There was a rustle in the leaves. Fain came swooping down on slate-grey wings. He snatched up the small dead animal from the grass and went winging back into the trees with it dangling from his claws. Blodwedd would not benefit from her kill, but the morsel would not be wasted.

Branwen turned away and walked back to the fire. She was torn between being sickened by Blodwedd and feeling the first inklings of pity for the poor creature. If only she had remained an owl, she would not be so difficult to come to terms with. Branwen knew that at this very moment Fain's curved beak would be pecking and ripping at warm flesh – she had no problem with that. That was nature. But Blodwedd? There was something demonic about her. But she was not to blame – neither for Branwen's problems, nor for what Govannon of the Wood had done to her. She was as much a cat's paw as Branwen herself. But all the same . . .

Branwen picked up the jug that had held the milk – it was now half full of fresh, cool river water. She walked back to where Blodwedd sat huddled in Rhodri's arms.

'Here,' she said. 'Water. It will soothe your throat.'

Blodwedd took the jug from her. She drank in an odd, jerky way, filling her mouth then throwing her head back to swallow.

'Is that better?' Branwen asked.

Blodwedd nodded, water trickling down her chin.

'And now, come back to the fire,' Rhodri said to her. 'There's a little bread and cheese left.' He looked up briefly at Branwen, before turning back to the owl-girl. 'I will teach you how to chew food and swallow it without choking. And I'll check your wound. And while I am doing that, Branwen will go and hunt for our supper.'

Branwen slipped her slingshot out of her belt. Whatever happened to them on their journey, Blodwedd's presence with them would surely have a profound effect – but whether it would be for good or for bad, she was not yet sure.

Branwen could not help feeling a little pleased with herself as she threw the small wild pig down by the fireside. She had come stealthily upon it in the forest as it rooted under an oak tree, quite oblivious to her presence as she crept close enough to use her slingshot. She had stunned it with a single deadly accurate blow to the side of the head and then quickly finished it off with a neat cut of Geraint's knife across its throat.

Blodwedd was huddled by the fire. She seemed to have fully recovered now, and Branwen noticed that all the bread and cheese was gone.

'Get some sticks for a roasting frame,' she told Rhodri. 'I'll prepare the meat for the spit.' She crouched down, taking the pig by a hind leg and turning it over to begin dressing it. She was aware of Blodwedd's eyes on her as she worked.

'Do you want your meat raw or cooked?' she asked without looking at her.

'I do not know,' Blodwedd said quietly.

Branwen grimaced. 'I ate raw meat once, when I was a child,' she said, still concentrating on her delicate knife work. 'Afterwards, I was very sick. I think human stomachs cannot cope with raw meat.' She glanced at last at Blodwedd. 'Try it roasted,' she said. 'I think you'll like it better that way.'

Blodwedd nodded. 'I shall try,' she said.

Branwen looked across the flames at Rhodri. Blodwedd was still at his side, sitting up awkwardly on her thin haunches, holding a bone in both hands and snapping at it with her teeth. Watching her eat was not pleasant – she chewed like a dog, loudly and openly, her lips drawn back and the juices dripping down her chin and on to her dress. The intent look of pleasure on her face showed she was clearly relishing the taste of roasted pig, so at least Branwen wouldn't have to suffer the sight of her trying to swallow live rodents whole again.

'I've been thinking about the idea of wearing diguises,' Branwen said, averting her eyes from the slavering owl-girl. 'I think I know how it can be done.' She threw a gnawed bone into the fire. 'At first light we hunt for another of these pigs, or for a deer or something similar. Then we take it to the nearest village or farmstead and barter fresh meat for clothing.'

'And if we are recognized?'

'I do not think we will be,' Branwen replied. 'The prince's soldiers will not have had time to visit every hamlet and farm.' She glanced at Blodwedd. 'We can leave *her* in the forest with the horses and with my war-gear. We enter on foot, a fresh-killed deer or two over our shoulders and leave the rest to luck and destiny!'

Rhodri grinned. 'That is a good plan,' he said.

'But if we're to go hunting at first light, we should sleep now.'

They piled more wood on the fire so it would keep burning through the night. Then Branwen made herself as comfortable as possible, curled on her side, her face to the warmth of the flickering flames, Geraint's cloak pulled up to her ears.

She woke once in the night. Blodwedd was sitting hunched by the fire, her arms folded around her up-drawn shins, her chin on her knees, her eyes closed.

Sleeping sitting up, Branwen thought drowsily. *Like a bird on a branch!*

She looked for Fain, but the falcon was invisible in the night-shrouded tree. Branwen dropped her head and fell quickly asleep again, but the silent, soaring shapes of owls haunted her dreams.

CHAPTER NINE

'Keep out of sight, do you understand?' Branwen said to the owl-girl. 'And don't let the horses stray. We'll be as quick as we can.'

Blodwedd gazed at Rhodri with worried eyes, as though the thought of parting from him disturbed her.

'Don't be alarmed,' Rhodri said. 'No harm will come to us.'

Blodwedd made a curious snapping motion of her lips and teeth, as though in her mind she was fretfully closing a beak. 'Very well,' she murmured. 'But do not leave me over-long with these great beasts – I do not know how to control them.'

'They're tied fast,' Branwen reassured her. 'Just make sure the knots on the reins do not slip.'

They were in the eaves of a patch of forest that skirted the ridged foothills below the mountains. Ahead of them the land rose and fell in buckles and ripples, much of it still wild, but some parts showing the hand of man. Coppiced woodlands could be seen, the tall straight, slender branches thrusting up like spears in the silvery early light. And there were muddy pathways crisscrossing the land, and fields where wheat and flax and rye grew.

The hill fell away at their feet. Below them in a cupped valley, they could see the huts and pens and houses of a small hamlet.

Branwen looked at Rhodri. 'Ready?' she asked, hefting the young female roe deer that lay across her shoulders.

Rhodri nodded. He had the doe's kid over his shoulder: a buck, no more than two moons old. It would make sweet eating.

The hunting had gone well – they had come upon mother and child at first light, feeding upon leaves and shoots. Branwen had paused for a moment, regretting the necessity of harming the gentle creatures, but she had a hunter's instincts and knew she had no choice but to go for the kill. The best she could do for the two animals was to make sure they died quickly and painlessly.

So now they had two fine deer to offer in exchange for clothing. The people of the hamlet would be eating venison that night, and Branwen and Rhodri would have new clothes to fend off prying eyes.

At least, that was the plan.

Branwen's eyes narrowed as she took a last look back

at Blodwedd. Could they trust her? Did they have a choice? She was uneasy about leaving her brother's sword and shield and chain-mail coat behind with the owl-girl, but those were things they would not have been able to explain – no more than they would have been able to account for why two young travellers should be in possession of such fine horses.

But Branwen still had her slingshot, and Geraint's hunting knife was at her hip. No one would find that odd. Anyone seeking game in the forest would carry such things.

Branwen and Rhodri trudged side by side down the hill towards the hamlet. Branwen heard a soft swishing sound behind her.

She turned and saw Fain following.

'No!' she called to the bird, gesturing it away. 'You can't come. People would be suspicious if they saw you with us.'

Fain circled them, his eyes staring down, his wings barely moving.

'We will not be long,' Branwen called up. 'Go! Wait with Blodwedd.'

Fain gave a single harsh croak and then flew back into the trees.

'Remember,' she said to Rhodri. 'Speak as little as possible. It was your accent that gave you away as a half-

75

Saxon before. These people are unlikely to be as well travelled as Gavan, so they may not know a Northumbrian accent when they hear it – but the less said the better.'

They came down into the hamlet. The ground was bare and a little muddy underfoot. Chickens scratched for grain. Goats bleated in pens made from wattle hurdles. There were only three buildings in all, low huts with shaggy thatched roofs hanging close to the ground. The walls were wattle and daub. Two men were making repairs to the wall of one of the huts, scooping the wet paste of mud and straw from wooden buckets and slapping it over cracks and holes where the weather had got in and the wattle framework was visible. Once firm and dry, the daub would insulate the house against the worst that winter could throw at it.

A boy and a young woman were busy threshing, their arms rising and falling as they wielded their long wooden flails to beat the grain loose from the ears of corn that were spread thickly upon the ground. Chaff and straw stalks danced in the air as they worked. Branwen knew that this must be the remnants of the previous year's harvest, hoarded and stacked and kept dry to provide bread through the year.

A woman in a brown apron and white linen wimple stood by the doorway to the nearest hut. There was a wooden crib at her feet. She was spinning wool, letting the cone-shaped bobbin dangle down for a small infant to grab at ineffectively.

'That's my good strong boy,' she crooned as the pudgy fingers snatched. 'That's my clever one.' The infant gurgled and blew bubbles in delight.

She looked up as Branwen and Rhodri walked towards her.

'Good morrow,' she said, a tinge of suspicion in her voice, although Branwen guessed it was no more than the normal caution reserved for strangers. She eyed the carcasses stretched across their shoulders. 'Those are fine-looking beasts, fresh from the forest, if I'm any judge.'

'That they are,' said Branwen with a smile. 'We killed them ourselves before the sun came up this very morning. Mother and child caught napping in the twilight. I felled them with my slingshot.'

'*You* felled them?' the woman said with an arch of her eyebrows. She looked at Rhodri. 'And what were you doing, my fine young fellow, while this girl-child was at the hunt?'

Rhodri hesitated for a moment.

'He helped,' Branwen said quickly. She stepped forwards, stooping and letting her burden down. She crouched, patting the golden red hide. 'They would make good food,' she said, smiling up at the woman. 'Would you be interested in a trade?'

'I might,' said the woman. 'If you can prove that you have come by these beasts honestly, and are not thieves and vagabonds.'

'And how would I prove that?' Branwen asked lightly. Usually she would have bridled at such a suggestion, but she was wise enough to keep her temper with the doubtful woman. Anger and hard words would get them nowhere.

The woman gestured to the slingshot that hung from Branwen's belt. 'Show me your skills,' she said.

Branwen stood, slipping the slingshot out of her belt and feeling in her pouch for a stone. 'Tell me what to hit,' she said.

The woman looked around. 'That wooden pail yonder,' she said, pointing to a pail that stood by the goat pen some fifty paces away.

'Hmmm,' Branwen said, eyeing the easy target. 'You mean to test me well.' She smiled. 'I can but try.' Then, quick as a flash, she spun the slingshot twice around her head and let fly. The stone cracked on the side of the bucket.

A smile broke on the woman's face. 'A skilful maid indeed,' she said. 'And who taught you such skills?'

'My brother,' Branwen replied. She straightened her shoulders and looked the woman keenly in the eye. 'These carcasses are mine, and I would take it badly if anyone disputed it. Shall we trade?'

'Aye, lass, we shall,' said the woman. 'Come inside, and we shall speak at our ease.' She glanced at Rhodri. 'And will your silent companion enter too? I have stew prepared, if the two of you are hungry. I can heat it while we come to some fair agreement.'

Rhodri laid the young buck deer down beside its mother and followed Branwen and the woman in under the low lintel of the door. The windows of the house were unshuttered, and the interior was full of light. As was usual among such dwellings, the rectangular house had a beaten earth floor with an oblong firepit in the centre, girdled with stones. A ladder stretched up to a hayloft under the thatch. There were straw mattresses against the walls and to one side of the firepit, a pair of quern stones were set in a wooden frame. A young girl of seven or eight years old was slowly turning the stones, and fine white flour was trickling into a stone trough. She glanced up curiously at them as they entered.

'Stop that now, Ariana,' said the woman. 'Go and feed the goats – and milk them too. Don't you hear them bleating, girl?'

'Yes, Mama,' said the girl, getting up and trotting from the hut.

'Now then, sit you down,' said the woman. 'Bartering is made easier in comfort, I find.' She took a pair of black iron tongs and lifted a stone out of the fire. 'You look healthy and hale,' she said, carrying the smoking stone over to a large wooden bucket of stew. 'So I don't take you for beggars.' She looked at Rhodri. 'Despite your rags and tatters. Whence come you? Whose daughter are you, maid?' She lowered the stone into the bucket. There was a hiss and a gout of steam.

Branwen leaned forward, watching the thick brown stew already bubbling from the heat. They hadn't eaten so far that morning, and a bowl of stew would be very welcome.

The woman put down the tongs and folded herself up to sit on the floor. Branwen and Rhodri sat in front of her.

'My father is a farmer of Cyffin Tir,' Branwen told the woman, reciting a tale she and Rhodri had worked out earlier that morning. She was aware of Rhodri staring intently at her, his lips moving a little as though he was mouthing silently to himself the words they had rehearsed together. 'We met with bad fortune. The Saxons came raiding and our home was burned and all our possessions along with it. I was sent over the mountains to seek for clothing and goods to help us build our life again.'

The woman's face clouded. 'Ach! Saxons,' she spat. 'The devils that they are! Would that King Cynon were a stronger man – a great bold leader like our prince – then maybe those ravaging dogs would be sent to the rightabouts!' She looked at Rhodri. 'And what is your tale, boy?'

'I worked on the farm with Branwen,' he said, his foreign accent all too obvious in Branwen's ears.

She winced inside – she wished he had not used her real name. She wished they had thought to come up with aliases. But the woman showed no sign that the name had any significance to her.

'Did you? Did you indeed?' said the woman. 'Well now.' She leaned over, stirring the stew with a wooden spoon. 'So, you wish to trade meat for clothing and . . . *what*? Pots? Farm tools? What else?'

'Clothing would suit us best,' said Branwen. 'Perhaps a dress and a wimple, and a jerkin and leggings and maybe a woollen cloak or two, if you are willing to part with them.'

'We have spare garments,' said the woman, hooking her head to a simple wooden box under one of the windows. 'But it is a lot you ask for only two deer, my child. If your need is so great, maybe you would be willing to work to make up the difference? The boy could be set to with winnowing, and perhaps you could spend a morning at the loom?'

Branwen glanced at the tall wooden loom that stood against the wall. There was already cloth in the frame.

Branwen had seen women at the loom daily in Garth Milain, but she had never been asked or expected to join in the time-consuming and laborious task.

All the same, if a morning of weaving would get them what they needed, she was willing to accept the woman's offer and try her hand at the loom. But could they afford that kind of time? Neither her vision of the coming carnage, nor Blodwedd's message from Govannon of the Wood had given any indication of when Ironfist's attack was due to fall on Gwylan Canu. Today? Tomorrow? By the new moon? When?

'I see you have your doubts about my offer,' said the woman, now spooning the steaming hot stew into two bowls. 'Eat now and think it over. For the two deer, I can offer little more than a cloak or two and a gown. If you need more, you know what I'd have you do.' She handed the bowls to Rhodri and Branwen then heaved herself to her feet. 'I must check on the babe,' she said. 'Talk it over – you'll find it's a fair offer, and the longer you are prepared to work, the better you will serve your folk back in Cyffin Tir.'

So saying, she went stooping out through the low doorway.

Branwen waited until she was sure the woman was out of earshot. 'You shouldn't have called me Branwen,' she hissed to Rhodri.

'I know,' he said, his face troubled. 'The moment I said it, I knew it was a foolish thing to have done.' He shook his head ruefully. 'You were right, I should have kept quiet. We should have told her I was mute!'

'All the same, no harm was done,' said Branwen. 'Just be more careful from now on.' She lifted a spoonful of the stew. The meat was chicken, and she could smell cabbage and onions too, as well as parsley; and a hint of rosemary and savoury. It smelled wholesome and appetizing and she ate it with pleasure, speaking between mouthfuls. 'But what are we to do? Can we afford to spend time here? There's little purpose in us telling our tale to Iwan ap Madoc if we arrive in Doeth Palas too late for it to do any good.'

'I think we have a few days,' said Rhodri. 'It will take Ironfist a little time to organize his men and take them to the coast – it's not something that can be done all of a rush.'

'So you think we should stay here and work?'

'I would rather not, if we had the choice.' Rhodri glanced over to the wooden box of clothes. 'I'm thinking that if I were a little less honest, I'd be sorely tempted to grab what we need and make a run for it.'

'Steal from her?' said Branwen in dismay. 'How can you think such a thing while you're filling your belly with her food?'

'Not steal,' said Rhodri. 'Borrow. As we did the horses – remember, you said when you took them that you would be glad to bring them back to their rightful owners when your need of them was done. So it would be with this woman's clothes. That's all I was suggesting.'

Branwen shook her head. 'It's work or nothing,' she said. 'We could offer to bring them more game – but it's hard to catch deer or wild pig in full daylight, and we'd be as well off working through the day as wandering the forest till dusk. But I'm concerned about Blodwedd. What might she do if we do not return soon?'

'She's not our enemy, Branwen,' said Rhodri. 'You should learn to trust her. If we . . .'

He was silenced by a shadow across the doorway. The woman had returned. But she was not alone. The two men who had been repairing the walls came in after her – and Branwen saw to her dismay and alarm that their faces were set and grim and that one was armed with a heavy wooden club while the other held a hunting spear in his two hands.

'Do you think the eyes of Bras Mynydd are blind?' spat the woman. 'Last night a rider came from Doeth Palas, speaking of two runaway Saxon spies – a black-haired girl dressed in hunting clothes, and a boy in rags.'

Branwen and Rhodri scrambled to their feet, their bowls spilling their contents across the floor. The woman knew who they were! She had tricked them – putting them at their ease while she fetched the men.

'Our prince has offered a rich reward for you treacherous swines!' snarled the man with the spear. 'And the offer holds good – whether you be alive or dead.' He grimaced with anger. 'So? What is it to be? Delivered alive and in bondage to Doeth Palas – or dragged there lifeless by the heels?'

CHAPTER TEN

Branwen backed away from the two men, almost stumbling over the stew bucket as she fumbled for her slingshot. Her knife would aid her only in close combat – but with the slingshot maybe she could keep the two men at bay until escape was possible.

She could not believe she had been taken so completely by surprise. She, the stealthy, keen-witted hunter, caught by the farm woman's pretence like a fly in a spider's web.

Rhodri held his hands out. 'Whatever you have been told, it is not true,' he said. 'We are not spies. We mean you no harm.'

'Listen to his voice!' snarled the man with the club. 'He tells us his lies in a foreign accent!' He spat. 'Saxon cur! You should not be given the offer of life – you should be killed where you stand.'

Branwen's eyes moved quickly from man to man. Their expressions were cold and hard – this was not a situation she would be able to talk her way out of. She ground her heels into the earth floor, balancing herself, quickly fitting a stone into her slingshot and lifting her arm above her head. 'The first man to approach me will regret it,' she said, her gaze flickering from the spearman to the man with the ugly knobbed club. 'My aim is true – ask the woman. Make a move on me and you will lose an eye!'

' 'Ware!' called the woman, stepping in behind the two men. 'She's a devil with that thing.'

Rhodri took a quick step forward and picked up the iron tongs from beside the firepit, jumping back again as the spearman made a stab at him.

'There's no need for this,' Rhodri said, his voice trembling a little. 'Let us go on our way and all will be well.'

'You'd have us let you go and tell your tales to Herewulf Ironfist?' scoffed the man with the club. 'Betray us to the Saxon pestilence? Do you think us fools?' The man pounced, lunging at Rhodri with the club. Rhodri fended it off with the tongs, but they were struck from his hands and as he tried to avoid being hit by a second swing of the club, he lost his footing and fell backwards with a gasp.

Branwen swung her slingshot and loosed the stone. It cracked off the man's wrist and he shouted in pain, dropping his club and reeling sideways, his hand clutched to his chest.

'That could have been your eye if I'd wished it!' she shouted.

The spearman surged towards her with a roar of rage. She felt for another stone, but he was on her before she could reload the slingshot. She shifted her weight, sidestepping as the spearhead skimmed past her. Bringing her arm up, she caught the man across the throat as he staggered forwards from the impetus of his missed blow. She ducked down, her shoulder hitting him in his stomach.

Flexing her legs, she heaved upwards, using all the power of her limbs and back to lift him off his feet. His own momentum betrayed him and he was tossed on to his face behind her. She turned quickly, coming down heavily on him, straddling his back. Snatching the spear from his hand, she threw it out of reach. Now she slipped the knife from her belt and held it to his neck.

'Be still!' she shouted. 'Or I shall cut your throat where you lie!'

He lay gasping, his face in the dirt. She knew he was no match for her – he was a simple farmer who had probably never wielded a weapon in anger before. Not that he wouldn't have run her through if she had given him the opportunity – she was all too well aware of that. But he could do her no harm now, and she wished to avoid hurting him further. Keeping the knife blade steady against his skin, she turned to see how Rhodri was faring.

It was not good. He was lying on his back and the woman stood over him with the iron point of the spear against his throat.

Branwen cursed herself for not having thrown the spear out of reach! *Fool!*

'Let Baddon up, or I'll skewer your friend like a pig,' the woman said grimly.

Rhodri shot Branwen an apologetic glance – as if he blamed himself for the turn of events. Blood trickled down his neck where the spearpoint had nicked his flesh. From the look in the woman's eyes, Branwen had no doubt as to whether she would make good on her threat. One wrong move on Branwen's part and Rhodri's life would be ended.

'Leave him be!' gasped Branwen. 'See! Your man is safe and sound!' She took the knife from Baddon's neck and stood up, stepping back to let the man scramble to his feet. His face was red with anger, his eyes blazing.

'Drop the knife,' the woman said. Branwen hesitated. Geraint's knife was her last hope of survival. With it she might be able to slash her way to freedom. Without it she would be bound and delivered over to the justice of Prince Llew.

But she only faltered for a moment before letting the

knife slip from her fingers. She could not make an escape for herself and leave Rhodri's corpse as proof of her faithlessness. Better to suffer at his side than to live with that burden on her soul!

'And the slingshot, if you please,' said the woman.

Branwen let the strip of leather fall.

The man with the wounded hand moved towards her, his face livid with pain and ire, his lips tight. 'You will wish we had killed you!' he spat, coming close. She stood her ground, gazing levelly at him, expecting the worst. He drew back and struck her hard across the face with his fist.

She staggered, her whole head exploding into pain, white lightning stabbing across her field of vision.

'A taste of what is to come!' he raged, spittle flecking on his lips. 'I hope your death will be a slow and lingering one, and I hope I am there to see it.'

Branwen straightened, holding up her aching head, looking into his face. Refusing to show him any trace of fear.

'It's cowardice to hit an unarmed prisoner!' shouted Rhodri. The woman spun the spear in her hands and struck him in the stomach with the butt end. Rhodri doubled up on the ground with a stifled moan.

'Have your revenge on the girl later, Newlyn,' chided the woman. 'Fetch rope now – tie them both up.' She turned to Baddon. 'And when they are secured, go you and harness up the ox cart. I'd have us drive to Doeth Palas and turn them over to the prince as soon as we can.'

'And take our reward,' Baddon said.

'Aye, lad, and take our reward!' said the woman. 'It will be some recompense for the hardship and loss of this past winter.'

Newlyn turned to leave the house, but he had not taken two steps before he was halted by the sound of scuffling from close outside. A moment later there was a shrill cry of pain. The young boy who had been threshing the grain came stumbling through the doorway, grimacing and holding a hand to the side of his face.

He stared at the woman. 'Mama!' he cried, 'she hurt me!' Then he fell on to his knees, blood showing between his fingers. Sharp nails had raked four cuts across his cheek.

'Fodor!' cried the woman, rushing forwards, her arms outstretched. But before she could reach him, the sound of a crying baby could be heard outside the hut. And a young woman's voice, weeping in fear: 'No! No! Please don't!'

Another shape stood in the doorway, casting a long ominous shadow into the house.

'Blodwedd!' breathed Branwen. 'By all the saints, *no*!'

The crying baby hung from the crook of the owl-girl's arm, held as carelessly as a bag of grain. In her other hand she held Branwen's sword, its edge steady above the baby's bent neck.

'Release them or I will cut its head off,' Blodwedd said, her deep voice cutting through the wailing from outside and the sobs of the woman as she flung her arms around the kneeling boy.

'Put the child down,' said Baddon, moving away from Branwen. 'See? Your friends are unharmed.' His voice was filled with dread.

'He's only an infant!' gasped Newlyn. 'An innocent babe!'

'What is that to me?' demanded Blodwedd.

'Let us go free,' said Rhodri desperately. 'She will do as she threatens.'

The woman pulled Fodor to his feet and drew him away from Blodwedd, her face grey with fear. 'Do not harm the babe,' she said, her voice quavering. 'If you must spill blood, kill me.'

Branwen crouched to pick up her knife and slingshot. 'Stand back against the wall,' she said. 'Let us leave, and there will be no more bloodshed.'

The two men backed away.

'You will pay for this deed,' said Baddon. 'Escape now, but you will be hunted down and slaughtered.'

Branwen walked over to Blodwedd. 'Give me the baby,' she said.

Blodwedd hesitated for a moment then nodded. Branwen drew the crying infant out of her arm and turned to the woman. 'Take him,' she said. 'And thank the saints that you are all still alive!' She looked into the woman's anguished face, feeling pity for her, regretting that her own lack of foresight had put them into this situation, wishing the boy had not been hurt, wishing none of this had happened. But the wishes were fleeting – she dared show no remorse or compassion to these people. They would see it as weakness, and she could not afford to have it spoken abroad in Bras Mynydd that she was weak – she had no doubt that she would need to show a ruthless face in times to come.

The woman stood and grasped the squalling baby to her chest, her eyes hollow and her cheeks wet with tears.

Branwen held out her hand for the sword. Blodwedd's eyes narrowed momentarily then she handed it over.

The owl-girl turned in the doorway. 'Get you inside!' she said. The little girl Ariana and the young woman who had been at the threshing with Fodor came cringingly into the house. They ran quickly to be with the two men.

'Look in the chest,' Branwen said to Rhodri. 'Take what we need.'

Rhodri knelt by the open wooden chest and began to go through the piled clothing.

Blodwedd's eyes shone eerily as she stared at the men. 'Do any more live here?' she asked.

'No,' said Baddon, glaring at her. 'This is all of us. Go, take what you wish and leave us.'

Blodwedd looked at Branwen. 'It is not safe to leave them alive,' she said. 'They will raise the alarm. We must kill them all.'

Branwen stared at her, revolted by the indifference in her voice as she condemned these people to death. But she realized the truth of what the owl-girl was saying. If these folk were left alive and free, they would spread the alarm.

'No!' gasped Rhodri, looking up at Branwen in horror, as though sensing her indecision. 'No matter how great our cause, nothing good can come of such a cruel deed. Tie them up, gag them – but we can't kill them.' His voice rose with his emotions. 'These are not Saxons, Branwen. These are your own people – the people you are destined to protect!'

'I will not kill them,' Branwen said. 'But they must be tied hand and foot.' She looked at the huddled family. The woman was now with the others, the baby swaddled in her clothing, his crying turning to sobs as she rocked him in her arms, Fodor clinging tightly to her skirts.

Branwen hated the look of fear and loathing in the woman's face.

'Where is there rope?' Branwen demanded.

'In the barn yonder,' said Newlyn. 'But if you leave us tied, you may as well kill us now – seldom and few are the folk who come nigh our farm. Belike we should be dead of starvation before we were found.'

Branwen pointed her knife at him. 'Be silent!' She turned to Rhodri. 'Go to the barn – fetch the rope.'

Glancing uneasily at her, Rhodri left the house, dropping a pile of clothing by the door as he went.

Branwen was angry; it was a fiercer, more wrenching anger than she had felt even on the battlefield when the Saxons had swarmed around her. A deeper anger than she had ever felt towards Rhiannon. It was an anger that gnawed in her belly and boiled in her mind. An anger ignited by the fact that for a few terrifying moments she had actually considered heeding Blodwedd's words – because for that fleeting time she had weighed in the balance these people's lives against her own safety.

'It would be safer if we cut their throats,' Blodwedd said, her voice totally emotionless.

Branwen turned on her. 'You've hurt the boy and terrified the others – aren't you satisfied with that?'

The great golden eyes blinked. 'Satisfied?' she echoed, as if she didn't understand what Branwen meant. 'I will be satisfied when our quest is done and the place of singing gulls is swept clean of the Saxon hawks,' she said. 'I will be satisfied, Warrior Child, when I am set free to soar the open skyways once more.' Her eyes glowed. 'And until that glorious time, all who block my path will be struck down.'

'She is surely not human,' Branwen heard the woman murmur. 'See! Her eyes! She is a demon.' She turned to look at Branwen, and there was dread and disgust in her face. 'You have called up demons to aid you,' she said, her voice shaking. 'I have heard of such things from my mother's mother − of creatures that have slept long in forest and stream and mountain. Things that slumber deep and should never be awoken.' Her eyes flashed. 'Beware, girl − they will only serve you while it pleases them. Such creatures have their own dark purposes and desires.'

Branwen gave a harsh bark of laughter. 'You think I do not know that?' she said. 'You think I would choose the life of a hunted fugitive if I was free to do otherwise? You have no idea of the burden I bear! Think yourself lucky that the demons did not choose you or yours for their *dark purposes and desires*!'

Rhodri came back into the house, lengths of hempen rope in his arms. He looked sharply from Branwen to Blodwedd.

'Branwen, I think the man spoke true,' he said. 'If we tie them up, they may well die of thirst and starvation before they are found.'

'Blodwedd would have me slaughter them, you'd have me set them free to condemn us,' said Branwen. 'And I am left with the weight of decision.'

'And what is that decision?' asked Rhodri.

Branwen frowned, considering his question. She turned to the gathered family. 'Ariana,' she said. 'Come here.'

The girl clutched at the woman, whimpering.

'I will not hurt you,' Branwen said. 'Be brave and true and you will be the protector of all your family. Come!'

'Go to her,' murmured the woman. 'Do not be afraid.'

Trembling and unsteady on her feet, Ariana walked to where Branwen was standing. 'You will come with us for part of our journey,' Branwen said, resting her hand gently on the child's head. 'And when we release you, you will come back here and set your kindred loose. Can you do that?'

The girl's eyes were huge as she looked up into Branwen's face. 'Do not let the demon kill me,' she said, her voice quavering.

'She will do you no injury, I swear,' said Branwen. 'Rhodri, tie the others up good and tight.'

Slowly and methodically, Rhodri moved among them,

97

getting them to sit and then tying them securely, passing the ropes around their ankles and wrists with many tight knots. He found a piece of clean cloth to bind the wounds on Fodor's cheek before tying him as gently as possible and seating him with the men. He left the woman's hands free so that she could keep hold of the baby, silent now in her arms. But he took her away from the others, and had her sit with her back to the quern stones, winding the rope around and around the heavy milling block and tying it beyond her reach.

He stood up, his task complete. 'There,' he said. 'And now let us get away from this place.'

'Take some food,' Branwen told him. 'Only what we need.'

Rhodri explored the house and found bread and cheese. He walked to the door and picked up the bundle of clothing, wrapping the food in a fold of cloth.

'Do not fear,' Branwen murmured to Ariana as she led the girl from the hut. She rested her hand on the girl's shaking shoulder. 'All will be well.'

CHAPTER ELEVEN

The horses were waiting, still tethered to a low branch.

Fain watched from a stump as they sorted through the bundle of clothes. Rhodri flung off his old rags and drew on a woollen jerkin and leggings, new-made it seemed, and unworn. He knelt, slipping on a pair of soft leather shoes, cross-gartering the thongs up his calves.

Branwen saw the doubt and concern in his eyes as he glanced occasionally at Blodwedd. A bond had been growing between him and the owl-girl, but Branwen wondered if that bond had now been broken.

Branwen picked out a simple brown gown for herself, and a white linen wimple that she could use to cover her hair and keep her face in shadow if necessary. She pulled the gown on over her hunting clothes, thinking it prudent to wear the dress on their journey, just in case they were seen from afar. It would be hot, she knew, once the sun was up, but she was not prepared to leave her leathers behind. She tied the gown at the waist with a strong leather belt with an iron clasp. Her more precious belongings she kept hidden away, but into the belt she thrust her sword and knife, along with her slingshot and the pouch for her stones.

Precious belongings indeed, these hidden things were. Everything she cherished was tucked away under that gown. Firestones and tinder in a leather pouch. Other items, less practical but vital to her nonetheless. A small bag containing a handful of white crystals that Geraint had found on the mountains, a comb gifted by her mother and a small golden key her father had given her on her tenth birthday. A key found in an old Roman temple, he had told her, although no one knew what lock it might open. These last things were virtually all she had left of her old life; they pained her and comforted her at the same time, and she would never be parted from them.

Folding the wimple and tucking it into her belt, she looked around and saw that Rhodri was helping Blodwedd into a dark-green gown. The owl-girl stood like an awkward child while he settled the gown into place on her small body, tugging at the hem to straighten it, then taking a rope belt and knotting it around her waist. He had picked a wimple for her too, so that her face could be shaded and her uncanny eyes hidden from view.

A dull wave of confusion sickened Branwen – how could Rhodri bear to have anything to do with her? She wasn't human. She was just an animal in human form – a cruel, murdering *thing*, with no compassion, no mercy or kindliness in her heart.

Branwen saw Ariana watching the owl-girl with frightened eyes.

She knelt, resting her hands on the small girl's shoulders and looking into her face. 'Have no fear,' she said softly. 'You will not be hurt, I promise.'

'She hurt Fodor,' Ariana replied, her eyes still on Blodwedd. 'She wanted to kill all of us.'

'Your brother's injuries are not severe,' Branwen said. 'He was more scared than hurt, I believe.'

Ariana shook her head. 'He is not my brother,' she said.

Branwen frowned.

'Fodor is my cousin,' the girl said in a whisper. 'His mother was my aunt – she died in the winter. My papa died, too. And Teithi died, and Aunt Yestin and Hafgan. They got ill and they all died.'

'I am sorry,' said Branwen. 'My papa is dead too. And my brother. The Saxons killed them.'

The girl's forehead crinkled. 'Saxons are bad people,' she said. 'Papa used to tell tales of the Saxons. He said they want to kill us. Why are you helping them?'

'Believe me in this, Ariana,' Branwen said solemnly. 'We are not Saxon spies. We hate the Saxons as much as you do. More, probably, because you hate only what you have been told, but my friend Rhodri and I have *seen* their brutality. We know the deeds of which they are capable!'

'Why do they wish us harm?' asked Ariana.

'They envy us the good fortune of living in such a beautiful land, Ariana,' Branwen said, her heart going out to the little girl. 'But I will not let harm come to you or to this land, not if I can help it. Now, have you ever ridden a horse? Do you know how?'

Ariana shook her head.

'Then I shall show you. You will sit in front of me and I will keep you from falling.'

The girl's worried eyes turned to Blodwedd. 'Was Aunt Aberfar right? Is she a demon?'

Branwen stood up, avoiding the question. 'She will not hurt you,' she said. 'Come, now – let me help you mount up.'

'Are you going to kill me?'

'No! I promise you, no.' On a sudden impulse, Branwen took her knife from her belt. 'Here, take this. Hold it tight, it is heavy.' Ariana grasped the long hunting knife in both hands. 'Keep it with you as we ride,' Branwen said. 'Hold it against my throat if it makes you feel safer.' She grasped the little girl under the arms and lifted her up into the saddle. 'We will ride until the sun is high,' she said. 'Then you will be let down and allowed to return home.'

The girl looked down at her from her perch on the horse's back.

'I wouldn't want to kill you,' she said. 'I don't think you are bad.'

Branwen put her hand on her knee, deeply moved by the girl's faith in her.

If only she had the same faith in herself – the faith that she could fulfil the burdensome destiny that the Shining Ones had thrust upon her. But perhaps she needed to *find* that faith – despite her misgivings, despite her feelings of inadequacy – if only to justify the look of trust in Ariana's eyes.

'Listen to me, Ariana,' she said. 'My name is Branwen ap Griffith. One day you may hear my name again – perhaps. People may speak of me as the saviour of Brython because that is, apparently, my destiny. To save this land from the Saxons.' She lifted her hand and touched her fingers against the girl's heart. 'But if that day ever comes, and people sing songs of the deeds of Branwen ap Griffith, remember how very brave and strong you have been today – remember that Ariana the farmer's daughter is as courageous as any hero in the ballads!'

So saying, she mounted, and with Fain flying over her

head and Rhodri and Blodwedd following behind, she curled one arm around Ariana's waist and sent her horse off at a brisk walk, along the forest eaves and into the north.

The beat of the horses' hooves was soft in the dense grass and the air was still and quiet, hardly a leaf stirring as they passed. Branwen could hear Rhodri speaking with Blodwedd as they rode. As before, the owl-girl was seated behind Rhodri, her thin arms around his waist.

'How did you know to come to our aid when you did?' he asked.

Branwen turned her head a little to better hear the owl-girl's response, realizing she had been too caught up in her anger at Blodwedd's callous behaviour to give any thought to that question – but it was a good one. What had caused her to come to their rescue when she did?

'Lord Govannon spoke in my mind,' said Blodwedd. '"Blodwedd of the Far-seeing Eye," he said, "you fail in your duty to the Warrior Child. You have let her go into great peril. Go now to the habitation of the humans and do what you must to bring her back to the safe path." So I took the sword and came down to the place. And I looked in through a window and saw you upon the floor with a spear at your throat, and I saw everything.' A kind of bitterness entered her voice. 'The Warrior

Child believes I struck the boy out of malice, but it is not so. I did not wish him pain, but the others needed to know that I was resolute – that if they sought to harm the Warrior Child, then my retribution would be swift and deadly.'

'Because unless you look after her properly, you will never be an owl again,' Rhodri murmured. 'I understand.'

There was a keen edge to Blodwedd's response. 'You think that is all?' she asked. 'You think I care only for myself? Do you not know the peril that this land is in? Lord Govannon has shown me horrors, Rhodri. He has shown me what will come to pass if the Saxons rule here. How the land will suffer and groan. Forests cut down or burned. Rivers dammed and fouled. The green hills scarred and gouged and riddled with maggot holes where the humans gnaw at the rock to feed their fires and to forge their weapons and to fill their pockets with pretty gems. The entrails of the world spewed up in a black slurry that will kill all things, bird and beast, tree and flower. And the air choked with filth and the fish dead in the rivers and lakes and nothing, *nothing* of beauty and grace left in the land.

'That is why the Warrior Child must not fail,' said the owl-girl. 'That is why her destiny must be fulfilled. That is why no one can be allowed to stand in her way.'

* * *

They rode silently on through the morning, keeping to the forest edge while the sun rose bright in a clear blue sky. A little before midday, Branwen brought her horse to a halt. She swung down from the saddle, reaching up to help Ariana dismount.

Wordlessly, Ariana held out the knife. Branwen took it and slipped it in her belt. She walked over to where Rhodri had halted his horse.

'Give me one of the loaves,' she said, avoiding eye contact with Blodwedd. He passed down a wheaten loaf and she tore it in two, handing half back to him.

'Take this for your journey home,' she told Ariana, going back to her and giving her the bread. 'You know the way, don't you?' She pointed south along the forest.

Ariana looked at her. 'I have never been so far from home,' she said uneasily. 'Must I go back alone?'

Branwen frowned. What other choice was there?

'*Caw!*'

She turned at Fain's sharp cry. The falcon was perched on the saddle of her horse, his eyes glittering. He rose into the air, his grey wings spreading.

'Caw! Caw!'

The bird flew higher and turned southwards, back the way they had come. He flew for maybe a single bowshot, then swooped down and landed on the bare limb of a gorse bush. He turned to stare at them.

'Caw!'

'Fain will lead the child,' said Blodwedd. 'He will see her safe home.'

Ariana stared after the falcon, her face uncertain.

'Trust him,' Branwen said. 'He is a wise creature. He will lead you true.' She called. 'Fain! She is under your protection. Take her to her folk, then return to me as swift as you can.'

'Caw!'

'Go, little one,' said Branwen. 'Have no fear.'

Giving her a final look, Ariana turned and ran.

Branwen stood on the hillside, watching the little girl as she raced through the tall grass. As she came close to where Fain was perched, the falcon flew up and winged its way further southward.

He came down in the grass, very small now to Branwen's eyes, just a dark fleck on the ground.

The little girl turned and gave Branwen a last look before following the bird.

Branwen mounted up again. Now they could travel at speed. With good fortune, they would arrive at Doeth Palas before nightfall.

CHAPTER TWELVE

Their luck held. Or perhaps luck had nothing to do with it, Branwen thought. Perhaps it was fated that they should reach Doeth Palas without being caught by Prince Llew's soldiers. She hoped that it was so. She hoped the Shining Ones were watching over her.

She had given a lot of thought to what she had overheard the owl-girl saying to Rhodri. *That is why the Warrior Child must not fail. That is why her destiny must be fulfilled.*

She still questioned her ability to live up to the Shining Ones' expectations – but she now found herself clinging to the hope that she *could* be the person they thought she was.

They travelled quickly through the afternoon, avoiding any sign of human habitation – passing hamlets and farmsteads at a distance, moving into the cover of trees or valleys or behind hills at the first sight of smoke or thatched roofs or men and women working tilled fields. And they avoided the roads, keeping always to deep countryside as they headed north-west across Bras Mynydd.

Sunset found them in the forest that spread at the very foot of the huge mound upon which the great and formidable citadel of Doeth Palas was founded. As they slid between the trees, Branwen saw torches ignite atop the high stone ramparts. More lights flickered to the south, where an ancient Roman wall ran along a sharp ridge, lined with iron braziers.

The sight of the mighty fortress of Prince Llew brought memories swarming into her mind. Although it felt like a lifetime ago, it was only a short time since that night when she had first arrived here, raw with the pain of Geraint's death, overawed by the size and the grandeur of the citadel, her whole life overthrown in a day. Doeth Palas was to be a staging-post on her journey south to be married to a boy she had only met once, ten years ago, when she had been five and he had been a mean-spirited and spiteful child of six. Her marriage to Hywel ap Murig was intended to cement an alliance between Powys and Gwent. She was meant to be the great hope of the House of Rhys – the *mother* of heroes!

But she had hated life in Doeth Palas, kicking against the rules and the pointless daily rituals of the existence she was forced to lead while she waited there for the roads south to be safe to travel. She could still see the prince's wife, the lady Elain – her mouth puckered with disapproval. And she could still hear the harping voices of their two daughters, Meredith and Romney, high-born princesses who had done their best to make Branwen feel like an uncultured barbarian.

And then there was Iwan, handsome son of the House of Puw – a thorn in her side from the very night of her arrival. He seemed to delight in tormenting and criticizing her. And here she was, risking her neck to warn him of a Saxon attack on his home.

Branwen was vividly aware that they were close to Rhiannon's pool – the ring of bright water set in a forest clearing where she had wrestled with the enchanted salmon, where she had first encountered the Shining Ones and learned of the fate to which they wished to guide her. She did not try to find the clearing again; she remembered Rhiannon's parting words.

My part is done, Warrior Child. Let others now light your path.

As night gathered under the trees, the three travellers huddled together, eating cheese and bread and drinking from the water bottle filled recently from a bubbling spring.

'Why do we not build a fire?' asked Blodwedd, sniffing

sceptically at a piece of cheese that Rhodri had given her. 'Why do we not hunt and cook?'

'There are too many men about,' Rhodri explained. 'They come and go upon the road from the citadel to the outer wall – they may see the flames. It's not safe.'

'A pity,' said Blodwedd. 'The roasted meat is good in the mouth.'

'You like cooked food then?' said Rhodri. 'I thought you might be more used to the taste of raw meat.'

Blodwedd frowned. 'The food I ate had no taste,' she said. She reached out a hand, two fingers pointing. 'I see it move.' She linked her thumbs and spread her fingers in mimicry of a bird's wings. 'I float on the wind.' She almost smiled. 'A snap of the beak. I swallow, and it's gone. There's no taste, Rhodri. No taste at all. Human food is . . .'

'Better?' Rhodri offered.

'Different,' said Blodwedd. 'Perhaps I shall miss it when I get my true form back.'

'So being human isn't all bad?'

Blodwedd tilted her head, her eyes thoughtful. 'It is hateful to be without flight,' she said at last. 'You folk, you crawl along the ground – bound to the earth – never feel the keen north wind in your faces as you rise high into the sky.' Her voice took on an almost elegiac quality and Branwen found herself gazing at the owl-girl in surprise.

'Never know the joy of the silent swoop. Ahh!' Blodwedd sighed. 'To glide above the forest roof on a moonless night. There is joy indeed – there is contentment.'

'You wouldn't be able to do much soaring with your injured arm,' Rhodri said. 'Not for a while yet.'

'You think not?' Blodwedd pulled the bandage loose from her arm.

'Branwen, look at this!' Rhodri exclaimed in amazement. 'There's no inflammation and the wound is already scabbed over and healing.'

'Good,' Branwen said curtly. 'I am glad.'

'Did I not tell you, Rhodri?' said Blodwedd. 'We heal quickly or not at all. Were I in my true form, already I would be winging over the treetops.'

'Do you not hate Govannon for taking that away from you?' Branwen asked quietly.

Blodwedd gave her a startled look. 'Hate Lord Govannon?' she said. 'How could that be? I *am* Lord Govannon!'

Branwen almost choked on a piece of cheese. 'What do you mean?' she coughed, half rising.

'All creatures of the woodlands are a part of the great Lord of the Forests,' said Blodwedd. 'He is in all of us, warm as blood, rich as rising sap, sharp as claws and thorns, bursting with life like a new-hatched chick or a seedling striving for the sun. We are his children and his limbs and his heart and eyes, his fingers and his arms and legs, his muscles and sinews and bones. We are all of him, the great Lord, Lord of the Forest – Govannon of the Wood.' Her eyes turned to Branwen. 'How could I hate him?'

Branwen sat down again, swallowing hard. 'Does he have no physical form, then?' she asked. 'I have heard that he was like a man – or half-man, half-stag. A man with antlers.'

Govannon of the Wood. He of the twelve-points. Stag-man of the deep forest, wise and deadly . . .

'I know nothing of that,' said Blodwedd. She touched a finger to her forehead. 'He comes into my mind as a great eagle – greater than all others – greater than any that have ever been. His wings span the land from sea to sea, and when he rises into the sky, the sun is dimmed and his shadow covers the world.' Her eyes shone. 'With one claw he could pluck a mountain out by its roots, and when he lifts up his voice, the stars shiver and the moon cracks. That is the Lord Govannon.'

'I don't understand,' said Branwen. 'Rhiannon was a woman – a woman in white who rode a white horse. But . . . but you say that Govannon is a *bird*?'

Blodwedd gave a throaty laugh. 'The Lady Rhiannon is not a woman,' she said. 'The Shining Ones are not *human*, Warrior Child.' She laughed again, as if the absurdity of the idea delighted her.

'You mean the Shining Ones can be anything they wish?' said Rhodri. He looked at Branwen. 'Do you see?' he said. 'Rhiannon showed herself to you as a woman – because you're human. For Blodwedd, Govannon is a bird. A huge eagle. They change their appearance to fit their surroundings.'

Blodwedd nodded enthusiastically. 'That is the truth, Rhodri,' she said. 'To the fish of the wide rivers, Rhiannon is an ancient pike. To the trees of the forest, Govannon is a mighty oak.' She raised her hand. 'Lord Govannon is *all* trees, he is *all* birds, he is *all* creatures: deer, shrew, wren and raven, oak ash and thorn. The lark in the morning and the owl at night. The white snowdrop in spring and the acorn of the late summer. Open your eyes, Warrior Child – see truly who the spirits are that guide you!'

'We will sleep tonight in the forest,' said Branwen. 'We must take it in turns to keep watch. If there is any sign of people in the woods, we must avoid them.' She glanced at Blodwedd. 'We cannot risk being discovered.'

'I will watch through the night,' said Blodwedd.

'No, we should take turns,' Rhodri suggested. 'We all need to get some sleep.'

Blodwedd smiled. 'I can sleep and watch both together,' she said. 'Not a mouse shall stir but I will know of it, no matter how deep my slumber.' Her eyes turned to Branwen. 'I will serve as lookout through the night – if the Warrior Child trusts me.'

Branwen looked at her. The owl-girl was a dangerous and disturbing creature, and Branwen was certain that she would never grow to like her, but she had no doubt Blodwedd could be relied on to be a safe and vigilant lookout.

She nodded. 'Do it then – and wake us at the least sight or sound of people. And in any event, wake us before first light. If we are to mingle unseen with the folk who come to Doeth Palas daily to trade, then our disguises will require some items for barter. A few fresh hares should suffice.' She lay down, wrapping Geraint's cloak around herself and bringing the warm woollen cloth up over her head. 'And then we shall learn whether Iwan ap Madoc is to be trusted!'

CHAPTER THIRTEEN

Once again, flying shadows and the sinister beating of wings haunted Branwen's dreams. There were golden eyes too, round as wheels, rimmed with flame, watching her unblinkingly from out of the black pit of the night.

She awoke in darkness to the flutter of wings. Fain had returned. He came to rest close to her head.

'Is the girl child safe?' she whispered.

Fain bobbed his head as though to say yes.

'Good.' She reached out and gently stroked the bird's chest feathers. 'You did well. I'm glad you're back.' She turned her head. She could see the dark hump of Rhodri nearby. Blodwedd was in her usual pose at his side, sitting up gawkily with her limbs gathered up, her chin on her knees. Her golden eyes were wide open, staring straight at Branwen.

The owl-girl's head tilted and an accusatory glint came

into her eyes, as if she assumed Branwen was checking on her and resented it.

Branwen nodded to acknowledge Blodwedd's gaze, her lips spreading in a tight smile intended to convey that it was no lack of trust that had awoken her. Then she turned away and drew the cloak over her head again.

There was a pale mist in the forested valley in the still, cool time before dawn. Branwen crouched, shivering a little and staring through the trees. She had taken off her brown gown and was in her hunting leathers. The long skirts of a gown were useless for forest work, and woollen garments were for ever snagging on twigs and branches. Fain had disappeared into the mist, sent ahead to scout for quarry. Rhodri had stayed behind with the horses – he had no skill at the hunt and he was not especially adept at moving with stealth and silence.

But someone else was. Branwen watched the slim shadow of the owl-girl glide through the mist like a wraith, passing in absolute silence from tree to tree. Adept as she was in forestry, Branwen felt heavy and clumsy in comparison.

Blodwedd turned and beckoned. Branwen followed, moving forwards on tiptoe, making sure that every step was soundless.

Blodwedd's hazy form slid forward, heading deeper

into the forest. A dark winged shape exploded out of the mist at eye level. It circled the owl-girl twice then vanished again. Fain. On the hunt.

Blodwedd turned and beckoned again, this time waiting until Branwen caught up to her. The owl-girl pressed her lips to Branwen's ear and whispered in a barely audible voice.

'Fain has found two hares. I will go around. You wait here and be ready.'

Branwen nodded and Blodwedd sped away as silently as a shadow and was swallowed in the mist.

Just like an owl on the hunt! Branwen thought, stepping cautiously forwards. The dawn was close now, she could feel it in the air and see it in the way the deep dark of night began to soften to shades of slate grey. The mist coiled its tendrils around her legs as she moved, the air still cold in her lungs.

She came to a place where the trees thinned a little and the mist was fading. A shape stirred on a branch above her head. Fain. He stared down at her.

She crouched, her head low, her eyes scanning the ground.

There!

A grey-brown hump in the grass. A crouching hare. She took in a shallow breath and held it, taking her slingshot and fitting in a stone, her pouch at her elbow, the mouth open to allow her to quickly take out another stone.

Then she waited, judging from experience how long it would take Blodwedd to circle the hare. She saw a long ear twitch.

Geraint's tutoring came back to her.

Be calm, be silent, be swift, be still . . .

She rose, twining the leather ends of her slingshot between her fingers. She lifted her right arm above her head, the left stretched out in front of her, the elbow locked, her hand flat, her fingers pointing towards the hare – creating a line along which she could aim.

Twice she spun the slingshot, her eye never leaving the dark hump – her focus aimed on the long narrow head from which the ears folded back along the spine.

She flicked her fingers open, loosing the stone. Even before it struck the animal, she was reaching for a second stone and fitting it to the slingshot.

The hare slumped into the grass with barely a sound. A second hare – an animal Branwen had not even noticed – bolted from the shallow depression in which they had been resting. It raced to Branwen's left, dashing for the cover of denser trees. Branwen spun and threw – but the hare jinked at the last moment and the stone missed.

Annoyed at herself, she snatched up a third stone. Blodwedd appeared suddenly in the hare's path –

appearing as if out of nowhere – lifting her arms and shouting.

The hare turned sharply, scudding back through the long grass, zigzagging so it was almost impossible for Branwen to aim at it.

Fain was suddenly in the air, arrow-fast on his scythe-shaped wings. He rose then stooped, stalling in the air and plummeting down towards the hare. The terrified animal turned again, its wide eyes desperate. Blodwedd came running forwards, her arms spread wide.

The hare sped towards where Branwen was waiting. Her stone struck it between the eyes. It flipped, tumbling through the grass, dead before it came to a slithering halt almost at her feet.

Blodwedd picked up the other hare by the ears and walked towards Branwen, holding it aloft. 'That was well done!' she said, smiling her pointed smile. 'As an owl, I might have taken one, but never the pair. You hunt well, Warrior Child.'

Branwen almost smiled – the rigours and focus of a good, clean hunt had cleared her mind. 'Another half dozen, maybe, and then we go to the citadel. Pray that good fortune attend us.'

'I don't like this plan,' said Rhodri. 'I should go into Doeth Palas with you.' He gave Branwen an uncomfortable look.

'I don't want to lurk uselessly in the forest with the horses while you walk into who knows what dangers.'

'What would you do, Rhodri?' asked Branwen. 'Even if you pass without any of the gate-guards recognizing your face, you cannot speak to answer their challenges – your accent would give you away before you spoke a handful of words.'

'Then I shall be dumb,' said Rhodri. 'And this hooded cloak will hide my face as well as those wimples hide you and Blodwedd from prying eyes.'

'Prince Llew's soldiers are hunting for a male and a female travelling together,' said Branwen. 'Two females travelling together will not arouse their suspicions, but add a man and our chances of succeeding are diminished.'

Rhodri stared at her for a long moment, then his eyes dipped. 'Very well,' he said. 'Rhodri the beggarly runaway will skulk in the forest with Fain and our two horses while the brave young women go alone into the wolves' lair!'

'Do not fear for the Warrior Child,' said Blodwedd, lifting her hand, her fingers crooked, her white nails sharp as claws. 'Any that look askance at her will lose their eyes.'

'No!' said Branwen. 'We only fight if all is lost.'

Blodwedd gave her a curious look. 'I will defend you *before* all is lost, Warrior Child,' she said. 'Thus *all* shall never be lost. But have no fear, I will not kill needlessly

'– and I will touch no child, if you wish it so.'

'Good. That's good then,' said Branwen. She turned to Rhodri. 'We should return before midday – but if we have not come back by nightfall, flee this land. If we are captured, I want to know you will not share our fate.'

Rhodri's eyebrows rose. 'You think I would run and hide and leave you to the mercies of Doeth Palas?' he asked.

'No, I don't,' said Branwen, curling her mouth in a faint smile. 'But it would be wise.'

'I've never been known for my wisdom,' said Rhodri. 'But for now, good luck go with both of you. Be wary and cunning and take no risks – and if Iwan proves false, do not hesitate to cut his throat.'

'It will not come to that,' Branwen added quickly.

'It may,' Rhodri warned.

Branwen saw the apprehension in his eyes. She rested her hand on his chest. 'We will not be long,' she said. 'Keep yourself safe!'

'For you, always,' he murmured.

Nodding, Branwen stooped and picked up the long slender branch to which they had tied three of the hares they had caught. Blodwedd already had a second branch over her shoulder, four hares dangling from it, blood clotted on their muzzles.

Branwen glanced down at her shield and sword and

chain-mail shirt, lying on the ground with her leathers and hunting knife. She and Blodwedd were dressed now in gown and wimple, but Branwen had her slingshot and stones with her, tucked well out of sight. But two young peasant women would not draw undue attention from Prince Llew's guards. Two women from the farms and hamlets of Bras Mynydd would pass unnoticed in among the crowds that made their way every day into the markets of great citadel.

Or so Branwen hoped.

CHAPTER FOURTEEN

'So many humans!' murmured Blodwedd, her eyes wide in the shadow of her wimple. 'Such danger!'

'Stay close to me and all will be well,' Branwen said. 'Do not speak unless you have to, and keep your eyes on the ground at all times.'

'Why?' asked Blodwedd.

'Because you have an owl's eyes!' Branwen hissed. 'Do you think they will go unnoticed if anyone looks directly into your face?'

They were in a slow-moving crowd of peasants, jostling and shuffling and knocking and barging as they came up the steep narrow road that led to the rearing white stone ramparts of Doeth Palas, citadel of Prince Llew, lord of Bras Mynydd.

The citadel towered above them, its blanched ramparts shining in the light of the sun as it climbed over the eastern mountains. The massive fortifications of Doeth

Palas were cloven by a deep passage, the road to the gates passing through the gap, rising sharply, the earth beaten iron-hard by the passing of thousands down the years.

Branwen and Blodwedd were pushed together as the traders, hawkers, and farmers pressed towards the gates. Some rode in ox-carts, others had their wares packed in wicker baskets suspended from the backs of donkeys. Some drove geese and goats and pigs. The rising heat of the day filled the air with the heavy, pungent smells of grain and of animals and close-packed sweating people. There was shouting and grumbling and the honking of geese and the squeal of pigs and the calling of traders greeting one another.

The procession slowed almost to a stop as they came to the bottleneck of the open gates. Branwen waited impatiently to be let through. This would be the first test of their disguises. Armed guards stood atop stone slabs on either side of the road, scrutinizing the people as they made their way through. Others shoved their way roughly in among them, spears in their hands, keeping some semblance of order and checking that all was well.

Branwen linked her arm with Blodwedd's, determined that the bumping and barging of the people would not separate them. They were almost through now – she could see the wide paved road that led deep into the heart of the citadel, and at the path's end, she saw the high thatched roof and the stone walls and gold-sheathed doorways of Prince Llew's Great Hall.

Stalls and carts already lined the road as those at the head of the line began to set out their wares and prepare for trade.

A burly man elbowed Branwen aside and she stumbled into one of the guards.

'Now then, maid,' growled the guard, fending her off with the shaft of his spear. Branwen swallowed her irritation as he pushed her back. She kept her head down, the white linen wimple drawn over her forehead.

Still clinging to Blodwedd, she passed the guard and the mass of people began to loosen. They were within Prince Llew's fortress and all was well.

'Ho! You there – maiden!'

Branwen's heart pounded. It was the voice of the guard she had bumped into. Was he calling to her? She didn't dare look around. Keep walking! Just keep on walking!

'Hoi! Stop when I speak to you!' A hand came down on her shoulder, bringing her to an abrupt halt.

'I will kill him,' muttered Blodwedd in an undertone. Branwen was grateful that the general hubbub prevented the guard from hearing the threat.

'No! Wait!' Branwen whispered under her breath. She turned, her head still lowered. 'What do you want of me?' she asked aloud.

'Use a less haughty tone with me, girl,' said the guard. 'Those are fine hares you have for sale. I'd have a brace for the cookpot. What price are you asking?'

Branwen had to think quickly. Money was seldom used in the less sophisticated cantrefs east of the mountains; in Garth Milain virtually all trade was for barter – a fine plump goose for two bags of rye grain, or a wheel of fresh-churned cheese for a basket of tench or trout or grayling. She had no real idea of the value of coins here.

'What would you consider a fair price, sir?' she asked.

'An eighth of a silver piece for the pair,' said the guard, his fingers delving into the leather pouch at his waist.

'A half would be closer to the mark, sir,' she said, keeping her voice low and humble. She assumed the guard had named a price lower than the true value of the animals – to agree to his first offer would rouse his suspicions.

'Ha! Would you make your fortune out of me, girl? A quarter and no more.'

'Done!' Branwen shifted the branch off her shoulder and took off two of the hares. She hoped the guard did not see how her hands were shaking as he dropped the cut silver coin into her palm.

She bowed her head, hefted the branch back on to her shoulder and walked on, away from the gates. Her racing heart slowed and she blew out a relieved breath.

'What did he give you?' asked Blodwedd. 'Show me.'

Branwen displayed the quarter-circle coin on her palm.

'*That* – for two hares? What purpose does it serve?'

'I'll explain another time,' said Branwen. 'We must find Iwan.'

'There are many people here,' Blodwedd said, staring out across the thronging market. 'Where is he to be found?'

'I have an idea,' said Branwen. 'Follow me.'

She led Blodwedd into the heart of the market. It was a noisy and boisterous affair. People crowded and elbowed and jogged and jarred one another, some laden with panniers from which they traded, others arguing and bickering over the stalls. Stilt-walkers and jugglers and acrobats entertained the passers-by. Metalsmiths came with heavy carts, selling pots and pans and knives. Grain traders cried their wares, fighting to shout louder than their neighbours. A hundred different smells filled the air, sweet, sour, savoury and foul, rising from the uneasy animals and from wicker baskets and hempen sacks. There was the clank of metal on metal as goods were weighed on hand-held balances, the slap of palm against palm as deals were done. Ox carts rumbled, gaggles of geese got underfoot, wattle pens were set up to house sheep and goats and pigs. There were earthenware jars of honey fresh from the hive; wheat and rye and barley by the poke, beans and peas and lentils. And in the odd corner, rings of men and women watched cock fighting and wrestling bouts.

But Branwen only wished to pass through the mêlée as quickly as possible. She had in mind a courtyard, hidden away close to the walls. A dusty square where she knew the young men of the court often gathered to practise archery and to hone their battle skills.

The noise of the market formed a constant backdrop as Branwen led Blodwedd away between the huts and dwelling-places.

As they turned a few corners, moving away from the market-place, Branwen recognized the long building whose wall formed one side of the courtyard.

'Stay back,' she murmured to Blodwedd. The owl-girl nodded. Branwen slid along the wall and peered around the corner.

Three lads were in the courtyard. There was gangly Andreas, red-haired Bryn and Iwan ap Madoc, tallest and most handsome of the three. Branwen felt a strange fluttering in her stomach as she caught sight of him, smiling his usual cock-sure smile as he leaned on his bow and watched Bryn aiming for the wicker target.

'Elbow up more,' Iwan remarked.

'I do not need your advice,' said Bryn, his lips to the bowstring, his arms shaking a little as he strained against the tension of the bow.

He loosed the arrow. It struck the head of the wickerwork figure with a sharp *thuk*! 'Now you do better!' demanded Bryn.

'With pleasure,' said Iwan, setting an arrow to the string and pulling back on his bow.

Branwen didn't bother waiting to see his shot. She knew he would hit the target with ease.

'He is there,' she whispered to Blodwedd. 'But he is with others. I need to speak to him alone – the others cannot be trusted. One of them in particular has no love of me: a big red-headed lad who thought he could best me with a staff in his hand.' Her fists clenched as she remembered their fight. 'I proved him wrong, but he would delight in giving me up to the prince if he knew I was here.'

'Then what shall we do?' asked Blodwedd.

'We'll leave the hares here – they have served their purpose, I hope.' They laid the two long poles down against the wall. 'Now, I want you to watch and wait,' Branwen continued. 'Be my lookout – I need to know if any others approach. Look out especially for an older man with grey hair and a white scar down the left side of his face.' Gavan ap Huw, warrior and hero of Powys

– briefly her mentor, the man whose teachings had saved her life in the battle outside the gates of Garth Milain. How he must hate her now! He must think her a traitor – to have released a condemned spy and to have fled with him.

He often schooled the lads of the prince's court in weaponry and battle skills. Above all others in Doeth Palas, Branwen did not want to come face to face with him. She didn't want to see the disgust and abhorrence in his flint-dark eyes; she didn't want to suffer his disappointment and displeasure, and she did not want his to be the hand that dragged her to Prince Llew's feet!

She crept back to the corner. Skinny Andreas was aiming at the target now but as Branwen had seen before, his stance was all wrong – it was obvious to her that he would miss.

He did, and his two companions roared with laughter.

She watched from behind the wall as the three boys took turn and turn about. Her intention was to follow Iwan once the training session was done and to somehow get him alone.

A fourth boy came running into the courtyard. 'Hoi! Come quickly – Padraig has challenged Accalon of Rhufoniog to a wresting bout in the market. Gold coins are being gambled.'

'On Padraig's swift slaughter, surely!' laughed Iwan. 'Accalon is unbeaten in fifty matches. He will pound our little Padraig to a sticky paste.'

'Padraig is as slippery as an eel,' said Bryn. 'I'll risk a silver half-piece on him!' He hooked his bow over his shoulder and strode off.

Andreas followed.

'Oh, it will be amusing, I suppose – albeit brief!' said Iwan, following the others.

Branwen had to act quickly. She fumbled under her gown for her slingshot. Bryn and the fourth boy had already left the courtyard by the time Branwen loosed a stone.

It skipped on the hard earth a fraction away from Iwan's foot. He paused, staring down at where the small white pebble had come to rest. Then, quick as an adder, he turned and stared along the obvious trajectory of the stone.

Branwen leaned around the corner, pulling back her wimple so that he could see her face. His expression changed from puzzled curiosity to amazement as he caught sight of her. She beckoned to him, then slid out of view before any of the others saw her. She leaned against the wall, heart hammering, legs trembling. Blodwedd looked questioningly at her, but Branwen gestured for her to keep silent.

Everything depended on Iwan's reaction to seeing her. Would his instinct be to call the guard? Would he give her away?

'Go on ahead,' Branwen heard him call. 'I will follow shortly. Put a quarter gold piece on Accalon for me.'

Branwen bit her lip. Soft against the distant hubbub of the market, she could hear footsteps padding towards her across the courtyard.

Iwan turned the corner. 'Well now,' he said, an arrow point aimed at her heart. 'The Barbarian Princess has returned to the scene of her great treachery. How very interesting. Prince Llew will think better of me now, when I bring him such a prize!'

CHAPTER FIFTEEN

Branwen gazed into Iwan's eyes. 'Kill me now rather than hand me over to the prince,' she said.

'As you wish,' said Iwan. He glanced for an instant at Blodwedd, his arrowhead still aimed at Branwen's heart. 'But I'd like to know first why you threw your whole life away for that Saxon vagabond – and what madness brought you back here.' An uncharacteristic urgency entered his voice. 'Prince Llew *will* have you hanged, Branwen, have no doubt about that, princess or no. And your feet will be dangling long before your father could bring a force over the mountains to seek your rescue.'

'My father is dead,' said Branwen.

Iwan let out a long, regretful breath and grimaced in dismay, lowering his bow. 'Then it is true.' There was sympathy in his eyes now. 'One of the men sent to seek you in the mountains returned here on a foaming and exhausted horse late yesterday eve. He came staggering into the Great Hall, speaking of battle and disaster in Cyffin Tir. He said Garth Milain was burning and all were slain. The prince and Captain Angor bade him be silent and we were sworn to speak nothing of his grim tidings. The prince and the captain took the rider to the private chambers and we were told nothing more.' He frowned. 'But how do *you* know of this?'

'I was at the battle, Iwan,' said Branwen, her voice trembling at the memory. 'I have travelled far since last we met. I fought at my mother's side. The Saxons were beaten back.'

'So Garth Milain is not lost?'

'Not lost to the Saxons,' said Branwen. 'But it was burning when I left, and my father lay dead upon the battlefield.'

Branwen had been aware of Blodwedd chafing at her side all the time while they spoke. At last, the owl-girl couldn't keep silence any longer. 'Tell the boy why we are here,' she said. 'Tell him of Lord Govannon's prophecy.'

'Lord Govannon?' breathed Iwan, staring at her. 'Govannon of the Shining Ones? There is no such creature! What madness is this, Branwen?'

'A great madness indeed,' said Branwen.

Blodwedd's eyes suddenly narrowed. 'It is not safe here,' she said. 'People approach. I hear their voices – I smell them – they are close.'

There was a wooden entrance in the wall of the long building. 'What's beyond this door?' Branwen asked.

'A storage hut for animal feed,' Iwan replied. He walked rapidly towards the door. 'Come. We will speak within, away from prying eyes.' He gave her a wry look. 'And if our discussions turn bad, we shall see whether I can loose an arrow more speedily than you can a stone.'

He opened the door and they entered a long room piled with sheaves of wheat. The air was stuffy under the thatch, smelling strongly of the dry wheat. Iwan swung the door to behind them, leaving it open a fraction so that a strip of bright light was thrown across the piled sheaves. Branwen blinked, her eyes slowly adjusting to the dimness.

'Tell me your tale,' Iwan said. 'Although if you truly believe you have come here as emissaries of dead gods, then I fear there is little I can do for you.' He looked closely at Blodwedd. 'Who *is* this, Branwen?' he asked, lowering his head to look into Blodwedd's wimple. He gave a low gasp at the sight of her wide golden eyes, bright in the half-light. He looked at Branwen. 'By all the saints, what is she?'

'Her name is Blodwedd,' Branwen said. 'If I told you more, you would think me out of my wits.' She looked into his confused face. 'I have come back here to give you a warning, Iwan.'

'A warning?' An eyebrow arched. 'Of what would you warn me?' he asked. 'To be more vigilant when I am put as sentry on a Saxon spy? That is a lesson I have already learned, Branwen, to my discomfort. I got Captain Angor's rod across my back for allowing you to make a fool of me like that. I'll not be duped by you a second time.'

'I'm sorry you were beaten,' said Branwen. 'I would not have wished that upon you. But I had to save Rhodri. He would have been tortured and hanged otherwise, and he is *not* a spy. It was his warning that took me to Garth Milain in time to beat the enemy back. I told the prince that Garth Milain would be attacked, and he called me a fool and a dupe!' Her eyes blazed. 'He knows otherwise now.' A thought struck her. 'You say the horseman came last night with the news of the battle? What has the prince done? Is he gathering a force to pass over the mountains and come to the aid of Cyffin Tir?'

'Not that I know of,' said Iwan. 'I am not privy to the prince's high counsels, but I have seen and heard nothing to suggest that he intends to send a troop of men into the east. And word has certainly not gone abroad in Doeth Palas of the battle. The people here go about their daily lives, and the only fear they have is that their throats may be cut by a Saxon spy and the lunatic Barbarian Princess who set him loose!'

'The prince does nothing!' Branwen said bitterly. 'A noble ally in times of woe! The Garth burns and he sits on his hands!'

'You want me to go to the prince and ask him to ride to the aid of Cyffin Tir, is that it?' asked Iwan. 'He would not heed me, even if I were allowed to speak with him. But no – you said you were here to *warn* me of something.'

'The Saxon hawks circle above the house of the singing gulls,' said Blodwedd. 'That is the warning we have come here to give you. How will you act, boy? What will you do?'

Iwan stared incredulously at her, clearly nonplussed by her enigmatic speech. 'She talks in moonstruck riddles!' he snapped, turning to Branwen. 'What does she mean?'

'She means that Gwylan Canu is in danger of Saxon attack,' said Branwen.

'As are we all,' replied Iwan. 'This is no news.'

'Herewulf Ironfist already leads an army northwards,' said Branwen. 'They will come upon the fortress of your father by land and sea. All will be slaughtered. A Saxon pennant will fly over the broken gates of Gwylan Canu.' She chose not to mention that, in her vision, Iwan himself was also slain and mutilated.

'How do you know of Ironfist's movements?' Iwan demanded. 'And how are you so sure that my father will not throw the Saxons back from his walls? You cannot know for certain that defeat will be the outcome of a battle that has not yet been fought.'

'I was shown it!' cried Branwen. 'Please, Iwan. Trust me!'

Iwan hesitated, his face twisted by confusion and doubt. 'What do you mean when you say you were *shown* it?' he asked. 'Branwen! If you want me to believe you, I must know more.'

'Would you know more, boy?' growled Blodwedd, drawing back her wimple so that her inhuman eyes caught the strip of sunlight and reflected it like molten gold. 'Would you have me show you more?'

She moved forwards, silent and swift, deadly as a feathered barb. Iwan gasped and stepped back, his eyes staring in his pale face.

'Blodwedd! No!' breathed Branwen, pressing quickly between Iwan and the owl-girl. 'Do not do this!' She knew what was coming – she knew what the owl-girl intended to do to Iwan.

Blodwedd pushed Branwen aside with ease, her clawed fingers coming up on either side of Iwan's startled face. She pulled his head down, her eyes staring into his.

'See now, and *understand*!'

Branwen saw a look of horror burn itself on to Iwan's face as he was caught and held by Blodwedd's intense gaze. He stopped struggling and dropped heavily to his knees, his arms hanging limp – a marionette with its strings cut, held up by the owl-girl's two thin hands, and by the power in her blazing eyes.

And as he knelt there, transfixed by Blodwedd's gaze, his expression grew ever more alarmed and appalled.

His lips moved. 'No . . . no . . . no . . . father! They come from all sides! 'Ware! 'Ware!' Then he cried out, tears running from his eyes. 'No . . . ! Father – *no*!'

'Blodwedd, stop!' gasped Branwen, pulling at the owl-girl's arm.

Blodwedd let out a low, threatening hiss.

'No!' shouted Branwen. 'Enough!' She clasped her arms around the owl-girl's waist and heaved her backwards, breaking her grip on Iwan and severing the dreadful link between them.

Iwan groaned and fell forwards on to his hands, panting, his head hanging.

Blodwedd looked at Branwen. 'It was necessary,' she said. 'It is done.'

Iwan lifted his head and stared at her. 'What are you?' he gasped.

'I am Blodwedd of the Far-seeing Eye,' replied the owl-girl. 'I was sent by Lord Govannon to guide the Warrior Child on her true path. The Shining Ones have chosen her to be the saviour of Brython. The Old Gods do not sleep – they are watching over her.'

'But is . . . is my father already . . . dead?' gasped Iwan. 'Is Gwylan Canu fallen?'

'No!' exclaimed Branwen. 'I do not believe so. You must go to Prince Llew, Iwan – speak with him. Tell him of your father's peril and beg him to send a force of warriors along the coast to Gwylan Canu.'

Iwan gaped at her. He staggered, still disorientated and dazed from Blodwedd's vision. Branwen caught his arm. He leaned heavily on her, panting for breath.

'This is madness,' he gasped. 'Visions and dead gods? Am I a gullible child to be told such things and believe?' He glared at Blodwedd. 'This she-devil is a sorceress!'

'Believe me,' said Branwen, her fingers digging into his arm. 'I know how your mind must revolt. I too denied these things until denial became impossible.' She tugged at his arm. 'Look at me, Iwan. Have I lost my wits? Am I a stranger to truth and reality? Is that how I seem to you?'

He rubbed his arm across his face and stared at her.

His eyes were on her for a long time, as though he was trying to pierce her mind and stare deep into her soul.

'Even were I fool enough to trust you, Branwen,' he said at last, his voice slow and heavy. 'The prince will not send warriors to Gwylan Canu on my word alone – and be quite certain, I would not go to him with the tale you tell, not unless I wanted the madness whipped out of me.'

'Then tell him a different tale,' said Branwen. 'Tell him you met with a messenger riding hard from your father's fortress – a messenger with grim and urgent news! Tell him you learned that Gwylan Canu is in deadly danger, that the Saxons are coming in force. Tell him you told the messenger that you would pass this news on to the prince – tell him you sent the rider back to Gwylan Canu with all the speed he could muster, back to your father to let him know that he should hold firm, for aid would swiftly follow. Tell the prince that!'

'A messenger from Gwylan Canu?' murmured Iwan. 'Dagonet ap Wadu, perhaps, he would know me well and take orders from me. But no! He could not have entered Doeth Palas without drawing the attention of the guards on the gate.'

'Then tell the prince you met him on the road, outside the citadel,' urged Branwen.

'Yes, yes,' muttered Iwan. 'It is possible that I could have met with Dagonet on the east road, while wandering abroad – exercising my horse.' He ran his hand over his forehead. 'Ach, but to take such a tale to the prince? Would I be able to convince him that I am telling the truth?'

'You have shown no difficulty in being plausible in the

past, Iwan,' Branwen said. 'You played me for a fool with ease the first time we met.'

Iwan nodded. 'I can playact most blithely, for sure,' he said. 'But this is a deadlier game by far, Branwen. And if I am believed, and you prove false, it will be the end of me at Prince Llew's court. I will be disgraced – or worse.'

'I will not prove false,' said Branwen. 'You have looked into Blodwedd's eyes, you have seen the things she showed me. The danger is real. Ironfist is coming for Gwylan Canu – you cannot think otherwise.'

There was a long silence. Branwen could see Iwan was thinking hard – deciding whether or not to give credence to what he had been told. At last, he took a long, slow breath. 'No, I do not think otherwise,' he said. 'I will go to the prince. I will make him listen – I will make him believe. But what of you, Branwen? You cannot show yourself in Doeth Palas.'

'I shall not,' said Branwen. 'We only came here to speak with you – to convince you that your home is in peril. We will go now.'

'Will this Prince of Men believe and act?' asked Blodwedd. 'Is it certain that warriors will be sent to the place of the singing gulls?' She looked sharply at Branwen. 'Unless our actions work to the salvation of the citadel on the seashore, we will have failed in our task. Should we not go with this boy to the prince and add the weight of our words to his argument?'

'You cannot do that,' said Iwan. 'Branwen is a condemned fugitive – the prince would never listen to her.' He looked at Blodwedd. 'As for you.' He shook his head. 'One glance into your eyes and he would know you for a demon of the Old Times. You would be slaughtered on the spot.'

'That would not be such an easy task,' Blodwedd growled.

'Nevertheless, I doubt even you could hold out against fifty warriors,' Branwen said. 'You would die and I would hang and all would be lost. No. Iwan must go alone.'

'I shall,' said Iwan. He stood in the doorway; the door half open, so that he was bathed in sunlight and his long shadow stretched across the floor. He looked at Branwen. 'Thank you,' he said. 'Thank you for trusting me.' He gave her the ghost of a smile. 'Did I not say you would have an interesting life, Branwen? I never knew till today that I was gifted with prophecy! But if it is so, then here's one last foretelling – we *will* meet again, Barbarian Princess, and you will see you were right to put your faith in me. But for now – farewell.' He turned and ran from the building.

Branwen watched until he turned a corner and vanished, but all the time that her eyes were on him, she could feel rage rising within her. She had kept it suppressed so long as Iwan was with them, but now she turned to Blodwedd, free to give voice to her fury. 'Did you show him his own death?' she demanded, her voice trembling. 'Did you make him see his own head hanging from a Saxon fist?'

'No, I did not,' Blodwedd said. 'All but that, Warrior Child.'

'I'm grateful for that at least,' Branwen said, her anger abating a little. 'We should go now. I'd be out of this place before Prince Llew's warriors begin to gather.'

'We cannot depart,' said Blodwedd. 'Not until we are certain that the boy's warnings will be heeded.'

'It will take time for a host to be mustered,' said Branwen. 'Yet we will know soon enough. We will keep watch from the forest.' She thought for a moment. 'If soldiers have not taken the road to Gwylan Canu by the time the sun is low in the west, we will know Iwan has failed. And then . . .' Her voice faded.

And then?

Return to Doeth Palas. Give herself up to the guards. Hope to be taken to the prince. Hope to convince him where Iwan failed.

Hope to live long enough to do what she came here to do.

CHAPTER SIXTEEN

Branwen had been nervous and apprehensive ever since coming on to the road that led up to the citadel; and once within Doeth Palas she had been on edge, wary of every shadow, of every eye turned towards her. But true fear of capture did not strike her until she saw the gates ahead through the crowds, and knew that escape was close. It was overwhelming and terrifying – the thought that safety lay so near but that danger could still strike her down at any moment.

The market bustled, riotous and unruly and she had to force her way forward, forging a path in the opposite direction of the mass of people. Blodwedd was close behind her, struggling to keep up. Branwen could see from her stumbling, uncertain walk and her hunched shoulders that the owl-girl was having trouble coping with the crowds that pressed in all around her. A woman crossed Branwen's path, leading a donkey loaded with sheaves of flax. Branwen was pushed to one side as the woman barged through the crowd. The donkey came between her and Blodwedd. More people shoved past, knocking her aside, forcing her to use her arms to fend them off. She was made breathless by the crush, unable to see where she was going.

She fell over an earthenware pot, her hands over her head to avoid the trampling feet. There was something nightmarish about the surging crowds. She had to get up again. She had to find Blodwedd.

A hand plucked her from the ground. Her arm was twisted roughly behind her, the fingers locked on her wrist, wrenching the joints of her arm as she was forced out of the crowds and into a narrow passage between two buildings.

'Release me!' she demanded, wincing from the pain in her arm and shoulder.

The fingers loosened from her wrist. She turned and looked up into the face of Gavan ap Huw. His grey eyes glowered down on her, his mouth set in a grim line.

'What are you doing here?' he asked, and Branwen was surprised to hear a quaver in his gravely voice. 'Are you moonstruck to come back here, girl?'

She didn't know what to tell him. The truth? Gavan did not believe in the Old Gods – he would not listen to talk of Rhiannon of the Spring and Govannon of the Wood.

'Do you know what happened at Garth Milain?' she asked him, her own voice shaking.

'The battle? Aye, I know. All dead, child – all burned. Your home . . . gone. Is that why you have returned? It was lunacy to do so. Do you not know what kind of welcome the prince will have prepared for you, Branwen?'

'No! You're wrong about the battle,' said Branwen. 'Not all are dead. My mother still lives, and although the Garth was burned, the Saxons were thrown back. I was there, Gavan. Rhodri spoke the truth, everything he told me was true. He is no spy.'

'That is not for you to decide,' said Gavan. 'Come, I must take you to the prince.'

'No!'

'Be calm, girl. I will speak on your behalf in front of the full counsel. The fell deeds in Cyffin Tir will weigh in your favour. The prince is not a tyrant, Branwen. He will treat you justly when all is known.' His eyes glittered. 'Where is the boy?'

'Far from here,' said Branwen. 'Where you will never find him.'

'So?' Gavan's voice was thoughtful. 'He means us naught but good, and yet he flees us?'

'You would have hanged him,' said Branwen. 'He has no reason to trust to kinder treatment were you to capture him again. Let me go! Let me leave Doeth Palas. I give you my word neither I nor Rhodri will do anything to cause harm to a single soul of Bras Mynydd.' She looked fiercely into his eyes. 'I have a task to perform, Gavan ap Huw – you would do well not to hinder me in it. You do not know what peril you put yourself in!'

His great hand gripped her shoulder. 'Tell me of this peril.'

'You would not believe me.'

'You are the daughter of Alis ap Owain. Open your heart and speak honestly with me and I will believe you.'

Branwen paused, uncertain of how Gavan would react to the things she was about to tell him. 'The Shining Ones have awoken,' she said at last. 'They would use me to beat back the Saxons. They call me the Emerald Flame of my people. They call me the Bright Blade. They call me Destiny's Sword. Release me, Gavan ap Huw, or you stand in the way of the Old Gods!'

A look of alarm crossed Gavan's face. 'No!' he gasped. 'It cannot be. You are deluded, Branwen. Tell me that you know this to be untrue.'

She laughed without humour and his face became even more grave and troubled.

'She is telling you the truth,' said a man's voice from

behind the old warrior. 'Now, do nothing foolish. Do you feel the blade in your back? Twitch but the tips of your fingers, and I shall be the end of you.'

'Rhodri?' breathed Branwen, as stunned as Gavan. Her companion had come up behind the old warrior without a sound.

'Yes, and not a moment too soon, it seems,' said Rhodri. 'Hoi! Hold still, old man – I may not be a great swordsman like you, but it will take little skill to skewer you like a wild pig!'

Gavan's eyes narrowed. 'So he is not so very far from here, after all, my lady,' he said. 'Boy? Do you know the danger you are in? Were I but to cry out, a hundred men would fall upon you like thunder before you could run ten steps.'

'I am sure you're right in that,' said Rhodri. 'But you'd not be alive to enjoy the sight!'

Gavan winced as Rhodri pressed the tip of the knife into his back.

'I have offered my life to my liege lord many a time,' said Gavan, speaking without a trace of fear or anger. 'Think you I fear death if my duty requires it of me?' He twisted in an instant, taking Rhodri completely by surprise, and before Branwen was able to react, the knife was wrested from Rhodri's grip and he was pressed up against the wall with its keen edge against his throat.

'Now, boy, let's see how *you* face certain death,' said Gavan.

There was dread in Rhodri's face as Gavan pulled his head back by the hair to stretch his neck under the blade. 'Kill me if you must,' Rhodri croaked. 'But let Branwen go. She has told you the truth.' He swallowed hard. 'My life for hers, old man. Willingly.'

For a few long moments Gavan held Rhodri against the wall, his slatey eyes staring into Rhodri's brave, frightened face.

Branwen didn't dare move – nothing she could attempt would be quick enough to prevent the cold iron from slicing across Rhodri's flesh.

At last, Gavan took the blade from Rhodri's neck, turning the knife in his hand and offering the handle to him. 'Three fine fools together, are we, I think – but I will not be the cause of the downfall of the House of Griffith,' he said sombrely. 'I will not have it weigh on my heart that the daughter of Alis ap Owain died because of my actions.' He turned to look at Branwen. 'I fear for you, child, truly I do. But for all your ravings, I cannot believe you mean us harm. Go now, return to your mother, and seek her wisdom, for pity's sake. For you are mad, Branwen, if you believe you are guided by gods.'

'If I had my way, I would be by my mother's side at this

very moment,' Branwen said. 'My heart aches to be with her.'

'Then go to her!'

'I *cannot*!'

A slender figure appeared at the end of the alley. She walked forward, drawing her wimple back and looking keenly up into Gavan's face.

'Beware, Warrior of Powys,' Blodwedd murmured. 'Beware lest your eyes be opened by the gods themselves – for they will pour their truth into your heart like molten iron, and you will be seared and destroyed by it!'

Gavan stared at her, his face blanching.

'What are you?' he gasped.

'I?' Blodwedd's voice was a low rumble. 'I am the silent wing in the still of night, I am the swift slaughter in twilight. I am the claw that clutches the heart, the beak that pecks the soul. Would you know me better, Warrior of Powys?'

Gavan shook his head. 'No,' he murmured, and for the first time Branwen heard fear in the powerful old man's voice. 'No, for the life of me, I would not. I know now what you are. But the world has changed since your kind walked abroad. You are wrong for these times. You come here from beyond sanity's shores.'

'You thought we would slumber for all eternity?' Blodwedd asked him. 'You thought that if you never spoke our names, you would be free of us? Free of the ache for air in your lungs? Free of the need for earth beneath your feet? Free of the howling hunger? Free of the unslakable thirst? Free of all things that bind you to this land?' She smiled. 'Not while you breathe and walk and eat and drink, Warrior of Powys.' She turned to Branwen, her head bowed. 'I failed you again, Warrior Child,' she said. 'I should not have let us become parted.'

'No harm was done,' Branwen said. She looked into the disturbed face of the old warrior. 'Gavan? Will you let me go now? Do you see that I am not mad?'

'I will not stop you,' said Gavan. 'But heed my words, Branwen – these powers that call you are like a mighty river, and you but a leaf on their flood. They will bear you to your doom, child.'

'Perhaps,' Branwen said. 'But if you honour me for my mother's sake, tell no one that you saw me here – leave me to walk the path the Shining Ones have laid out for me.'

Gavan bowed his head. 'I will pray for your soul,' he said.

'For that, much thanks,' Branwen replied. She looked from Rhodri to Blodwedd. 'Come, he won't give us away.' And so saying, she pulled her wimple close over her face again and led her two companions along the narrow alley between the two huts and out into the marketplace.

CHAPTER SEVENTEEN

'What Goraig goblin put it into your mind to risk your life like that?' Branwen asked Rhodri as they moved through the trees. 'Don't you know that Gavan could have slaughtered you in an instant if he had so chosen? I told you to stay with the horses and be safe.'

'I left Fain to watch over the horses,' said Rhodri. 'And here they are, safe and sound. And your armour untouched. And as for the rest.' He shrugged. 'I asked myself, what would Branwen do in these circumstances?' He smiled. 'The answer came very easily.'

'Then perhaps such questions are better not asked,' said Branwen.

The two horses were quietly grazing.

'Caw! Caw!'

Branwen smiled at the falcon, perched on a branch, watching them with its clever, knowing eyes.

'Thank you, Fain,' she said. 'You are more true to your duty than some I could mention.'

Blodwedd looked from Branwen to Rhodri. 'Why do you chide him so?' she asked. 'He acted out of loyalty and concern.'

'He could have been killed,' Branwen said.

'Well, I was not,' said Rhodri. 'Now, tell me all that happened in Doeth Palas. Did you find Iwan?'

'We did,' said Branwen. 'He will speak with the prince.'

'And will Prince Llew act, do you think?'

'That we shall see,' said Branwen, staring up through the leaves at the midday sun.

The afternoon wore slowly away. The forest was full of drowsy air, the light thick and golden through the canopy of leaves. An insect buzzed in Branwen's ear. She flicked her hand at it, fretting at the delay.

She and Rhodri and Blodwedd were seated under the trees. Blodwedd was sitting as she always did, bolt upright in the grass, her legs folded, her arms wrapped around her shins, her chin on her knees. Her eyes were open, but she did not seem to be looking at anything. She had not moved for some time. Watchfully asleep, perhaps, Branwen wondered, as the owl-girl had been the previous night.

Rhodri was whittling a stick with the hunting knife,

his head bowed in concentration. Branwen envied his calmness. She felt anything but calm. She had no idea how long ago it was that she had sent Fain to gather news, but it seemed like a whole lifetime. And still they hid in the forest, and still they knew nothing of what was happening in Doeth Palas.

And what if Prince Llew did not act? What were her choices then? She had gone over this many times in her mind, turning her thoughts like heavy rocks, not liking what was revealed beneath.

A grey sickle-shape came winging through the branches.

Branwen jumped up. 'Fain!'

The falcon burst out with a succession of sharp calls as it circled her.

She looked over to Blodwedd, alert now, also on her feet. 'What is he saying?'

'Horsemen,' said Blodwedd. 'Many horsemen have left the citadel, armed and caparisoned for warfare. They have taken the coastal road to the east, travelling swiftly.'

Branwen let out a breath. 'Then it is done!' she gasped, relief thrilling through her body like a rush of cool water. 'The prince has sent soldiers to Gwylan Canu. Ironfist will be thwarted!' She looked over to where Rhodri was standing. 'It's done!' she called to him.

He smiled, looking at Blodwedd. 'The place of singing

gulls will be safe from the Saxon hawks, Blodwedd,' he said. 'You will be a bird again!'

'When all is fulfilled, with my Lord's blessing, I shall,' said Blodwedd. 'The bird is on the wing and the prey is under the claw, but the kill is not yet certain.' She looked at Branwen. 'We must go to the place of singing gulls,' she said. 'We must know for sure that all is well. Only then is our duty done. Only then will Lord Govannon release me.'

The stone-clad citadel of Doeth Palas stood on a lofty peak rising from a forested valley at the northern limits of the Land of Brython and the Kingdom of Powys. The solitary hill sheared down in precipitous cliffs to the restless sea, and from its shoulders, long undulating bluffs of timeworn limestone stretched into the east.

A road ran along these cliffs, hugging the coastline, rising and falling like a pale ribbon as it threaded its way into the cantref of Teg Eingel, long home of the House of Puw, a narrow stretch of land between the Clwydian Mountains and the sea.

It was a road much used, traversed by merchants, hawkers and travellers in peaceful times, a conduit for trade and commerce. And in unsettled and violent days, the hooves of war-horses and the feet of soldiers echoed among the cliffs and glens as armies swept back and forth with the tides and fortunes of battle. Although Branwen had no patience with dry lists of names and dates, she had always loved the thrilling tales of the old wars as they were told and retold around the hearth in the Great Hall of Garth Milain. And so she knew it was almost twenty years now since a Saxon warrior had walked this road. Twenty years since Powys had been in such peril as now haunted these regions.

Branwen and Rhodri and Blodwedd tracked the horsemen of Doeth Palas as they made their way along the road. They were careful to keep out of sight, wary not to show themselves against the horizon or to come close enough for a vigilant eye to catch a glimpse of them.

Fortunately the northern reaches of Bras Mynydd were less hospitable than the fertile lowlands, and there were no farms or hamlets to be avoided. There were hills and forests enough to provide cover, and when the difficulties of the landscape forced Branwen to lead them away from the warrior band, there was always Fain to keep watch from on high and guide them back to the road.

They shadowed the horsemen through the long afternoon and on into evening. They were drawing close to the mountains now and their dark-green bulk filled the eastern sky as the sun set, the highest peaks turning to gold in the fading light.

* * *

Night fell. The horsemen made camp in a sheltered dell south of the road, building fires and setting the horses to graze while they prepared their evening meal.

Branwen and Rhodri watched from a high ridge, lying flat on their stomachs as they peered down the wooded slope to where the flames of the cooking fires flickered. Branwen was in her hunting leathers again. She felt much more herself now that the disguise had been shed – and she was glad to feel the knife and slingshot at her belt.

Her sword and shield were with Blodwedd and the horses, further up the hill, well out of sight. It had been difficult to convince Blodwedd to let the two of them patrol alone, but in the end the owl-girl had agreed to remain behind while they scouted out the land.

'How many men, would you say?' asked Branwen. 'Fifty perhaps?'

Rhodri nodded.

'Why so few?' Branwen wondered aloud. 'He has twice ten times that number of armed men in Doeth Palas. What can fifty men do against Ironfist's army?'

'They can hold the tide till the foot soldiers can get here,' said Rhodri. 'My guess would be that these are just an advance party, sent as a show of force – to let Ironfist know that the Prince of Bras Mynydd is coming for him.' Rhodri grinned, his eyes bright in the darkness. 'Ironfist will be livid to find his tactics have been discovered. His whole purpose was to strike without warning – first, Garth Milain, then another citadel, and another and another, his enemy never knowing when or where he will come at them next. This will sour his milk for him! Closed gates and men armed and ready. Ha!'

'The prince is not with them, I think,' said Branwen, staring down through the gloom. 'But who is leading them? We have never come close enough to find out. And is Iwan with them? That's something I'd like to know.'

'Go down and ask,' Rhodri suggested. 'And while you're at it, beg some food from them. We have hardly anything left to eat. I have to say, being linked to your high destiny would be more comfortable if the Old Gods gave thought to our bellies once in a while.'

'Don't joke about such things,' Branwen warned.

'Was I joking?' Rhodri sighed, lifting his head to gaze off into the east. 'How far is it to Gwylan Canu, do you think?'

'Why ask me? I don't know these lands,' Branwen replied distractedly. She was staring down the long slope and calculating how close she could get to the encampment without being spotted by the sentries. 'Another day? Half a day? It cannot be too close, or they would not have made camp for the night.' She lifted herself on to one elbow, looking at Rhodri. 'I'm going down there,' she said.

'Are you out of your wits?' Rhodri hissed. 'Why would you want to do that?'

'I may learn how soon they expect to come to Gwylan Canu,' Branwen replied. 'And find out whether you are right – whether more warriors are coming, or whether fifty is all Prince Llew is willing to spare for a neighbour in peril.'

'What are you saying? I don't understand.'

'Neither do I,' said Branwen. 'But doesn't it seem odd to you that the prince did not send his warriors over the mountains to Garth Milain when he learned of the Saxon attack? Why did he not come to our aid?'

'The battle was done, so far as he knew,' said Rhodri. 'Your army scattered or slain, your mother and father dead, and the triumphant Saxons warming their hands as Garth Milain blazed. It was too late to help.

There's little purpose in you going down there and risking your neck in the hope of learning otherwise.'

'I'll be careful,' said Branwen.

'All the same,' Rhodri said, 'you'll probably find they're talking of nothing more elevated than saddle sores, or grumbling about having to sleep under the stars instead of snug in their own beds with the furs piled high.'

'We shall see,' said Branwen. 'Wait for me, I shan't

be long. And don't let Blodwedd know I've gone. The last thing I need is for her to go crashing down there causing chaos.'

Rhodri gripped her arm. 'Branwen, be careful.'

'I will, I promise.' She pulled away and slipped silently over the ridge and down the forested slope.

'Be calm, be silent, be swift, be still.' Branwen mouthed the familiar instructions to herself as she made her way down the steep fall of the hillside. Occasionally the bulk of trees blocked sight of the fires down in the vale, but most of the time she could see the flames flickering through branch and bole as she slipped lithely from trunk to trunk, her fingers running over the rough and ridged bark. The acrid smell of smoke drifted up to her, tingling in her nostrils, blotting out the other night-time forest scents.

She began to hear the voices of the warriors, the clank of metal against metal, the restless thud of a horse's hoof, the crackle of the flames. And with those sounds rose the rich aroma of cooking meat, filling her head, making her belly growl. She had not tasted hot food since the half-finished bowl of stew in the farmhouse where they had almost been captured.

She rested her back against a wide fir, listening intently. The nearest campfire was no more than twenty paces away, and now she could clearly hear the voices of the soldiers.

'I'm telling you there's a storm coming,' one was saying. 'I can smell it on the air. We'll sleep cold and wet this night. We should have found a more sheltered spot to make camp.'

'We should have ridden on through the night,' said another voice – one that Branwen knew. Iwan. So he *was* travelling with them. She felt uneasy, remembering the vision of his severed head dangling from a Saxon fist. Was he riding to his death? A third voice interrupted her troubled thoughts.

'And arrive to fight red-eyed and yawning,' it said. 'That were wisdom, indeed, young pup!'

'Captain Angor knows his business, lad,' said the first voice. 'Don't you fret, we'll be up and on the move with the dawn. It makes no sense to travel by night. Look you at those hills – wooded from end to end; trees enough to hide an army! You'd have us ride such terrain at night? Why, if old Ironfist was lying in ambush, we'd not stand a chance.'

'Aye, I don't like the look of these forests,' said a different voice. 'Pass that pig's foot, Digon, fetch it out of the flames before it's charred. Mark me, boys, there's something uncanny about these old woodlands. Don't you feel it? *Eyes watching? Minds turning.*'

Branwen felt a shiver run down her spine. There was

something almost sinister in the way that flecks of firelight trembled and danced on trunk and branch and leaf all around her. But what did the man mean? Eyes watching. Minds turning.

'They say there was a Druid temple hereabouts in the way-before times,' said the first voice in a husky growl. 'They performed strange rites and rituals in these hills, sacrificing to the Old Gods . . .'

Ahhh! The Old Gods . . .

'Be silent, you fool,' the third voice said angrily. 'Do not name them. Not here. Not in this place. Are you moonstruck?'

'Why do you fear them?' asked Iwan. 'Do the Old Gods hate us?'

'How would you feel, boy?' commented the first voice ominously. 'To be a god no longer worshipped or feared?'

'Speak no more of these things!' snapped the third voice.

There was a lull in the conversation for a few moments. Branwen could hear the sounds of meat being gnawed from the bone and of drink being swallowed.

'I still say we should have pressed on through the dark,' Iwan said at length. 'Scouts could have ridden on ahead to scour the road for danger. And isn't it as dark for Saxons as it is for us? My father could be lying slain this very moment, while we sit cramming our bellies and gossiping!'

'If your father is already slain, there's little need for haste, boy,' said the first voice lightly. 'He won't begrudge us our respite – not where he'll be watching from!'

There was some laughter at this, but Iwan broke angrily into it. 'If Gwylan Canu is taken while we slumber and snore, every death will be on our heads.'

'Calm yourself, boy!' ordered the third voice. 'Dagonet ap Wadu will have reached the citadel by now. They will know of our coming. The gates will be closed. Why do you fret? Gwylan Canu is a strong fortress and your father a fearsome warrior. We will arrive in time, Iwan, have no fear.'

Branwen heard Iwan give a snort of anger. She knew why he was angry and frustrated by the delay – he alone knew that Dagonet would not be arriving at Gwylan Canu with hopeful tidings. He had not come to begin with.

'Don't stray, lad,' called the first man.

Branwen realized that Iwan must have got up from the fireside and walked away from the men.

'I'm going to check on the horses,' called Iwan, his voice further away now. 'Perhaps they'll make more sense than you bunch of old women!'

The soldiers roared with laughter.

Branwen moved stealthily across the hillside, careful

not to rustle a branch or snap a twig. She peered around a trunk. The horses were gathered a little way off from the fires, haltered by reins looped around fallen branches and large stones. A slim shadow moved among them.

She slipped from cover and was in an instant in among the horses, smelling their distinctive scent, listening to their breathing and their night-time movements. She ran her hand over flank and neck, enjoying the rough texture of their hair, wishing she had some morsel – an apple or something – to offer them as they turned their huge, noble heads towards her.

And then one horse in particular nuzzled against her and even in the dark of night she knew him. A tall bay stallion, the bold and true friend she had been forced to leave behind when she fled. Her own horse.

'Stalwyn!' she breathed, lifting her hands to stroke his neck and run glad fingers through his glossy black mane. 'I thought I'd never see you again, boy.' She pressed her face into his neck and breathed in deeply, her head filling with his warm horsey scent. 'So they knew your worth, did they, the men of Doeth Palas? Who rides you now to war, boy? Someone equally worthy, I hope.' Stalwyn lifted his head, his liquid black eye shining. He pushed his soft nose into her shoulder, as if glad to be reunited with her. 'I'd ride off with you now, if I could,' she murmured. 'But we'd be seen and that would not be good. Be brave and steadfast and with luck we will be together again in time.'

Oh, but the smell of him brought back such memories! There was a thickness in her throat and a prickling in her eyes as she remembered carefree days riding on the heaths with Geraint, the wind slapping her skin red as berries, Stalwyn's body moving powerfully under her and she gripping tight with knees and thighs as they raced the long summer days away.

And in deep winter, fetlock-deep in snow, his breath white like the smoke from a smith's fire when the bellows are blown. The trill of a hunting horn. The chase for a stag. And Stalwyn sweating in the paddock afterwards, leaning into her as she wiped him down with sacking, his hot horse smell filling her head.

Lost times. Never to be recovered, except with the bittersweet stab of memory.

'Branwen?' The voice was a low murmur, breaking the reverie that Stalwyn's scent had thrown her into. She looked around sharply, her fingers gripping her knife. Iwan was staring at her, his face just a pale blur in the night. He came closer, his voice lowered to a whisper. 'You followed us?'

'I had to know your home would be saved,' Branwen whispered back. 'But why are there only fifty of you?

Prince Llew could have spared more, surely?'

'More are coming,' murmured Iwan, his head close to hers, his eyes dark and deep. 'Two hundred or more, on foot, as soon as they can be mustered. But fifty horse was all that the prince could bring together on such short notice.'

So Rhodri's guess had been right – these were only the vanguard of the force that would be sent. Good. Very good – so long as they came quickly!

'At least Prince Llew believed you,' Branwen said.

'Aye, I played the part well. But you should not be here. It isn't safe. What if you are discovered?'

'Don't worry on my behalf,' Branwen replied.

He looked closely into her face, his breath warm on her cheek. 'Oh, but I do,' he whispered, his eyes glinting in the dim light. 'I knew from the first time I saw you that you'd stamp a heavy foot on my heart, Branwen.'

She stared at him. Confused. Not understanding what he meant. Was he playacting again?

'You should not have come, Iwan,' Branwen murmured.

He looked puzzled. 'Why so?'

Because I fear you will be killed!

A deep voice called. 'Hoi! Iwan!'

He spun, his face perturbed. 'Here, Captain – I'm coming.' He glanced briefly at Branwen, moving away, holding his arm out towards her, warning her to stay hidden. Almost without thinking, she reached out and their fingers touched for a moment.

Then he was gone among the horses.

'Who were you speaking to, Iwan?' came Captain Angor's voice.

Branwen shrank away between the horses, a cold sweat starting on her face, the blood throbbing in her ears.

'Gwennol Dhu was fretful,' Iwan replied smoothly. 'I calmed her with a few gentle words.'

'The horses are agitated, for sure,' said the captain. 'They like not this forest. It has an ill name in legend. It used to be called the Ghostwood. Perhaps ancient memories linger.'

'Memories of the Old Gods, do you mean?' asked Iwan.

'There are no Old Gods, boy,' Angor said abruptly. 'There are Saint Cadog and Saint Dewi and Saint Cynwal. Look you how they watch over us. We need no others.'

'But the saints have gentle hands and they watch from afar,' Iwan responded. 'It is said the Saxons have terrible gods. Gods of thunder and lightning, blood and iron. Gods of death and mayhem. Can the saints protect us against such gods?'

'Aye, lad – that they can, have no fear on that score. Come now, get you to sleep, Iwan ap Madoc. It is stern work that awaits us with the coming of the new day.'

Branwen heard them move away, back towards the campfires. She let out a long, slow breath.

She waited among the horses until it felt safe for her to slip away into the sheltering darkness under the trees and up the long hill to where her companions were waiting.

The Ghostwood. Haunted by memories of ancient things. But *what* ancient things, Branwen wondered as she climbed. Perhaps Blodwedd would be able to tell her more. Yes, if anyone knew the secrets of this place, it would be Govannon's messenger.

CHAPTER EIGHTEEN

'Are you thistledown that you think you can move among men without being seen?' Blodwedd's eyes were like angry fires in the darkness under the trees.

'No one saw me except for Iwan,' Branwen retorted, stung by the owl-girl's rebuke. 'And I won't answer to you for my movements. You're here to be my guide, not my master.' She held Blodwedd's eyes, refusing to be browbeaten by her.

'Did you find out anything of use?' Rhodri asked, obviously wanting to break the tension between the two.

'More soldiers are coming,' Branwen said, turning to Rhodri. 'Iwan told me that. And one of the soldiers thinks there's a storm coming.' She peered up through the branches. 'But I'm not so sure.' Stars were twinkling, cold and remote.

'He is right,' said Blodwedd, looking at Rhodri. 'I can

smell it on the air. It rides in on a brazen west wind. There will be rain before dawn.'

'Then we should get what sleep we can,' said Rhodri. 'For a while before the heavens open, hopefully.' He pulled his cloak around his shoulders and curled up on his side.

Branwen settled back against a tree trunk, pillowed on dead leaves, her knees up, feet splayed and her arms folded over her chest. She closed her eyes, but was vividly aware of Blodwedd's presence on Rhodri's far side, bundled up like a grasshopper or a stoop of hay.

Did the girl never lie down? *Girl? Is that what you called her? Careful, Branwen, don't forget what she truly is.*

Branwen opened an eye. She was surprised to see Blodwedd gazing at Rhodri with a curious, conflicted expression on her pale, wide face. It seemed part fascination, part joy and part . . . what? . . . *longing*, almost. Yes, that was it exactly – a look of quiet, almost regretful yearning.

Has she fallen in love with him? Branwen wondered. She found the idea faintly repellent. And what feelings did Rhodri have for the owl-girl? He was kind to her, as was his nature, and he was obviously intrigued by her. But surely no more than that? Surely he could not have deep feelings for a creature so inhuman that she had come close to slaughtering a helpless baby?

Blodwedd's eyes turned towards her and her face became blank and unreadable again. 'You may speak freely,' Blodwedd said. 'He will not wake.'

'Why?' Branwen asked sourly. 'Have you put a spell on him?'

'Not I,' Blodwedd replied. 'There are things you wish to ask me, but you fear the answers. Ask anyway, Warrior Child – it is the fears that are never faced that gnaw the deepest.'

'The men were talking about this place,' Branwen began hesitantly. 'About this forest. Something about it scares them. Like children frightened of the dark, except not quite that. One of them started to talk about the Old Gods, but he was told to hold his tongue.' She sat up now, strangely sleepless. 'Do the Shining Ones live in this forest?'

'I have told you already,' Blodwedd said, as though speaking to a child. 'The Shining Ones live in all things, trickle and torrent, shoot and tree, pebble and crag, breeze and blizzard. *All* things.'

'So why do the men call this place the Ghostwood?'

The huge eyes shone. 'Perhaps because this was a place of worship in the young days, in the days before the counting of days. It was here they venerated the guardians of the land and gave thanks for their stewardship.'

Branwen tried hard to understand what the owl-girl

was telling her. 'You mean there was a temple here – a Druid temple – before the Romans came?'

'A sacred place,' said Blodwedd. 'A blessed place. A glorious place. If men fear it now, it is only because they know in their hearts that they have turned away from the father that seeded them and the mother that bore them and watched over them. They fear to come here because it speaks to them of who they once were, and shows them the folly of the path upon which their feet are now set.' Blodwedd rose to her feet. 'It whispers of their peril, Warrior Child. It murmurs of their doom.'

'A Saxon doom?' Branwen asked, gazing up into the owl-girl's face. She trembled as Blodwedd stared at her, feeling in danger of losing herself once more in those golden eyes. But she could not tear herself free.

Her head throbbed and white lightning flashed at the edges of sight. Her skin prickled hot and cold and she felt dizzy and disorientated, as though in a nightmare or a high fever. And Blodwedd seemed somehow to have grown taller – towering over Branwen, her head among the stars, her feet sunken deep into the earth, her arms as wide as the night sky.

'The riddling Saxons will come, Warrior Child,' cried Blodwedd, her voice booming in Branwen's mind. 'And the high-hearted Angles and the flaxen Jutes and the rune-wise Danes.' Lightning flashed around her like knives, and white sparks rose from her hair, forming forked shapes almost like antlers against the dark sky.

'What are you talking about?' shouted Branwen. 'I don't understand!'

But Blodwedd didn't seem to hear her.

'And also will come the butchering Vikings,' she raged. 'Steeped to the shoulder in crimson gore, cutting the blood-eagle and sprinkling salt in the wounds. And in their wake will come the courtly Normans and Owain Gwynedd, first Prince of the Walha. And in time upon bad time, Edward Longshanks will waken, to slaughter the four brothers of Gwynedd and to hack off the head of Llewellyn Ein Llyw Olaf – the last leader of our people – and carry it as a trophy through the streets of London.'

'Stop! Stop!'

'And then, in the reign of Henry Plantagenet, third of that name, the great hero Owain Glyndwr will arise – warrior descendent of warrior stock, far-flung son of the daughters of the sons of the women of the House of Griffith!'

'For pity's sake – enough!' shouted Branwen, screwing her eyes tight shut, pressing her hands to her ears to try and hold back the thundering and crashing of Blodwedd's voice in her head.

And suddenly the voice was gone – and all Branwen could hear was the hiss and spatter of rain. She held her breath for a few moments to be sure. Yes! Blodwedd's rantings were done.

She could still hear the thunder, but there were no longer words in it. She could still see the cold fire of the lightning through her closed eyes. She could feel rain on her skin.

She opened her eyes. Blodwedd was standing over her, small and slender again, gazing unfathomably down at her through a curtain of slanting rain. Branwen gasped, her head aching and her limbs tingling as though the lightning had got into her body and was burning her from within.

Blodwedd stretched down a thin hand. Branwen took it and got up. She glanced at Rhodri, sleeping still in all the tumult, curled under his rain-speckled cloak. The horses stood close by, lost in imperturbable horse dreams.

Wordlessly, Blodwedd led Branwen through the trees. The rain tapped on the leaves like impatient fingers, but beneath their feet the ground was still dry. Thunder rumbled and growled, and blades of lightning bleached the world black and white – sable trees standing stark against a backdrop of blanched nothingness, like a veil thrown across eternity.

They came to a grove where there was no rain and no thunder. The sky above was vibrant with uncountable stars. The air was sweet and warm. Branwen saw that the skulls of animals had been nailed high on the trunks of the trees that ringed the glade, their staring eye sockets black in the light of flickering torches.

A rhythmic drumming filled the glade, throbbing in the air and making the ground shudder under Branwen's feet.

A circle of grey standing stones dominated the glade, shoulder high, rough-hewn into shapes like pointed leaves or spear-heads. Designs and patterns had been engraved on the stones, but the hollows and ridges were blurred by lichen and funguses.

Branwen had the certain feeling that the stones had been there for a long time – girdled with snowdrops in festive spring, scorched by the sun in high summer, marooned in an ocean of brown leaves in autumn, snow-crowned in deepest winter – enduring and outlasting all that the shifting seasons offered for years beyond count.

A woman stood in the middle of the stone circle, dressed in deep-blue robes, her arms spread and her face lifted towards the starry night sky. She was chanting, her deep, resonant voice keeping time to the drum.

In the summer comes love and devotion
Like a stallion galloping, courageous for his lady and his lord
The sea is booming, the apple tree in bloom

The thirsty earth drinks deep
The sun shield-shining
Lightning comes as arrows from the blue sky
Cloudless rain like a falling of spears.
I long and I crave for thee, Guardians of our land
Eternally renewed from ever was to ever will be
Earthshakers, with the sky on your shoulders
With your feet in the sea
Movers of the rolling world, the Shining Ones.
I stand among the slender hemlock stems
In bright noon and in blessed night
Awaiting the fair, frail, fragile form
Awaiting thy light.
See, silent she comes as the deer's footfall
Comely and bountiful,
See, mighty he comes, root deep, leaf bright
Loving and giving,
See, solemn she comes from out the hollow hills
Constant and true,
See, merry he comes, the liquid acrobat who carves the
quartered sky
Laughing and leaping.

As the woman threw her words up into the immense
darkness, four figures moved around her in a slow
ritual dance.

One was a woman, turning and turning, dressed in white and with long fine white hair, carrying in her hands the white skull of a horse. The second was a man dressed all in green, stamping with heavy feet, antlers bound on to his forehead. The third was bent-backed, stumbling forwards, gnarled fingers clutching a twisted stick – masked with an ancient, ugly wrinkled wise face. And the last of the four was a man in grey who tumbled and cavorted and pranced and leaped like cloud-wraiths in a gale.

'What is this?' Branwen asked, her mouth dry, her head hammering.

'The midsummer rites from the years of man's innocence,' said Blodwedd. 'Do you recognize the players, Warrior Child?'

'The woman in white is like Rhiannon,' said Branwen. 'I imagine the green man is Govannon of the Wood.'

'Yes. And the crone is Merion of the Stones and the cloud-man is Caradoc of the North Wind. This is from the days of belief, Warrior Child – from the days of bone-deep faith and of loyal blood. This is from the days of *understanding*.'

'Geraint told me that the Druid priests sacrificed children to the Shining Ones,' Branwen said. 'That they used human blood to placate the Old Gods. That they were terrible and full of vengeance.'

'Do you see spilled blood, Warrior Child?' asked Blodwedd. 'Do you feel fear in the air?'

'No.' There was certainly no sensation of fear in the glade, Branwen sensed joy and awe, as though this worship that she was witnessing was a pleasure and a privilege. She turned to look into Blodwedd's golden eyes. 'Why did we turn our backs on them?'

'You are human – you tell me.'

'I don't *know*!'

'Humans are weak and changeable,' said Blodwedd. 'All the same, the parent loves still the wayward child, foolish and errant though it be. But when danger threatens, then the children must return and guard the home, lest the house fall and all are consumed in the flames.' A sinister, dreadful light glowed in Blodwedd's eyes. 'The Shining Ones dread the coming of the Saxons, Warrior Child. They dread the things they bring with them.'

'What things?' Branwen whispered.

'The dark and brutal gods that dwell in their hearts,' Blodwedd murmured. 'Gods of warfare and avarice who have no love for Brython nor its people. Gods with iron teeth and hearts of stone, gods whose footsteps burn, whose touch withers, whose breath is plague and damnation. Gods who will enter the hearts and minds of the people of Brython and destroy them.'

Branwen felt her eyes widen in horror. 'So they'd have me fight not only the Saxons, but their gods as well?'

Blodwedd smiled. 'Now you have wisdom, Warrior Child,' she said. 'Now you see all! But the task is not as heavy as fear makes it. The Saxon gods follow behind the armies, feeding on death and despair as carrion birds feed on the fallen in battle. Hold back the Saxons and their gods will never darken this land. Do this thing and you will turn the long hard winter into glorious summer, Warrior Child. That is what you must do. That is why the Shining Ones have called you. That is your destiny!'

CHAPTER NINETEEN

The stars were snuffed out by a mass of seething black cloud. Thunder roared. Branwen blinked the teeming rain out of her eyes, trying to see in the sudden darkness.

'Blodwedd?' she screamed as storm-winds buffeted her and tore her hair.

Forked lightning cracked the sky open and showed Branwen the world.

She was at the edge of the glade still, but it was overgrown now, bereft of magic, the stones half buried in fern and flower, their heads mantled in climbing plants. Tall trees grew where the woman had chanted and the four god-players had danced. But from high on the trunk of a nearby tree, the dead black eye sockets of a goat skull stared down mournfully, the last remnant of lost love and failed devotion.

'I am here,' came Blodwedd's crackling voice. 'We

must return – there is mischief afoot! I smell wolves in the night! Rhodri cannot fight them alone.'

Wolves!

Branwen drew her knife as she ran, the dark ecstasy of impending combat thrilling through her body. Here at last was an enemy she could strike at! Here was a prey to vent her frustration on! She gripped the knife tightly, chasing hard after the owl-girl as she flitted through the trees, praying Rhodri had not been caught unawares.

She could make out the frightened neighing of horses and the keening screech of Fain the falcon – but she could also hear harsh snarling and growling of wolves.

Rhodri was on his feet, freed now from whatever spell had caused him to sleep so deeply earlier on in the night. He was at bay against a tree, his face twisted in fear, his clothes and hair saturated from the rain. He was holding off four or five wolves, the sword gripped in both fists as he swung it to and fro in a wide arc in front of him. As the blade scythed the rain, the wolves backed off, then came snapping forward again.

Fain was doing his best to help, wings fluttering as he rose and swooped, flying into the wolves' eyes with outstretched claws, screaming, distracting them from their prey.

Even had Branwen been in a position to shoot a stone into a wolf's eye, the rain would make it impossible for her to aim accurately with the slippery wet leather slingshot. No! It was knife work that was needed now – and quickly too, before one of the wolves got close enough to Rhodri to draw blood.

Blodwedd let out a fearsome shriek, throwing herself forwards, her arms raised, fingers crooked into claws. Seeming at that moment far more owl-like than human, she came down on the back of one of the wolves, sending it tumbling, the two rolling over and over, Blodwedd's arms and legs wrapped around the creature's shaggy body, its vicious head twisting and the wide jaws snapping red.

Branwen sprang forwards, stabbing fiercely, catching a wolf in the hindquarters. Blood spurted as the wolf turned, howling in anger and pain, its eyes poison-yellow, its black lips drawn back from slavering fangs. She slashed again with the long hunting knife, rending the wolf's shoulder to the bone. As lightning flashed, she saw a second wolf turn and leap toward her.

She dropped to her knees in the wet earth, mud spraying up around her. Claws raked across her back as the flying wolf overshot. Branwen lunged forwards and sank her knife deep into the wounded wolf's throat. It gave a hideous yowl as dark blood gushed from the wound and the wolf crashed in front of her in a tangle of twisted legs.

She took one quick look into the dead eyes, seeing

the jaws still open, the tongue hanging, red with blood, and then she stumbled to her feet, dashing the rain out of her eyes, twisting as she heard a scrabble of claws behind her.

She had no time to use her knife as the huge creature pounced. She thrust her forearm between its jaws, forcing the mouth wide so that it could not bite down, fighting to stay on her feet as the weight of the animal came hammering down on her. There was the stench of its breath and the horrible smell of its rank, wet fur, the scrape of its hooked and broken claws. She wrenched her arm to one side, forcing the creature's head to twist on its powerful neck, and drove her knife upwards, cutting through flesh and sinew and throbbing veins. Hot blood splashed over Branwen's face as the bulk of the wolf suddenly became lifeless, bearing her down into the mud.

Using all her strength, she pushed and kicked the hairy corpse off her. She scrambled to her feet, her shoes slipping, her face whipped raw by the rain. She saw Blodwedd rise from a dead wolf, her arms blooded to the elbow, her mouth red and dripping, her eyes ferocious. The wolf's throat had been bitten out.

Branwen turned away from the dreadful sight, desperate to get to Rhodri's side. He was still fighting for his life, but he was managing to hold off the last two wolves, slashing and swiping at them as if the sword was a stick. He had no battle skills, no training as a warrior – all he had was courage and the strength of his two arms. Fain was still with him, plunging with outstretched claws, rising in a flurry of wings as the deadly teeth snapped at him.

Behind the tree against which Rhodri was trapped, Branwen saw the two horses, rearing on their hind legs, kicking the air, their eyes terrified as they dragged at their tethers.

'Hold on!' she yelled to Rhodri. 'I'm coming!'

Screaming in rage, she flung herself on the nearer of the two remaining wolves, using her momentum and weight to drive her knife up to the hilt in its back. It twisted and writhed in its death agonies, ripping the knife from her fist, knocking her feet out from under her, sending her slamming hard to the ground.

She blinked as she lay gasping on her back, pain wracking her body, the rain filling her eyes, mixing with blood, veiling her sight with a red haze. She heard snarling. She felt blindly for her knife. A great dark shaggy head appeared above her. Claws dug into her chest. Crimson jaws opened, yellow eyes gleamed. Fetid breath blasted in her face.

Her fingers scrabbled in mud and grass, finding no weapon. She dashed the red water from her eyes as the gaping maw plunged towards her throat. There was a shout from above her. The wolf's head jerked up, the neck arching back. It fell sideways, kicked for a few moments, then lay still.

Branwen sat up, coughing and choking. Blood bubbled from a wound in the wolf's back. Rhodri was standing over her, panting for breath, the sword in both his hands, the blade swimming with gore.

She got up, grimacing, aching from her fall. Blodwedd walked towards them through the rain.

Rhodri gave Branwen a wry smile. 'A fine time to go walkabout, Branwen!' he said. 'If not for Fain waking me up, you'd have returned to find me being enjoyed as a late supper by those fine fellows!' He looked around at the five dark corpses. Fain had come down to perch on one unnaturally bent head. Branwen looked away as the curved beak pecked for juicy morsels among the bloody fur.

'Do you think the soldiers in the valley below will have heard us?' Rhodri asked. 'I'd rather we did not have to face them as well!'

'The storm is loud enough to drown all else out,' said Branwen. 'And I doubt they would come to investigate the howling of wolves.'

Blodwedd came up to Rhodri, looking into his eyes. 'Are you hurt?' she asked.

He flinched for a moment at the gruesome sight of the owl-girl; her teeth and lips still red with wolf's blood, her long fingernails dripping.

Blodwedd saw his dismay and her forehead wrinked in concern. She crouched quickly and washed her hands in the long wet grass, passing the back of her hand across her mouth to wipe the gore away before standing again.

'No. I'm not hurt at all,' Rhodri said, his face softening as though he was touched that Blodwedd should have cared enough to clean herself for him. 'You arrived before my strength gave out. I was more worried for the horses, truth be told. I thought they might . . .' His voice trailed away. He turned and Branwen became aware of something that she had not noticed until that moment.

The horses were gone. In their dread of the wolves, they had torn loose from the stump to which they had been tied.

'Curse the luck!' groaned Branwen. 'We cannot follow their trail in the dark, and there's little chance of hearing them in this storm.' She pulled her cloak around her shoulders. 'Let's hope they do not stray far. We must find what shelter we can from this downpour and with good fortune we may find them in the morning.'

'We may,' Blodwedd said. 'If we live out the night.'

'Why shouldn't we?' Branwen asked her. 'The wolves are dead.'

'Five is a small pack, is it not?' Blodwedd asked. 'I have lived in these mountains all my life, and I have observed many things and counted many beasts, both great and small. This was not the whole pack, Warrior Child. These five were but outrunners – scouts sent abroad to lead the pack to food.'

A cold fear swept over Branwen. The owl-girl was right – and she should have known it! She had often accompanied her father and brother and the warriors of their court, hunting the starving winter wolf packs that came ravaging down from the mountains through the deep snows. Even in the frozen heart of the worst winters, when their numbers were thinned by starvation and unendurable cold, the packs were always large: twelve or fifteen wolves – sometimes as many as twenty.

'Perhaps this was a single family,' Rhodri suggested.

As though to mock his wishful words, a long-drawn howl sounded through the rain. Not the distant baying of a wolf on a lone crag, but the blood-chilling howl of a rapacious predator, sounding out his rallying call from far, far too close.

'They come!' hissed Blodwedd.

Branwen stared into the heavy curtain of the rain. Yellow eyes shone like jewels in the darkness. She turned slowly, her heart beating fast under her ribs. Two pairs of eyes – five – ten – twenty! *Even more!*

They were all around them, those eerie, luminous eyes, surrounding them in a deadly, unblinking ring.

There was a second ghoulish howl, rising and falling in the night, scraping at the inside of Branwen's skull like fingernails drawn down slate.

As the howl faded, the eyes began to move forward.

CHAPTER TWENTY

The wolves began to take form through the rain, moving in from all directions. Branwen took two swift steps and grasped the hilt of her knife, still jutting from between the ribs of her last victim. It would not come easily loose, and she had to press her foot down on the carcass and pull to rip it free.

She moved back to be with the others, her eyes flickering from wolf to wolf, from eye to gleaming eye. These were nothing like the half-starved, bony animals of winter; they were large and well fed, these wolves, powerfully muscled and filled with the courage of the pack. Their narrow shoulders were easily as high as her waist and, from their bulk she guessed they probably outweighed her. Formidable foes indeed, especially in such numbers.

Five had been killed, taken by surprise and from behind. But twenty-five?

'Can you communicate with them?' Branwen asked Blodwedd. 'Animal to animal? Tell them we are under Govannon's protection?'

'Owls do not speak with wolves, Warrior Child,' hissed Blodwedd, and Branwen could hear terror in her voice. 'You must escape. See you the scar-faced old grey? He is their leader, I think. I will attack him while you break out of the circle. Run fast and swift, Warrior Child. If you hear pursuit, find a tall tree and climb for your life. I will come to you when I may, and if not, Lord Govannon will send a more worthy creature to watch over you.'

'I'm not leaving you to be killed!' exclaimed Branwen.

'You must!'

'*No!*'

'Branwen, she's right,' Rhodri's voice was dull, as though he already knew Blodwedd was lost. 'I'll stay with her. Hold them off – you must get away if you can.'

Branwen eyed the massive grey wolf that Blodwedd had indicated. He was old, she could tell, but there was strength and murderous intent in his yellow eyes and when he came to a halt, maybe five paces away from them, the rest of the pack stilled also, their heads down, watching and waiting.

Branwen spread her feet, grinding her heels into the mud, squaring her shoulders. She lifted her knife-hand above her head, the blade running with rainwater.

'Come, old grey-muzzle!' she shouted, staring into the wolf's deadly eyes. 'Do you know who I am? I am Branwen ap Griffith! Come if you dare – I don't fear you.'

The wolf's eyes burned into hers, lurid as candlelight, ravenous, impassive, unknowable.

Rhodri raised his sword, the hilt held firm in both hands. Blodwedd's fingers curved and her lips drew back. Death hovered above them. Impatient. Expectant.

Branwen took a step forward, ready to fight for her life.

A peal of thunder shook the world, and at the same moment the whole mountain seemed to rock, taking Branwen's feet from under her and throwing her in the mud. Gasping, her hair plastered against her face, she got to one knee, her ears ringing.

Lightning split the sky into fragments. A fizzing whiplash of blinding white fire struck a tree, bursting the trunk open, sending the tall branches tumbling in flames.

Branwen was dazzled by the lightning flash, but in the blur of partial vision she thought she saw a pathway opening through the trees – a shimmering pathway of coruscating green light. She knelt, her mouth open, her shoulders down, staring in wonder as the pathway unwound itself into the distance.

Surely the trees were bending away from the green pathway, their branches bathed in the flickering emerald light, every leaf and bud sparkling. The path ran up a hill, and on the crest of the hill, caught in a mesh of trapped lightning, she saw a standing shape.

A man, but huger than a man. A great silhouetted man standing spread-legged, dark as caverns, tall as mountains, and from his head rose twelve-point antlers flickering with lightning. And although she could not see his face or his eyes, Branwen knew he was looking at her – looking into her. One massive arm rose and the hand beckoned.

Then the thunder rolled again and she had to close her eyes against the noise. When she could open them again the green path was no more and the stag-man was gone.

'Branwen!' It was Rhodri's voice, calling through the numbness that clouded her ears. 'Quickly! Get up!' There was joy and relief and disbelief in his voice. 'The thunder frightened them away! The wolves have gone!'

A hand helped her up. The rain was falling like spears, splashing knee-high, beating into her face. She turned to Rhodri, her mind full of green clouds.

'Branwen?' There was a sudden alarm in his voice. 'What's wrong? What's happened to you?'

She stared at him, groggy and befuddled. Suddenly

Blodwedd was also looking into her face.

'She has seen marvels,' said the owl-girl.

'What . . . is . . . it . . . ?' Branwen asked.

'Your eyes!' said Rhodri. 'They're . . . they're filled with green light.'

'This is not good,' said Blodwedd, her voice fearful. 'Few are they whom the wendfire light does not change.'

'Why?' gasped Rhodri. 'What is it?'

'It is the light that fills those who have looked into the eyes of the Lord Govannon,' said Blodwedd. 'Alas! Death lies often in that light.'

'What did you see, Branwen?' urged Rhodri. 'Tell us. What did you see?'

'I . . . don't . . . know . . .' Branwen mumbled, trying to think. 'A man . . . with antlers. He beckoned . . .' She turned, pointing through the trees. 'That way!' she said. 'We have to go that way!' A few ragged thoughts managed to come together in her head. 'The wolves!' she gasped. 'What of the wolves!' She stared around, lifting her knife.

'Did you not hear? They're gone,' Rhodri said. 'Branwen, can you *see*?'

'Yes.' She caught hold of his arm. 'Come on – we must go this way.'

Without waiting to see whether they were following, she began to run unsteadily over the slippery ground, her body battered by the rain.

She went stumbling into dense-packed trees, the ground rising sharply under her feet. Beneath the sheltering arms of the forest, the full fury of the storm was lessened, the rain splashing down all around her in huge heavy drops. The beating of the rain on the leaves above her sounded like ten thousand spears pounding against ten thousand shields.

There was a cave. She had not known what she was running towards till she saw the black mouth open in front of her – and then she knew as if she had known all along. A deep cave. Shelter from the storm.

She stood in the wide cave mouth, her head suddenly clear again.

Rhodri and Blodwedd were running towards her through sheets of rain, his arm around her shoulders, their heads down, backs bent against the torment of the weather.

'Where is Fain?' she shouted above the din of the pounding rain.

'He will have found a safe place to weather the storm,' called Blodwedd. 'Have no fear for him.'

They came into the shelter, panting and dripping. Rhodri pushed his hair out of his eyes. 'It's gone,' he said, looking into her face.

Branwen frowned. 'What has?'

'The green light – it's gone from your eyes.' He shook his head. 'You saw Govannon?'

'I don't know.' She turned to Blodwedd. 'Did I?'

'I believe you did,' said the owl-girl. 'Indeed so.' She looked even thinner and stranger with her saturated clothes clinging to her body, and her long hair flat against her skull. Her round eyes seemed to fill half her face.

'He led me here, I think,' said Branwen. 'Look!' She pointed. There was brushwood and small branches and twigs strewn across the cave floor. 'We can build a fire.'

'If we can see what we're doing, we can,' said Rhodri staring into the black depths of the cave. 'Are you sure we haven't been led to a wolf's lair or a bear's den?'

'I'm sure,' said Branwen. She gathered the brittle branches and twigs and set them in the centre of the floor, just deep enough into the cave that she could still dimly see what she was doing. She took tinder and firestones from the leather pouch at her belt and knelt to arrange the wood. Picking the thinnest twigs, she made a nest into which she placed a small amount of the dried moss tinder.

She held the firestones close to the tinder and struck one against the other. Sparks flew, flashing and fading in an instant. The rain hammered down. Rhodri and Blodwedd stood close by.

Strike and chip.

Flying sparks.

Patience and concentration.

Strike and chip.

Watching for the spark that would live long enough to cause a smoulder in the tinder. Smoulder to scorch to smoke to flame.

Branwen could see from the corner of her eye that Blodwedd was shivering. She saw Rhodri put a tentative arm around her shoulders. The owl-girl pressed close against him and Branwen saw him wrap his arms protectively around her. She could even see how Blodwedd's skinny body relaxed against him, her head resting against his chest.

She tried not to care that her friend's hand had come up gently to rest on the owl-girl's head. Rhodri was only showing kindness to the bedraggled creature – even a stray dog would deserve comfort on such a night. And besides, she did not envy Blodwedd the warmth of his embrace – it was only the thought that his affections were leading him astray that caused her concern. The last thing Rhodri needed was to lose his heart to something that was not human. Despair lay waiting at the end of that thorny path!

Clear your mind.

Concentrate on the stones.

Strike and chip.

Watch for the one heroic spark.

Strike and chip.

A wisp of smoke curled. She leaned low, doubling over to blow gently on the smoulder. A tiny white flame quivered. She blew again, nursing the budding flame, carefully feeding it more moss.

More flame now, leaves of fire with red and yellow edges. She offered twigs to the flame. Soon they would have a fine leaping fire. Soon they would be warm and dry.

They huddled around the fire while the rain fell like molten iron and the thunder bellowed all around them, beating the hills like drums. The incessant noise made Branwen's teeth ache. Garish lightning came and went, turning the rain from black to silver.

The fire gave light enough to illuminate the whole of the small, round cave. The walls were of stooping grey stone, striated with bands of minerals sparkling blue and yellow in the light. The floor was of pebble-strewn earth, sloping slightly towards the mouth so that the rain did not seep in.

They had spotted one thing that disturbed them – scattered among larger stones at the back of the cave they had found human bones. A skull. A complete rib cage. Other long bones. Evidence, perhaps, of some poor soul devoured by wild animals. Maybe dragged in here from the forest, maybe attacked within whilst sheltering from bad weather.

It was not a comforting discovery.

The fire spat and crackled fiercely, making Branwen's eyes smart.

'I'm hungry,' Rhodri said, gazing into the flames.

'So am I,' said Branwen.

'What little food we had is with the horses.'

'Rhodri, I know.'

'At least we don't need to go thirsty,' he said, turning his head to the cave mouth, where torrents of water splashed and foamed. 'That's a good thing.' He looked at her. 'Where were you when the wolves attacked?' he asked. 'Where did you go?'

'I don't know,' Branwen said. 'A place . . .' She shook her head. 'An *old* place.'

'A young place,' said Blodwedd. Branwen gazed into her eyes for a moment then looked away.

'Yes. A young place.'

'I don't know what you mean. What kind of place?'

Branwen gnawed a torn fingernail. 'It was a clearing in the forest – but we were seeing a scene from a long time ago. Lifetimes upon lifetimes ago. There was a woman . . . she was singing – chanting – a song about the Shining Ones. It was wonderful . . . glorious . . .'

200

'One of the druades, she was,' Blodwedd murmured. 'Woman priests of the old ways. Wise heads. Full throats. Great hearts.' There was sadness in her voice. 'Long gone now. Hunted down. Betrayed.' She clutched at her arms. 'The smooth-faced conquerors came. But theirs is not the blame. They had their own shrines and wells – their own gods. The Druid blood they shed had no divinity for them. It was her own followers who led them to her. Wickedness.'

Blodwedd became silent, her head down, her eyes darkly reflecting the fire.

Branwen spoke hesitantly, drawing her thoughts out like tangled and knotted threads. 'People fear the Shining Ones,' she said. 'They say: these Old Gods, they are not real. They never *were* real. Stories for children! Make-believe! And yet they fear them – fear to talk of them – fear to have their names spoken aloud.' She looked at Rhodri. 'I think I begin to understand why that is.'

'They turned their backs on the old ways,' said Rhodri.

Branwen nodded slowly. 'My father told me once: always be honest and true in your dealings with others, because you can never trust a man you have betrayed – you will always fear his revenge.'

'And if a man's revenge is fearsome, how much worse would be the revenge of a betrayed god,' said Rhodri.

'Yes. I see the problem.'

'The Shining Ones are not vengeful,' said Blodwedd. 'They are wild and perilous ... like an avalanche ... like deep water ... like a thunderstorm. But they are not cruel – not vengeful.'

'No, maybe they aren't, but they're pitiless all the same,' said Branwen. 'Pitiless in shaping people to their needs.' She stared across the fire. 'Why did they choose *me*, Blodwedd?'

'You think the Shining Ones chose you, Warrior Child?' said Blodwedd. 'No. They did not choose you. The mountains chose you. The forests and the rivers chose you. The land of your birth chose you, Warrior Child. Be honoured!'

'I want you to stop calling me that,' said Branwen. 'Use my real name.'

Blodwedd gave a mysterious smile. 'Ahh, but what is the real name of the Warrior Child?' she asked in a low, thoughtful voice. '*Now* she is Branwen ap Griffith – but it was not always so. Once she was Addiena the Beautiful, daughter of Seren. And before that she was Ganieda, forest girl and sister to Myrddin Wyllt. Celemon was her name in the long-ago – Celemon, daughter of Cai the Tall.' Blodwedd smiled again. 'Many are the names of the Warrior Child down the rolling years,' she said. 'Many the names and many the lives. You are but a thread in the tapestry, Branwen ap Griffith, a single footprint upon the eternal road.' She laughed, low and soft, a sound that made Branwen shiver. 'But I shall call you Branwen if it gives you ease.'

CHAPTER TWENTY-ONE

Branwen lay curled on her side, her head pillowed on her arm, her eyes half open as she gazed into the dancing flames.

Blodwedd's words had given Branwen a lot to think about. *What did she mean – I am but a thread in the tapestry? And who were those other women she named?*

An odd image came into her drowsy mind, as though formed in the flames. She saw herself standing on a hilltop under a bright sky. Standing on the crest of a long white road. And all along this road, women were walking. Women armed and armoured. Women with strong, proud, glad faces. A line of women stretching back along the road for ever – a line of women stretching onwards down the road for ever. A thousand generations of warrior women.

The image faded, but it left Branwen with a feeling of deep well-being – of *belonging*.

The fire cracked and fizzed. Beyond the flames she could see Rhodri, bare-chested, leaning against the cave wall, his face peaceful in sleep, and one hand resting on the shoulder of the small figure that lay with her head in his lap, the huge amber eyes closed for once, the limbs relaxed.

So Blodwedd had finally learned the art of sleeping like a human. *Good for her.*

Inhuman and monstrous as Blodwedd could be – and Branwen was still haunted by the image of her impassive face as she held the sword over the neck of that baby – the owl-girl had offered without hesitation to give her life in exchange for Branwen's safety when the wolves had surrounded them in the forest.

That was something to remember.

Her eyes closed.

Her mind drifted off into velvet darkness.

Branwen dreamed that it was day. A bright morning. She stood at the cave mouth, gazing out over the forest. The breeze was fresh and cool, but there was an ominous feel in the air, as though the hills and the woods were holding their breath in anticipation of horror.

She heard voices calling through the trees. Urgent, excited voices.

One rang out above the others. 'This way, masters!

She goes this way! Follow close – she may shape-shift to evade us!'

Other voices called in response, male voices, breathing hard and speaking a language she did not know, a strange silken language of words that seemed to flow together without pause or break.

Now she could see movement in among the trees – dark blundering shapes under the arching branches. The smell of fear wafted up to her, knotting her stomach. Something dreadful was about to happen.

A woman burst from the forest, dressed in ragged and stained blue robes. Her face was livid with fear, her mouth open to gulp in air, her eyes wild and staring. There were cuts and bruises on her face, and her hands were bloody with torn and dirty fingernails.

Branwen stared at the fleeing woman, her heart beating fast.

I know you! I saw you in the glade, speaking those beautiful words to the Shining Ones. You're the chanting woman – the druade from the ancient forest. But who is chasing you?

The woman scrambled desperately up the long slope. A spark of faint hope came into her eyes as she looked up towards the cave. At first, Branwen thought the hunted woman had seen her – but then she realized she was looking straight through her, staring into the cave mouth. Perhaps she hoped the cave wound on deep into the hills

– perhaps she hoped to escape her pursuers that way.

A forlorn hope. The cave was no more than a rounded hollow in the hill – once in, there was no other way out.

Don't come this way. It's a dead end. You'll be trapped.

The woman ran on with renewed strength, passing Branwen as if she didn't see her and entering the darkness of the cave.

Perhaps they would not look there for her. Perhaps they would search elsewhere.

A man plunged out of the trees. He was dressed all in furs and untanned animal skins and his hair was ragged and unkempt, but he had on his top lip the thick drooping moustache worn by the men of Brython.

'I see her! She has gone into the cave! Now we have her!'

He came pounding up the slope.

No! She didn't come this way! Go back! Go back!

Five more men came out of the trees.

Branwen could see that they were soldiers, although their clothes and weapons were unfamiliar to her.

They wore grey iron helmets with thick ridges and curved cheek-guards, and there were curved plates of iron over their shoulders and around their chests. Underneath the armour they wore short-sleeved tunics of a vivid red, and instead of trews or leggings they had short red kilts that left their legs bare save for leather sandals with thongs tied to the shin. Their shields were oblong, curved and painted deep red with iron bosses stamped into them. Short broad-bladed swords bounced at their hips, and in their free hands each carried a long wooden javelin with an iron point.

The skin-clad man paused, waving back to them, pointing towards the cave mouth. 'Come, my masters, she is trapped now!'

He was speaking Branwen's own language – a man of Brython, guiding alien soldiers to the woman's hideaway. *Traitor!*

They came plodding up the hill, breathing heavily, sweat running down their faces. Olive-skinned faces, Branwen could now see – far swarthier than the hunted woman or the man in the animal skins.

One pulled his helmet off and wiped his face – and Branwen saw that he was clean-shaven and had dark hair clipped short around his head.

One spoke to the others in a voice of authority. He handed his javelin to one of them and drew his sword.

No! You cannot do this! What harm has she done to you?

The soldier pushed the skin-clad man aside, his face grim as he strode into the cave, his sword jutting forward.

No!

Branwen could not bear to look. She heard the

woman pleading. The man spoke harshly. There was a scream, cut short.

Then silence.

The soldier came out of the cave, wiping his sword on a piece of blue cloth.

'That is the last of them, Principalis Optima Flavius,' said the skin-clad man. 'All the old priesthood is dead now, my master – dead and gone for ever.'

The soldier said something to his companions. He sheathed his sword and took back his javelin. He strode down the hill, the other four falling into line behind him.

The skin-clad man of Brython peered into the cave, a look of woeful regret disfiguring his face for a moment before he turned and trotted along in the soldiers' wake like an obedient dog.

CHAPTER TWENTY-TWO

'Caw! Caw! Caw! Caw! Caw!'

Branwen awoke at the strident, insistent cry. Daylight filled the cave, sparkling on the embedded minerals so that skeins of moving light wavered across floor walls and roof. Cool morning air flowed in. She had slept close to the fire, and she saw that it was finally dead, the rowan branches transformed to a lace-work of white ash on the blackened ground.

'Fain!' Branwen gasped, dream-drunk still, and fighting to gather her wits. She sat up and saw Rhodri and Blodwedd lying together close to the cave wall, Blodwedd curled on her side with her arms across her chest and her knees drawn up, Rhodri at her back, an arm thrown protectively across her.

'I'm glad he survived the storm unharmed,' came Rhodri's sleepy voice. 'But I'd wish for a more melodic introduction to the day!' He lifted his head and gazed at

Blodwedd, his face amazed – almost as if he had awoken from an outlandish dream to find it real. He withdrew his arm from her and pulled himself up against the cave wall, rubbing the heels of his hands into his eyes and yawning.

'Caw! Caw! Caw!'

The falcon was in the cave mouth, moving impatiently from foot to foot, ruffling his feathers and bobbing his head.

'The horses have returned,' said Blodwedd, her eyes opening sharp and bright, moving from sleep to waking in an instant.

Puzzled but relieved, Branwen got to her feet and stepped out into the day. Fain rose into the air and circled high above the cave, calling loudly.

It was early and the sun was low in a sky banded with innocent white clouds running before a strong west wind. Of the black storm clouds of the night there was no sign, although the ground was still wet underfoot and the rocks and the leaves shone jewel-bright.

The two horses were standing side by side, just under the trees, their heads down to tear the grass. When they had made camp last night, Rhodri and Branwen had taken their saddles off, but now they were strapped on to the horses' backs once more and all the things that had been left in the clearing were slung over them – cloaks and clothing, Branwen's chain mail and shield, even their bag of food.

'How could this be?' Branwen wondered aloud, walking quickly down the hill towards them. *Who brought them here? Who put their saddles on? Who gathered our things?* The horses lifted their heads as she approached. Branwen gasped and stopped. An eerie green light flickered in their eyes.

But as she moved closer, the light paled and went out and the large eyes were brown once more.

She stood between the horses, touching them, stroking their hides, as though to reassure herself that they were real.

'Did Fain bring them back?' called, Rhodri, coming out of the cave, pulling on his jerkin.

'I don't think so,' Branwen called back. 'Govannon maybe?'

'Govannon indeed,' said Blodwedd, emerging behind Rhodri. 'Fain says the soldiers have already broken camp. They are riding hard to the place of singing gulls. We must be swift if we are to keep track of them.'

'Then we will follow now,' Branwen said as she ran back up to the cave to retrieve her sword and her knife and leather belt.

'What of the things we left in the forest when the wolves attacked?' asked Rhodri as she moved past him.

'Your shield and chain mail and our cloaks.'

'Look more carefully, Rhodri,' Branwen called back as she entered the cave. 'Someone has already seen to that.'

He peered down at the horses. 'Even our bag of food was remembered,' he said with wonder in his voice. 'At least we shan't go hungry.'

'We'll eat in the saddle.' Branwen buckled the belt around her waist and slipped the sword and knife into place. She paused for a moment. The early light reached all the way to the back of the cave, splashing her shadow over the rocks and up the far wall.

She walked deeper into the cave and gazed down at the scattered bones, consumed by an aching sense of sorrow and loss.

Suddenly she was aware of Blodwedd at her side. 'Did you dream her death, Branwen?' the owl-girl asked. 'The chanting woman from the holy glade?'

Branwen's throat was thick. 'Yes.'

'The cave remembers – old stones do not forget,' sighed Blodwedd. 'Ah, but man is fickle and full of fear. It was ever so.'

'Does that excuse him for leading them to her?'

'No,' murmured Blodwedd. 'And yes.'

Branwen turned her back on the pitiful sight and walked out into the daylight once more. She strode down the hill, staring up into the sky. 'Fain! Fain! Guide us!'

she called, and leaped into the saddle. A sudden urgency had filled her, a burning need to be on the move.

Fain glided down, flying so close his wingtip almost brushed her shoulder. He gave a single commanding cry.

'Come on!' Branwen shouted as Rhodri and Blodwedd came racing down the hill. Hardly waiting for them to mount, she urged her horse to follow the falcon. She had the feeling that before this day was out, they would be caught up in events both great and deadly.

'Gwylan Canu,' Branwen murmured, gazing down with narrowed eyes. 'The place of singing gulls.'

It was a little after midday. Fain had led them through the long warm morning, winging away under trees that dripped still from the previous night's storm. At times he would leave them, rising up and up till he was only a dot against the blue sky. Occasionally he vanished altogether – but always he came back with news of the progress of the prince's horsemen as they travelled along the coast road.

Down through valleys he guided them, where ferns curled like reaching fingers through a waxen ground-mist and where the trees were garlanded with spiders' webs. Up to summits where the wind sang and played and flicked their hair into their eyes.

Down again, through bleak ravines running with white

water, and around brown peaks that tore the clouds. Northwards, always northwards, till, rounding a blunt, fern-clad knob of rock, Branwen heard for the first time through the trees the sound of surf breaking on rocks, and smelled the evocative tang of the sea.

They came to a high ledge where the pines stood like sentinels at the world's end. The ocean stretched out before them like a sheet of blue silk strewn with diamonds. At their horses' hooves, the land crumbled away in rugged, boulder-strewn precipices down to a rubbled shoreline of pocked and fissured rock where the waves broke in plumes and flurries of white foam.

And standing proud and strong on a narrow outcrop of sea-worn limestone, the citadel of Branwen's vision – the fortified village of Gwylan Canu. Its back was to the ocean, and its landward side was protected by a long, sloping rampart of dry-laid stone, pierced by a massive timber-framed stone gatehouse.

There were many houses and huts huddled beyond the wall, and on a high-point near the sea she saw the Great Hall of the House of Puw, thatched and stone-clad, rising proud above the other dwellings.

As Branwen gazed down, the endless tide pounded in on the black rocks, sending up spouts of foam that gushed from sea-gnawed blowholes and cracks, so that it almost seemed that the entire shoreline was boiling like a cauldron in a firepit. To either side of the rocky headland, the land fell back to form deep sandy bays. Some way westward along the shore, sheltered a little from the full fury of the sea, a small knot of huts was gathered – a sparse fishing village, its boats drawn up on to the beach like black leaves. There was no sign of activity or movement in the village. It seemed deserted.

Beyond the fishing village, Branwen saw the pale tongue of the road from distant Doeth Palas, skirting the cliffs, winding in and out to follow the contours of the land. She traced it all the way to the gatehouse of Gwylan Canu.

Now Branwen turned her eyes eastward where the road continued, chasing away along the coastline. Somewhere, out of sight in that direction, she knew the road branched and sent a tributary striking southwards into the wild lands of Cyffin Tir, where it would lead a weary traveller at long last to Garth Milain.

Branwen felt an ache like savage hunger as she thought of her homeland and of her dear, brave mother bereft of son, husband and daughter at the furthermost end of that long pale road.

By all the saints, when will this be over? When will I be allowed to go home?

'That's strange.' Rhodri's voice brought her back to the present. 'Why are they waiting outside the walls?'

To the west of the gatehouse and a little way from the sloping walls of the citadel, the rocks formed a flat plateau blanketed with scrub and wild grasses. It was here that the fifty horsemen of Doeth Palas had come to a halt at the roadside. The horses had been gathered together as though Captain Angor had ordered them to make camp.

'I do not know,' said Branwen, shading her eyes against the glare of the sun-struck sea. The men were marshalled in rows, but she could not make out enough details to understand what was going on.

'This is all wrong,' Rhodri said, his voice uneasy. 'It makes no sense. Why are the gates closed? And look – there are armed men on the gatehouse. Why would the gates be closed against the prince's men?'

'Unless we have come too late and the Saxons have already taken the citadel,' said Branwen in alarm. 'By Saint Cadog! I wish I could see more!'

As though responding to her words, Fain took to the air and went wheeling in long, graceful loops down towards the citadel.

'Move back under the trees, just in case they look this way,' Branwen said. She dismounted and Rhodri and Blodwedd did the same, leading the horses a little way back into the woodlands.

Blodwedd stared back over her shoulder, her owl eyes wide and full of apprehension. Her expression was one that Branwen had never seen on a human – a kind of pure, primal unease.

'What is it?' Rhodri asked her.

'The sea,' murmured the owl-girl, as if struggling to find the words. 'It puts a chill in my heart!'

'Why is that?' Rhodri asked gently, his hand resting on her shoulder.

'My lord Govannon holds sway only over the land,' Blodwedd replied. 'Beyond the shore of Brython, he can no longer protect me.'

'I'll protect you,' Rhodri said. 'Trust in me.'

Branwen smiled to herself for a moment. The thought of gentle Rhodri protecting the wild owl-girl was as odd in its way as learning that there was something in nature that made Blodwedd afraid.

Blodwedd turned to him. 'I fear you cannot protect me, my friend,' she whispered.

Branwen left Rhodri and the uneasy owl-girl under the trees. She pushed forwards again to the cliff's edge, pressing herself against a tree, watching in growing apprehension as Fain zigzagged above the citadel.

What would he find? Echoes of her dreadful vision? Corpses and bloody Saxon banners?

It seemed an age till Fain came flying back up to them. She lifted an arm and he came towards her with wings curving and claws outstretched.

He landed gracefully on her wrist and she carried him to the others. Folding his wings, he stared at Blodwedd and gave a succession of carping cries.

'What is he saying?' Branwen gasped, staring at the owl-girl. 'Are we too late?'

'There are no Saxons in the citadel,' Blodwedd said. 'But there is fear and dismay. Women weep and the menfolk are armed and grim.'

'Why do they not allow the prince's horsemen in?' asked Branwen.

'Caw! Caw! Caw!'

'Fain does not know,' said Blodwedd.

'Then we must go and learn for ourselves why Iwan's father slammed the gates on his own son,' said Branwen. She looked into the falcon's bright black eye. 'Stay with the horses, my friend,' she said. 'You are a worthy guide and see much, but I don't want you to draw attention to us. Do you understand?'

At her words, Fain took wing, coming to land on the saddle of her horse.

'Blodwedd, I want you to stay here as well.'

The owl-girl looked levelly at her. 'Twice now have I left your side and let you walk into peril,' she said. 'It will not happen again . . . *Branwen.*'

Branwen held her eyes for a moment then nodded.

'Don't bother asking me to stay behind either,' Rhodri

said. He peered down the long boulder-strewn slope. 'But it will be a perilous descent, I think.'

'Then we must take great care,' said Branwen.

As Rhodri had pointed out, the way down was not easy, and it was all the more difficult because it was vital that they use every scrap of natural cover to shield themselves from Captain Angor's men. They climbed down in unspeaking file, Branwen first, then Blodwedd, Rhodri in the rear, crouching, often pausing, seeking a safe path, then moving forward again, sometimes on hands and knees. Branwen worked her way slowly and cautiously down the hillside, summoning all her powers of stealth and silence despite her eagerness to unravel the conundrum of the locked gates. On such a precarious hillside, one carelessly placed foot could easily send stones bounding down the slope to alert the soldiers below.

But at last they made it unseen to a deep, narrow cleft that ran just above the landward side of the plateau where the soldiers were gathered. From here, they could hear the men's voices on the fresh salt breeze that blew in from the sea.

Cautiously, Branwen climbed the side of the cleft and lifted her head above the sharp rim of dark rock. Ensuring her footing was secure, she edged up till she could see to where Angor's men were standing.

eglected to mention the long and painful road you would travel before it came to that.' He thrust his hand under Iwan's chin, wrenching his head up so their eyes met. 'You know me, Iwan ap Madoc, do you not?' he hissed. 'You have seen me at my work. Trust me when I tell you that I am an absolute master at the craft of teasing a man's soul from his body. You will beg for death long before I am done with you – unless you beg first for your father to open his gates to us.'

Iwan's face went ashen, but there was still contempt and audacity in his eyes as he stared at the vicious old soldier. Branwen's heart went out to him – so brave and defiant against such terrible odds.

'That will never happen,' Iwan said thickly, his lips bubbling with blood.

'A bold claim,' said Angor. 'But make no rash promises, boy – not until you have learned the full extent of your courage.' He patted Iwan's cheek. 'It's a rare privilege, Iwan, that I offer you. Few are the men given the opportunity to be taken to the uttermost end of their endurance. It will be an interesting journey.'

He stepped back, turning to the two men holding Iwan upright. 'Come, we have wasted enough time on this. Let's see if Madoc ap Rhain has yet come to greater wisdom.'

He strode towards the gatehouse, the two men

Branwen stared down in shock and alarm. Iwan was being held between two of the men, and ropes bound his arms at the elbow and wrist. His usually impassive face was pale and angry and there was a trickle of blood at the corner of his mouth, as if he had been struck.

Captain Angor was speaking. 'If they will not heed the voice of reason,' he growled, 'let us see whether threats will force their hand.'

'They will never surrender Gwylan Canu to you!' It was Iwan's voice, filled with rage. 'My father will die first, traitor!'

Angor turned on Iwan with a snarl. 'You had better pray your father sees sense, boy,' he said, grasping Iwan's hair in his fist and forcing his head back. 'Because if he does not, then the next sight he will witness will be his son's severed head dripping blood as I raise it up in front of his gates on the end of my spear!'

CHAPTER TWENTY-THREE

Branwen's mind reeled. She had risked the dangers of Doeth Palas in order to warn Iwan of the coming Saxon attack. He had trusted her word – he had gone to Prince Llew and the prince had sent fifty horsemen to Teg Eingel. But now the gates of Gwylan Canu were bolted against the prince's men – and Captain Angor was threatening Iwan with death!

There was treachery afoot, that much was certain and all but Iwan were party to the betrayal. That at least explained the small number of men sent riding east – all had to have been hand-picked! But it was madness that in such times men of Powys would fight one another!

An insistent tugging at her tunic made Branwen look back. Rhodri had climbed part-way up the slope towards her. His anxious face stared up at her, his eyes questioning. She shook her head and gestured for him to leave her be.

Iwan was speaking again, his voice defi... the saints that you have among your men su... cannot hold their tongues!' he spat. 'If I had them speaking of your intentions to take my mo... father captive, I would not have been able to call... warn them to bar the gates against you! As it is, yo... sit here till you rot, you treacherous dog! Gwylan ... will never fall to you!'

Branwen winced as Captain Angor swung his ar... round and brought the back of his fist hard into Iwan... mouth. 'Be silent!' he shouted. 'Unless you wish to share the fate of those men whose loose lips came close to ruining all!'

It wasn't until then that Branwen realized that what she had taken for a bundle of bags and provisions thrown down in the grass, was actually two dead bodies. Her stomach churned and she had to press her lips together against a rising sickness as she saw that their throats had been savagely cut.

Iwan spat blood. 'Kill me quick then, and have an end to it!' he shouted.

Angor grinned crookedly. 'Oh no, my fine young cockerel,' he said, and now his voice was deadly calm. 'That would never do. Kill you quickly? That will not serve my purposes at all. When I said that the next thing your father would see would be your dripping head, I

following close behind, half dragging Iwan between them. Branwen's soul ached as she saw the way Iwan struggled to keep to his feet.

Anger blazed through Branwen and she closed her fingers around the hilt of her sword. She couldn't leave Iwan to the vile practices of Captain Angor. She would reveal herself and come to his aid – even thought she knew her chances of surviving a reckless assault on so many armed men were limited.

She started along the cleft, knowing she must keep hidden for as long as possible. But her rage betrayed her. As she made her first move along the gully, her foot came down on a loose stone and it spun away, cracking against others and sending a small flurry of rocks tumbling noisily down to the bottom of the cleft.

Angor spun around, his eyes searching along the ridge. 'What was that?' he shouted. Branwen ducked, her heart hammering.

Fool! Clumsy fool!

'Loose rocks, Captain,' a voice called. 'Nothing more.'

'Be certain!' shouted Angor. 'Go up there and check. Madoc may have men on the ridges, waiting to fall on us unawares!'

Branwen grimaced at her blundering stupidity. Now men would come up here and scour the hillside. If they were discovered, all would be lost.

Something touched her leg. She looked down. Blodwedd was just below her on the slope. 'Do not fear,' whispered the owl-girl. 'I know I said I would never leave your side, but now I must. I will give them something to chase!'

Branwen nodded and the owl-girl slid away down the slope. She paused for a moment, her gaze lingering on Rhodri's face. Then she went running along the cleft, her long thick hair flying.

Branwen watched as Blodwedd scrambled lithely up the far slope. She came into clear view, leaping and bounding among the rocks, moving more swiftly than any human as she skimmed the loose scree, turning this way and that along the face of the precipice, kicking up clouds of grey dust that billowed in her wake.

But even as she watched, Branwen could not quite believe her eyes. Clad in her simple gown of dappled brown, and only dimly visible through the dust, Blodwedd's shape suddenly seemed quite different. Was she still a slender woman – or had she now somehow taken on animal form?

Stone and rock rained down. Branwen heard the men shouting out.

'There! There it is! On the hill!'

'What is it?'

'A hare, I think!'

'No, it's too large. A fox maybe?'

'A young deer? No – see how it throws up the dust as it runs! A wolf of the mountains? What is it?'

'Whatever it is, it moves with rare speed! See? It's in among the trees already.'

'Captain Angor, did you see? It was only an animal.'

'Yes, I saw it,' came Angor's voice. 'A wild dog, I thought.'

The voices dropped to murmurs.

No men came up the hill towards them. Blodwedd's diversion had worked – for the moment, Branwen and Rhodri were safe.

Paying close attention to her footing, Branwen moved across the face of the cleft. Rhodri kept pace with her at the bottom.

A strident voice called out.

'Madoc ap Rhain! The time for thought is done! What is your answer? Will you open your gates and surrender to me, or will you look on as I torture your son to death?'

A woman's voice responded. 'For pity's sake, Captain Angor, do not harm my son!'

'Get you from the walls, Alfrun ap Rhain,' shouted Angor. 'It were best you did not see what is to come if your husband does not relent!'

Branwen lifted her head over the ridge again. She was almost opposite the gatehouse of Gwylan Canu. Angor stood under the great wooden gates, staring up at the high ramparts.

Many armed men lined the walls, but no weapons were drawn and there was a deathly silence from the battlements.

A portly, elderly man with long grey hair and a grey moustache stood above the gates – a warrior past his prime – a man Branwen vaguely recognized from her childhood. He had visited Garth Milain once, this merry-faced old lord. She remembered that he had roared with laughter that day, till his round belly shook. But there was no laughter in him now. His face was grey and drawn, as though he was looking into the very pits of Annwn!

A woman was at his side, clad in green and with plaited flaxen hair. A young woman, she seemed, many years the old man's junior – and by the look of her, a woman of old Viking stock. Even from a distance, Branwen could see that she was weeping.

'Angor, I implore you,' Madoc called down, his emotions clear in the quavering of his voice. 'Look not through your master's greedy eyes. He can take as many lands as he wishes, but he creates enemies out of his countrymen. You must see this. What of the old alliances? What of our long fight against the Saxon hordes?'

'What of them?' Angor shouted. 'This is not about territory. Too many years lie on your grey head, Madoc ap

Rhain! You are aged and faint-hearted and weak. You cannot defend this cantref. Step aside now! What Prince Llew commands, is done for the good of Powys – and any who stand in opposition to that greater good will suffer the consequences! Open your gates and all will be well. You have my word on that!'

'Old I may be, Angor of Doeth Palas, but faint-hearted I never was!' shouted Madoc. 'You shall not usurp me, nor enter my citadel, though you come at my walls with ten times your present number. Do your worst! If my son dies, I will unleash such vengeance upon you that the very stones of Gwylan Canu will sicken at it!'

'We shall see,' called Angor, drawing his sword. 'I have many skills, Madoc. Your son shall not die – not for a very long time.' He turned. 'Bare his chest!' he ordered the two men.

Iwan struggled as the two men tore his tunic open.

Branwen's fist tightened on her sword hilt.

A long-drawn wail sounded from the gatehouse. Iwan's mother was leaning out over the old stones, her hands reaching uselessly towards her son.

'Let me tell you what wonders await the boy,' Angor called callously, turning towards Iwan and pressing the point of his sword into his abdomen just above his belt. Iwan winced as the point cut his skin and a thin thread of blood trickled down. 'A small cut made here will give access to his innards. I have a tool – a clever little hooked implement forged for this very purpose.' He drew a thin loop of iron from his belt and held it up for the watchers from the battlements to see. 'It goes into the belly, do you see? It takes care and skill to turn it just so – allowing it to hook around the boy's guts. And then very slowly – very carefully – I draw it out again, and the guts come unravelling with it.' He stared up at Iwan's mother. 'I will draw your son's guts out, Alfrun ap Rhain. You will be surprised how much of a man's innards can be pulled out without causing him to die on the spot.' His voice rose to a fearsome roar. 'No, my lady, even then your son will live for half a day and in that time, he will learn how to scream – trust me on this – he will learn how to scream his lungs out!'

Branwen felt sickened by Angor's threats, and she could see the horror that swept over the faces of Iwan's parents. Iwan himself was white-faced, staring blankly ahead of him as though in utter disbelief.

'Lie him down,' snarled Angor. 'Let the carnival begin!'

'Enough!' shouted Madoc ap Rhain, his whole body shaking as he glared down at the barbarous captain. 'Release my son.' His head bowed in defeat. 'Name your terms.'

'Father, no!' screamed Iwan.

'The terms are simple,' Angor called. 'You will open your gates and your menfolk will come forth, bearing with them all arms and armour. They will lay their weapons at my feet, my lord, and you will cede to me the lordship of Gwylan Canu.'

There was a dreadful silence from the gatehouse; Madoc ap Rhain's grey head was bowed low. His wife turned, resting her hand on his arm.

Branwen bit her lip, as torn as the old lord by the impossible choice. Even if she leaped up, sword swinging, running as fast as her strong legs allowed, she could never cover the ground between her and Iwan before Angor's men caught her and cut her down.

She would die in vain. Her death would make no difference. No, deeply as it went against the grain of her nature, she lay hidden and did nothing save tighten her grip on her sword hilt till her knuckles were white and bloodless.

'So be it,' called Madoc.

'No!' Iwan howled, struggling in the grip of the two men. He fought so fiercely against them that he broke free on one side. With wild eyes he threw himself at Captain Angor. Branwen understood that he meant to impale himself on the captain's sword – to die rather than allow his father to surrender the citadel.

But Angor pulled the blade back as Iwan lunged at

him. Iwan pivoted in the grip of the other soldier and fell heavily to his knees. Angor stepped back, laughing.

'Self-murder, is it, Iwan?' he mocked. 'The ultimate sacrifice to save the honour of the House of Puw! No, lad, I'll be the one who decides how and when you die.'

'Father – no!' Iwan shouted. 'I'm not afraid! I'd rather die.'

But he was too late, Madoc ap Rhain had disappeared from the gatehouse and Branwen could hear the rasp and grate of timber bars being drawn back from the gates.

She was wracked with guilt and despair.

It was her warning that had brought Iwan to this place – and although her intention had been the opposite, her actions had brought this calamity upon the citadel of Gwylan Canu.

What can I do? How can I stop this?

And all the while, the vision of Iwan's severed, dripping head darkened her mind. She had seen his death in Blodwedd's foretelling – was she now to see it in reality?

CHAPTER TWENTY-FOUR

B ranwen could hardly bring herself to watch as the gates of Gwylan Canu swung slowly inwards, creaking and cracking on their hinges. For a moment all was still, then Madoc ap Rhain strode out, his soldiers following in sombre silence.

Captain Angor stood over the kneeling Iwan, his sword resting on the back of the subdued boy's neck, a threat to ensure his father's continued compliance.

'Neb ap Mostyn!' Angor called to his men. 'See that these fine men are disarmed. Have them pile their weapons together and then have them stand in ranks.'

The man called Neb ap Mostyn began to organize the men of Gwylan Canu, herding them on to the plateau, while the soldiers of Doeth Palas gathered their swords, spears, shields, and axes and began to pile them in a great heap with much ringing and clanging.

Branwen guessed that Madoc ap Rhain's force

consisted of about two hundred and fifty men – easily enough to do battle with Captain Angor's warriors, if not for that sharp blade held at the nape of Iwan's neck. She stared up at the ramparts. A few women were gathered there, watching in deathly silence as their menfolk gave up their weapons and stood in grim, sullen rows while Angor's soldiers guarded them, swords at the ready.

'You have all that you wished for,' called Madoc ap Rhain. 'Give me back my son!'

Angor wrenched Iwan to his feet. 'Take him, my lord, and be welcome.' He shoved Iwan between the shoulders. Iwan stumbled, tripping and falling heavily with a cry, his arms still tied at his back.

Branwen's agony diminished a little – perhaps Iwan would not die here after all! Perhaps there was some hope.

Iwan's father ran to him and helped him to his feet.

Branwen heard Iwan's voice, shaking with anger and dismay. 'You should not have bartered Gwylan Canu for my life!' he cried. 'You should have let these dogs do their worst.' He turned, spitting at Angor. 'Worse than the Saxons, you are, Angor ap Pellyn! May the curses of all the saints come down on you!'

'Keep the boy quiet, my lord,' Angor said without emotion. 'You have surrendered your citadel to me on his behalf. Do not make that a vain sacrifice.'

Madoc ap Rhain put a protective arm around Iwan's shoulders. 'Only the weak of heart threaten those who cannot fight back, Angor of Doeth Palas,' he said. 'You have had your way. What will now become of my people?'

'That you will learn in good time,' said Angor. He called to his lieutenant. 'Neb ap Mostyn, take a detail into the citadel and make sure that no men lurk there. Search for any weapons that may have been kept back from us. And any man of sword-bearing age that you find beyond the wall – kill him!'

'What of the women and children and old folk, Captain?' Neb replied.

A cruel smile slithered over Angor's face. 'On the promontory behind the Great Hall you will find the ground is dug with many deep pits,' he said. 'In the wars of Madoc ap Rhain's youth, these pits were used to imprison Saxon captives, although I'll guess they are unoccupied now. Have them thrown into the pits. Kill any that resist, be they woman, child or ancient.'

'Yes, Captain.' Neb ap Mostyn called ten men to follow him and they entered the citadel while the women watched from the ramparts with hollow, frightened eyes.

'One more thing,' Angor called after him. 'There will be Saxon servants – do them no harm. They are not for the pits.'

Branwen had become so immersed in the distressing and unfathomable events that were unfolding out on the plateau that she was startled when Rhodri came crawling quietly up alongside her.

'Do you hear it?' he whispered urgently.

She ducked her head down below the ridge before replying. 'Hear what?' she hissed softly.

'Listen! Marching feet!'

Branwen frowned, straining her ears.

Yes! She could hear it now, echoing faintly among the rocks – the steady tread of many feet.

'Are they the rest of Prince Llew's men?' she wondered aloud. 'No, surely not. It's too soon for them to have got here.'

'And the sound does not come from the west, Branwen,' Rhodri murmured. 'Listen more closely: they are approaching from the east!'

It was hard for Branwen to pinpoint the exact direction of the noise as it bounced from rock face to rock face. But at last, as it grew gradually louder, she knew that she was hearing a force of soldiers coming in along the coastal road – and, as Rhodri had said, they were coming from the east.

A small figure appeared suddenly among the rocks. It was Blodwedd. She must have circled through the trees and come down into the gulley from their right. She scrambled along the cleft and crawled up towards them.

'Saxons,' she hissed. 'I saw them from the hilltop. Many Saxon warriors, led by horsemen. One was a great black-bearded man on a tall black stallion. He has gold on his helmet. Pennants fly at his back – a white dragon on a field of red. Those that follow are savage men. Their eyes brim with the lust of slaughter and conquest!'

'Herewulf Ironfist!' said Rhodri. 'He's the black-bearded man who leads them – and it is his flag that flies over them.' He looked at Blodwedd. 'Did you have time to count their numbers?'

'I would guess they be five hundred men strong,' she said. 'Maybe more.'

Branwen remembered the line of Saxon soldiers that she had seen in her vision. All too soon, it seemed, her vivid dream was becoming reality. She closed her eyes, seeing again Iwan's dripping severed head in her mind.

Here you are at last, Branwen, but too late . . . the west is lost. All is done. All . . . is . . . done . . .

She opened her eyes. If all were truly lost, then she would go down fighting, not skulking among the rocks. 'We must go to Angor's aid,' she said, drawing her sword. 'Ironfist must not come upon him in the open.' She narrowed her eyes. No matter what disputes had riven Powys over the years, the great princes of her homeland had always come together to fight their age-old foe. It was impossible to think Agnor and Lord Madoc would not now join forces against Ironfist!

'Now this madness will end!' she said. 'The men of Powys will unite against the Saxons. Angor cannot leave the men of Gwylan Canu unarmed now. He will need every able-bodied warrior if he is to hold the citadel against Ironfist's attack.'

Blodwedd's small hand gripped the wrist of Branwen's sword-arm. 'Do not show yourself yet,' she said, looking into Branwen's eyes. 'One of the horsemen who leads the warriors was not a Saxon, I think. He had no beard and he was dressed in the fashion of the men of Powys. My heart tells me there is more to learn before you act.'

'The man you saw was likely a captive,' said Rhodri. 'A man of Brython, forced to lead Ironfist to the citadel.'

'It is of no matter,' Branwen hissed. 'I will not stand idly by while Gwylan Canu is taken!' She tried in vain to drag her hand free from the owl-girl's deceptively strong grasp.

'Branwen, heed me,' murmured Blodwedd. 'Watch and wait. All has not yet been revealed.'

Branwen grimaced as Blodwedd's fingers tightened about her wrist. She knew Govannon's messenger was duty-bound to keep her from harm at all costs – but surely not if it meant allowing Gwylan Canu to fall to the Saxons? What was the purpose in her being brought here, if all she did at journey's end was to stand aside while a Saxon army overran the citadel?

The hurried percussion of hoofbeats sounded – a horse, galloping along the road from the east.

Branwen glared at Blodwedd. She twisted her arm, ripping the owl-girl's fingers away. 'I will not reveal myself,' she said. 'But I must see what is happening.'

She lifted her head above the rock-edge once more. Yes! A rider was coming in fast along the road, and Blodwedd had been right if this was the man she had seen riding alongside Ironfist – he was no Saxon; it was a warrior of Powys. It was a man of Doeth Palas.

Angor raised a hand in greeting. 'Adda ap Avagdu!' he called. 'You return in good time. Is all well?'

'All is well, Captain,' replied the horseman, bringing his horse up short.

Angor knows him! He must be a scout sent ahead of the warrior troop. But why has he been riding with the Saxons? Has he betrayed his captain?

Hardly had the words of greeting left the horseman's lips than the brazen blare of Saxon war horns sounded, echoing and re-echoing among the precipices.

'Ironfist!' cried Angor, lifting his sword and turning to his men. 'General Ironfist is upon us, warriors of Powys!' he called. 'How would you greet the great Saxon Warlord?'

Captain Angor's men hammered swords on shields as though in defiance of the approaching hoard, but Branwen could see consternation among the unarmed men of Gwylan Canu.

Lord Madoc stepped forwards, ignoring the swords that pointed towards him. 'Angor ap Pellyn!' he shouted. 'Give us our weapons, man! You cannot fight Ironfist alone!'

As though spurred on by his lord's words, one of the men of Gwylan Canu broke free of the others and ran towards the mound of spears and swords and shields.

'Bring him down!' snarled Angor.

Neb ap Mostyn hefted a spear in his fist and let it fly.

Branwen stared in utter disbelief as the spear caught the running man in the back. He fell on to his face with a short-cut cry.

A murmur of shock and anger ran through the other men of the citadel. One stepped forwards, shouting in protest.

A sword slashed down and he fell to his knees, his head half severed from his body. He dropped on to his face, and now the other men of Gwylan Canu were hemmed in with a hedge of swords.

While Branwen was still trying to come to terms with what she had witnessed, the rumble of marching feet grew suddenly louder. She turned her head. Several horsemen had rounded a crag of rock and at their head was the man from her vision.

Horsa Herewulf Ironfist, lord of Winwaed, Commander of the armies of King Oswald of Northumbria, a huge, hulking man with a bristling black beard and blue eyes as bright and hard as stones. On his head was a round, crested helmet of iron, inlaid with silverwork and gold. A red cloak hung from his shoulders, covering a leather jerkin and a long coat of fine iron mail. At his hip was a sword and in one fist he clutched a silver-tipped spear.

He rode forward, and behind him came the bearded Saxon warriors, some in chain mail, others in leather trews and brown woollen cloaks, barefoot and with helmets of beaten iron. Clouds of dust rose as they marched, and the sunlight glinted coldly on spear tip and helmet.

Ironfist lifted a hand and the marching men came to a halt. The sudden silence was shocking. The brown dust wafted away on the wind. Branwen's thoughts were thrown back to the hoard of Saxon warriors who had come down upon Garth Milain, reckless in their battle-fever, war-skilled and deadly. She tasted iron on her tongue and felt a terrible pressure growing in her head as she stared into those brutal bearded faces. So many men – so much hatred.

Herewulf Ironfist rode on alone, slowly, without drawing his sword.

Angor walked forwards to meet him, his sword in hand.

Ironfist brought his great black stallion to a halt on the road. It stood pawing the ground and snorting, dark eyes rolling.

Angor stood for a moment in front of the horse, then dropped to one knee, his head bowed. He turned his sword in his hands and offered the hilt to the Saxon general.

'Greetings, my lord,' Angor said. 'In the name of Prince Llew of Bras Mynydd, I offer you my allegiance and my fealty.' He looked up now. 'I give to you a great prize, my lord. The gates of Gwylan Canu are open to you. Ride in and take the citadel for your own!'

CHAPTER TWENTY-FIVE

Branwen bit down hard on her lip, tasting blood, her jaw clenched, her whole body knotted in horror as she stared at the kneeling Captain of Doeth Palas and the Saxon warlord who loomed over him, haughty and powerful on his huge black stallion.

Herewulf Ironfist leaned out of the saddle and closed his fist around the hilt of Captain Angor's offered sword. He turned, lifting the weapon, brandishing it in the air.

A roar came from the Saxons, a bellow of triumph accompanied by the clash of swords on shields and the stamping of feet.

Tears of rage and despair started from Branwen's eyes. This could not be happening. There could not be such treachery in Powys!

And then something came into her mind. Something that Rhiannon had said to her when they had first met, by the silvery pool in the forest outside Doeth Palas.

Something that had not meant anything to her at the time.

'If you turn from me, child, the enemy will sweep over you like a black tide. There is a festering canker at the heart of this land.'

A festering canker at the heart of Powys!

Greetings, my lord. In the name of Prince Llew of Bras Mynydd, I offer you my allegiance and my fealty.

Prince Llew ap Gelert had turned traitor! The richest and most powerful lord in all of Powys had gone over to the enemy. How could Powys survive such a betrayal? How could Brython endure such deception and perfidy?

Branwen had set out on this journey with no clear vision of how it might end. Failure and death had been her worst nightmare. In the dark of night she had sometimes seen her own slaughter. In bright sunrise, her hopes had risen, she had imagined herself on a field of battle, bloodied but victorious. But not for one moment had she dreamed of witnessing such a villainous deed as this! To surrender to the age-old enemy – to bend the knee to a Saxon general!

'No,' she murmured, her heart drumming in her chest, the blood pounding in her ears. 'No, this shall not be!' She lifted her sword and made to stand up – to reveal herself, to put an end to this insanity!

She was vaguely aware through the thunder that filled

her mind of Blodwedd's voice, a frantic whisper.

'Rhodri! Stop her! Hold her back.'

Hands took hold of her, pulling her down from the ridge, dragging her to the bottom of the cleft. A hand came across her mouth as she struggled to get free. Another wrenched her sword from her fingers.

She fought wildly, but Rhodri's body was across hers, his weight holding her down. Hands gripped vice-like on either side of her head.

'Branwen, be calm!' She stared up into Blodwedd's huge golden eyes. 'This is not the way,' the owl-girl said. 'You cannot reveal yourself at this time. Your death will be for nothing if you do! Heed me, Branwen!'

'Branwen, please, listen to her.' Rhodri's frantic, breathless voice. 'You'll be killed.'

Branwen panted, staring up into Blodwedd's face. The red rage began to subside. She became still, her taut muscles relaxing. Through the throbbing of blood in her ears, she could hear the Saxons howling and beating their weapons.

'Get off me,' she gasped. 'Rhodri, I'm all right. There's no need to hold me down.'

Rhodri knelt up. 'It's a good thing they're making such a racket down there,' he breathed. 'They'd surely have heard us else!'

Blodwedd's eyes glowed. 'You must not throw your life

away, Branwen, not in futile despair,' she murmured. 'Your life is not your own to do with as you please! Has everything I have told you meant nothing? You are the Warrior Child! Latest in a great line. Brython needs you to live!'

A frozen anger began to take the place of Branwen's fiery rage. 'Did you know of this all along?' she asked Blodwedd. 'Did you know *this* was waiting at the end of our road?'

Blodwedd shook her head. 'I did not.'

'And your master? Did he know?'

Blodwedd's head lowered. 'That I cannot say.'

Branwen frowned at her for a moment then turned to Rhodri. 'Give me back my sword!'

He looked uneasily at her. 'You can't fight them all.'

'I don't mean to,' she replied, sitting up and holding her hand out. 'The sword, Rhodri!'

Reluctantly, he handed it to her. She stood up, sliding the sword into her belt and taking a long, slow breath.

'If we are to turn back this day's evil tide, we will need to know what plans have been laid,' she said, and the calmness of her voice surprised her. Her anger was like a stone now, cold and heavy in her chest.

She climbed the slope again. The din of the Saxon warriors had subsided.

Ironfist was speaking, using the language of Brython,

albeit with a strong Saxon accent. 'I am grateful to you, Captain Angor,' the general said. 'You came in good time to save me the hardship of bitter blows and loss in the taking of Gwylan Canu. I had not looked to you for this – the messenger from Prince Llew did not speak of him sending men to aid me in this endeavour.'

'We looked to find you already embattled,' said Angor. 'A messenger was sent to Doeth Palas, telling of your coming.' He frowned. 'And yet . . . how could that be? How could they have known so soon that a Saxon force was marching on Teg Eingel?' He turned. 'Is Dagonet ap Wadu among those captured?' he called to his men.

'Dagonet is not here,' said Lord Madoc. 'He is with the King in Pengwern. Thus is one brave warrior of Powys saved from your treachery!'

Angor's eyes turned to Iwan. 'How did you know, boy?' he shouted. 'If it was not Dagonet who told you, who was it?'

Iwan gave a bruised smile. 'A power greater than you know,' he said. 'A power that will see you trodden into the dust ere all is done, traitor!'

'What does he mean?' snarled Ironfist. 'What power is this of which he speaks?'

Iwan lifted his head, standing suddenly proud and straight once more. 'Do you not know?' he shouted, his voice ringing in the hills. 'Do you not hear them? They are awake, they are stirring, they are coming – and they will be the death of you all!'

Angor strode forwards and struck Iwan, knocking him to the ground. But still there was defiance in Iwan's eyes as he looked up at the treacherous captain.

'Do you feel fear yet, Angor ap Pellyn?' he cried. 'The Shining Ones have awoken! Harken! They are close! They will—'

A second brutal blow sent him crashing on to his face before he could say any more. His father knelt at his side, his face livid with anger, his arms protectively around his son's shoulders.

'What does the boy mean?' demanded Ironfist.

'His wits have turned, my lord,' said Angor. 'He speaks madness. It is of no consequence.'

'Then let us about our business, Captain Angor,' said Ironfist. He turned in the saddle gesturing to his men. Two burly warriors strode forwards, carrying between them a heavy iron-bound wooden chest.

At the general's command, they bore the chest forwards, throwing it down and opening its heavy lid. Branwen saw the sparkle and glint of coins heaped within, a mountain of coins, more coins than she had ever seen in her life. A king's ransom, she guessed.

'Are your men loyal to you, Captain Angor?' Ironfist asked.

'They are, my lord,' Angor replied. 'They are hand-picked and will die in my service if need be.'

'And what of the others of the Court of Prince Llew?' asked Ironfist. 'How many know of the treaty that has been agreed between our realms?'

'These men under my command have long known the truth, my lord,' said Angor. 'And so do some intimates of the prince, but they are all close-mouthed men and trustworthy to our cause. No hint of what is to come has yet been spoken abroad in the citadel, and outside its walls the folk of Bras Mynydd know nothing. The prince deemed it better that way, lest some fools chose defiance.'

'Wise thinking,' said Ironfist. 'Until all is in readiness, I would not have word of our plans come to the ears of the other lord of Powys, nor those of the king, weak and cowardly as he may be, lurking within the walls of the citadel at Pengwern. I'd not have word sent to the southern kingdoms either. We want no armies arrayed against us before we are secure in Powys.'

So that's the scale of their ambition, Branwen thought bitterly, her fists balling, her nails digging into her flesh. *To use Prince Llew's cantref as a base from which to strike King Cynon, and then to eat up the rest of Brython piece by piece!*

Captain Angor spread his arms. 'We are yours to command, my lord.'

'And the men of Gwylan Canu – how go their hearts in this?'

Lord Madoc got to his feet and stepped forwards. 'Know me, accursed Saxon dog,' he spat, his fist hammering his chest. 'I am Madoc ap Rhain, lord of Gwylan Canu. I know not what lies you have used to sway Llew ap Gelert to your cause, but hear me now! The men of Gwylan Canu are loyal and true to their king. They will not do your bidding, Herewulf Ironfist – they would die a thousand times first.'

Ironfist smiled coldly. 'A thousand deaths will not be necessary, my lord,' he mocked. 'One death for each man will suffice.' He lifted his voice, addressing now the gathered warriors of the citadel. 'Listen well, men of Powys. Against the forces that gather in Mercia and Northumbria there can be no victory for you. Brython will fall to us – our destiny wills it so! Only a fool goes willingly to a battle that cannot be won. See wisdom, as has the Lord of Bras Mynydd, for all who swear allegiance to King Oswald, I will give great riches.' He gestured towards the teeming chest. 'Find wisdom, men of Teg Eingel.' His voice rose to a guttural snarl. 'For those who defy me, death will be their only release. Choose swiftly! Come!'

Madoc ap Rhain stared into Ironfist's face, his arms spread wide. 'Kill us now, Saxon filth. None will take your tainted gold!'

A kind of bleak pride welled up in Branwen as she saw that not one of the men of Gwylan Canu stepped forwards. She could see fear in the eyes of many of them, and anger and hatred and despair in others. But it spoke well of Lord Madoc's leadership that every man chose loyalty to him and their homeland over the offer of the Saxon general.

There was a long, dreadful stillness, broken only by the constant beating of waves on the rocks and the lonely cries of gulls.

'So be it,' Ironfist said at last. 'Let Lord Madoc and his kin be taken captive and held in the citadel. Their lives may prove useful if it comes to bargaining. For the others, they will be taken east – to captivity or death.'

'What would you have me do, my lord?' asked Angor.

'Return with your warriors to Doeth Palas,' said Ironfist. 'Make it known in the citadel that you have scored a great victory against the Saxons and that Gwylan Canu is secure and Ironfist sent packing with his tail between his legs. Let no man speak of the things that have passed here, on pain of certain death.' He leaned forwards in the saddle, a savage smile stretching his lips. 'In the privacy of his court, tell the prince I am well pleased with him. He has shown foresight and wisdom. King Oswald will be generous when the time comes. If all goes well, Llew ap Gelert will one day sit upon the throne of Powys. Tell him that.'

'I shall, my lord.'

Ironfist sat upright again. 'Tell your men to take from the chest what coins they can carry before they depart.'

He handed Angor's sword back to him, then turned his black stallion and rode back to his men, shouting commands in his own harsh, guttural language. Captain Angor stood, sheathing his sword, staring after the Saxon general.

Branwen tried to imagine what thoughts must be going through his mind. Was it really the hopelessness of warfare against the Saxons that had made him and the prince agree to betray their homeland? Was this treachery fuelled by despair? Or was it something else that spurred Prince Llew to join hands with Ironfist? Even greater wealth? The promise of the crown of Powys?

Whatever it was, it left a taste like gall in Branwen's mouth; it soured her stomach and burned her heart. Somehow she would find a way to fight this!

Things began to move quickly. A detachment of Saxon warriors led the men of Gwylan Canu away down the road into the east. At their captain's word, the men of Doeth Palas ran forwards, scrabbling for gold and silver in the chest like pigs at a trough. Then Angor had them mount, and with a final hand raised in farewell to Herewulf

Ironfist, he led them at the trot back to spread their lies in Doeth Palas.

Finally Madoc ap Rhain and Iwan were taken into the citadel by the Saxons. The foreign warriors gathered the weapons left by Lord Madoc's men, then they poured into Gwylan Canu, stone-walled bastion of Teg Eingel, which had been taken without a fight. Fallen to bloodless treachery.

Branwen saw the gates pulled closed. There was the thud of the great doors as they slammed, the crash and boom as the bars were put in place. Saxon warriors appeared on the gatehouse. A banner was quickly unfurled – the white dragon on a field of blood.

And then there was a terrible stillness and Branwen tasted salt tears on her tongue as she made her way down from the ridge.

CHAPTER TWENTY-SIX

Branwen, Rhodri and Blodwedd were among the trees once more as the evening shadows lengthened. They had eaten a bleak meal together, Rhodri and Branwen almost too shocked by the turn of events to put their feelings into words. But no matter how deeply they were hurt by Prince Llew's treachery, they could not remain silent.

'If the prince knew all along that Ironfist was marching on Gwylan Canu, why did he send fifty horsemen to its rescue?' Rhodri asked. 'How does that make sense?'

'It was for show, that's all,' Branwen replied. 'What else could he do? If Iwan told people that his homeland was in danger and that Prince Llew had done nothing, how would that look? No, he sent Angor here with a troop of warriors who already knew the truth. But not to help Gwylan Canu – simply to ensure that all was going as planned. The moment Iwan rode with them, his fate was sealed!' Branwen shook her head, still enraged and overwhelmed by what she had witnessed. 'In fact, it was Iwan's presence among them that made it so easy for Angor to force Lord Madoc to give up the citadel!' She glared at Blodwedd. 'If we had not gone to Iwan, perhaps Gwylan Canu would still be holding out against Ironfist's army! We did no good at all. We only caused harm – and made it easier for Ironfist to take the citadel without even having to fight for it!' She glared at the owl-girl. 'Your master has only made things worse!'

Blodwedd had not spoken for some time. She sat huddled on the brink of the hill, staring down at the fires and torches that were igniting in the citadel as the evening deepened. 'Lord Govannon did not set your feet on the path that took you to Doeth Palas,' she said.

'She's right,' said Rhodri. 'That was my idea.'

'Then we should have been sent a sign or something to show us it was a *bad* idea,' said Branwen.

'I don't think it works like that,' Rhodri said in a subdued voice.

Blodwedd looked around. 'Lord Govannon will show us the way to thwart that Saxon general's ambitions,' she said softly, almost as though talking to herself.

'Then share his plans with us,' Branwen said bitingly. 'All he's done so far is to bring us here too late to do anything other than watch Gwylan Canu fall! What are his plans, Blodwedd? Will he conjure up an army for us, so we can sweep down and assail the citadel? Can he put a battering ram into our hands for us to beat down the gates?' She stood up, anger taking her again. 'What will he do for us, Blodwedd? *What?*'

The owl-girl looked up at Branwen with wide, calm eyes.

'What more would you have him do, Branwen?' she asked. 'Are you without hope, without thought? His will brought you to this place at this time with a purpose, Warri— *Branwen*. Use your skills, use your mind.' Her eyes sparked. 'It is for us to find a way!'

'We should try to get word to the king,' said Rhodri.

Branwen nodded. 'You're right, the king must be told of this. An army must be assembled and Gwylan Canu retaken before Ironfist can bring yet more Saxon warriors here.' Branwen had not forgotten the other element of her bleak vision. Not only had she seen Ironfist holding up Iwan's head, not only had she seen the white dragon flying over the citadel and Saxon warriors triumphant on the walls – she had seen a fleet of Saxon ships cleaving the waves and she knew they were coming.

It was no more than a day's march from Ironfist's great encampment outside Chester to the mouth of the River Dee. If her vision was true, then hundreds more Saxon warriors could already be on the open sea. The morning could see a whole host of their low, square-sailed ships riding the surf off the coast of Teg Eingel.

'The trouble is we could spend four days on the journey to Pengwern,' Branwen said. 'And when we came to King Cynon's court, would we be believed? Will the king accept our word that his most powerful prince has turned traitor? What proof could we offer him?'

'The proof of our own eyes,' said Rhodri. 'What more could he ask?'

'A great deal more,' said Branwen. 'You are half Saxon, Rhodri – who would trust you? And for all we know, the prince already has conspirators at the royal court. How am I to be trusted if Prince Llew's men are there to give the lie to my every word?' She paused for a moment as the glimmerings of an idea came into her head. 'But he would surely trust the word of the lord of Gwylan Canu.'

'Doubtless he would,' said Rhodri. 'Except that he is being held captive behind the walls of his own citadel.' He lifted an eyebrow. 'Or are you suggesting we three should attack Gwylan Canu and rescue Madoc ap Rhain from under Ironfist's very nose?'

'Not attack, no,' said Branwen. 'I see no way through that wall. But is it impossible to approach the citadel from the sea?'

'Those who built it must think so,' said Rhodri.

'Otherwise walls would surround the entire headland. I would say they think themselves quite secure from a seaborne attack.' He turned, listening to the drum roll of the surf. 'Can't you hear the noise the waves make when they break on the rocks?' He shook his head. 'That will be the sound of our bones cracking if we attempt such a deed.'

'And that is why no one within will expect such an assault,' Branwen insisted. 'There are boats drawn up on the beach a little way along the coast. One of those may serve us, if a way on to the rock could be found.' She looked eagerly into Rhodri's face. 'Couldn't a single boat make secret landfall on a dark night? Couldn't three people enter the citadel unseen? And could they not rescue Madoc and escape with him before the alarm was sounded?'

Rhodri pursed his lips. 'What are we, flies and spiders to cling to sheer rock?' he said. 'The land drops straight into the sea all along the headland.'

'We don't know that for sure,' Branwen persisted. 'We should send Fain to scout the land for us. He can bring back news of any possible landing place.'

Rhodri stared dubiously at her for a few moments. 'Yes,' he said at last. 'We should do that.'

Branwen stood and walked over to where the horses had been loosely tethered. She peered up into the darkling branches, but saw no sign of the bird. And then, as though he knew he was needed without Branwen even having to call, a dark scythe-shaped shadow came flying through the trees.

Branwen held up her hand and Fain came to rest on her wrist. She lifted a finger to stroke his feathers.

Blodwedd was standing suddenly behind her. 'Ask him to fly down to the citadel to learn whether it can be approached safely from the sea,' she said. 'I will tell you what tidings he brings.'

Branwen turned to the bird. 'Fain, do as Blodwedd says.' She lifted her wrist higher and the falcon lurched forwards, wings spreading and curling. 'Be swift and sure, my friend!' Branwen called after him. 'Bring us back good news!'

'No one has lived here for some time,' said Rhodri as they walked among the huddled huts.

Branwen could see that he was right. From afar the little hamlet looked like any other, but now that they had come down out of the hills and made their way across rough scrubland to the sandy bay, it was clear the huts were derelict and tumbledown.

In many places their wattle and daub walls had crumbled away to reveal the broken mesh of wickerwork beneath. Some of the thatched roofs had fallen in, leaving the walls standing like the shards of a hollow tooth. There were long-cold firepits and scattered pieces of cracked earthenware, dimly discernable in the growing night.

'What took the people?' Branwen wondered, looking uneasily around herself. 'This place has a sad and mournful air to it.'

'Disease perhaps?' ventured Rhodri. 'Or it could have been overrun in the old wars and none ever returned to fish its waters. Who can say?'

Branwen shivered and pulled her cloak around her shoulders. The wind was coming in cool off the sea.

She glanced over to the east. Across the bay, Gwylan Canu was a great dark hulk against the sky, cragged and uneven, the roofs of huts and houses cut sharp against the stars. Taller than all other buildings was the Great Hall, stark and black on its hill. But the citadel twinkled with lights, yellow and red and white, and there were torches lit on the wall, flickering as guards passed in front of them.

'Let's see if the boats are still seaworthy,' Branwen said. She looked sideways at Rhodri. 'Can you swim?'

'No.'

'Neither can I,' she said. 'Let's hope we find a watertight boat.'

Fain's news had been . . . *hopeful*. Speaking through

Blodwedd, he had made it clear that he had found no landing posts or jetties along the headland, and that in most places the black rock dropped straight into the waves without step or handhold. But all along the promontory, the endless pounding of the sea had gnawed and corroded the ancient rocks, leaving cracks and breaches where the water churned white and deadly. And in other places the waves had eaten deep into the rock, mining out blowholes and apertures from which the surf spouted.

It was one such chasm that had taken Fain's attention. At the headland's very point, beyond the buildings, even beyond the Great Hall, a deep sloping tunnel led from the sea up on to the land.

How easy it would be for a person to climb this borehole and get safely above the fury of the breakers, Fain could not tell them. But there was some hope that this perilous way might take them safely into the very heart of Gwylan Canu.

Either they took this chance, or they had to admit defeat – and Branwen was not prepared to do that.

The boats were above the tide-line, but as they moved from one to the next, they quickly saw that most were falling to pieces, the wooden slatted hulls long rotted, the oars snapped and useless.

'What about this?' Rhodri asked. He had moved away

from Branwen and Blodwedd and was standing by a boat that was turned upside down in the sand.

Branwen went to look. The boat was narrow and leaf-shaped, not much longer than Branwen was tall. Its hull was made from tough old leather, thick and durable. So far as Branwen could see in the darkness, the hull had no breaches or tears in it.

'Let's turn it over and see if it's sound,' she said. They tipped the vessel on to its back. It rocked in the sand. The timber framework seemed solid enough, and there were also two paddles that had been under the boat and looked to have survived the ravages of wind and rain and bad weather.

She saw Rhodri's eyes on her. 'We have to make our minds up,' he said. 'I think it's this one or nothing.'

'Then it's this one,' Branwen said. She turned to where the owl-girl was standing, her arms wrapped tight around her chest, her forehead creased, her anxious gaze fixed on the sea. 'Blodwedd, help us,' Branwen called.

Between them, they carried the boat down to the water's edge. As they waded into the surf, dragging the boat with them, Blodwedd hung back, unwilling to set foot in the foaming wash of the incoming tide. Branwen was aware of small, sharp sounds coming from the owl-girl. She realized that Blodwedd's teeth were chattering.

Branwen looked back at her. 'Come,' she said. 'What's wrong?'

'I cannot.' There was deep terror in Blodwedd's voice, and her eyes were haunted in her pale face. Pure animal eyes they seemed now – as though Blodwedd's true spirit was staring through them. She shook her head.

Branwen left Rhodri to keep hold of the boat. She splashed back to the shore, remembering the owl-girl's anxious words from earlier in the day. 'There is nothing to fear,' she said.

'I am Lord Govannon's child,' Blodwedd murmured, her voice little more than a fearful whisper. 'I dare not leave his realm.' Branwen could see that she was shaking from head to foot.

'What do you fear?' asked Branwen, looking into Blodwedd's terrified glowing eyes.

'Beyond the reach of his hand, the sea will drown me,' Blodwedd murmured. 'My feathers waterlogged, dragging me down – down and down – never fly more – never feel the wind – cold water in my mouth, in my body – choking me!' Her voice rose to a wail. 'Lord Govannon, forgive me. You ask too much! I cannot! I cannot!'

Before Branwen could act, Blodwedd turned and ran headlong up the beach, the sand kicking high from her heels.

'Blodwedd! Wait!' Branwen chased after her, but the

lithe owl-girl sped away into the darkness and before Branwen had a hope of catching up with her, the slender form had vanished into the night.

Branwen stood in the sand, panting, staring blankly after her. She felt no anger at Blodwedd's flight. Not long ago she would have been relieved to be rid of her, but she didn't feel that either. She felt pity, that was all. Pity for the inhuman creature and for the terror that had caused her to run away from the duty that Govannon of the Wood had laid upon her.

At length, she shook her head and made her way back to where Rhodri was waiting, knee deep in the sea, clinging to the bucking boat.

'Don't put too much blame on her,' he said. 'At heart, she's an animal still. A bird of the forests – she could not help herself.'

'I don't blame her,' Branwen said. 'But I hope her master is as forgiving. The Shining Ones ask for impossible sacrifices – and make us pay a terrible price if we fail them.' She was thinking of her father lying dead and of Garth Milain in flames. If she had not turned her back on Rhiannon of the Spring when the woman in white had first called to her, might those tragedies have been averted?

'Perhaps she hasn't entirely abandoned us,' Rhodri said, scanning the shadowed hills, his face hopeful. 'She may wait for us with the horses.'

'Let us hope so,' Branwen said. 'Because if she has deserted us, then I fear she will never be an owl again.' She glanced at Rhodri. 'Although, would that upset you, I wonder?'

Rhodri didn't reply, and turned his face away so she could not see his expression.

So now I know for sure, she thought. *A strange affection, and I don't envy him the pain it will surely cause, whether she returns to us or not.*

Unspeakingly, they pushed the boat into deeper water, struggling all the time against the breaking waves. It was a hard, exhausting task and it felt as though the sea was fighting them, working with all its tireless might to prevent them from using the boat. Branwen's muscles ached from the strain of keeping the leaping boat secure. The rush of the undertow around her legs made every step an effort.

At last she was waist deep and they were out beyond the breakers. She hauled herself up and over the side, gasping and clinging on as the light vessel rocked and bobbed. A moment later Rhodri came surging up over the other side.

'The paddles – quick!' she panted.

They knelt in the bottom of the boat, Rhodri behind her as they gripped the wide-bladed paddles and thrust them into the water. Branwen bent her back, attacking the sea with the paddle, the muscles in her shoulders and arms knotting as she battled against the tide.

She could hear Rhodri grunting and gasping behind her. But still the surge of the sea drove them back towards the beach. She renewed her efforts, refusing to be beaten, using every fibre and every sinew as she plunged the paddle down, dragged on it and lifted it again – down, back, lift. Over and over while the surf spat in her face and her muscles screamed in protest.

At last she felt able to look over her shoulder. Rhodri's face was running with sweat and seawater, his jaw clenched, his lips parted in a snarl of effort and pain. But beyond him, the pale line of the coast had fallen away into the distance.

She let out a gasp of breathless laughter. They had beaten the sea!

Rhodri looked at her, too spent to speak.

Over to their right, the great dark bulk of the headland loomed with grey foam at its feet.

'We need to get further out,' Branwen gasped. 'Come at it from the seaward end. Yes?'

Rhodri nodded.

They plied the paddles once more. Down, back, lift. Branwen tried to ignore the fatigue that made her arms feel leaden. She did her best to blot out the pain that bunched across her back and bit into her neck.

Gradually they crawled along the headland until they came to the outermost point – a huge blunt forehead of black rock thrusting out into the sea. The waves broke white, spurting and spewing into the air.

It looked impossible. They would be dashed to fragments.

'There it is!' came Rhodri's gasping voice. She glanced back, following the line of his pointing hand. Yes! She saw it. A gaping black hole in the rock face, its lower lip just above the swirl and spit of the sea.

She drove her paddle deep, making for the deadly headland.

The dark cliff reared above them. The noise pounded in Branwen's ears – far louder than the surge of her own blood or the harsh pant of her breath. A wave took the little boat and sent it careering forwards. An unseen rock scraped the leather hull, pushing them aside, sending the boat spinning.

Foam spat. The boat heeled over. Water came pouring in, swirling around their feet, cold and deadly. Again, the waves lifted and twisted the boat, jerking Branwen's body, jarring the paddle out of her hands.

With a cry she lunged sideways, frantically trying to retrieve it. But the sea sucked it away from her and as she hung over the side of the boat, more water flooded in.

She heard Rhodri shout. Another wave slapped down hard on them. The boat tipped, and Branwen was hurled headlong into the thrashing sea.

CHAPTER TWENTY-SEVEN

Branwen found herself struggling in deep water, fighting to keep her head above the surface, her arms and legs flailing in the turmoil of the sea. She gaped for breath, kicking, clawing, desperate in the wild darkness.

She felt something solid under her foot and pushed herself upwards. Her hands grazed over wet rock. Seawater filled her mouth, choking her. The waves pulled at her, trying to drag her off the rock. Coughing and retching, she clung on grimly, using all her failing strength to keep from being dragged to her death.

A wave beat on her back, pushing her forwards, pummelling her, spreadeagling her on the rock. But now she was half clear of the water, for a moment at least. She kicked out and heaved herself upwards.

She hung on, spat at by the angry waves, but above the tide-line. Foam blinded her, and she lifted her head. The roaring of the sea almost deafened her. 'Rhodri!'

A hand took hold of her ankle. She reached down and snatched at the wrist. Surf burst all about them. Branwen looked down into Rhodri's eyes as he struggled to pull himself up the slippery rock.

It was agony for her to keep hold of him. The effort of rowing through the choppy water had all but drained her muscles of strength, and now she had to cling to Rhodri while the tireless sea fought to rip him from her grip. But she would not let him go. She would *not*! She gritted her teeth, forcing her fingers to tighten around his wrist. She twisted around, grabbing his hair with her other hand, yanking him up, ignoring his cries of pain.

At last he was at her side and they clung to one another, gasping and almost weeping with relief.

'A little further up,' Branwen panted. 'I don't want to be washed off if a big wave comes.'

Side by side, they clambered on hands and knees further up the rock, struggling on until they were beyond the bluster and boil of the sea.

Branwen wiped her eyes. They were sitting in the mouth of the long sloping borehole. Against all the odds, they had made safe landfall on the headland of Gwylan Canu.

But all had not gone as planned.

Their boat was lost. There was no way back.

Rhodri looked at her, his eyes creased in the gloom.

'What's that stink?' he asked.

Branwen wrinkled her nose. He was right. There was a foul stench in the air. The disgusting smell of rot and purification – the unmistakable reek of a midden.

And then she realized that the slippery, slithery surface beneath her was not wet from the sea, but from the accumulated slime and muck and ooze of discarded waste: cast-away filth from the cookpot and the trencherboard.

'They must use this shaft as a garbage chute,' Rhodri gasped. 'Ugh! I cannot stand it!' He turned and began to climb up the slope.

Trying her best to hold her breath against the appalling fetor, Branwen scrambled up after him.

They came up out of the offal-chute and crouched among the rocks that lay beyond its upper rim. The landscape directly ahead of them was pocked with holes and ridges – a bleak end to the promontory, houseless and deserted, a place where the fleshless rock dropped stark into the sea.

An arrow's shot away from them, the rocks rose into a long-backed, flattened hill, and upon its high summit stood the Great Hall of the House of Puw.

'Listen,' murmured Rhodri, his head close to Branwen's. 'Can you hear them?'

She nodded. She could hear well enough: laughter and shouting and the noise of musical instruments and thumping drums. Smoke was pouring from the roof of the Great Hall. A fire was burning in the hearth – food was being cooked – a feast was taking place.

General Ironfist and his warriors were celebrating their easy conquest of Gwylan Canu, carousing on into the night, swigging ale and gorging on roasted meats.

'I have served at feasts like this,' Rhodri said. 'Ironfist likes to indulge his men when battles have gone well. It will go on all night, I expect. That's the usual way with such debauches.'

Branwen narrowed her eyes. 'Will they all be in there?' she asked.

'All save for a few guards on the wall,' said Rhodri. 'But what do we do now? The plan was to free Lord Madoc and use the boat to take him ashore. But the sea has put paid to that intent. Even if we can rescue him, how do we get out again?'

Branwen looked at him. 'We must hope that the Saxon's eyes are blurred with too much ale, my friend,' she said. 'Our only choice now is to cut our way through whatever gate-guards have been posted and have faith that once we are beyond the wall, the old lord can run faster than his girth would suggest.'

Cautiously she lifted her head over the rocks and scanned the barren landscape. 'I see no one,' she said. 'No guards, here nor on the hill. You guessed right, Rhodri –

they don't fear attack from the sea.' She smiled grimly, her fingers patting the hilt of her sword. 'We will make them regret that oversight.'

'We must find where Lord Madoc is being held,' Rhodri said. 'And we should expect to find guards watching over him.'

'Perhaps,' Branwen replied. 'But Angor said something that gives me some hope. When he ordered his men to search the citadel for weapons, he spoke of pits dug into the ground beyond the Great Hall – pits that were used in the old wars to hold Saxon prisoners.'

'Ahhh,' breathed Rhodri. 'And if good fortune is with us, you think Ironfist's captives will have been put into these pits? If they're beyond the Great Hall, then surely they must be close by.'

'Close by and unguarded, it seems,' said Branwen. She looked at Rhodri. 'Even though his messenger is gone, Govannon of the Wood may still be guiding our footsteps to good fortune.'

A look of anguish passed over Rhodri's face at the mention of Blodwedd. Branwen reached a hand towards him but withdrew it again without making contact. What comfort could she give him if the owl-girl was truly fled?

She crept forward, slow and silent as a shadow among the shadows, ignoring the discomfort and chill of her wet clothes, refusing to be thwarted by fatigue. All her attention was focused now on the ground directly ahead of her. If this cape of bitter rock was indeed riddled with pits, she did not want to stumble into one of them unawares.

She paused, holding her breath. Listening.

'What?' Rhodri murmured, close behind.

She held a hand up. 'Hush!'

She listened again. She fancied she had heard a new sound above the steady rumble of wave on rock and the rumour of the revelries taking place atop the hill. The subdued sound of voices.

She crawled forwards, turning her head to try and track down the elusive whispering. She moved between two large rocks. Her hand came down on something other than stone. She looked down. It was a coil of rope, knotted at one end and secured to the ground by a great black iron spike driven into the rock.

And then Branwen saw that the ground fell sharply away in front of her into a wide, black pit. And it was from the depths of this pit that the mutterings and whisperings were coming.

She lay flat on her belly, edging closer to the lip of rock.

Voices! Several voices, both male and female.

Branwen lifted her head, looking around quickly.

Then she hung out over the black void and called in a low, urgent voice.

'Is Madoc ap Rhain among you?'

She heard gasps and then a sudden silence.

'I am a friend,' Branwen called again, trying to be heard without raising her voice. 'I seek Lord Madoc. Is he with you?'

'Branwen?' A familiar, astonished voice spoke from the black pit.

'Iwan! Yes, it is me!'

'Look for a rope, Branwen,' came Iwan's voice, filled now with hope. 'You will find one attached to the rocks.'

Branawn fumbled for the rope, feeling its length rough and hard under her fingers 'Yes, it's here. I have it.'

'Throw it down to me. Say nothing more. There may be guards.'

Branwen knelt up and, taking hold of the thick, hairy rope, began to feed it down into the gloom. Suddenly the rope went taut in her hands, slithering through her fingers. It had been grasped from below.

She leaned over the hole. The rope was tight now, thrumming, shuddering as someone began to climb.

A hand came down on her back, pushing her to the ground. She twisted her head in surprise. It was Rhodri, kneeling close behind. His voice hissed softly. 'Stay down. Do not speak.'

So saying, he stood up. '*Hael!*' she heard him call out. '*Hael – freon! Liss, freon – cniht betera latteow Herewulf! Liss freon!*'

He was speaking in the Saxon language! She did not know what the words meant, but she recognized their sounds.

A slurred, guttural voice replied out of the night. '*Nama cniht!*'

A Saxon.

Rhodri must have seen him approaching and had revealed himself to try and prevent Branwen from being discovered. The rope had become still – whoever had been climbing it had paused.

'*Nama Rhodri,*' called Rhodri, giving Branwen a warning nudge with his foot as he moved away from her and towards the voice. He continued speaking, the tone of his voice conciliatory and submissive.

She heard a harsh gush of words from the Saxon, then a low, dull thud. Rhodri gave a gasp of pain, as though he had been hit. Branwen's instinct was to draw her sword and throw herself on the Saxon – but then she heard a third voice. The Saxon was not alone.

Rhodri spoke again. There was harsh laughter. He must have said something to amuse or appease the men.

Branwen listened as the two Saxon debated. She

guessed they were trying to decide what to do with this unexpected interloper.

Rhodri spoke again, his voice servile now, pleading and whining. There was more laughter. Branwen heard scuffling sounds, then Rhodri again, his voice now relieved and thankful. Whatever he had said to them, it had saved his life by the sound of it.

Rhodri's voice faded.

Branwen lifted herself up cautiously. She could just make out three shapes moving off towards the Great Hall.

Her stomach twisted into knots. To protect her and to save their plans from being revealed, Rhodri had given himself up to the Saxons. She hardly dared think of what terrible fate might await him in the Great Hall. How would Herewulf Ironfist choose to reward a runaway servant who had allowed himself to be recaptured?

CHAPTER TWENTY-EIGHT

The rope quivered under Branwen's hand. Whoever was hanging from the rope had begun to climb again now that the voices had faded.

Iwan's pale face showed at the mouth of the pit. Branwen held out a hand, bracing herself as he snatched at her wrist and hauled himself over the edge of the hole.

There was dried blood on his chin and the bruises were livid on forehead and cheek, but there was still an unquenchable light in his brown eyes.

'I'd ask how you got here, Branwen,' he murmured. 'But as you are aided by Old Gods, I shall assume you were flown here on wings of air to rescue us and to drive Ironfist into the sea.' He saw her wet clothes and the hair plastered to her skull. 'Or perhaps you were transformed into fishes and swam here?' he added wryly.

'Not quite,' Branwen whispered. 'The Old Gods do

not make life that easy for their cat's paws. We came by boat, but the boat is lost.'

'We?' Iwan asked. 'Is the demon girl with you still?'

'No, she is not. I spoke of Rhodri.'

'Ahh! It was his voice I heard speaking with the Saxons, yes?'

'He must have heard the Saxons coming. He gave himself up to prevent them from finding me.' She looked urgently into Iwan's eyes. 'We came here to rescue your father so that word could be sent to the king. But I will not leave this place without Rhodri.'

Iwan eyed her dubiously. 'What hold does that Saxon rogue have over you that you should consider risking everything for him yet again?'

Branwen frowned. 'He is only half Saxon,' she said. 'And is friendship not enough? For good or bad his life is bound up with mine – I will not abandon him.'

'Listen to me, Branwen.' Iwan's voice was low and insistent. 'My father was not thrown into the pits,' he said. 'I think he is held captive in the Hall – a trophy for the sport of Ironfist and his men. We have no hope of rescuing him and surviving.' He looked hard into Branwen's eyes. 'I am not a coward,' he said. 'But I will not die for no reason.'

'I know you're not a coward,' Branwen replied.

Iwan nodded. 'I see that you carry a sword and a knife,'

he said. 'Give me the knife and between us we may be able to get past whatever guards have been posted on the gate and break out of this place before the alarm is sounded. You must have horses – let's get to them and fly away south to Pengwern and the king. We need an army at our backs if we're to snatch Gwylan Canu back from Ironfist's grasp.'

'No.' Branwen shook her head. 'I won't leave Rhodri behind.'

'It's pure madness! We cannot free him!'

'I do not care – we must try.'

Iwan's eyes narrowed. 'Your stubborness will be the death of us, Barbarian Princess.' He looked at her for a few long moments, his face undecided. Then he let out a hard sigh, as though he knew his fate was sealed. 'If you intend to enter the Great Hall with a sword in your fist,' he continued slowly, 'do me this one favour – give me your knife, as I asked, so that I can at least defend myself for a few brief moments before I am slaughtered at your side.'

Branwen stared at him. 'Are you mocking me, Iwan?'

'No, I am not.' For once his voice sounded entirely sincere and his eyes were on her face, dark and glittering like agate stones. 'If you insist on throwing your life away, I will fight beside you. Do you think I would watch you walk to your death and do nothing?'

'A selfless act, is it, from the boy who from the moment I met him cared for nothing but his own amusement?' she asked gently.

'Possibly,' Iwan said. 'Or perhaps it amuses me to care for something other than my own amusement, Branwen. Perhaps I'd have you think as well of me as I do of you.'

Branwen sat back on her haunches, perplexed by Iwan's words. She shook her head, deciding against asking him exactly what he meant. There was more important business to hand.

'Are there no able men left among the captives?' she asked. 'A few fighters to even the odds?'

'None,' Iwan said. 'The pits are crowded with women and children and the elderly. Some of the women were taken – to serve in the Great Hall, I guess. But all my father's warriors are gone, marched into the east – to their deaths, I fear.' A moment of pain showed in his face. 'And they were good men, Branwen. Friends and companions of my childhood. I remember every face, every voice.'

Branwen looked thoughtfully at him. 'Where are the weapons that were taken from the men of the citadel?' she asked.

'I do not know,' said Iwan. 'Piled high in the Great Hall, I suspect, or divided among the Saxon dogs. But why do you ask? Even with fifty swords apiece, we two would be no better off.'

She looked closely at him. 'Are there no brave women in Gwylan Canu?' she asked. 'None that will fight for their homeland?'

'Many, I don't doubt,' Iwan replied.

A plan was beginning to formulate in Branwen's head – an uncertain and perilous plan, but one that offered at least a thread of hope. She turned her head to look up at the Great Hall. 'They are celebrating their victory,' she said. 'Rhodri told me that such feasts often carry on till dawn, or until all are so drunk that they fall witless to the floor and roll snoring amongst the rushes.'

'I've heard the same,' said Iwan.

'And you say that women of Gwylan Canu were taken to the Hall to serve them?'

'I think so.'

A grim smile touched Branwen's lips. 'Then maybe we shall find a way to take back the citadel after all,' she said. 'I must speak with your women, to find out whether their hearts are strong enough for the hazard I'd lead them to.'

'There are many women in the pit below,' Iwan said.

'More guards might come if I speak too loudly. I'll descend. You stay here – keep watch. If you see any Saxons, pull the rope up and hide yourself.' Branwen gripped the rope and lowered herself over the edge of the pit. She felt for a toehold. There – under her left foot – a tiny ledge, but enough to take her weight while she searched about for another. She found that the wall of the pit was ribbed and cracked, allowing meagre footholds to help her most of the way down.

Moving slowly and feeling her way carefully, she went hand-over-hand down into the darkness.

She looked up, seeing Iwan's face against the night sky. It was good to know he was there, keeping watch.

It was good to have him close by.

The pit was maybe four times Branwen's height – not so deep that all was pitch-black at the bottom, but deep enough that escape was impossible unless the rope was thrown down. As she came close to the ground, the wall became smoother and her legs swung free, but she felt hands reaching to help her.

She found herself surrounded by women, some close to her own age, others more mature and a few quite elderly and grey haired. In the deep shadows, other women sat with children gathered around them, and a few held babes in arms.

'I am Branwen ap Griffith,' she told them.

'The daughter of Griffith ap Rhys,' she heard one woman murmur. 'Yes, child, I have heard your name before.' A haggard face came close and withered hands touched her skin.

'I've come to bring you hope.' Branwen replied.

'Hope?' repeated another woman, tall and clear-eyed, carrying a swaddled babe in her arms. 'What hope do we have? To be carried east in chains is our only destiny now.'

'Or to be left to die of starvation in these pits,' said another, her round face pale and full of fear. 'Or to be the sport of our captors. I have heard that the Saxons delight in torture and cruelty.'

'They will throw our babies into the fire!' wailed another. 'Our heads will be hacked off and our corpses hurled down into the sea. We are all doomed.'

More voices lifted, crying and weeping and calling out to the saints for rescue.

'Be still!' called Branwen. 'I have hope for you – for those of you who are willing to follow me. But I can do nothing for you if you despair! Heed me well before you surrender your spirit to the enemy.' She stared around at the desperate and frightened faces that surrounded her. 'Who will listen to me? Who among you will fight with me?'

'Do not heed her,' said the old woman. 'She will lead you to certain death. Our only chance is to bend the knee to the Saxons. Prince Llew has abandoned us. He is a wise leader, he knows it is pointless to struggle against such odds.' She pointed a crooked finger towards

Branwen. 'This child will lead you to your deaths!'

Branwen narrowed her eyes. She could see even in the darkness of the pit that many of the women were in agreement with the old woman. She had hoped to persuade the womenfolk of Gwylan Canu to fight at her side, but few seemed willing to trust her. She did not blame them, the consequences of fighting and failing would be dire indeed.

Then one young woman stepped forwards, a bright-eyed girl of maybe fourteen summers, slim and erect. 'I will join with you, Branwen ap Griffith,' she said.

'Linette, do not be a fool,' cried the woman with the baby. 'Carys speaks the truth. We will die if we resist.'

'I fear death,' Linette responded. 'But I fear it less than I fear a life of servitude. I will not be dragged away by these dogs if I can fight against it.' She turned to Branwen, her eyes burning. 'What would you have me do?'

'And I, too,' said another young woman, stepping forwards. 'Linette is right – a quick death is better than a life on our knees.'

'Yes!' said a third, pushing out of the throng. 'I will follow you, Branwen ap Griffith, no matter what the cost!'

And then it was as if a dam had been breached. More and more women stepped forwards until Branwen found herself surrounded by a ring of valiant, eager faces. She looked into their bright, undaunted eyes, her heart swelling with pride that so many were prepared to risk death rather than succumb to the Saxon yoke.

The old woman, Cerys, shuffled off to the far side of the pit, muttering dire warnings. Many of the other women followed her, distancing themselves from Branwen and Linette and the others, now about fifteen strong.

'Do any of you have training in weapons?' she asked.

'I have some skill with a bow,' said Linette.

'That's good,' said Branwen.

'And I have some battle skills,' said another, a slight, compact young woman with a mass of black hair and with deep-set dark eyes that looked keenly into Branwen's face. 'My name is Dera ap Dagonet. My father is one of Lord Madoc's lieutenants.'

'I am Banon. I know something of the hunt,' said another.

'And I can spear a moving fish underwater at ten paces,' said yet another – a big, powerful young woman with piercing eyes. 'I am Aberfa. Lead me to the Saxon dogs, Branwen ap Griffith, and see how well I fight!'

A slow smile spread across Branwen's face. 'We *shall* fight, my friends. And with good luck and bold hearts, perhaps we shall show Herewulf Ironfist that there is daring yet in Gwylan Canu.'

'What would you have us do?' asked Dera ap Dagonet.

'I'd have you be patient yet awhile,' said Branwen, staring up at the night sky far away above the black mouth of the pit. 'Rest until the night is almost done. And then we shall see.'

CHAPTER TWENTY-NINE

Branwen lay on the long slope of the hill. Silent, holding her breath, listening intently. Linette and Dera lay on either side of her. Iwan and the other women were a little way behind. Far, far away to the east, the night sky had a grey hem – the first intimation of the coming day.

Despite being wakeful all through the night, Branwen felt keen-witted and alert. She had given her sword to Iwan, whose task was to stay back and to deal with any guards who might come to the Great Hall while the women were busy within.

The din of the night-long revels had dwindled. Branwen could hear snatches of singing and the occasional shout or peal of laughter from the Hall, but the music and the stamping of feet and the roar of drunken voices was done.

She stood up, knife in hand, and led the women up to

the crest of the hill. They were at the back of the long Hall. Branwen turned to her followers, pressing her finger to her lips. Then, quiet as a cloud, she slipped around the side of the Hall and ran fleet-footed under the hanging thatch of the high roof.

She could hear the patter of feet behind her as the line of women came snaking along in her wake. She paused, holding a hand up. There was a shape at the far corner of the Hall. A man – swaying unsteadily, relieving himself against the wall. Too far away for a slingshot stone to finish him, but close enough for a well-thrown knife.

The man was singing to himself, hardly able to keep upright. Branwen took the blade of her knife between her fingers and drew her arm back. Stretching her left arm out as a guide, she leaned back and then brought the weight and strength of her shoulders into the throw.

The knife hissed through the air. The white blade stabbed deep into the darkness of the man's throat. He dropped like a sack. Soundlessly. Branwen pounced after the throw and was on him in an instant. His eyes were wide in the gloom, as though he was surprised to find himself dead.

She pulled the knife out and wiped it on his tunic. She glanced back, seeing a new confidence in the faces of her followers. They had seen how a Saxon could be brought down! Gesturing to them to follow, Branwen turned the corner.

Braziers were burning on either side of the open doors of the Great Hall. Branwen crept to the doorway and risked a quick glance inside.

She leaned her head back against the door, her body trembling with suppressed excitement. She could not have hoped for better! In the aftermath of the victory feast, the main chamber of the Great Hall was a scene of excess and overindulgence. The fire was burning low now in the huge stone hearth at the centre of the long chamber, the flames flickering red on charred logs, reflecting on bloated sleeping faces and on bleary eyes, throwing up dancing shadows along the walls, as if the ghosts of the feasters played on while the Saxon warriors snored and wallowed in their debauchery.

Branwen leaned to take another look. Not all were lost in drunken slumber. A few were wakeful still, swigging from mugs, picking morsels from food bowls. Here and there men squatted or sat, playing at dice and knucklebones and from the odd corner the occasional snatch of song swelled for a few moments before subsiding into laughter and calls for more ale.

Branwen saw that the women of Gwylan Canu who had been brought to the Hall to serve were mostly gathered together against the wall, their faces gaunt and sleepless, their eyes empty of hope. A few moved unsurely among the Saxon warriors, pouring drink and trying to avoid being struck as they passed. Even as Branwen watched, one young girl – not even her own age – was kicked as she walked past a sprawling man. She fell to her knees, dropping the ewer she carried. It smashed, spilling foaming ale over the trampled rushes. The man snarled an oath and clumsily drew his sword, swiping feebly at her as she scrambled to get away. She ran to the others and was held in another woman's arms, while the drunken Saxon kept swinging his sword and muttering curses as if he did not realize she was out of his reach.

On the far side of the hall, General Herewulf Ironfist sat in a wide chair spread with animal furs, his legs thrown out, a mug in one fist and the end of an iron chain in the other. His eyes were hooded with drink and he leaned over the high arm of the chair, speaking to a prisoner who sat helplessly on the floor at his side.

The prisoner was Madoc ap Rhain, his face bruised and bleeding, his body wound about with chains, his hands wrenched around behind his back.

From the way that Ironfist leaned back and opened his wide red mouth to bellow with laughter every few moments, Branwen assumed the Saxon general was taunting his defeated rival, revelling in Lord

Madoc's downfall. But Lord Madoc just stared ahead, his face expressionless.

On Ironfist's other side, Branwen caught sight of another bound prisoner. Lying on his side, stripped to the waist, his arms and legs tied, his back showing the signs of whipping. It was Rhodri. White-hot anger seethed in Branwen's mind and rage clenched hard under her ribs, but she could not rush to Rhodri's rescue, as she desperately wanted to do, not yet. Not until her plans were well and truly laid.

She turned to the women, gathered now at her back, and gestured for them to follow her into the hall. Stepping into the open, Branwen pulled her cloak close around herself to hide her hunting leathers, keeping her knife hand under the swathes of cloth.

They crept along the walls of the Great Hall. A few groggy and fuddled eyes lifted as the women passed the drink-addled Saxons. A slurred voice called for more ale, a mug was raised, but no one seemed to sense the danger creeping in among them. No one drew a sword or called the alarm.

Branwen made her way cautiously around the chamber towards Ironfist.

He was leaning even further over now, spittle flying from his mouth, getting caught in his beard and hanging there thickly as he heaped more abuse on the helpless

Lord of Gwylan Canu. Now Branwen could hear his harsh taunts.

'My men will wish for sport in the morning, my lord,' he sneered. 'Perhaps your son could offer his services in entertainment? Have no fear that he will not have the talent to amuse – I am expert in drawing vivid performances from the most reticent of actors. Have you heard of the blood eagle, my lord? It is most engaging. The performer is laid upon his belly on the ground and the ribs along his spine are cut through and wrenched upwards to form wings. And then his lungs are drawn out of his body to lie throbbing upon his back.' Ironfist gurgled with laughter. 'Alas, the performance never lasts as long as my men would wish. But we have many captives to practise on. It will while away the time till the remainder of my army arrives.'

Revolted, Branwen glanced around. The women had placed themselves at all points along the walls of the hall and were watching, waiting for her to act.

She nodded and stepped up to Ironfist.

He lifted his head and peered at her with glazed eyes. 'More ale, woman,' he said, holding out the mug. 'Be swift, or I'll have you whipped raw to the bone.'

'You will not, my lord!' Branwen snarled.

His eyes narrowed, but his wariness came too late.

Branwen smashed the mug out of his hand with a

single blow of her fist, then sprang forward, the knife in her hand, grabbing him by the hair and dragging his head back, the blade hard against his throat.

She leaned over him, her mouth close to his ear. 'If you value your life, call to your men to throw down their weapons – those few with wits enough to understand you, that is!'

Ironfist breathed hard, his breath foul with ale, his bloodshot eyes glaring under heavy black brows.

'Who are you, woman of Gwylan Canu, to threaten me?' he snarled.

'I am Branwen ap Griffith,' she replied calmly. 'And if my name means nothing to you now, you will know me better hereafter, Saxon! Tell your men to disarm or there will be bloodshed here – and yours will be the first throat to feel a blade!' She turned to the women. 'Get weapons! Arm yourselves. These fools are without their wits, but there will be sober guards on the wall.'

At her words, the women ran out into the body of the hall and began to search among the drunken warriors, taking swords and knives and axes. Seeing what was happening, some of the serving women came forward, stepping among the drunkards to find themselves weapons.

A Saxon who had been playing knucklebones surged to his feet, an axe in his fist, swinging at Dera ap Dagonet's head. She ducked and thrust a new-found sword into his belly. He went crashing to the floor, but others rose, their weapons ready.

Using all her strength and bodyweight, Branwen heaved Ironfist up out of the chair. Once he was on his feet, she stepped behind him, the knife sliding across his throat, drawing a thin trickle of blood. 'Speak to them, General.'

'You are a fool, child,' grated Ironfist. 'Drowsy from our revels, you may take us unawares – but against the forces that are gathering, there can be no hope of victory.'

'I've heard that speech before,' said Branwen. 'I do not need to listen to it again. Have them drop their swords, General.'

Ironfist called out something in his own language. Those few warriors who were able to stand on their feet dropped their swords and axes, their drink-sodden faces wrathful but wary as the armed women moved among them, picking up weapons by the armful.

Iwan appeared in the doorway, the sword ready in his fist.

He looked across at Branwen and smiled darkly. Then, seeing his father, he sprang forwards with anger and concern on his face.

'Take all the weapons out of here,' Branwen called to

the women. 'Cut down any man who tries to stop you. Show no pity – they would have none for you. Dera ap Dagonet, come here. Watch over Ironfist.'

The slender young woman came bounding across the room, her eyes glowing with the wild, feverish light of battle-lust. She stared up at Ironfist, a fierce grin spreading across her face, her bloodied sword pointing up at his chest.

'Do him no harm unless he tries to escape,' Branwen said. 'He's more use to us alive than dead.' She went to Rhodri and knelt at his side. Gently, she turned him over. His face was battered and bloody, his hair matted with gore.

'You are too brave for your own good, my friend,' she whispered, leaning close over him, carefully peeling back the sticky hair from his forehead and cheeks. 'Look what they did to you!'

Rhodri's eyes opened. They swam for a moment. 'Ahh,' he murmured. 'A sweet dream to ease my torment. Are you a hand-maiden of the gods, sent to bear me to Wotan's hall?'

'Hardly that,' said Branwen. 'A hand-maiden of the gods would look more fair, I think.'

'You do yourself injustice.' His hand rose and touched her cheek. 'I'm alive then, am I?'

'I think you are, yes.' She smiled. 'Can you stand?'

'I will try.' He smiled weakly. 'I hoped to persuade old Ironfist that I came back to him of my own free will, but I think he did not believe me.'

'But how did you explain your presence here?'

As Rhodri began to speak, Branwen busied herself sawing through the ropes that tied him. 'I said I found refuge in Gwylan Canu, and that when the warriors were sent out to surrender, I hid myself away among the rocks,' he said. 'He knocked me about a little while for sport then had me whipped for running away.' With Branwen's support he got to his feet. He rubbed his wrists, red and sore with welts from the tight ropes. 'I expected you to find Lord Madoc and escape, but not under these circumstances.' He stared around the Hall. 'I underestimated your ambition, Branwen. What now?'

She turned to see Iwan helping his father to his feet.

Madoc ap Rhain stared at her in astonishment. 'You are the child of Griffith ap Rhys and the lady Alis,' he said. He looked around the Hall. 'How have you come here – and how have you done such deeds!'

'I have powerful allies, Lord Madoc,' said Branwen. 'But all is not yet won – there will be guards on the wall. We must look to them before Gwylan Canu is in the hands of men of Powys once more.' She frowned, seeing how the old man leaned on Iwan's arm. 'You are unwell, Lord. Take rest if you can. All shall soon be done. In the meantime, let's bind the hands of this general and take him out to meet his few remaining warriors. And then we shall shut and bar the gates of the Hall and leave these drunken sots to their hoggish dreams.'

Branwen stood under the high stone wall of Gwylan Canu, her knife to Herewulf Ironfist's throat. Iwan and Rhodri were at her side and most of the armed women of the citadel stood at her back. Some few were missing, led by Lord Madoc to the pits to rescue those still imprisoned, and two more had remained behind, beyond the huts and houses of the citadel, busy piling rocks against the doors of the Great Hall so that none should escape from within.

'Order your men down off the wall, General,' Branwen said. She turned her head, looking into the east, to where the soft light of dawn was suffusing the sky. 'Do you see the light growing? It's a new day – and your overlordship of Gwylan Canu is done.'

Ironfist smiled. 'A new day and a new hope,' he said. 'But not the hope of Powys, girl-child. Do you feel the east wind?' He gave a harsh laugh. 'It blows ill fortune upon you. Release me and maybe I will allow you to die swiftly. Continue with this folly and you will linger to see your body torn to quivering shreds.'

Branwen narrowed her eyes. She had not for a moment

expected to see any trace of fear from him, but there was a casual bravura in his words that made her uneasy. He had only six armed men on the wall. All the rest were captives in the Great Hall. And yet he spoke as though he was assured of victory.

'Call your men down,' Branwen ordered, pressing the knife to his flesh. 'I will kill you if I need to.'

But before he could speak the braying of war horns tore the air. The Saxons on the ramparts ran to the far edge of the wall and stared down, shouting greetings in loud, exultant voices.

Ironfist gave a howl of laughter. 'Too late, girl-child!' His voice rose to a commanding roar. 'Warriors of King Oswald, get to the gates. Open them to our most welcome brothers!'

'No!' Branwen yelled. 'Make no move! I'll cut his throat!'

'Do as I order!' bellowed Ironfist. 'And then avenge my death!'

The men on the walls drew their swords and came pounding down the stone stairs of the gatehouse. Iwan and the women rushed forward to meet them.

Branwen stared for a moment into Ironfist's defiant eyes. The general was unarmed. His hands were bound. She could not bring herself to slit his throat when he could not defend herself. She pulled her knife away.

'Rhodri, watch over him. See he does no harm!'

Rhodri nodded grimly, grasping Ironfist's tied hands.

Branwen ran forward.

Iwan and some of the women were already fighting, but the Saxons were huge men and strong and they were beating their way steadily to the gates. Beyond the wall, the war horns were braying continuously, and Branwen could also hear the commotion of men shouting and of swords being hammered on shields.

Branwen threw herself into the battle, leaping in front of the warrior closest to the gates. He was a great scarred beast with a yellow beard and with eyes like blue diamonds. He swung a two-handed war axe at her. She ducked, feeling the air sing as the sharp iron swept a hair's-breadth over her head.

She lunged forwards, her knife stabbing upwards. Its blade was deflected by the man's chain-mail jerkin and she found herself falling on to her knees with the impetus of her wasted blow. He roared, lifting his axe high and bringing it down. Branwen curled up, rolling in against the brute's legs, knocking him off balance. He staggered, his face red with wrath, his open mouth spraying spittle.

She turned on to her back on the ground, her head between his feet. Taking her knife in both hands, she thrust upwards. Blood sprayed down on her as the man tottered sideways and fell. She leaped on his back, plunging her knife into his neck.

A hard blow sent her reeling. Another warrior had come up behind her, but he had stuck first with his shield rather than his sword, otherwise she would have been dead. Groggily she crawled away, picking up the dead man's fallen axe. Twisting her torso and opening her shoulders, she threw the axe behind her. She saw the curved blade strike the man full in the face. She looked away as he fell.

But another man sprang over her and ran to the bar that held the gates closed.

'Stop him!' she shouted, staggering to her feet despite the ringing in her head.

An arrow cut the air. It struck the man in the shoulder. Dera ap Dagonet ran forward, sword swinging, shouting. The man grasped the bar with both hands, leaning down on it, too consumed with battle-lust to heed his wound.

Branwen could hear a tumult from outside. There was the sound of men hammering on the gates.

A shrill voice called out. 'Ships! Saxon ships!'

Branwen gasped. The voice came from one of the women on the hill of the Great Hall. She was staring into the east. The buildings of Gwylan Canu blocked Branwen's view out over the sea, but the woman's terrified alarm was clear enough. Her hellish vision was coming true. Ironfist's fleet had arrived.

And even as she despaired, Branwen heard the crashing thud of the gate bar being pulled aside. She turned back in time to see the doors swing open and a whole host of Saxon warriors come pouring in.

Ironfist had been right – the sea's wind had indeed brought ill fortune to her. And now all that she could hope to do was to die valiantly and take with her as many of these Saxon dogs as possible.

CHAPTER THIRTY

'Fall back!' Branwen cried. 'Fall back to the hill!'

Her instinct had been to hurl herself at the Saxon warriors as they came whooping and howling with bloodlust flooding through the open gates of Gwylan Canu. But when she saw how the women she had urged to fight were being driven back, she knew she had to do what she could to get them out of immediate danger. Then she could rally them in a good defensive position.

A sword swung and Linette fell. Branwen started to run to her aid, but feet were already trampling over her. There was nothing to be done.

The words from her vision hammered in her mind.

Too late! Too late!

She saw Dera ap Dagonet running towards her, blood streaming from a cut on her forehead. 'We cannot hold them!' she gasped. There was a kind of blazing resignation in her sable eyes – as though she knew she was going to die – but there was no fear. No fear at all.

'We must keep them from rescuing Ironfist!' shouted Branwen. 'If we have him, we may still be able to negotiate for his release.'

'But you heard him – he is willing to die!' exclaimed Dera.

'Let's hope his men are less willing to let him be slaughtered!' growled Branwen. 'Go! Gather the others! We will make a last stand on the hill if need be.'

Branwen ran to where Rhodri was still standing with the Saxon general.

Ironfist had an exultant, savage smile on his face. 'Kill me or don't kill me, girl-child!' he spat in her face. 'It will make no difference now. My army will sweep over you like the tide! Before the sun rises, every man, woman and child not Saxon born will perish here – and their deaths will be upon your head!'

Branwen refused to give him the satisfaction of a response. 'Bring him,' she said curtly to Rhodri. She strode rapidly between the huts and houses of Gwylan Canu, making for the hill of the Great Hall.

She would make a last stand there, with her back to the Hall of the House of Puw. Or maybe there was the chance that some lieutenant of Ironfist's army would be prepared to barter the lives of the women and children of Gwylan Canu for the life of his general. Even if *she* had to die in that place, it would offer her some solace to know that the women that had followed her to this ruin might survive.

She ran up the long slope. A spear grazed her shoulder and glanced off the stony ground. She turned. The Saxons were streaming up through the buildings. She saw another of the women fall with an axe in her back.

Ironfist was dragging back as Rhodri forced him up the hill. With a hissed curse, Branwen ran down to them, snatching hold of Ironfist's arm and pulling him forward.

They came at last to the doors of the Great Hall, piled high with stones and rocks. The timberwork rang to the sound of hammering fists and Branwen could hear the oaths and shouts of the imprisoned men within.

Let them howl! They at least will not join the battle – not till all is lost!

Branwen turned at the top of the hill, staring out over the sea. As she looked into the east, all hope left her. Six ships rode the foam, and a seventh was already beached upon the sand. She stood frozen in despair. The ships looked strangely elegant as they rose and fell on the waves, their low, wide hulls leaf-shaped with high prow and stern, their single masts holding belling white sails full of the sea-scented east wind.

Each ship swarmed with Saxon warriors – five, ten

times the number that had taken Gwylan Canu.

A second ship made landfall and the warriors poured from its sides in a dark flood. Branwen felt the chill of death come over her, almost as though Saxon iron was already piercing her heart. But why should she be surprised? She had always known in her heart that her great destiny would end like this – end in death.

The fates had acted foolishly when they had picked the girl-child of Griffith ap Rhys and the lady Alis to be their tool.

Their mistake would doom all of Brython.

'Branwen?'

She turned at the voice. It was Iwan. He looked keenly into her face.

'No!' he said sharply, as if he could read her thoughts. 'No! You won't give up! I won't let you!' He gestured to the women gathered on the hill – the ten or so that had survived the initial Saxon onslaught. 'They are yours to command!' he said. 'You cannot abandon them.' His eyes blazed. 'You cannot abandon *me!*'

She saw Rhodri looking at her, and beyond him the eyes of the warrior women were turned to her, waiting for some word.

'Take your sword back,' Iwan said, holding the hilt out to her. 'There are plenty of others for me.' In that he was right: all around her feet were scattered the weapons taken from the hall.

She closed her fingers around her sword hilt and at its touch a kind of wild elation poured like fire through her veins. Despair was the ultimate betrayal of life! She would not succumb to it! Her mind boiled. A red mist veiled her eyes. New strength surged in her muscles.

'We fight!' she shouted, lifting the sword and brandishing it at the Saxon warriors that were swarming up the hill. 'I am the Emerald Flame of my people! I am the Sword of Destiny! I am the Bright Blade!'

She swept up a shield and leaped down the rocks to meet the oncoming hoards. Striking a running Saxon with her shield, she used the whole weight of her body to crush him to the ground. Branwen looked for an instant into his savage eyes before bringing her sword down into the gap between his chain-mail jerkin and his black beard. Dark blood sprayed up.

A spear thrust at her from the side. She threw herself backwards as the iron tip sliced past her stomach. She was on her feet in a moment, digging in her heels, finding her balance, her knees flexed, her shoulders open, her shield up to her eyes and her sword arm bent back ready for a killing stroke.

Three Saxons came for her. Sword, spear and axe.

She sidestepped the spear-thrust and chopped down with her sword, snapping the spear in half, then stepping into the spearman and bringing the upper rim of her shield hard in under his chin. His head snapped up as he stumbled.

Already Branwen was turning to meet the swing of the axe. She angled her shield to counter it. The buffet numbed her arm and she had to throw one leg back to keep from being tossed off her feet. But the axe-blow was deflected off her shield and the warrior staggered forwards on to her swordpoint. He roared, red spittle spattering her face as he reached a clawing hand towards her.

She bent her back, pushing in closer, deepening the thrust of her sword under his ribs. Suddenly his dead weight came down on her, pressing her to the ground, her sword-arm trapped under him.

She fought to get out from beneath his body, but her arm was still caught as she saw a sword plunging towards her face.

She heard a shrill cry. Another sword drove the Saxon blade aside. A slim dark figure bounded in. It was Dera ap Dagonet, her face a ferocious mask, blood-smeared and feral. She spun on her heel, sinking her sword into the Saxon's belly.

Branwen heaved and managed to push the dead warrior off. Her eyes met those of her rescuer. There was no time for words. They were surrounded by Saxons. They stood back to back and it was good to feel Dera's strong shoulders against hers as Branwen fought, striking out with her shield, slashing and thrusting with her sword, constantly shifting her footing as the bearded warriors bore down on her.

The uneven ground beneath her feet became slippery with spilled blood. Three bodies lay twisted in front of Branwen, a fourth warrior was on his knees, his hands up to try and staunch the flow of lifeblood from his throat.

But as hard as they fought, Branwen knew they would not be able to survive here, out in the open where the Saxons could come at them from all sides. It would only be a matter of time before they were overwhelmed by sheer force of numbers.

'We must ... get to the ... hilltop ...' Branwen gasped.

'I'm with you ...' came Dera's voice.

Branwen drove her shield into a Saxon face. 'Now!' she howled.

Side by side they sprang back up the hill, and for a brief moment Branwen had the chance to see how the uneven battle was going.

It was not good. Rhodri was still with Ironfist, holding a sword at his neck. But he had been driven up against the wall of the Great Hall, and only four warrior women stood between him and the press of Saxons. Iwan had been forced to take a stand up on the rocks that blocked the doors. He was fighting stalwartly, and several more of the women were gathered there with him.

Branwen saw Aberfa there, swinging a Saxon axe in her powerful arms, sending the blood flying. Banon was also with him, leaping from rock to rock, thrusting down with a spear then dancing back as her opponent fell back with blood welling from his wounds.

But their courage could never be enough. What were they now – ten against hundreds? And all the while still more Saxons were surging in through the open gates.

Branwen felt a pang of anguished pride as she saw Lord Madoc appear at the corner of the Great Hall, sword in hand, leading a group of women and old men, armed only with staves and rocks.

They would die. They would all die.

There was only one shred of hope for them – and Branwen knew it existed only if Ironfist was kept back from his men long enough for her to reach him. She knew what she had to do. She had no choice.

Dera had run on ahead and was already springing up on to the stones to fight alongside Iwan and the others.

Branwen hacked her way along the hill, coming up behind the Saxons who were fighting to rescue their general, taking them by surprise, cutting them down with blow after blow of her sword. She saw with a rush of sudden joy that one of the women holding them back was Linette, her gown soaked with blood from a wound in her shoulder – but alive and fighting still!

Branwen fought her way through the Saxons and came face to face with Ironfist. He glared defiantly at her, no sign now in his flinty eyes of the drunkenness that had earlier blurred his vision.

'Kill me now, girl-child,' he hissed. 'You'll not get another chance!'

She knew in her heart that he was right. But his death would not prevent the Saxons from swarming over Gwylan Canu and slaughtering all who stood in their way – man, woman and child.

As she stared into those cold blue eyes, she thought of the warriors she had known in her short life. Bloodthirsty and cruel, many had been, but all of them had a code of honour – every one of them! Could such honour live in a Saxon warlord? Surely it could – surely even such a man as Herewulf Ironfist could be asked to take an oath so deep and strong that he would not dare to break it.

It was a weak hope – a fool's hope – but maybe if he accepted her as a leader of her people, as a true warrior ready to sacrifice herself for those who followed her, maybe then she could bring this horror to an end.

'How do I stop this?' Branwen shouted in his face, lifting her voice above the hideous din of the battle. 'These people do not deserve to be massacred. If I tell them to stop fighting – if I give myself up to you to do as you wish – will you then spare them?'

'Branwen, no!' gasped Rhodri.

Branwen ignored him. 'Well?' she demanded. 'Do we have an agreement? My life for theirs? Will you give me your word on the name of your greatest gods to honour such a pact?'

'I will,' Ironfist replied, his eyes gleaming with a savage light. 'By Wotan's Fiery Spear, I swear it! Your life forfeited for theirs saved!'

'Agreed!' said Branwen. She avoided looking into Rhodri's appalled face as she pushed his sword away from Ironfist's neck. She stepped behind the Saxon general and slashed through the ropes that bound his wrists.

He turned, his eyes burning into her face. Wordlessly she offered him her sword, letting her shield fall to the ground at her feet.

He took the sword from her.

'Keep your oath. Call off your armies,' Branwen said, hearing her own voice through a dense white fog. 'Bring this slaughter to an end.'

She felt a profound sense of calm and peace. A curious emptiness grew and grew inside her chest, as though her heart, her lungs, her very spirit was being absorbed and lost in an expanding void.

Ironfist's guttural laughter brought her tranquillity to a sudden and brutal end.

'Foolish child,' he hissed, lifting the sword and running its cold edge along her neck. She felt warm blood trickling. 'Did you truly believe I would honour such a pact?' he laughed. 'Know this, girl-child. You will die now at my hand, and before the sun is risen on this day of triumph, every man, woman and child of Gwylan Canu will die with you.'

Branwen looked into his eyes, furious with herself for having believed he may have held some honour. There was nothing in his eyes but lust and brutality and murder.

She had gambled her life and she had failed. There was nothing more to be done.

CHAPTER THIRTY-ONE

'No!' Rhodri's voice rang in her head, cutting through the white fog that blurred her brain.

She felt the sword jarred from her neck. She heard Ironfist spit a curse. She saw him turn savagely. She saw Rhodri's terrified, courageous face beyond the great general's shoulder. She saw Ironfist lift his sword arm. She saw his sword crash down across Rhodri's weapon, breaking the blade, jolting the hilt out of his fingers.

She saw Ironfist's other fist pound downwards, striking Rhodri in the face, driving him to his knees.

All this happened in the space of a single breath, and it was as if she could do nothing. The other young women fighting close by had not even seen what was happening – they were too busy battling to save their own lives.

Branwen saw the sword arm lift again. She saw Rhodri cringe from the deadly blow.

No! She could not let him be killed.

Gasping with the effort, she flung herself on Ironfist's back, one arm hooking around his throat, the other reaching to grip the wrist of his sword arm.

He spun, roaring in anger, trying to dislodge her, fighting to get his arm free. But the desperation that had jerked her out of her stupor had also given her new strength. Her arm tightened on his throat and he began to choke and cough as he stumbled. But he wasn't so easily bested. He dug in with his heels and threw himself backwards, crushing her against the wall of the Great Hall. He surged forwards then pushed back again, beating the breath out of her lungs. Two, three times he drove her into the wall, until the pain made her lose her grip on his wrist and she was no longer able to keep the pressure against his windpipe.

His hand groped over his shoulder for her face, fingers stretching as though to find her eyes and gouge them out. She jerked her head back, but he caught her hair and brought her head down so that her face smashed into the chain mail that covered his shoulder. She tasted blood. His elbow came into her stomach and he twisted as she fell to her knees, spitting red, her mind reeling.

The hand caught her hair again, yanking her head up. She knelt as he raised his sword.

Forgive me. Forgive me. I've led you all to your deaths.

A sudden sound shivered the air.

A howling. A braying. A whooping noise, skirling and swirling, rising above the sounds of battle.

Ironfist paused, turning, his face confounded by the strange noise coming from beyond the wall of Gwylan Canu. He stared off towards the distant mountains, glowing now, touched by the first light of the new day's sun.

And then the wind came.

It came down from the mountains, screaming like a thousand lost souls, shivering through the crags, bending tall trees like meadow grass before its rushing breath. It came down from the high places of the Clwydian Range, ice on its lips, driving all before it. It came rushing down through the ancient forests, ripping boughs from trunks, sending branches whirling, filling the air with leaves and twigs and flying debris.

It raced out over the bare rock and the long beaches and burst upon the Saxon hordes like a hammer, whipping their feet out from under them, tearing the swords and shields from their hands, tossing them through the air, piling them up against the outer wall of the citadel like stalks of wheat at the harvest.

As Branwen watched in silent awe, the wind fell upon the beached ships, ripping their sails to shreds, cracking their masts, splintering their timbers, throwing the terrified Saxons into the seething sea.

316

Roaring, it came surging over the wall of Gwylan Canu, dislodging stones, tearing the gates from their hinges, howling through hut and home and pen and paddock, ripping the thatch from the roofs, lifting wickerwork hurdles and throwing them like leaves across the sky in front of Branwen's stunned eyes. It blasted up the hill, rolling the Saxons before it, their heads cracking on stone, their swords and spears and axes skimming the ground, their cries drowned out in its wild halloo. Branwen's body tensed for the impact as the wind swept towards her.

Ironfist staggered back, his arm up to shield his face as the wind beat its way up to the very doors of the Great Hall.

Branwen felt its force hit her like an avalanche. It lifted her, plastering her helplessly against the wall of the hall, holding her there, her clothes glued to her body, her hair pulled back hard on her scalp, her skin lashed and pricked and scourged.

It bellowed in her ears, its ear-splitting pandemonium heaping and piling in her head until she had to open her mouth in a soundless scream from the pain and the fury of it.

And then – stunningly – the wind was gone, the noise and the mayhem with it, and Branwen could breathe again. She alone was still standing. She saw Rhodri close by, getting unsteadily to his feet. Iwan and the fighting women were picking themselves up around her, their faces stupefied, their eyes uncomprehending.

Ironfist was sprawled against the wall of the Great Hall, panting for breath, the sword gone from his hand – blown away by the wind.

Then, as though the wind had been no more than a prelude, there came a new sound and a new wonder. From her vantage point on the hill, Branwen could see shapes moving down from the southern foothills. Strange shapes, dark and sinister, moving with a swaying, rolling gait.

Branwen gasped as the great forms came swarming down the beach. They were *trees* – huge trees, walking on gnarled and angular roots, their heavy leaf-laden heads tossing from side to side as they jerked and lurched towards the sea.

And running among the spindly and crooked roots she saw wolves and stags, bears and wild boar, howling and belling and roaring and snorting as they came surging through the sand. It seemed to Branwen as if all the beasts of the mountains had been summoned to drive the Saxon army back into the sea.

Some Saxon warriors tried to stand against the ravaging animals, but they were brought down by teeth and claws and stamping hooves, overrun by tusks and stabbing antlers and champing jaws. Others fled in terror, floundering helplessly in the surf, trying vainly to get back to their ships.

But the wind had smashed the beached ships to shards, and those still on the open sea were being tossed like eggshells on the surge of the waves.

Then a different sound caught Branwen's attention – the crack and crumble of tumbling stonework. She stared beyond the wind-ravaged huts of Gwylan Canu and saw that the wall of the citadel was falling inwards, thrust down by the living trees. The gatehouse crashed in ruin as the unwieldy and awkward creatures climbed and clambered among the fallen stones. And as on the beach, animals came leaping and bounding and crawling and running among them, falling on the warriors of Ironfist's army as they scattered in horror.

Flying like a dark cloud above the moving trees, Branwen saw flocks of birds – crows and eagles and hawks and falcons; buzzards and goshawks and harriers and kites – sweeping down on the Saxons, claws stretching, beaks open, eyes bright with a predatory light, all led by a great wide-winged eagle owl and by another bird ... a bird she knew well.

'Fain!' she shouted, although she knew he would not be able to hear her voice in all the tumult. '*Fain!*'

'And Blodwedd,' said Rhodri's awed voice at her side. 'Surely that owl is Blodwedd!'

'Yes, perhaps it is,' Branwen gasped. 'Rhodri – oh, *look*, Rhodri.' Her voice trembled. '*Look!* He has come!'

A new form came striding through the wreckage of the gatehouse.

It was a tall brown-skinned figure, as tall as the trees, man-like but in no way human. He was clad in a simple green tunic that hung down to his massive thighs, the mossy cloth stretched taut over a great, deep chest. The muscles of the bare arms and legs were huge and knotted, the skin lined with coiling greenish veins. Solemn eyes flashed like emeralds from beneath heavy brows and the wide mouth was open to show rows of pointed teeth. Tawny hair tumbled over the towering head, and from the temples there grew massive, branching antlers.

'Govannon of the Wood,' breathed Rhodri, taking Branwen's hand. 'The Shining Ones have come to our aid.'

Branwen saw pure terror now on the faces of the Saxon warriors as they turned from the huge man-like form and ran, tripping over one another, as they hastened to get away.

Branwen gripped Rhodri's hand tightly. 'I see it,' she murmured, her eyes riveted on Govannon as he strode among the animals like a king.

She heard the clash of weapons close by.

She pulled her eyes away from Govannon of the Wood

and saw that Iwan and the warrior women were fighting with those few Saxons that had survived. But the fight did not last long – even those Saxons who had clung on to their weapons had seen the moving trees and the armies of beasts and birds that were falling upon their comrades, and for most of them the only thought in their minds was to seek a means of escape.

'Ironfist!' Branwen hissed in sudden remembrance. He was gone. He must have realized his cause was lost and had stolen silently away while all eyes were on the marvels that followed the unearthly wind.

She ran to the corner of the Hall.

There! She saw him.

A solitary figure, darting among the rocks, running towards the rear of the headland, a shield on his arm and a spear in his hand – weapons he must have picked up from the ground as he fled.

Perhaps he hoped to hide there, among the tumble or raw rocks – hide from the wrath of Govannon until all was done and he had the opportunity to slip away unnoticed.

But Branwen had other ideas. She would not let him escape so easily. She snatched up a sword and shield.

'Branwen, no!' It was Rhodri's voice. He was at her shoulder. 'Let him go!'

'I can't,' Branwen hissed. 'He has to pay for what he

has done!' She stared into his eyes for a moment. 'Stay back, Rhodri. You can't help me with this.'

So saying, she sprang away after Ironfist, her long legs quickly eating up the distance between them.

'Coward!' she shouted. 'Come back and fight me!'

He was at the farthest point of the headland now, standing on the last ridge of wind-blown rock. A single step further and he would plunge into the pounding sea.

He turned, grinning.

'Would you have single combat with me, child?' he called. 'Do you long for death? Do you ache for it?'

Branwen came to a halt, eyeing him carefully. She walked slowly up the slope towards him, her shield up, her sword angled across her back as Gavan had shown her, her muscles tensed and ready to uncoil.

'*Deadain, andgietleas cild!*' shouted Ironfist, leaping down at her, the long spear thrusting.

She brought her sword sweeping over her shoulder, aiming for his neck. But he fended it off with his shield and, as he leaped past, stabbed his spear at her side. She snatched her shield back to cover herself, dancing away from him as he ran past her.

She turned as he came for her again, thrusting the spear at her belly, his eyes burning, teeth bared. Branwen brought her shield down hard on the shaft of his spear, hoping to break it. But he pulled back and she stumbled forwards and only just avoided falling on to the spearpoint.

She dived headlong, curling up, rolling across the uneven ground as he stabbed at her, missing and missing again until she bounced to her feet, bringing her sword sweeping in under his shield, hoping to take his legs out from under him.

But he was too wily a fighter. With a cry, he leaped over her scything blade and came down heavily, his shield pounding on hers, his weight forcing her to her knees, while she ducked this way and that to avoid his jabs and thrusts.

Her limbs were weary, her muscles aching, but there was no possibility of rest or respite until this fight was over. She surged upwards, using all the power of her legs and back to push him off so that she could bound away and get briefly beyond the reach of his spear.

She glanced behind herself – she was on the very edge of a dark cliff that dropped straight down into the foam. If she could enrage him so that he threw his spear, and if she could react quickly enough when he did, then perhaps she could leave him weaponless.

'Do you know me now, Herewulf Ironfist?' she howled, spreading her feet and brandishing her sword. 'I am the saviour of Brython! Drop your weapon and kneel to me, Saxon dog, and perhaps I will spare your life!'

But Ironfist was not to be taken so easily. Grinning wolfishly, he moved up towards her, his spear reaching out, the point darting from side to side as he sought to find a way past her shield.

But she had planned for this also. She leaped sideways, allowing his spearpoint through, then bringing her arm down hard into her side, trapping the shaft before Ironfist could withdraw it. Springing down on him, she aimed a deadly blow at his head. But his shield came up under her blade and it was swept aside.

Betrayed by her own momentum, she plunged past him. He turned and struck her on the back of her head with his shield. The pain flared in her skull and down her neck as she stumbled forwards. But she caught her balance again and turned, angling her shield downwards so that as he thrust at her his spearpoint was sent stabbing into the ground.

With a scream of agony and rage she lifted her foot and brought it down hard on the shaft of his spear. It snapped, but he was hurtling towards her, his shield up, all his weight behind his charge.

He struck her and took her clean off her feet. She felt dizzy and sick, the pain throbbing through her head and jaw as she crashed on to her back. But she had wits enough left to keep her own shield up as he loomed over her. His face twisted into a malevolent grin as he pounded his shield down on her again and again until her arm was numb and her whole body shrieked in pain. Her sword arm dropped, her weight bearing down on her bent elbow as she tried to rise.

He stamped down on her wrist, forcing her fingers to fly open, then kicking her sword away. Agony flared through her wrist as he brought his shield hammering down on her – and he was laughing now – sure of her death.

She gasped, lightning flaring across her eyes, the pain crowding down on her senses. Using her last shred of strength, she rolled away from him, crawling through the rubble, seeking only to escape the pain and the thunder in her head.

She tottered to her feet, swaying, her eyes half closed.

She saw him snatch up her sword.

She braced herself, her shield up to her eyes, the upper rim angled outwards to block the sword and perhaps, if chance allowed, to punch up into his throat.

He came for her, the sword swinging like a scythe.

But then, in the fleeting moment before he would have fallen upon her, a grey shape soared down out of the sky, shrieking and clawing, wings beating and a hooked beak stretched wide open to rip flesh to the bone.

Straight into Ironfist's face the falcon flew, furious and savage, wings flurrying, claws raking. Dizzy with pain,

Branwen saw blood spurt and heard Ironfist give a howl of agony as Fain tore at his eyes.

Staggering backwards, Ironfist dropped his sword as he brought both hands up to try and protect his face. But his feet stumbled on the rocks and he lost his balance. For a moment he hung on the very edge of the black cliff, then, with a wavering shout, he lost his footing and plunged downwards.

Branwen staggered to the cliff edge. Fain was descending in slow circles, but the restless foaming waves had already swallowed up the great general. Branwen stooped forwards, her hands on her knees, panting as she looked down at the seething waves far below.

Fain turned and came soaring up. He gave a single cry as he passed her.

She turned, watching as he flew back over the Great Hall.

She stood there for a few moments, gathering her breath, waiting until the pain in her head lessened to a dull throbbing. Then slowly and painfully she picked her way back over the rocks.

Branwen and Rhodri stood side by side on the hill of the Great Hall, overlooking the scene of carnage below. Dera ap Dagonet stepped in front of Branwen, her face pale with wonder, her eyes haunted. 'What are these things that come to our aid, Branwen – are they known to you?'

'Did I not tell you I had powerful allies?' Branwen replied. 'They have been guiding my footsteps, Dera. It's their path that I walk.' She shook her head. 'But I had not dared hope for *this*!'

'And can they be controlled?' murmured Dera, staring down the hill to where the forces of Govannon swarmed among the buildings, seeking out and pulling down those few Saxons that remained alive. 'I am glad of their help, but I fear them also.'

'I don't think they will harm us,' Branwen said. But she shuddered as she watched the animals of Govannon at their dreadful work. It was brutal, that final hunt, and none were spared. Even those Saxon warriors who cast down their weapons and threw up their arms in surrender were killed.

Govannon was standing just inside what remained of the gatehouse, and as the last Saxons were hunted down and destroyed, the animals turned and went back to him, surrounding him, their heads turned towards him, as though awaiting some word. The trees, too, came to a halt, as though knowing their task was done, and as Branwen watched, their roots dug down into the ground and they seemed to settle and become still, so that the whole area between the citadel's huddled village and the ruined wall was dotted now with full-grown trees.

The sky cleared of birds as well, all save for one solitary slate-grey shape that climbed the air up to where Branwen stood.

She held up her arm and Fain came to rest heavily on her wrist.

'Caw! Caw! Caw!'

Branwen smiled. 'My life is yours, Fain, my dearest companion,' she said. 'What would you have me do now? I cannot understand your speech.'

The falcon turned its head, staring down the hill to where Govannon stood in a quiet flood of animals.

'Caw!'

She looked and saw that Govannon was gazing up at her.

'I must go to him,' she murmured. But even as she spoke, her heart faltered and it felt as though her legs might give way under her at any moment.

'I'll come with you,' said Rhodri, his voice trembling. His hand reached for hers and their fingers twined together.

'And I,' said Dera. 'I would see this marvel up close, though it be my death!'

Branwen nodded, grateful for their offer.

The thought of approaching Govannon alone had filled her with unease but with these two companions at her side, she believed she could muster the courage to stand in front of Govannon and look up into those daunting green eyes.

Fain spread his wings and went swooping away down the hill.

Her heart crashing in her chest, Branwen followed.

CHAPTER THIRTY-TWO

The congregation of animals parted to allow Branwen and Rhodri and Dera to pass through. Branwen saw fresh blood on fangs and claws and tusks and antlers as she made her way towards the centre of the gathering – to where Govannon of the Wood stood waiting for her.

He was twice her height; a giant creature who radiated such power and authority that it was all Branwen could do to gaze up into his noble face. His immense arms reached down, his broad hands stroking the backs and heads and shoulders of the animals that crowded around him. Branwen saw in the eyes of every beast there a flickering green light that was only a pale reflection of the blazing emerald radiance that filled Govannon's own eyes.

The three of them came to a halt a few paces away from him.

As Govannon looked down at them, Branwen could

discern no expression on his face – no more expression than might be found on a tree or a bear or a cloud. But there was lordliness and ancient knowledge and an aching sadness in his profound eyes that wounded her heart.

'So, Warrior Child,' he said, and his voice was deep and sonorous. 'We meet on the battlefield. Is this victory honey to your tongue?'

Branwen's mouth was dry, her throat constricted. 'No, it is not,' she said. 'It is not, and I would have done anything to have prevented this slaughter. The death of Saxons gives me no pleasure, Lord. I did only what I had to do.'

'That is good, Warrior Child,' rumbled Govannon's voice. 'Dark is the heart that delights in killing. But it was not of your doing that the enemy came into Brython, and without you, great harm would have been done this day.'

Branwen narrowed her eyes. 'Without me?' she said. 'I didn't win this battle, Lord – the victory is yours. Had you not come, I and all who followed me would be dead now.'

There was a pause and Govannon's eyes were thoughtful as he stared down at her. 'Do you not know why I was able to come, Warrior Child?' he said at last. 'Do you not know the sacrifice that was made?'

She looked up into his eyes, confused now. 'I don't, Lord,' she said.

'Do you think that I have the authority to breathe sentience into my trees as I will it?' Govannon asked. 'Do you think I have such dominion that I can light wendfire in the eyes of my birds and my beasts without consequence? No, Warrior Child, I am but a guardian, the steward of the forests. Greater potencies than I must be appeased. A sacrifice must be offered.'

'What sacrifice was offered?' asked Dera. 'Who gave their life so that you could come to our aid?'

The huge green eyes turned to her. 'Death is not the ultimate sacrifice, child,' Govannon said gravely. 'To live sundered from your true self – to live a half-life of loss and willing surrender – that is true sacrifice.' His head turned, the spreading antlers that branched up from his forehead seeming to scrape the sky. 'Come forth, my daughter. Take the first step on this new path that you have chosen and which you must endure now till the end of your days.'

From somewhere at Govannon's back, from in among the animals, a small slender figure emerged and stood in front of them, her head bowed, her eyes hooded.

'Blodwedd!' breathed Rhodri, letting go of Branwen's hand and taking a step forward. 'But . . . I saw you . . .' he stammered. 'It *was* you, surely? Leading the birds.'

She lifted her head, her huge sombre eyes gazing into his. 'Yes, it was me you saw,' she murmured. 'My lord gifted me one last moment of flight – one final chance to feel the wind beneath my wings before I renounced myself for ever.' She looked at Branwen. 'I learned much from you, Branwen, in the time we spent together. I learned of duty and loyalty and I learned of the burden of responsibility and the weight of grief.'

'I don't understand,' said Branwen. 'When the quest was done, you were to be given back your true form. You were to become an owl again.'

'That is so,' said Blodwedd. 'But I saw the same vision that was given to you. I saw ships filled with warriors sailing to the place of singing gulls. I knew you would not be able to stand against such numbers. I knew you would be lost, so I went to my lord and I begged him to come to your aid. And I offered myself in your place – offered my life. It was forfeit anyway – I fled your side in fear, Branwen. I failed in my duty to you. I would willingly have taken death as my punishment.'

'Death is not the ultimate sacrifice!' Rhodri murmured, as though understanding now what Govannon had meant. He looked at Branwen. 'She gave herself up to save us. She will be human now for the rest of her life.'

'No,' Branwen said in dismay. 'It's worse than that – she will be an owl trapped for ever in a human form.' She looked up at Govannon. 'Can this be undone?' she asked. 'Can I do anything to change her fate?'

'The bargain has been made,' Govannon replied sadly. 'It cannot be unmade.'

'I did this of my own free will, Branwen,' said Blodwedd. 'Do not weep for me. I am reconciled to my exile. I will roam the forests and know that my loss had purpose. It will be enough.'

Filled with pity and gratitude, Branwen reached out her hands to the forlorn owl-girl. 'I would rather you stay with us,' she said. 'Will you do that?'

Blodwedd slid her slim fingers into Branwen's, her eyes glowing. 'Gladly,' she said softly. 'Gladly.'

'But what new purpose do you have?' asked Dera. 'For I see that yours is no easy destiny, Branwen ap Griffith, and that great deeds await you.'

'I must go to Pengwern – to the court of King Cynon,' Branwen replied. 'He must be told of Prince Llew's treachery. An army must be gathered, one strong enough to lay siege to Doeth Palas and bring Llew ap Gelert down.'

'No, Warrior Child, that is not your path,' said Govannon. 'Let others go to the king.' He turned, pointing up to the mountains. 'Thither wends your path. Warrior Child, up into the cold peaks, into the high places of the land to seek for Merion of the Stones.' He turned to look down at Branwen again, his eyes smouldering. 'My part in the great tale is done for now,

Warrior Child,' he said. 'My sister shall show you your next task.' He raised a hand. 'Farewell, Emerald Flame of Brython. I leave you now.'

'But how am I to find Merion of the Stones?' Branwen asked.

'Fain will be your guide,' replied Govannon.

So saying, the great lord of the forests turned and strode away. And as he went, the animals followed after him and the birds that had rested on stone and thatch and upon the ground all around, rose into the air and flew southward back into the forested foothills of the Clwydian Mountains. Only the trees remained, their roots sunk deep into the ground, their leaves stirring in the gentle sea breeze.

Branwen stood high among the ruins of the gatehouse of Gwylan Canu and watched the last few animals melt away into the forested hills. As they went, it was as though she was waking from a feverish dream. But she knew this could be no dream – her head still throbbed with pain and her hands and arms and face were sticky with blood.

She was about to turn and climb down again when she heard the distant rhythm of galloping horses coming along the winding road from the west.

Puzzled, she stared along the coast. At that moment five horses came speeding around a bend, saddled and bridled, but with no riders and with their reins flying.

Branwen jumped down and ran to the road. She knew the leading horse!

'Stalwyn!' she cried, throwing her arms up.

Stalwyn came to a clattering halt in front of her. He rose up, neighing loudly and beating the air with his hooves.

Iwan came running to her side as the other four horses all came to a stamping and whinnying halt on the road.

'What does this mean?' Iwan gasped, staring at the horses. 'These are steeds of Doeth Palas. Why have they come riderless back to this place?'

Branwen laughed as she caught Stalwyn's reins and pressed her face into his sweating neck, breathing him in.

'He came back to me,' she said. 'Don't you see? He must have thrown his rider and bolted! He knew I needed him!' She thumped the great stallion's flanks. 'Good boy – great friend!' she said. 'And you brought companions!'

Stalwyn nodded his head and snorted, his eyes bright and knowing.

'Why so many?' Branwen mused. 'I have need of but two.'

'Three at least,' said Iwan. He gave a sweet, tuneful whistle between his teeth and one of the other horses, a dun mare with a creamy coat and black mane, tail and muzzle, came trotting obediently forwards and nuzzled his shoulder. 'Welcome back, my beauty,' he said, stroking the mare's nose. 'This is Gwennol Dhu. She also must have known I would have need of her.' He smiled at Branwen. 'She has a wise head on her and is sure-footed among the mountains.'

'But your journey lies south, along the road to Pengwern,' Branwen said. 'There are no mountains in your way.'

Iwan gave her a crooked smile and for a moment she was reminded starkly of the teasing lad from the Great Hall of Doeth Palas. 'Oh, but I am not going to the king,' he said. 'My father can undertake that errand. There are brave men of Gwylan Canu – elderly but hale – who can accompany him. No, I have decided on an altogether more amusing journey.' He cocked his head and his eyes sparkled. 'I'm going with you, Barbarian Princess. Don't you remember what I said to you when you bound me and escaped with the half-Saxon?'

She gazed at him. She remembered it very well. 'You said you thought I would have an interesting life,' she said quietly. 'You said you wished you could have shared it with me.'

'And now I shall.' He lowered his head and gave her a sideways look. 'If you will have me as a companion.' He turned his head and glanced over to where Rhodri and Blodwedd were standing. Rhodri seemed to be watching them carefully. 'The half-Saxon is a good fellow, I am sure, but he spent most of his life as a captive servant, Branwen. He has no learning, no culture. On this strange journey of yours, I think you could do with a man of wit and intelligence – and thus I offer my services.' The bantering tone left his voice and his eyes fixed on hers. 'I want to be with you, Branwen, at your side no matter what. Will you let me ride with you?'

Before Branwen could answer, she heard the patter of running feet.

Dera came up to her, a determined light in her eyes. 'I have spoken with the women of Gwylan Canu,' she said briskly. 'I have told them I wish to journey with you wherever you go. I wish to share your adventures and your destiny, Branwen. And Linette and Aberfa and Banon wish it also.' Branwen opened her mouth to speak, but Dera gave her no time. 'You will meet with many perils and dangers on your path, Branwen – we can help you. We fight well. We are unafraid. You cannot sweep Brython clean of Saxons alone. A princess needs followers – let us be the first of your warrior band!'

Branwen let out an astonished breath. She did not know what to say. But then, words spoken to her by Rhiannon of the Spring came into her mind. *All of*

Brython will be your home and you will gather to you a band of warriors who shall keep the enemy at bay for many long years.

'It seems that Stalwyn was wise to bring companions,' said Iwan with a wry smile. 'Even if we double up, five horses will only just be enough.'

Rhodri strode up. 'Are we departing soon, Branwen?' he asked. 'Blodwedd says we should not leave it too long before we take the path to Merion of the Stones. She fears that any delay may be costly.'

Branwen turned to him, a smile widening on her face. 'We are leaving very soon, my friend,' she said. 'But not we three alone.'

Rhodri gave her a confused look, but before she could explain, a single, shrill, compelling cry came down out of the air.

'Caw!'

She looked up, seeing Fain hanging in the sky, borne up by the sea wind, his wings spread wide, his black eye on her.

He too was eager to be going.

Branwen turned, gazing up into the mountains, and as she stood staring out at those distant peaks, the words of the old song rang in her head. The song of the Shining Ones. The song of the Old Gods.

I sing of Rhiannon of the Spring
The ageless water goddess, earth-mother, storm-calmer
Of Govannon of the Wood
He of the twelve-points
Stag-man of the deep forest, wise and deadly
Of Merion of the Stones
Mountain crone, cave-dweller, oracle and deceiver
And of Caradoc of the North Wind
Wild and free and dangerous and full of treachery.

It was time to take the path to Merion of the Stones. It was time for the Shining Ones to reveal to her the next stage on the long road to her destiny.

The Bright Blade! The Emerald Flame of her people! The Saviour of Brython.

Branwen ap Griffith – the Warrior Princess.

Enjoy a sneak peek at the next part of
Branwen's adventure:

Merion of the Stones

'Are you managing to keep awake, Branwen?' Iwan ap Madoc asked. 'I'm told a spur of hawthorn in the britches is a fine way to stay alert on a long ride.'

She looked at him, sitting erect in the saddle, his light brown hair falling over his lean, compelling face. His eyes met hers, and he gave her a crooked smile.

'I'll be fine, thank you,' she said. 'This is not such a night that I will have trouble with drowsing.'

'No.' His eyes were bright and wakeful. 'I imagine not.'

She gazed back beyond him to where the rest of her band rode, two to a horse. Four young women of Gwylan Canu: fiery Dera, riding with lithe little Linette; and bringing up the rear, flame-haired Banon and heavyset Aberfa, with her dark, brooding eyes.

In the dying embers of the day just passed, this wayfaring band had won a great victory. The Saxon warlord Horsa Herewulf Ironfist had sought to come with speed and stealth to conquer the seagirt citadel of Gwylan Canu, guardian outpost of the coastal road that led into the very heartland of Powys.

But speed and stealth had not been the only weapons

in Ironfist's arsenal. He had deep and dreadful treachery to help him on his way.

Prince Llew ap Gelert – the richest and most powerful of the nobles of Powys, second only to King Cynon himself – had turned traitor!

Branwen still did not know the reason for this terrible betrayal. It was almost beyond belief that a lord of Powys would side with the ancient enemies of Brython. For two hundred years the people of the Four Kingdoms had battled wave after wave of Saxon incursions, yet they had always thrown the butchering invaders back. But never had defeat been closer than in the battle Branwen and her band had just fought. And if not for the aid of the Shining Ones, all would have been lost.

Govannon himself had joined in the battle – bringing even the trees of the forests to life to sweep the Saxons into the sea, beating down upon them with an army of birds and beasts that had utterly defeated them.

And upon a rocky promontory Branwen had done her part – fighting furiously with Ironfist himself. Almost bested by him, she had been saved at the last by the beak and claws of her faithful companion Fain the falcon, who had flown into Ironfist's face and sent him plunging over the cliff and into the raging sea.

Then had come the momentous meeting with Govannon, towering above her, wild and dangerous and yet strangely benevolent. He had told her what she needed to do next – what new effort her great destiny required of her. He had pointed the way up the mountains. *'Thither wends your path, Warrior Child, up into the cold peaks, into the high places of the land to seek for Merion of the Stones.'*

Faithful, kindhearted Rhodri had insisted on coming with her, of course. And Blodwedd, too. But it had been Iwan's insistence on journeying alongside her that had filled Branwen with a heady mix of joy and confusion.

'Don't you remember what I said to you when you bound me and escaped with the half Saxon?' he had asked, his eyes shining.

'You said you thought I would have an interesting life. You said you wished you could have shared it with me.'

'And now I shall. If you will have me as a companion.'

She had no control over her destiny. It was pitiless and relentless, and people had died on the way.

But these people shan't die. I won't let that happen. I am Branwen ap Griffith. The Emerald Flame of my people. I will keep them safe from harm.

But the responsibility weighed heavy on her. Into what perils was she leading them on these high mountains?

She knew virtually nothing of Merion of the Stones. In a mystic glade that had been shown to her in a vision, she had seen a devotee dressed as Merion – bent backed,

343

stumbling, clutching a stick – masked as an ugly, wrinkled old woman.

But Branwen had learned not to trust appearances. The forms that the Shining Ones took when they interacted with humans were not their true ones. But what would Merion want of her? So far the requirements of the Old Gods had all been for the good of Brython. Surely, the most vital task now was to unmask the traitor Prince Llew ap Gelert and to bring him down before he could do any more harm.

To that end riders had already been sent from Gwylan Canu, racing pell-mell down the long road to Pengwern – to the court of King Cynon – with urgent warnings from Iwan's trustworthy father.

Hopefully that would be enough to thwart Prince Llew's grim ambitions. But even with Llew's duplicity laid bare, there was still a great Saxon army on the border of Powys – less than a day's march from Branwen's already embattled homeland of Cyffin Tir.

And here she was – a thousand lifetimes away from the world she had once known – treading again the veiled path of her destiny . . . riding through the impenetrable night with seven souls in her care.

'Ware!' It was Blodwedd's scratchy voice, its low pitch at odds with her small, slender body. An owl's voice in a human throat.

Branwen snapped out of her thoughts, alert in an instant. 'What is it?'

Blodwedd had by far the keenest eyesight of them all. That was why she had taken the lead through the forest once the night had grown too dark even for Fain's sharp eyes. The falcon was at rest now, perched upon Branwen's shoulder, his claws gripping her chain-mail shirt.

'I am not sure,' called Blodwedd.

Branwen urged Stalwyn on with a touch of her heels to his flanks. She came up alongside Rhodri and Blodwedd. The owl-girl's amber eyes were circular in her pale, round face.

'I smell something not of the forest,' Blodwedd said, arching her back, lifting her head to sniff, her long thin hands resting on Rhodri's broad shoulders, the nails white and curved.

Branwen heard a metallic scrape. Dera ap Dagonet, daughter of a Captain of Gwylan Canu, had drawn her sword.

'No beast shall come on us unawares!' she growled, peering into the fathomless dark that lurked under the trees.

'It is no beast!' said Blodwedd. 'It is worse than beast!'

Her head snapped around, and she let out a feral hiss.

Branwen drew her own sword. There were shapes in

the forest. Large, fast-moving shapes, blacker than the night.

Moments later, with a rush and a rumble of hooves, a band of armed men came bursting into view, their swords glowing a dull gray, iron helmets on their heads, and their faces hidden behind iron war-masks.

Curriculum Continuity: primary to secondary

Ray Derricott

With contributions by

Mary Atkins
Jennifer Nias
Eric Steed
John Stephenson
Philip Sudworth
Bill Szpakowski
Les Tickle

Edited by Ray Derricott

Published by The NFER-NELSON Publishing Company Ltd.,
Darville House, 2 Oxford Road East,
Windsor, Berkshire SL4 1DF
and in the USA:
242 Cherry Street, Philadelphia, PA 19106–1906.
Tel: (215) 238 0939. Telex: 244489.

First published 1985
© Schools Council Publications 1985
ISBN 0-7005-0671-3
Code 8181 021

This title, an outcome of work done for the Schools Council before its
closure, is published under the aegis of the School Curriculum Development
Committee, Newcombe House, 45 Notting Hill Gate, London W11 3JB.

Photoset in Plantin by Illustrated Arts Limited, Sutton, Surrey
Printed by Billing & Sons Limited, Worcester.

Contents

Introduction

The purpose of this book is to examine the notion of curricular continuity as it applies to children crossing what has been called the 'great divide' in education in England and Wales: that is, as they move from primary into secondary education. Curricular continuity can claim to have been achieved when the experiences provided by a school ease the social, emotional and cognitive adjustments that pupils have to make when transferring from one class to another or from one school to another. Problems of transition and continuity occur throughout the whole of a pupil's educational career but they appear to be more acute at the primary-secondary interface.

Chapter One provides a backcloth to the discussion on continuity through a review of the use of the idea in educational writings – official reports, local authority documents, Schools Council publications, books and articles that have appeared particularly during the past ten years.

Chapter Two uses this backcloth to present a conceptual ground-clearing. Much of the discussion on continuity is at the level of rhetoric with words used loosely and as slogans. The chapter explores the meanings of concepts such as 'transition', 'liaison', 'consistency' and 'continuity'.

Chapter Three, entitled 'The Humpback Bridge' is written by two local authority advisers and it describes some of their work with teachers. The teacher considering problems of continuity between primary and secondary schools has to proceed with caution in the same way as the driver approaching the humpback bridge.

Chapter Four comprises a series of descriptions, some with accompanying analysis, of the *practice of continuity* in primary, middle schools and lower secondary school settings.

Chapter Five contains case-study material which takes a closer, analytical look at continuity.

Chapter Six reviews several examples of documents published by local authorities which are judged to be worthy of wider publicity than they could normally expect to receive. These are concerned with mathematics, science, religious education, humanities and social studies.

Chapter Seven reflects on the idea of establishing continuity of curricular experience as an innovation. Inevitably, in a work of this nature more questions are raised than solutions proffered. However, the questions listed in this chapter are an attempt to suggest starting points for inservice activity and staff development, whether this be fashionably school-based or whether it is located in a teachers' centre or is the agenda of a specially organized conference. Emphasis is given to ways of handling the *processes* involved in establishing curricular continuity.

Finally, the bibliography not only serves to support what is written but is also intended as a rich source of ideas on continuity for those pursuing practical, professional and academic activity in this area.

The book has grown out of the activities of Programme 1 at the former Schools Council. These activities were instigated by Ron Abbott, then programme director, and several of the contributors were members of the original working group.

Ray Derricott
University of Liverpool

CHAPTER ONE

Curricular Continuity: the rhetoric

Ray Derricott

> May I ask whether these pleasing attentions proceed from
> the impulse of the moment, or are the result of previous study?
> (Jane Austen, *Pride and Prejudice*, Ch. 14)

> Transplanted to new ground, and set in a new environment,
> which should be adjusted, as far as possible, to the interests
> and abilities of each range and variety, we believe that they
> will thrive to a new height and attain sturdier fibre.
> (Board of Education, 1926, *The Education of the Adolescent*.)

There is much that is common sense about the notion of continuity in education. It can be taken for granted that continuity in education is naturally good and desirable. Lay opinion (if such exists in relation to education) may well assume that if a curriculum is planned and purposeful then continuity from one year or one stage to the next will have been an essential part of the programming of children's experiences. Yet, when we examine 'informed' professional opinion we are likely to find more rhetoric than reality about continuity. Dean (1980) indicates that it is a concept to which the profession pays only 'lip service'. Marland (1977) wonders whether all the attention that is paid to the topic is worth the effort.

The focus of the study is on continuity at the traditional age of transfer, 11+, between primary and secondary schools. Eleven may be the traditional age of transfer but only became so after the recommendation of the Consultative Committee on *The Education of the Adolescent*, the Hadow Report of 1926. The second quotation at the beginning of this section indicates how the 1926 committee used the metaphor of growth to imply that a new age structure would strengthen what they clearly saw as a continuing process.

The Hadow Report on *The primary school* that followed in 1931 reinforced the idea of education as a continuous process:

> It is true indeed that the process of education from the age of five to the end of the secondary stage should be envisaged as a coherent whole, that there should be no sharp division between infant, "junior" and post primary stages, and that the transition from any one stage to the succeeding stage should be as smooth and gradual as possible.
>
> (p.70)

This style of rhetoric or exhortation has little effect on practice. The same report went on to advocate a form of streaming into three tracks. (Hadow Report, 1931). Although it is not the concern of this study, it is important to remember that post 1926 reorganization of education saw the emphasis on eleven as the age of transfer into a selective secondary system. A consequence of the selective system was the pressure felt by junior schools to emphasize their preparatory function (Blyth, 1967). In preparing their children for an appropriate secondary education, many junior schools concentrated their curricular activities on those areas that were tested, namely English and mathematics. The spread of comprehensive schools has taken much of this kind of pressure from primary schools. Indeed, the period immediately before the publishing of the Plowden Report in 1967 to the mid 1970s saw considerable development in the establishment of progressive primary education under what some writers have called 'the Plowden ideology' (Hargreaves and Tickle, 1980).

One of the main tasks assigned by the Secretary of State to the Plowden Committee was an investigation of transition between primary and secondary schools. The Report devotes a whole chapter to *Continuity and consistency between the stages of education*. The report puts forward the view that junior schooling ends too early:

> . . . . . for many children the changes of curriculum and method associated with a break at 11 cut across a phase in learning and attitude to it. An unselfconscious period in art, dramatic movement and writing, for example, may last till 12 or 13. Many children too, at the top of the primary school develop confidence in devising experiments and using books in specific situations. Their progress may be slowed down by premature emphasis on class instruction, adult systematization and precision in secondary schools.
>
> (Plowden Report, para. 371)

Assumptions and assertions of this kind about the nature of primary and secondary schools were at the basis of Plowden's advocacy of 8 – 12 middle schools which were to extend the education of childhood beyond the traditional age of transfer (Peters, 1969). Middle schools were seen to be the meeting points of the primary and secondary traditions. According to the report the middle school was to:

> develop further the curriculum, methods and attitudes which exist at present in junior schools. It must move forward into what is now regarded as secondary school work but it must not move so far away that it loses the best of primary education as we know it now.

> · (Plowden Report, para. 383)

The Plowden committee therefore, put its faith in changing the age structure of schooling in order to ease problems of transition from education of childhood to the education of adolescence. However, recognising that change, if it came at all, would come slowly, the report made twelve recommendations about *continuity* and *consistency*. Those that are most relevant to the present study are:

(iii) The initial and inservice training of teachers should overlap more than one stage of education.

(iv) There should be a variety of contacts between teachers in various stages of education.

(v) Local education authorities should close schools for one day to arrange conferences for teachers where there is evidence of lack of contact between those in successive stages.

(vi) Authorities should call area conferences of teachers to consider the information passed on within the primary stage and from primary to secondary schools and the use made of it.

(vii) There should be a detailed folder on each child which could provide a basis for a regular review with children's parents of their progress. The folder should accompany the child into the middle and secondary schools and should be available to the child's class or form teachers. Information about former pupils should be sent back from secondary to primary schools.

(viii) All children should make at least one visit to their new school in the term before they transfer.

(xi) Authorities should send parents a leaflet explaining the

choice of secondary schools available to them and the courses
provided within them.

(x) All secondary schools should make arrangements to . . . meet
the parents of new entrants.

(xii) Discussions should be held between primary and secondary
teachers to avoid overlap in such matters as text books and
to discuss pupils' records.

(Plowden Report, para. 448)

At almost the same time as the publication of the Plowden Report
and serving to support many of its ideas, a middle years of schooling
movement gathered momentum. Strong support for the middle years
movement came from the Schools Council who funded major projects
which enabled teams of developers to produce ideas and materials for
teachers of 8 to 13-year-olds. In addition the Lancaster University
Middle Years of Schooling Project directed by Professor Alec Ross
sought to review the *whole curriculum* for children between ages 8
and 13 (1975). The beliefs underlying the middle years of schooling
movement were that the period 8–13 represented a discernible,
separate phase in cognitive, social and emotional development. The
curricular needs of these children were the same whether they were
being educated in junior, secondary or middle schools. The
curriculum was seen as providing opportunities for *learning how to
learn*. Process was more important than content. The curriculum for
the middle years was to avoid early specialization and keep open the
options of children in terms of what they studied for as long as possible.

The Lancaster Project set up five working party/study groups. One
of these groups investigated problems of transfer between primary
and secondary schools that arise when children face differences in
methods and content. Working Paper No. 42, *Education in the
middle years* (Schools Council), was published in 1972. On continuity
the report had this to say:

Continuity implies making assumptions about what has gone
before and about what has yet to come, preferably in concert
with teachers responsible for the earlier and later stages of
schooling, and then deciding what may best be done in the
middle years. To achieve continuity it is desirable to base the
work on the methods of learning that are most productive (for
long term development) in the middle years and to leave to later
that learning that can be more appropriately done in those later

years . . . Problems of continuity may more easily be solved where children move upwards from school to school within a compact area.

(pp. 18–19)

Thus the notion of continuity between stages received legitimation from a national report of the Central Advisory Committee and from a major Schools Council project. The task of establishing continuity throughout the middle years and particularly between stages was also written into the briefs of a number of national curriculum projects. In 1971 I became involved in *Schools Council Project, History, Geography and Social Science 8–13.* During the initial four years of the Project we made several unfruitful attempts to establish joint planning and development groups of primary and secondary teachers. There are many possible reasons for our lack of success in establishing continuity practices during this period. Project teams, like teachers, need time to develop their ideas and materials and it is often easier for this to happen, in the first place, *within* separate schools. Working across stages demands additional levels of sophistication of use and additional skills of a teacher educator. During the second phase of the Project (1978–1981) when the essential ideas and materials were developed and available in published form, more progress was made in encouraging the setting up of continuity groups.

The problems of the implementation of curricular continuity remain great. Looking at the experience of the HGSS Project with hindsight it now seems clear to me that our Project (like many others) had multi-faceted and ambitious objectives. Naturally, we worked at trying to achieve as many of these as we could but during the development phase of a project it is often impossible (as it was in our case) to identify and predict *the levels of use of the innovation.* Some of our ideas, particularly those related to the organization and sequencing of skills and content, may have added unnecessary complexity to our message and probably led to low levels of implementation.

The establishment of curricular continuity between stages even when supported and legitimated as an approved activity by the rhetoric of prestigious groups (Plowden, Schools Council, individual projects) does not therefore just happen. Perhaps the national platform is an inappropriate one from which to launch such an exercise. Perhaps effort is needed at a much more local level. Thinking of this kind must have been at the basis of the initiative taken by the City of Birmingham in 1972. In that year the local authority's Educational

Development Centre set up their own Project 5: *Continuity in Education – Junior to Secondary*. The project under the chairmanship of Neal issued a report in 1975. The assumptions upon which the report is written were made clear:

> It is generally accepted that continuity of curriculum is highly desirable, and that the secondary school should as far as possible continue where the primary school leaves off. There should be every endeavour to avoid repetition of work, in particular the use of the same text books in primary and secondary schools. It is hoped as the consortium principle develops this will enable primary schools to work on more inter-related lines with the development of more comparable curricula.
>
> (Neal, 1975)

The Birmingham report listed the main barriers against the establishment of curricular continuity as:

1. Distances between schools discouraged contact.
2. Liaison with a view to establishing continuity is a time-consuming process and poor staffing ratios did not allow teachers to be released from classrooms to pursue contacts.
3. Liaison was often seen as part of the headteacher's role. Heads of Departments and class teachers were reluctant to take initiatives and to get involved.
4. Too few teachers were experienced in both primary and secondary schools and their parochial outlooks did not help in understanding each other's difficulties.
5. Some headteachers had little or no interest in establishing liaison with other schools.
6. Some secondary schools recruited from too many feeder primary schools and this made liaison difficult to establish.

The Birmingham Report made 36 recommendations on continuity. I have listed below the ten statements specifically related to the establishment of curricular continuity (Neal, 1975).

(1) Staffing ratios, particularly in primary schools, should be improved so that the major obstacle to liaison should be removed.

(2) . . . an opportunity has presented itself to standardise certain procedures such as transfer cards. With smaller catchment areas, freer access between primary and secondary schools should be possible.

(3) Secondary heads of departments, particularly mathematics, modern languages and remedial, *should ascertain the content and methods of the work associated with their particular discipline in the contributory primary schools.* *

(4) Every facility should be provided to encourage discussions about subject teaching between secondary and primary teachers.

(5) The LEA should make liaison conferences mandatory, unavoidable closures rather than occasional holidays. Indeed, it would be hoped that the officers of the LEA would provide the initiative for such conferences.

(6) Any opportunity should be taken for primary pupils to visit the secondary schools and vice-versa.

(7) The primary class teacher, whose pupils are about to transfer, should be given every encouragement to liaise with the secondary schools. This should not be the exclusive province of the headteacher.

(8) Every effort should be made to ensure that the courses are continuous. This would eliminate waste both in teaching time and in the use of materials. It would also promote a happier relationship between the pupil and his new school.

(9) Where possible, exchanges of teachers between primary and secondary classrooms should be promoted in the hope that a greater understanding of each other's problems may be fostered.

(10) Contributory and receiving headteachers should be encouraged to meet together on a regular basis to discuss problems and other matters of common interest. Even if these meetings appear to be of a social nature little but good can come from them. If properly conducted they could help to break down the recognised barriers between primary and secondary schools.

(p. 15)

There is little doubt that the Birmingham report on continuity is thorough in its treatment of the subject. Its recommendations aim at changing practice. The degree to which the programme is successfully implemented will depend, firstly, on the ability of the local authority

* my emphasis

to provide additional *resources* that will release teachers to establish liaison procedures and continuity of curriculum. Secondly, and perhaps as much of a challenge as the provision of resources, the programme depends upon changing attitudes, values and motivation. These will be taken up in Chapter Seven.

My historical treatment of the notion of continuity does not end in the mid-seventies. The period from 1974 has been distinguished by 'a heightened sense of interest in *the curriculum as a whole*'* (Richards, 1982). In the words of Mr. Bennet's question from *Pride and Prejudice* with which I began this chapter, 'these attentions' (to the curriculum) 'proceed from the impulse of the moment'. The year 1974 represents something of a watershed in the study of the curriculum in Britain (Richards, 1982). Previous study (to use Mr. Bennet's phrase) stemmed from the years of the national projects and expansion and development. From 1974 we began to feel the effects of falling rolls, a contracting economy, inflation and a call for schools to be account-able. The period from 1974 has added even more rhetoric to the dis-cussion about continuity.

The Bullock Report (1975), *A Language for Life*, saw language as the spinal cord of the curriculum. One of the report's main conclu-sions (para. 14.16) was that 'effective liaison is a priority need' and recommendation 162 spelled this out in more detail:

> There should be close liaison between the secondary school and the junior and middle schools from which it receives its pupils. In addition to joint activities of various kinds, this liaison should include such measures as:
>
> (i)   the appointment of a member of the secondary school staff to maintain contact with the contributory schools;
> (ii) an exchange of visits and teaching arrangements between members of the staffs.
>
> (p. 532)

Adding to the rhetoric on the need for curricular continuity between stages of schooling was the DES report on local authority arrange-ments for the curriculum (DES, 1979a). One of the major areas of investigation stemming from the questionnaire in Circular 14/77 was *transition between schools*. The report's findings on transition were summarized as follows:

---

* my italics.

Many replies place great emphasis on encouraging curriculum continuity between primary and secondary schools, while recognizing that some problems may be an inevitable consequence of individual schools having responsibility for curricular content and teaching materials. Some authorities promote guidelines on particular aspects of the primary curriculum to encourage a common approach among schools: others stress the role of advisers in forging links between schools, although a few advisers appear to have specific responsibility for curriculum continuity throughout the area. Most rely on direct *ad hoc* contacts between teachers in the different schools to promote smooth transition through visits, staff exchanges, and – less commonly – meetings of head teachers or the allocation of special liaison responsibilities to individual teachers.

(p. 134)

The point must be made that there is potential for a large gap to exist between what local authorities say they do in reply to a questionnaire from a central agency such as the DES and what they actually do. Nevertheless, the exhortations to establish smooth transition between stages and continuity of curricular experience have continued into the early 1980s.

Further limited empirical evidence about the practice of transition and the existence of continuity was provided by the primary school survey carried out for the DES (1978a). This survey by HMI acknowledged the considerable efforts being made to ease *transition* from school to school but indicated that 'the importance of continuity in the curriculum of schools was largely overlooked' (p. 39). This distinction between *transition* and *continuity* is an important one which will be taken up in Chapter Two. Clearly, the empirical evidence from the HMI's admittedly limited survey was able to produce more evidence about transition than about continuity. For example, about one fifth of the schools kept folders of individual children's work to be sent on to the secondary school; four fifths of primary heads surveyed, and occasionally other teachers, were able to visit their local secondary schools; 90 per cent of the children visited their future schools in the summer term before transition; roughly half the primary schools received information about the subsequent progress of children in their new schools. Efforts to ease *transition* were therefore clearly considerable. However, according to the primary school survey, continuity involved

> The planning of the curriculum and the preparation of schemes
> of work [which] should take into account the requirements of
> the next stage of education as well as the effects of the previous
> stage. This can only be achieved if there is regular and systema-
> tic consultation between teachers from the associated schools.
>
> (p. 39)

The years 1980 and 1981 saw the by now monotonously repeated
message and ritual rehearsal of the arguments for curricular
continuity, in three more official documents. Both the HMI discussion document *A view of the curriculum* (DES, 1981a) and the DES
document, *A framework for the school curriculum* (DES, 1981b)
argued for more thought to be given to curricular continuity and
progression and made suggestions attempting to clarify local authority
responsibilities and duties in relation to the school curriculum.
Perhaps the final version of the 'official' view in this chapter should be
left to the DES who in their statement in 1981 on the school curriculum (DES, 1981b) still felt it necessary to repeat the essence of the
message about continuity.

> Throughout primary and secondary education the curriculum
> needs to be viewed as a whole . . . Authorities and schools need
> to ensure continuity in pupils' programmes both within and
> between the primary and secondary phases . . . Records should
> be kept and transmitted with this in view.
>
> (pp. 8–9)

How far was the argument advanced from the statement with which I
chose to begin this review? The years since 1926 have seen very little
change in the views expressed about continuity. The Plowden Report
paid particular attention to continuity in 1967 but since then its arguments have been rediscovered, reworked and resurrected. The
message coming from a powerful part of the educational system is very
clear. Problems of transition, progression and continuity are
emphasized as important. How far has practice changed or how far is
it changing? I shall take up these questions in subsequent chapters.
Despite all the rhetoric, it was possible in 1981 for Schools Council
Working Paper, 70, *The Practical Curriculum* to make the point that
'Finding ways of monitoring continuity and progression would be one
of the best ways of providing children with an effective curriculum'
(p. 52). The sequel to *The Practical Curriculum* entitled *Primary*

Practice (Schools Council, 1983) devoted a whole section to the theme of continuity and concluded that the most difficult challenge was to promote continuity of teaching. However, the report could go no further than outlining the difficulties, exalting the need for progression in learning and giving hints about what was (or could be) going on in the field. Alongside this we must place the evidence of the ORACLE project (Galton and Willcocks, 1983) which indicated that when some measures of children's attainment in the basic subjects were used there was a falling off of performance as children crossed the 'great divide'. In the secondary schools used by the ORACLE project, 30 per cent of children did worse on tests at the end of their first year in a new school than they had done at the end of the last year in the primary school. On the surface this constitutes cause for great concern. However, the phenomenon of a dip in performance will be well known to many teachers and to constructors of standardized tests. The conventional explanation of the phenomenon is often given in terms of adjustments to a new regime or new teaching styles or school organization. In relation to the development of the argument in this book it indicates a need to explore much more closely the concept of continuity and the concepts that usually surround it, such as liaison and progression.

CHAPTER TWO

Curricular Continuity: some key concepts

Ray Derricott

In this short chapter I shall try to extract some important ideas that occurred repeatedly in Chapter One and examine their meaning in relation to curricular continuity. I shall give these important ideas the status of *key concepts* because an understanding of them and how they are used will help us to make sense of continuity.

The key concepts I shall examine are:

> transition
> liaison
> continuity
> consistency
> structure.

Transition

> We are born, so to speak, twice over; born into existence and born into life; born a human being, and born a man . . . Up to the age of puberty children of both sexes have little to distinguish them . . . But, speaking generally, man is not meant to remain a child. He leaves childhood behind him at a time ordained by nature . . . This is the second birth I spoke of . . .
>
> (Rousseau, *Emile*)

> . . . Professor T. Percy Nunn informed us that he had long been in favour of a 'clean cut' across our public educational system at the age of 11 plus . . .
>
> (Board of Education, 1926, *Education of the Adolescent*, p. 72)

I begin with these two quotations because they indicate the deep-rooted nature of differences between the education of childhood and the education of adolescence. Rousseau, writing in 1762, began the popularization of an idea that saw childhood and adolescence as requiring different educational treatment. The quotation from the Hadow Report of 1926 indicates how the clean break theory persisted well into the twentieth century helped by the early and, in those days, seminal writings of G. Stanley Hall. The best academic advice available in 1926 was, as we have seen, for a clean break at eleven and although there was a cautionary sentence added here and there about the need for links between stages in education, the view was clearly expressed and strongly held.

The *process* involved in moving from stage to stage is *transition*. Much of the material examined in Chapter One was a plea to make this process less of a clean break and more of a gradual adjustment to secondary schooling. A number of workers have explored the problems of adjustment faced by children entering secondary schools. Blyth (1967) states that pupils have

> to learn the many new roles of a secondary school pupil, with no previous experience . . . What is more the new role-complex is not just that of a secondary school pupil, but of a first year pupil. Having reached the pinnacle of importance in the junior school he must like Sisyphus begin to think all over again.
>
> (p. 139)

Brierly (1980) and Pigott (1977) make very similar points. Both emphasize that adjustments not only have to be made to a larger organization, specialist teaching and a tightly structured day but also to the physical demands of longer school days and in many cases more time spent in travelling to school. In an empirical study of pupils' adjustment to secondary schooling, Murdoch (1966) found that in a sample of 522 only 10 per cent enjoyed the experience of transfer from primary schools. In the same sample 5 per cent of the boys and 64 per cent of the girls had experienced identifiable problems of adjustment. The pupils' major fears were of getting lost and not knowing what to expect. Complex timetables and frequent room changes were also a source of confusion.

Youngman (1980) described the transition experience in terms of a pupil's need to adjust to the variety of influences encountered during transfer. He categorized these influences as situational (mainly school characteristics), biographic (pupil characteristics), intellectual (ability and achievement) and dispositional (covering attitude and personality characteristics).

Smith (1981) studied features within the school environment which concerned children after the transition, and the extent to which they were related to adjustment. He found that most first-year pupils were satisfied with school, although bullying, lesson-work, homework, school rules and discipline were unpopular factors.

Studying personal adjustment, Jennings and Hargreaves (1981) found that pupils experienced problems of adjustment arising from the changing of classrooms, school rules, punishment and having more than one teacher. They concluded that the transition had detrimental short-term effects upon the attitudes of the children involved.

Probably the largest and most comprehensive investigation into the transfer is that of Nisbet and Entwistle (1969), who studied the relationship between problems of adjustment and academic attainment. They found that the transition affected different children in different ways, that problems did exist, but that simple organizational innovations could help to ease the adjustment after transfer.

Anxiety, as a factor of adjustment, has received relatively little attention in the studies reviewed here. However, using a test of anxiety towards school, Campbell (1971) drew attention to the anxiety many children experience at the transition. He found that girls were more anxious than boys, and that the school's pastoral system was successful in reducing stress at the time of transfer. Simon and Ward's (1980, 1981) investigations are of interest in that they examine the anxieties of children both before, and after, comprehensive reorganization.

Of course, studies such as those quoted above are subject to social desirability of response. One has to keep in mind that children surveyed about their worries and anxieties may dredge up 'fears and anxieties' in order to present researchers with what they are obviously seeking.

It is important to point out when considering the process of transition that there is in most situations *continuity of social experience* in relation to group membership. Friendship patterns and small group membership established in primary schools often continue as friends move together to the same secondary school. Practices appear to vary. Some secondary schools encourage the retention of such friendship groups especially in the early adjustment period in a new school. Other schools *deliberately* break up existing friendship patterns. The justification given for this is the belief that transfer provides opportunities for new friendships to be formed. There are examples which are usually only talked about 'off the record' of secondary schools deliberately breaking up existing primary school friendship groups in order to try to minimize social and academic differences that are apparent in children who come from contributing primary schools. This is a minor form of social engineering designed to minimize school and environmental differences.

Liaison

The process of transition is accompanied by *liaison procedures*. If we examine the recommendations of Plowden or the Birmingham Report outlined in Chapter One we can discern different categories of procedures which are designed to make the process of transition a gentle one. These are:

(1) The exchange of documentation about pupils.
(2) The organization of activities for pupils and teachers.
(3) Staff consultations – pastoral.

(1) The HMI Primary School Survey (DES, 1978a) found considerable evidence of the exchange of documentation between primary and secondary schools. The administrative task of passing on individual record cards from one stage to the next and even the development of pupil profiles seems to be well established. In many cases this may be the only form of liaison. A great deal depends on how much importance is attached to the individual record, *what is done with it when it arrives in the secondary school*, and how accurate it is. As Cooper (1976) has pointed out, teachers do not automatically refer to their pupils' case-records when teaching them for the first time in the same way that doctors are trained to do. Teachers suspect their colleagues' judgements and prefer to rely on their own diagnosis. We must also note that the exchange of documentation can be two-way. Half the primary schools surveyed by HMI received feedback about the progress of their ex-pupils.

(2) The organization of activities for pupils and teachers with the aim of 'gradualizing' the process of transition can range from the now almost ritualized visit of pupils in their last term at primary school to their secondary school, to the planning for the transition group of (for example) a field trip in which both primary and secondary teachers take part. Activities under this heading would also

include visits (and perhaps some teaching) by heads of department or secondary specialists to contributory primary schools and a reciprocal arrangement for primary teachers in secondary schools. I distinguish visits of this kind, which are perhaps best described as diplomatic or courtesy visits, from those activities which aim at attempting to establish curricular continuity by evolving a joint curriculum plan across the stages. These visits may be essential preliminaries to such joint planning ventures but they do not necessarily lead in that direction.

(3)   Staff consultations on pastoral matters are usually undertaken by head of lower school or head of first year to the contributing primary schools. The agendas for these visits usually concern children with individual difficulties or special needs.

Continuity

Liaison procedures may ease the transition from school to school but they do not ensure continuity of curricular experience. Curricular continuity necessitates the presence of an agreed curriculum plan which is implemented in both the junior school or middle school and in the lower years of the secondary school to which children are transferred. The agreement between schools implies consultation amongst staff and the ability to plan together. This is a demanding process and will be the theme of Chapter Seven. Such a plan assumes teachers to shared technical language and the competencies to use this in inter-school professional activity.

Continuity implies agreement at the levels of
   aims and objectives,
   the selection and organization of content,
   skills,
   methods of assessment,
   and understanding if not agreement about approaches to reading.

The Birmingham document was controversial in its statement that:

Secondary heads of department, particularly mathematics, modern languages and remedial, should ascertain the content and methods of the work associated with their particular discipline in the contributing primary schools.

(Neal, 1975)

The case study material that I present in Chapter Four shows this to be an unacceptable situation to the teachers with whom I have worked.

Given the definition of curricular continuity outlined above, I have come across groups working to achieve such a framework but little evidence of a fully operational system. It is possible to achieve an agreement at the mesa level of decision-making, i.e. between a consortium of associated schools but it is much more difficult to implement such a plan at the micro curriculum level, i.e. the level of day-to-day decision making by individual teachers in their own classrooms.

Consistency

Agreements about curricular continuity imply the existence of consistency. Richards (1982) has argued persuasively that curricular consistency is a useful distinction to make. Richards defines curricular consistency in the following way:

> It is argued here that curriculum consistency is a short-hand term for a very important set of problems, which policy makers at *all* levels need to tackle if equality of curricular opportunity is to be a reality for all primary pupils. By 'equality of curricular opportunity' is meant the opportunity for all pupils to be introduced to some of the major concepts, skills, rules and underlying generalizations associated with established ways of knowing in our society.
>
> (p. 47)

Richards argues for agreement about curricular consistency at the macro (national), mesa (local authority or inter-school) and the micro (within schools and classrooms) levels. There are implications here, of course, for design. Who would be responsible for the design of such curricula? Clearly, as we have seen in Chapter One, the government, represented by the DES, has suggested a broad structure for the school curriculum, but local authorities are seen as having responsibility for curricula within their own areas.

Structure

A curriculum that provides for continuity and consistency is structured. Structure is a word that is over-used and under-explained. Take the following often heard phrases:

'Children need structure, it is my job as a teacher to provide it
for them'
'My classroom is structured'
'The children learn through structured play'
'I operate a structured day'
'There is only one structure that matters and that is the child's
own'.

In these quotations structure is used in a number of different ways.
Derricott and Richards (1980) in an analysis of the structure of the
curriculum identify three aspects of structure:

    (a) logistical;
    (b) logical;
    (c) psychological.

Logistical structure

The logistical structure of a school represents the way in which the
environment is organized for learning. This structure is apparent in
the timetable, in procedures for moving groups of children around the
school and in any system that is designed to facilitate the sharing of
space, resources and time so that potential conflict is minimized.
Within a primary classroom, for example, the logistical structure is
manifest in the separation of clean from messy activities, noisy and
quiet activities, and in the general organization of the learning
environment to avoid 'log-jams' of children.

Logical structure

The logical structure of the curriculum focuses on what is taught
and the sequence in which it is taught. Here, the teacher is concerned
with the content of the curriculum, how it is organized and in what
sequence it is presented to cater for the needs of children at different
ages and stages. There may be more of a consensus about what represents a logical structure in some areas such as mathematics than there
is in other areas, such as the social subjects. Some would question the
view that there is a need to pay careful attention to the selection and
sequencing of content in the primary years. I have argued elsewhere
(Derricott, 1977) that in the years 8–13 not only is learning how to
learn important but so is attention to the selection and organization of

content. In terms of the social subjects, history, geography and the social sciences, I hold that the transition years between primary and secondary education are years in which the pedagogy should emphasize a progression from pre-disciplinary experiences to disciplinary experiences using the resources of history, geography and the social sciences.

Psychological structure

This brings us to the third element in structure. The logical structure of a curriculum has to relate to its psychological structure. This structure uses knowledge we have about how children learn and how they develop to enable us to specify the most effective sequences in which to present the ideas and concepts to be learned.

A psychological structure will depend on what is known about cognitive development. The most persuasive models of cognitive development are provided by Piaget and Bruner. Piaget's stages of pre-operational, concrete operational and formal operational thought are echoed in Bruner's enactive, iconic and symbolic phases. Teachers who are seeking to design a course which offers continuity of curricular experience between the primary and secondary stages of education cannot ignore the powerful ideas of Piaget and Bruner. Derricott and Blyth (1979), when asked to make explicit the psychological bases of their suggested social subjects curriculum, produced the following list based on theories of cognitive development in children 8–13:

(i) Progression in learning is likely to be related to development from concrete to formal operations.
(ii) There is likely to be a wide range of individual differences in the pace of learning.
(iii) Logical thinking is possible if based on direct experiences or upon experiences skilfully described or evoked in words.
(iv) The ability to manipulate variables in the solving of problems will be limited.
(v) Coping with the uncertainty of there not being a single 'correct' answer to many of the questions posed by study in the social subjects will prove difficult for children in this age group.
(vi) There will be a developing interest in other people but the starting point will often be egocentrism which is the antithesis of empathy.

(p. 290)

There are dangers in relating these assumptions to objectives in a simplistic way to produce a suggested pedagogic progression. Let me illustrate this from the HGSS (Place, Time and Society) Project. The suggested intellectual skills of the project are well known, well used and apparently non-controversial in that very few teachers, over the decade in which the project has operated, have rejected them and produced a list which is radically different. This may be both the strength and weakness of the list. Positively, the list has provided a useful starting point for many planning groups; negatively, the list is a 'catch all' in that it can mean all things to all people. The HGSS Project's Intellectual Skills are as follows:

PLACE, TIME AND SOCIETY: INTELLECTUAL SKILLS

1. The ability to find information from a variety of sources, in a variety of ways.
2. The ability to communicate findings through an appropriate medium.
3. The ability to interpret pictures, charts, graphs, maps, etc.
4. The ability to evaluate information.
5. The ability to organize information through concepts and generalizations.
6. The ability to formulate and test hypotheses and generalizations.

The list has been useful, but it has also, *almost always been misunderstood*. The misunderstanding is the result, almost entirely, of our own lack of clarity. Anyone who has used objectives during the last 25 years owes a considerable amount to Bloom and Kratwohl. The taxonomy of educational objectives is *taxonomic*! Objectives are concerned with mastery learning. A stage is mastered and you then move on to the next stage. Our list of six intellectual objectives has been generally interpreted as taxonomic, i.e., ability at each successive level depends on mastery of previous and lower levels. According to this finding information is a lower level of skill than evaluating information, which in turn, is not as high a skill as conceptualizing. In terms of the 8–13 age group this has meant that Intellectual Skills 1 to 3 have been seen to be more appropriate for primary children and 4 to 6 for secondary children. Instead, we would claim, each of the skills has its own *relative levels of mastery* and some level of ability to evaluate information is necessary in finding information. Similarly, some level of generalization is necessary in order to interpret or communicate information. Progression in understanding through the six general objectives is *not linear*; rather it is complex and multi-dimensional. For an alternative interpretation of the same theme one should read Oliver's exploration, *A Proper Basis for Planning* (1982). Oliver's view is that:

> The teacher is not concerned with developing complete mastery, learning and understanding of a given skill or concept but with developing an adequate degree of both to enable further learning to take place, in the light of which, understanding of previously learned material will be refined.
>
> (p. 120)

Continuity and autonomy

The establishment of curricular continuity between primary and secondary schools has implications for the autonomy of the school and of individual teachers. Cooperative planning and teaching *within* a school has been shown to be unwelcome to some teachers because it exposes them unduly to the judgements and scrutiny of their colleagues (Blyth and Derricott, 1977). Much has been written about the freedom of the individual teacher and the individual school in the what, when and how of the curriculum. Cooperative planning and teaching *within* a school reduces individual autonomy. The establishment of curricular continuity between stages involving agreements amongst a number of primary schools and a secondary school must reduce even further the levels of autonomy. This threat to autonomy is perhaps one of the most formidable barriers against continuity.

Circular 14/77 (DES, 1979a) represented a determined attempt by the DES to discover the arrangements the local authorities were making for curricular provision in their schools. In formulating the questions seeking information about what *was going on* there were strong implications from the centre about *what should be going on* in schools. The Education Act 1980 requires local authorities to provide information about curriculum and organization in each of its schools for parents. The DES has indicated that schools should systematically review their curricula. These strong messages have placed considerable pressure upon local authorities and through them individual schools, to make public information that was previously regarded as the professional property of teachers. Some local authorities (for example, Salford) have produced schedules designed to guide schools through the process of self-evaluation. These pressures to produce curricular consistency and by implication curricular continuity threaten the traditional view of the autonomy of the school.

Summary

In this chapter I have tried to explore the meanings of five key concepts – transition, liaison, continuity, consistency and structure – which permeate the rhetoric about curricular continuity. What I have said, especially in the last section, also has implications for sequencing within a curriculum. The intention has been to raise awareness about some of the key words that are often passed over and taken for granted in professional discussions about continuity. If, after reading this chapter, one teacher develops the confidence to ask of a colleague from another school, or an adviser, 'Are we talking about liaison or continuity or both?' or 'You used the word "structure" a minute ago – how are you using it?' then I shall have achieved my objective.

CHAPTER THREE

The Humpback Bridge
Eric Steed and Phillip Sudworth

[The Humpback Bridge is written by two local authority advisers. The metaphor is used to indicate that liaison between primary and secondary schools is a topic that both *is* and *should be* approached with caution. The section provides us with quotations from primary and secondary school teachers that ring true to my own experience. The initial note struck in the paper is pessimistic but it does end in a more optimistic tone. The advisers indicate that in their experience the role of headteachers in establishing liaison and continuity is crucial. Perhaps the writers themselves are not in a position to indicate that bringing schools together in cooperative professional ventures also requires the legitimation of outsiders such as advisers and can also benefit from the motivating factor of attaching activities of this kind to award-bearing inservice courses.

The work of Steed and Sudworth is just one example of the many I came across which illustrates advisers and teachers working together in pursuit of continuity. Some groups working in local authorities concentrate on specific curricular areas such as language, English, maths or science but the work reported shows the two advisers taking on a wider 'across the curriculum' brief.]

Traditional in structure, the humpback bridge survives because the volume of traffic wanting to cross is not sufficient to generate demands for change to a more efficient form of bridge. Its narrowness restricts passage to certain categories of road users. Unable to see over it, one forms a view of what is going on at the other side by listening to reports brought back or by making surmises from those activities that create sufficient noise, unless one is prepared to venture across oneself. When crossing, a cautious approach is recommended lest one falls foul of counter flow traffic. Honking loudly is a common way of making those on the other side aware of one's presence.

If vehicles try to maintain their speed when crossing, they are likely to come down with quite a bump on the other side. It is more usual to drop down one or two gears and to proceed with caution until one is more certain of the new conditions. A disparity of road type or surface between two sides means that there is often a tailback and vehicles can expect to spend some time at a standstill or in low gear.

Similarly, many of the attempts to bridge the primary/secondary divide have resulted in structures more decorative than functional. There is still a major hiatus in the educational journey of most pupils and it takes time for them to adjust to a different set of conditions. All too seldom do their teachers have any real contact with, or insight into, what is happening on the other side of the 11+ gap. In consequence, attempts to establish effective liaison and transfer systems meet problems of misunderstanding.

In examining some of the attitudes which both form and contribute to this misunderstanding a number of quotations from both sides of the divide have been selected as illustrations. Those who have regular contact with primary and secondary teachers will recognize the sentiments expressed through them.

Some Secondary Views

'We have a good liaison system. Our Head of Lower School visits all the primary schools to talk to the children coming to us and they are brought up to the school for half a day. All the primary schools send us record cards.' Most schools recognize that the change from leaving as the oldest pupils in a 140 plus primary school with the security of one class teacher to arriving two months later as the most junior members of a 1400 strong comprehensive school can be quite stressful. They attempt to ease the new intake into the school by giving the pupils a name and a figure they can recognize and a sight of the new school. Some identification of potential pastoral or remedial problems is usually made as well.

Whilst commendable, this is a system of reception rather than of liaison, unless it is underpinned by a much greater interchange of information. Many schools have concerned themselves with preparing pupils for a fresh start rather than with attempting to provide some continuity or to build on what has gone before. Almost all teachers would agree that liaison between schools is important, but once one investigates the substance below the surface unanimity, one finds a wide variety of practice. The variations include the frequency of contact, the level at which the contacts are made and the nature of them. Meetings or visits may be formal and rather guarded, provide useful social hints, or even be joint planning sessions.

There may be a marked disparity between what happens at an official level between schools and the work done by classroom teachers. Some teachers may fail to act on the information available and avoid involvement, while others will use informal contacts with friends and relations on the staffs of other schools to obtain information which does not percolate through the official channels.

Teachers will encounter a warmer reception in some of their linked schools than in others and for any one school the picture will be rather a patchwork. Primary schools that feed into more than one secondary school will find different approaches to the information wanted and the use to be made of it. Their record cards may be used to divide pupils into homogeneous groups, trawled for possible problem cases, made available to all staff or locked away in filing cabinets as possible future evidence. Only rarely will they be used to determine the point from which individual children ought to proceed. Most secondary schools expect to be given an indication of the progress of each pupil at the primary stage, but there is variation between secondary schools, and frequently inconsistency within them, in the use made of this information.

At a recent liaison meeting between the senior staff of a secondary school and the heads of the feeder primary schools, the secondary headteacher was endeavouring to get the primary schools to use the same reading test, etc., so that the scores on the record cards were standardized on one set of tests. The individual secondary heads of faculty were asked what information they could use best and the majority response was, 'We like to give pupils a fresh start. We only look at the record cards, if there are any difficulties.'

One can sympathize with this attitude, although the primary headteachers were quick, not surprisingly, to enquire why they were being asked to spend so much time conducting tests, writing up records and reports and attending meetings, if the majority of staff teaching their ex-pupils were going to ignore the information. The idea of pupils starting with a clean sheet and not carrying labels from primary school is clearly attractive to many secondary teachers, particularly those who are concerned with subjects or approaches not normally found in primary schools.

Some schools have a policy of non-identification of pupils on transfer. 'We have a mixed ability system. We group the children according to alphabetical order of surname so that everyone can see the system.' This approach may help with administration and avoid queries from parents but it does not aid the staff. Grouping pupils by this or any other totally random method can in fact mislead teachers who are expecting a mixed ability class, since any even spread of ability within or across class groups is purely fortuitous. The allocation of children to what often becomes both their social and working groups is something of a lottery. If rigidly applied, such a system precludes acting upon information from feeder schools that Jack Barclay and Martin Barratt should be kept apart, that two previous loners, Fiona Anderson and Dawn Williams, had recently begun to form an effective relationship, or that John Matthews only works to capacity when faced with some competition in the class, such as that provided by Peter Burke and Jane Thomas.

It also poses problems for the classroom teacher who is faced not only with a wide-ability class – and for many secondary teachers matching tasks to individual pupils does not come easily – but with having to discover what he or she may reasonably expect of any individual child. Teachers may set the same work for all the class and wait for differences to emerge; they can plan diagnostic work to establish the skills and knowledge the pupils have already; or they can arrange open-ended tasks with no pre-conceived standard or expectation in terms of quality of quantity for any child on the assumption that each child will both want to and be able to perform at their best in a new school.

Many teachers will want to begin to divide or classify pupils into ability groups, either as separate sets or within classes, or at least to allocate differentiated work to individual pupils according to their perceived ability after a year in many schools, a term in others or even as early as the first half term in a few cases. At four lessons of 40 minutes' duration a week these periods of time are equivalent to one month, one and a half weeks or three days of the primary school class teacher's full day contact with his pupils. This is after rejecting the idea of 'labelling' based on perhaps seven years' experience of a pupil and, in the case of the previous class teacher, a full year of working across a range of subjects with the class. It is small wonder that the primary school teachers query the purpose of liaison in these circumstances.

Other schools equally sceptical of primary school assessment take a different approach: 'Primary schools vary so much in their standards that we give them all a test when we get them here.' To have some standard scores or the results of diagnostic tests as part of, or to supplement, the information passed from the primary schools seems a sensible way of achieving a balance between the objective and the subjective. To expect, as some schools do, that one set of test scores administered when the pupils are in a new environment will provide in a definitive form all the information you need about a child, on the other hand, is to misunderstand both tests and children. Information in the test manual about margins of error is largely ignored in these cases and if the test score differs from the primary school assessment, the tendency is to place more credence in the former. Secondary schools can help the primary schools that appear to be out of line in their assessments to be more realistic by giving them some feedback. High schools in one area send to the contributory schools both the test results and group placings achieved at the end of the pupils' first term in certain subjects and also in due course the external examination results. Many of the staff in these departments have made the effort to get to know the main feeder schools and can interpret the record cards that much more easily. One or two of the staff in these schools have worked with groups in the year of transfer while others have seen examples of work done by the intake. Not only does this help with the assessment of the potential of the pupils, it also provides the opportunity for linking up with the work that has been done at the primary level.

Liaison between primary and secondary schools leading to an effective dovetailing of curricula is a rarity: 'I know some of them have done it before but they come from fourteen different feeder schools, so we do it again to ensure a common baseline.' Even in these cases where some agreement has been reached on a common core element by a group of primary schools – often in mathematics in which the progression through to the secondary school is clearest – the hardwon, theoretical agreement on what will be the responsibilities of the primary and secondary stages can differ markedly from the realities of practice: 'The primary schools claim to teach fractions but half the class did not seem at all sure of them so we had to start the whole topic from square one.' Many of the children probably did benefit from approaching the topic again from a slightly different angle, while others needed reminding of work they had first encountered in the second or third year of the junior school. However, did that necessitate the whole class spending several lessons repeating work? Able young mathematicians who have been extended and challenged at primary level can mark time for much of their first year in the high school.

Mathematics is not alone in this. The inability of the secondary schools to capitalize on the oral and aural competence of many of the pupils coming from the pilot schools in the Nuffield French Project has been fully charted. Many of the receiving teachers had difficulty in coping with the organization of pupils arriving with a wide range of competence; they concentrated on what they saw as the neglected aspects and failed to develop the areas of competence; they did not take into account the methodology the pupils had experienced previously.

Despite all the moves towards mixed ability teaching in secondary schools and the theories of group and individual learning, many secondary teachers are tied to whole-class teaching and the idea of what the class as a unit knows or has covered. The specialist ought to be able to devise activities in his field which will enable the more able to apply the knowledge they bring with them, to encounter areas of interest and new challenges at the same time as practising skills, while others concentrate on mastering the basics of a topic.

A further factor is the dismissive attitude taken by some secondary specialists to the work of the general primary teacher: 'Of course, they may have done the Romans before, but now we shall do it properly.' The scepticism may be a fair comment on what passes for topic work in some junior schools but it leads to a failure to capitalize on valuable work that may have been done. Whilst the specialist is rightly conscious of the need to develop certain approaches, skills and attitudes within his subject area, there are often alternative or parallel topics which would give the advantage of a different content area while enabling the teacher to introduce his own technique and approaches.

Some secondary science teachers, aware of the limitations of the primary schools in terms of specialist knowledge and resources, have made available to their local primary schools suggestions, materials and equipment, sources of information and their own expertise. This positive and constructive approach could be applied in other areas of the curriculum.

Other secondary teachers see no need for any interlacing of curricula. The primary schools' task, for them, is to inculcate certain basic skills and knowledge. 'If they taught the four rules and the tasks properly, they could leave everything else to us.' This kind of thinking presumes that knowledge can be effectively separated off from concepts, skills and attitudes. Reasonable progess at secondary level depends at least as much on the children still being interested in learning, on their having developed a capacity for thinking, questioning and analysing, and on their having some understanding of the processes involved as on the number of facts they have acquired.

This tendency among secondary school teachers to consider the work that has been done in the feeder schools primarily in terms of factual knowledge relates to their lack of understanding of the classroom process in the primary school. 'Some of them even think they can walk about the classroom and talk.' Many primary school classrooms are arranged to facilitate individual or group work. Resources and equipment are set out so that a child can go and get what he or she needs or move to a piece of apparatus without fuss. This approach is alien to most secondary classrooms, although it might be encouraged in some practical areas. One secondary teacher related to incredulous colleagues recently how a first-year child having been given a written assignment got up and set off in the direction of the school library to look for the information he required. How many of our secondary teachers try to foster this kind of independence and the accompanying capacity to ask questions and how many see the ideal class as rows of compliant pupils soaking up the knowledge that is offered to them?

'I don't know what they do with them in the primary schools, but this lot can't even . . . .' The endings to this statement of exasperation are many and varied. The key to the problem lies in the first half of the sentence. Some secondary teachers have spent a nominal period of observation in a primary school but many others have not been into a primary classroom since they were themselves eleven years old. Their knowledge of primary education is limited to their own experience and possibly to that of their children plus the media's potted versions of research findings and national reports. Since they are unaware of the development that has taken place from the reception class, through the infant years and on into the juniors, they are unable to continue the process without a hiatus or to build effectively on the pupil's earlier experiences.

Some Primary Views

The comments coming from the primary schools often parallel the concerns of the secondary teachers but present obverse perceptions of the situation: 'We play our full part in liaison. We fill out the record cards conscientiously and give any other information that is requested.' The primary schools comply with the agreed format of completing records for transfer but vary in the extent to which they go beyond the formal requirements. Figures on record cards are the bare bones of information which need to be fleshed out by pertinent comments if they are to convey a meaningful impression of a child's personality and aptitudes. (The sales particulars of second-hand cars are usually accurate as far as they go but they do not give you all the information you really want).

Many primary schools put the onus on the secondary school to ask if they wish for more than the usual factual information plus the kind of innocuous remarks that would go on a school report to parents. 'They must realize that we cannot commit everything to paper.' The primary schools have built up knowledge about their pupils which is not automatically passed on as confidential information between professionals dealing with the same children. Certain elements of this are covered when the representative of the secondary school makes his annual round of visits but there is a limit to the amount that can be conveyed in one visit per year.

This infrequency of personal contact also militates against the development of a trust between the parties concerned. In the absence of a sure knowledge of what use will be made of information given in confidence, primary teachers tend, naturally enough, to err on the side of reticence rather than to risk labelling a child for the rest of his school career.

The confidence of the primary schools in liaison is also shaken by the way in which some secondary schools discount the information which has been carefully prepared for them: 'We have plenty of other things to do with our time than to compile records which are ignored.' Clearly, if the system of records is to be effective, the secondary schools must be clear in their own minds what information they can best use and communicate this fact to the primary schools in their area. Similarly, the primary schools should ensure that records are in a form that the secondary school can readily decipher.

As more parents take advantage of the provisions of the 1980 Education Act, primary schools will find themselves increasingly feeding several secondary schools and this will fuel complaints that 'the secondary schools do not seem to know what information they want.' Faced with this situation the primary schools can either restrict themselves to the minimal liaison required of them or make an effort to see that their former pupils start their secondary school with the advantage of their new teachers knowing a great deal about them. The problem of liaising on curricular issues, which as we have seen is an issue of some delicacy, will not be helped by the lack of defined catchment areas for secondary schools.

In any case, not all primary schools react favourably to suggestions of curricular discussions with the secondary sector. 'No secondary school is going to tell me what to teach in my school.' The assumption is made by many primary schools that 'discussions on matters of common interest' is a circumlocution for secondary schools telling their feeder primary schools what they expect their pupils to have covered on arrival, and the barricades are immediately manned. The primary schools are, on the whole, very jealous of their autonomy. Now that they have been freed from the shackles of the 11+ syllabus in most areas of the country, they are not prepared to consider anything which resembles an imposed curriculum. Each school has developed its own philosophy and ethos which it is reluctant to compromise and most primary schools could point to the use made of the freedom from constraints to develop units of work related to topical events or to issues which have caught the pupils' interest.

However, whilst approaches and organization may diverge and there will be differing emphasis on particular areas of the curriculum, one would expect a group of primary schools to be able to agree on certain aims in terms of skills, concepts and attitudes and on a common core of basic knowledge, at the very least in one or two curricular areas, which could be presented to the local secondary school for discussion. Mathematics and science are often perceived as the areas in which a large measure of agreement can be obtained fairly easily. It is often advisable for a group of schools to restrict initial discussions to one curricular area where agreement is not too difficult to achieve and only to proceed to other areas when mutual confidence has been established.

If a primary school feels that its autonomy is sacrosanct, one wonders in whose interests the defensive attitude is being taken. Certainly, the outcome will be that many pupils will mark time at the secondary school repeating work they have covered previously. 'One of our ex-pupils came back to see us at half term. He spends half his time going over old ground.' From our observations this complaint is justified in many instances. Yet secondary schools have to be sure of certain baselines before progressing further. Even where checklists are attached to record cards, it is not always clear what is meant by a tick against 'measurement of area'. It is always much more helpful for teachers to see examples of work that has been done or ideally to observe the children and work with them.

'What is the point of extending bright children at primary level if they are going to have to repeat everything in the high school?' Primary teachers find it particularly galling, when they have given time to providing extra work for a bright pupil, to learn that his or her progress seems to have been temporarily halted at the high school. If primary teachers were to think of enrichment less in terms of going further on and tackling material usually reserved to a later stage, and concentrate more often on giving additional experiences, this would be less of a problem. Some primary schools have involved staff from the local secondary school in devising programmes and providing materials for their brightest pupils and have found that this obviates many of the problems of repetition of work.

'The secondary school expects us to give them plenty of information about what we do, but they are not very forthcoming themselves.' Liaison is a two-way process. Many secondary schools do accept their responsibilities in this respect. They provide feedback to the primary schools on the achievements of their ex-pupils and information on what they are doing both generally and in specific areas. Heads of Departments from certain secondary schools give talks on their work to primary schools. There are still areas, however, where the only way the primaries know more than the general public about the local secondary school is through former pupils reporting back on their experiences. In many of these instances the primary schools have evinced no particular interest and it has simply not occurred to the secondary school that there is an information gap.

'They are enthusiastic and keen to learn when they leave us. Look what they are like by 15. What on earth do they do with them?' The transformation of the bright-eyed 11-year-old into a truculent teenager is a familiar picture, and the agonies of adolescence, which cause many parents to wonder what they did wrong, are accepted as a fact of life in secondary schools.

The size of a secondary school contributes to its differences from the primary schools in terms of relationships and organization, whilst the constraints of examination syllabuses restrict curricular thinking. The primary school teacher should appreciate that comments from secondary teachers about the standards of intake cohorts are not unrelated to the pressure on secondary schools to produce good examination results.

Towards Two-way Traffic

What form should real liaison take? How can one recognize that liaison underpinned by positive reasons for contact is taking place? Liaison between schools, whether primary and primary or primary and secondary, will spring ideally in a natural manner as the need to liaise arises. This natural gathering together will be based firmly on the mutual understanding and belief that teachers and ultimately children gain from liaison. The atmosphere which allows such meetings should be both professional and friendly, for the aim of such a meeting can only be to attain a means of moving forward which is acceptable to all parties.

For individual headteachers the prerequisite is that members of the school staff which they lead are working in harmony. To attain this state the headteacher must ensure that the aims and objectives of the school are known to colleagues and that an accepted and viable form of record keeping is in use. In order that the compilation of records about individual pupils should have a real influence on the teaching which takes place the headteacher will monitor constantly what is taking place within the school and organize inservice training for both the staff as a team and for individual members of staff, so that knowledge of what is being taught and why it is being taught is common knowledge and understood. Teachers cannot liaise one with another in a vacuum where information is not shared; headteachers can only liaise realistically with other headteachers when they know that their own school is functioning as near to its potential as possible.

The headteacher's role is the crucial factor in any school to school liaison process. The headteacher must support liaison in an active manner both as participant and as the major encourager of colleagues to be fellow participants. In those instances where the headteacher is not committed to liaison there can be very little chance that the school can be an effective partner in liaison, no matter how keen individual members of that school staff may be to make liaison work. Headteachers effectively control those aspects of school organization and resources which affect liaison directly. For example, it is desirable that colleagues from liaising schools not only talk about what happens in classrooms but are able to spend time in one another's classrooms to share the teaching processes. These desirable visits can be arranged only with the active goodwill of both headteachers.

Despite the fact that there are many schools where, because of a lack of stated aims, objectives or schemes of work, teachers receive pupils from a colleague within the same building without the benefit of adequate records, it is equally true that the reverse situation applies in many schools. Here each teacher will hold statements from the head-teacher and colleagues which make clear how the school should operate. In these schools staff meetings will be held as appropriate to discuss progress and to amend aims and schemes as necessary. In short, the school will be a living community which responds to each stimulus after due consideration and corporate consent.

One such school known to us has looked recently at its marking schemes. To the surprise of the staff it was discovered that pupils had to learn to cope with many different coded messages which were used by different teachers as signifying the same type of mistake. Once a new marking scheme had been worked out and accepted the staff set about considering the revision of other aspects of their teaching which, in the eyes of their pupils, could be construed as being designed to confuse rather than to illuminate their days. In these cases liaison could be seen to benefit both staff and pupils.

In one authority attempts have been made to bring together colleagues from infant, junior and secondary schools over extended periods to try to spread liaison between schools. In two examples the teachers who were brought together to take part in courses comprised colleagues from secondary schools together with their primary feeder schools. In another example, the science staff from individual secondary schools acted as a resource for colleagues from the feeder primary schools who wished to write graded science units for extra-curricular science clubs. In all three examples the teachers who took part were volunteers displaying a belief in liaison which had a useful end product.

One course, for a certificate in language and learning, was a modified version of a course designed and taught by a polytechnic in the area. In order to make the structure and content of the course more meaningful to the groups of teachers described above, two advisers liaised with polytechnic lecturers and produced a new structure which encouraged teachers of pupils between the ages of five and sixteen to follow a common syllabus. Two cohorts have so far completed the certificate and, thereby, have spent ninety hours each in contact with teachers of children differing in age from those they taught them-selves. Workshops and discussion sessions have helped to present the aims and objectives formulated for these various children.

Although insufficient data is yet available to make definite state-ments, there is some evidence to suggest that contacts made during the year-long, part-time course have fostered cross-school liaison. It is perhaps worth noting that although no headteachers were members of this particular course during the first two years it has subsequently been recognized that participation in the course would afford head-teachers a means of gaining understanding of liaison possibilities. Each feeder primary school for the third course is represented by its headteacher and one other member of staff.

The second initiative has been planned by an adviser and polytechnic lecturers as a 9–13 mathematics enrichment course involving secondary schools and their feeder primary schools. Further courses have been designed to include work with children of all abilities. The possibilities of gaining practical experience by working with children not normally encountered were welcomed by colleagues from secondary and primary schools alike.

The third authority initiative was organized by the science adviser. Each secondary school science department was asked to provide one of its members to act as the resource contact for those primary colleagues from its feeder primary schools who wished to cooperate in organizing extra-curricular science clubs. In effect the organization underpinning the science cells was designed to produce an array of science activities, graded for age and ability levels, which could be evaluated, collated and distributed to any primary school wishing to make use of them. The apparatus, expertise and knowledge held by secondary specialists was made readily available to primary schools.

There is, of course, nothing new about secondary, primary and infant school teachers attending courses together. What was unusual, although by no means unique, about the thinking behind the three inservice models outlined above, was the planning for active coopera-tion and liaison. It had been accepted by the organizers that no teacher would wilfully act against the educational needs of children. The problems surrounding the approaches to the humpback bridge were based in great measure on myth and legend. It was felt that much could be done to obviate misunderstandings by providing course activities which would not only enhance personal knowledge and performance but also provide course members with useful insights into the requirements of teachers working with age groups other than those normally encountered in their own schools.

Acting upon the positive nature of the authority initiatives, the school adviser to one secondary school liaised with the headteacher in an attempt to provide an atmosphere in which the school staff could liaise with the members of staff in its feeder schools. The fact that the school adviser was also the adviser to those feeder schools meant that he was not seen as a secondary adviser attempting to impose the wishes of secondary teachers on primary colleagues.

During a meeting with the senior staff of the secondary school many of the themes mentioned earlier in this chapter were repeated. There was, however, a common desire expressed to know what the primary schools as a body would expect the average child to know in terms of skills, attitudes, concepts and knowledge, when they ended their primary school courses. It was accepted that as there were a number of newly-appointed headteachers in the area it would be both impractical and untimely to expect the headteachers to have coordinated their aims and objectives. It was decided to offer the primary headteachers the same resource facility from every department within the school that they had received from the science department. In broad terms this meant that a group of primary teachers from various schools would be able to use the expertise and facilities of the secondary departments to help them to achieve those skills, attitudes, concepts and knowledge areas that they agreed were desirable for eleven year old pupils. This offer was placed before the primary headteachers and was accepted as being both realistic and worthwhile by everyone present. Varying degrees of prior liaison were claimed, explained and discussed; very little, however, related to curriculum matters but tended to support the borrowing of equipment and the attendance at one another's formal functions. It was evident that everyone was willing to make an attempt to make liaison work and to support members of staff who wished to participate in liaison.

The first meeting with a department has not yet taken place but the headteachers showed enthusiasm for this approach and unanimously decided to request a meeting with the science teachers within the department. It was further requested that the science adviser and the teacher/adviser for environmental education should also be present as it would make sense to know everything that was on offer to influence their curriculum thinking.

One may wonder why liaison had not occurred naturally between these schools especially as the desire and goodwill to make liaison work was so evident during the meetings. In many similar situations it may well be that the only missing element is a catalyst to bring the two sides together in order to begin a chain reaction leading to mutual understanding and ongoing commitment to liaison. It cannot be claimed that the viable catalyst is always the school adviser; the status, position or otherwise of the catalyst is unimportant. What is important is that he or she should appear.

Willingness to liaise, although extremely important, is not the only requirement of the headteachers and their colleagues. Time is a factor for which planning decisions must be made for it takes many hours of meetings before even committed colleagues feel secure enough to state what they really believe. From the point of security onward real liaison begins to take off. To illustrate this point, a group of secondary headteachers working on a curriculum project in the same authority have stated that their real work began after approximately sixty hours of meetings.

Making liaison work is difficult; early meetings will necessarily be given over to sizing one another up and sparring for openings. These are natural happenings and to attempt to hurry them may divert the course of liaison into a pathway which will become a mere talking shop and have no influence upon what happens ultimately. To span the primary/secondary divide with a structure more fitting than the humpback bridge takes time and effort. It presupposes a willingness both to contribute to and to learn from the work of colleagues and a preparedness to compromise in the interests of the pupils. The rewards are reaped not only by the pupils but by the teachers in terms of their professional development.

CHAPTER FOUR

Curricular Continuity: some examples

> Between the idea
> And the reality
> Between the motion
> And the act
> Falls the Shadow
>
> (T. S. Eliot)

Common Ground: establishing curricular continuity between a secondary school and its contributing primary schools

John Stephenson
Helsby High School, Cheshire

[The paper by John Stephenson affords us the privilege of sharing the thoughts, feelings and ideas that have emerged over a period of change, one in which the secondary school in question is in the process of taking on the traditions of two separate grammar schools and becoming comprehensive. As part of this process of change, liaison with contributory primary schools was given priority and the teachers began to consider the possibilities of curricular continuity. Stephenson provides us with an open and positive description of events at Helsby. He is essentially optimistic about continuity without losing sight of some key problems. A school and the individual members of staff concerned that take initiatives over continuity are likely to raise suspicion in some quarters. Who is creating the agenda for discussion and why? Is control of the direction of the primary school curriculum what the secondary school heads of department have in mind? How will such initiatives affect the autonomy of schools, and in particular the traditional freedom in curricular matters enjoyed by primary school head teachers? Stephenson's paper raises such questions both explicitly and implicitly. It also gives a clear indication of how an issue such as banding the 11+ intake can become the focus of an ideological stance which may hinder more effective communication between primary and secondary schools.

The details of the one-day conference at Helsby and the subsequent reports from the working groups as well as the expectations of heads of mathematics and English are included as examples of the useful and usable products of discussions across the primary/secondary interface. I also wish to add that Helsby High School is the actual name of Stephenson's school. Neither the head nor the authority saw any reason to hide behind anonymity. Stephenson presents the experiences at Helsby, not as a panacea but as a contribution to the debate on continuity.]

The creation of Helsby High School in September 1978 as a mixed comprehensive through the amalgamation of two single-sex grammar schools inevitably led to a contraction of the catchment area and as other schools were also reorganizing, a reorientation.

Previously the two schools had had a common catchment area of approximately 23 primary schools from which they had drawn their four-form entry: now the contributory schools were cut to ten with the loss of the town primaries in the 'Old Town' of Runcorn and the acquisition of the village schools lying to the South. The most important consequence of reorganization of the catchment area was that it gave a more coherent and monolithic blend to the intake in that it was now drawn from rural and semi-rural areas.

Initially there were two pressing tasks: to reassure the parents about the aims and teaching within the new school, and to make effective contact with the primary school heads in order to facilitate as smoothly as possible the transition to secondary school. (There was also a need to reassure parents of existing pupils that amalgamation and reorganization would have no detrimental effect on their children's education, but this was achieved by the headmistress who took every opportunity during the 18 months prior to reorganization to state publicly that there would be no change of curriculum for those who had embarked upon a grammar school course and that to this end single-sex classes for these pupils would remain so until the pupils entered the sixth form.)

It was decided to concentrate upon meetings with the parents of the ten primary schools on the assumption that any pupils from the old catchment area would enter as siblings and their parents would have heard the Headmistress' remarks in the previous 18 months. In the autumn and spring terms of 1977/78 the head and senior staff most closely involved with receiving the comprehensive intake visited the schools in the evenings and met parents and staff. In general parents were happy about the plans and especially pleased about the school's insistence upon a uniform, homework and an examinations-based curriculum: some needed assurance that equally good provision would be made for pupils with specific learning difficulties. The meetings also provided the opportunity to make close contact with staff and this was followed up by:

1. The Head of Lower School keeping in close contact with the primary heads
2. The Head of First Year and his assistant making arrangements to visit the primary schools to gather information about the pupils prior to their entry

3. Heads of key departments (e.g. Maths, English, Remedial) visiting some of the primary schools to acquaint themselves more closely with curriculum and methods.

On all occasions the visits were received with the greatest coopera- tion and every attempt was made to ease the transition, one head remarking that no longer did he feel his pupils were being thrown over a ten-foot wall at 11+ and others, notably those who had had contact with other comprehensive schools, offering advice, help and informa- tion which their experience enabled them to do. Information such as school calendars was also exchanged and primary heads were invited to High School functions.

In the meantime a prospectus was produced and copies sent to every parent of the first year's intake with courtesy copies to the primary school heads. Parents and pupils came to the school for an acclimatiza- tion visit in early July (tour of the school, meet form teachers and purchase uniform for pupils; tour of the school, meet officers of Parents' Society, purchase school uniform, and informed discussion with staff for parents) and the school opened in September 1978.

The question of grouping the new intake for teaching purposes pre- sented the greatest difficulty. Owing to the nature of the building, the subjects offered by the staff (recruited from the existing grammar school staff plus four extra for reorganization) and the experience of the majority of the staff plus the commitment to the existing pupils, it was not possible to divide the intake into two populations of four classes each and teach the pupils on a blocked timetable scheme. Instead pupils were to be placed in three broad-ability bands with promises for promotion and demotion according to progress. How- ever, this was not immediately possible as there were no common test results available. The pupils were therefore placed in mixed ability groups for one term, tested at Christmas and then banded. By the following July the LEA had introduced a common system of testing which meant that the 1979 and subsequent intakes were banded upon entry.

At about the same time (September 1979) it was considered that regular meetings between the High School and primary school senior staff would be useful on the argument that liaison and continuity were inseparable. The schools could liaise as much as they liked but the pupils undergo the education and its continuity or lack of it. Everyone wished to smooth the transition across the primary/secondary inter- face and active steps were taken. At the same time it was recognized that each school is an entity in itself and meetings must not be seen as attempts by the High School to dictate policy to the primary schools but rather as genuine, professional attempts to talk out ways and means to ease the lot of the pupils – the whole *raison d'être* of the schools.

After several general meetings it was considered worthwhile proceeding to a regular termly meeting which was subject-based to which the teachers of the fourth year primary pupils plus a secondary school head of department would be invited. Quite rapidly a programme to discuss English, mathematics and science to be followed by French and remedial teaching was operated. It soon became clear that the primary schools were unhappy about the banding system:

1. On principle, it was different from the common practice in primary schools of mixed ability classes and the use of friendship groupings within these classes.
2. They found themselves under much pressure from parents (as did the secondary school) anxious to see their children in a top band which they (the parents) equated (incorrectly) with a grammar-school stream.

As 'banding' appeared to be getting in the way of more fruitful discussion about pupils' needs and continuity of practice method and content, it was decided to postpone a further 'subject' meeting and spend some time on looking at how and why the High School grouped the pupils. This 'clearing the air' exercise at least made plain to the primary headteachers the High School's constraints, though subsequently one wonders how far this percolated through to their staffs. It was also agreed that in addition to its normal consultation about pupil banding, the High School would provide each primary school with notification of which band pupils would be placed in and also give them 48 hours to make representations before the placing became final. In most cases there were no representations made and in the few cases where a head did telephone, the pupils were borderline anyway or a better than average year tended to put pressure on places for Band I and forced a few able pupils into Band II. This action cost the High School little apart from the necessity of getting its lists ready 48 hours early and it certainly pleased the primary heads who felt that the consultative process had been improved. In addition, when the Head of First Year makes his preliminary visits to primary schools in the early summer term, he gives a verbal report on progress made by the previous entry. This again enables the primary school to assess how its pupils are fitting in and progressing within the larger intake of the High School, and also the accuracy of its assessment of last year's pupils.

Another area of cooperation which has proved very fruitful has been a joint musical venture. The High School has a strong Music Department and the Head of Department was most anxious that all pupils should be aware of the musical opportunities and take advantage of them. In the summer of 1979 it was decided to have a Musical Evening with contributions from all schools and with parents forming the audience. Each school was allotted ten minutes for groups and/or soloists (instrumental and vocal) and the High School also made a number of contributions. This proved to be an opportunity for participation and for explanation as well as being an extraordinarily successful musical evening. The event is now firmly on the school calendar, coupled with the idea that a number of songs might be rehearsed individually and then sung communally as a climax to the evening.

In early July 1981 the head of mathematics was expressing concern about the lack of common policy in the primary schools concerning the four basic operations. At the same time a feeling emerged that the primary heads felt they were being 'summoned' to the High School and had had no opportunity to determine the agenda of meetings. (No slight, of course, was intended.) The High School provided the hospitality and the clerical back-up together with facilities for a meeting, and clearly the mathematics policy topic might look very much like dictation. When the meeting was held, the Head of Department took the line that whatever method each school favoured for teaching the four operations it would be invaluable if, during the final primary school year, all pupils were introduced to the method used at the High School. This received general support and the Head of Lower School followed this up by suggesting that the venue of meetings should move around the schools whilst the High School would continue to provide administrative back-up. This also appeared to be acceptable and the Headmistress then suggested that the secondary schools' in-house conference in the autumn should be a primary/secondary meeting with all schools closed for the day and staff attending the conference at Helsby. This appeared to be generally acceptable although some heads expressed reservations about closing their school for a day. Given this general support, preparations were made for the conference, speakers were booked and catering arrangements made. At this point some schools began to back out but in the event all schools sent some representatives, some schools' managers attended, five schools closed altogether and six Heads attended.

The programme, entitled 'Common Ground', was as follows.

MORNING SESSION
   Lecture: 'Curricular Continuity – Rhetoric or Reality?'
                                                    Mr. R. Derricott

Discussion groups
   1. What is the child's experience of the curriculum 9–13?
        a) What facts/skills/attitudes does he/she learn?
        b) What teaching and learning methods are used? How was progress assessed?
        c) Is there any continuity?

   2. In view of the above:
        a) Is there need to establish common objectives?
        b) Is it possible to coordinate and so improve the continuity of learning? e.g. topics, skills, texts.
        c) Are there areas where practical cooperation would help?

AFTERNOON SESSION
   1. What differences do the 11-year-olds experience as they move from primary to secondary school?
   2. What can be done to ease the transition?
   3. What have primary and secondary staff to learn from each other's methods?

Lecture: 'The Primary School Curriculum' – Mr. D. Clare, HMI.

The digest of the reports that follow does not necessarily answer all or some of the questions posed, nor were answers intended or expected. As in any group discussion, teachers interpret, analyse and react according to their own experiences, ideas and expectations and the questions were 'stimulus' material only designed to provoke thought, discussion and hopefully, better understanding. Nonetheless some interesting ideas emerged. They are grouped below for convenience – many of the ideas emerged from more than one of the groups. Some of the ideas overlap but the group of schools felt that if it was to make any headway, such issues would have to be tackled in small groups rather than piecemeal.

Curricular Issues

1. Should the primary and secondary schools be regarded as one rather than each separate with its own philosophy?
   Should they teach skills across the 11+ divide?
2. Can a degree of common core curriculum be established? Perhaps Heads of Departments and primary school staff might investigate. Will the Cheshire Curriculum Review and Assessment Group give a firm indication of the particular skills which the secondary school might expect?
3. It is most important that changes in approach and teacher-expectation should be graded.
4. Thought should be given to easing the methods of primary into secondary and vice-versa.
5. Is there a possibility of pupils from individual primary schools visiting Helsby during the day and seeing it in action? Might they come in July for lessons?
6. Is it possible to establish a common terminology across all schools?
7. Can remedial help be made more effective? e.g. could a primary teacher come to Helsby for a year and teach the remedial group?

Administrative

1. Is enough time devoted to liaison? Would a couple of days (say residential experience) help?
2. Can the primary schools provide more information about pupils? Pupil profiles?
3. Could a joint project be started in the primary schools and completed in the secondary school?
4. Can Helsby provide a set of skills and concepts that could possibly be met by the primary schools?

Pupils' Experience

1. Should be ongoing rather than a complete break.
2. Should the secondary school be able to expect/ask for certain specific skills?
   Should the policy documents required by the LEA mention specific skills?

Ought the High School to draw up a list of skills it would hope new pupils had mastered?

3.   It is important to cut down the mobility of pupils in the early years – gives the pupils stability which they are used to.

4.   Pupils faced the following sizeable changes:
Coping with homework
Tiredness
Many teachers
Bottom of the school again
Movement round the school
A more formal structure
Not having one mother/father figure with whom to identify.

5.   Some staff believe that pupils are expecting a change – they are amenable to it and cope well with the challenge of new subjects and the stimulus and bustle of the secondary school.

6.   Pupils meet new subjects, e.g. history and geography, and these skills and concepts are not developed in the primary school.

7.   Pupils experience a change in teaching style from an informed to a more dictatic style.

8.   Pupils have to learn to focus on the teacher and concentrate for longer periods than in the primary school.

Teaching Staff

1.   Teachers should visit one another's schools and learn about one another's approach and methods.

2.   Staff should liaise more closely about method.

3.   Interchange of staff might help each group to understand one another better and why things happen in a particular way.

4.   There should be a possibility of 'middle school' – type teaching staff who teach across the interface and move with the pupils.

Primary Schools

1.   It might help the transition if parents had a greater understanding of the test scores, what they test and the use to which they are put.

2.   Should primary schools establish a more formal structure in the final term/year in order to prepare their pupils for the more highly structured situation in the High School?

3.   There was a suggestion that, as well as liaising with the secondary school, they should liaise among themselves 'to ensure that the necessary educational skills have been covered

and that all pupils are at the same "starting line" when they arrive at Helsby.'

Aims of the Head of First Year
The Head of First Year is a key link in the chain of transition and sees his role as possible having seven strands – no order of priority is implied.

1. Obtaining the pupil's scores. This works very well due to the authority's policy of testing all pupils in the final primary school year.

2. Obtaining social information, such as information about pupil background, parents, one-parent families, and maintaining contacts with social services, police, etc. This tends to work well for the socially deprived or the pupils where there are known domestic problems. What has been less successful is the use the High School makes of this information as the banding system will break up some friendship groups anyway and the pressure of time often prevents some fine tuning of the class groups to take into account all the information received. This time factor is of course compounded by the number of primary schools and their geographical isolation.

3. Passing back to the primary schools information about last year's intake.

4. Acquiring information about the nature of each primary school, its organization, what subjects are strong: does it teach French? How much science? reading, mathematics? Such information is subjective but over the years one acquires a 'feel' about each school and how it fits into the overall pattern.

5. Looking after inter-school relationships; acting as an ambassador for the High School; picking up and passing on fears and worries from the primary school. Facilitating the use of the High School's resources, e.g., duplicating and sports equipment; projectors.

6. Inviting primary schools to school functions and handing out the High School's calendar of events.

7. Keeping the primary school informed about progress of ...ific children and their background since the children ...the school.

Report From the Head of English

The Head of English, visiting the primary schools before and after re-organization, comments as follows:

> I was very glad to have the opportunity to visit several primary schools and to go into the classrooms and see class organization. I particularly wanted to observe how mixed ability groups were dealt with in the English teaching and felt that there was a great advantage in them all remaining in one room with all their materials, resources, exercise books, wall stimuli to hand. I was particularly able to observe:
>   pupils assisting each other
>   pupils confidently organizing their own work
>   the amount of central direction
>   the amount of corporate activity
>   the teaching atmosphere (informal/institutional)
>   the amount of learning, testing, correcting
>   creativity
>   displays of work.
>
> In general it would be advantageous to have the following information:
>   Time spent on practical/factual and imaginative writing
>   Methods of stimulating different types of writing
>   Quantity and subject of project work
>   Books used for 'formal' English work
>   Books used for reference
>   Books used for reading
>   How much time spent on drama
>   How written work is corrected.

Report From the Head of Mathematics

The Head of Mathematics comments that it would be useful to have the following information/cooperation from primary schools:

1. During the last primary school year all pupils should learn a common approach to the four operations (additions, sub-tractions, multiplications, divisions)
2. The content of the maths teaching in the final two years

3. The text books which are used in the primary schools in the final two years
4. Examples of pupils' work
5. Greater opportunity to discuss subject teaching between primary and secondary school teachers
6. What aids and stimuli are used.

The Future

The Day Conference was obviously valuable and there remains at the time of writing much 'unfinished business' to attend to. Clearly some ideas that emerged are impractical, others worth discussion and follow-up. It may be that greater contact at classroom teacher level will provide many answers but it will equally raise the question of how far classroom teaching in primary and secondary schools are autonomous and whether any measure of uniformity can be achieved across all the schools. There is also the question of the role of the LEA – what time and resources can/will it make available for further conferences and follow up? What pressures should/will it put on schools to work more closely? The question of philosophy remains. Should pupils have an abrupt break at 11+? Some are ready and swim; others flounder. Will closer liaison help the latter or will they emerge more mature through a little floundering? Does the answer lie closer to the concept that the pupils should come to the High School at 11+ having mastered certain skills? Which? Whilst the schools

Continuity in Geography Between Primary and Secondary Schools

Bill Szpakowski

[The next contribution is written by a geographer and focuses on problems of establishing curricular continuity within that specific subject area. Bill Szpakowski explores the literature on teaching geography mainly written over the last 30 years. His survey reveals not only changes in the subject itself but also changes in teaching which call for the identification of skills and the recognition of key ideas or concepts. Szpakowski uncovers frequent exhortations to establish progression in learning and continuity between stages but indicates that as in the general debate on the subject there is considerable rhetoric and little action.

The second part of the paper explores the efforts of one comprehensive school and four contributing primary schools to establish liaison and possible continuity. This case study may produce descriptions that readers will readily relate to their own situations. So far as curricular continuity is concerned, geography emerges from this study as a low priority area. 'Is it a cause worth pursuing?' seems to be the question asked by the secondary school headteacher, echoing the quotation by Marland in Chapter One. The vignettes from the four primary schools indicate as many approaches to geography as there are schools which appears to be a reflection of the national scene. What is also clear from Szpakowski's work is the gulf that exists between the influence practice in schools. In this chapter we examine some of the ideas about curricular continuity elaborated by writers on geography education and then through some small-scale field work we attempt to assess the influence of their ideas at the primary-secondary interface.

One advantage of using the community of geographers in the way we propose is that in the Geographical Association we have an example of an active subject association with effective networks and a clear objective of improving the teaching of geography.

In a report for the Geographical Association (GA), *Geography in the Secondary School*, Briault and Shave wrote, in 1952, 'Sound geography teaching requires careful progression, which means building on the foundation of materials already taught, and using the pupils' own environment to the full for reference and comprehension.' The authors of the report stuck strictly to their secondary school brief and assumed that careful progression and building upon materials already taught was the exclusive preserve of the secondary school. No mention is made of expectations at primary school level, the assumption being that geography education begins at 11 and the secondary school specialist treats new entrants as blank slates.

In 1953 the GA did turn its attention to geography in primary schools, concluding that local studies, mapwork and the lives of people in other environments should be major areas of focus with local studies occupying the core. The pamphlet *Geography in the Primary School* hinted at possible problems during transition, indicating that pupils' studies should '. . . increase in depth and quality as, with growing mental stature, the junior school child approaches the age of 11 years and over' (Geographical Association, 1959, p. 9). No other mention of transfer or secondary school provision was made.

In 1959 the Ministry of Education published an official statement about the state of primary education. In its review of geography teaching the ministry suggested that the study of the locality and of other lands should form the major content areas of a primary school syllabus. The report regarded maps and books as indispensable sources of information and emphasized the importance of systematic recording of information. It must be noted that much of the then contemporary writing used the term 'syllabus' rather than 'curriculum'. Teachers were being given guidance on appropriate geographical *content*, little attention, at that time, being paid to spelling out appropriate *skills* and *processes*. The authoritative ministry statement which emphasized the importance of recording was echoed in the GA's next publication *Teaching Geography in the Junior Schools*,

(Geographical Association, 1959). In stating the expectations that
geographers should have of junior school pupils as they transferred to
secondary education, the GA pamphlet borrowed a quotation from
the Board of Education Handbook of Suggestions for Teachers, 1944.
At the end of junior school, a pupil should have:

> . . . a good knowledge of the district in which he lives, its posi-
> tion, climate, neighbouring towns and villages, and local
> industries. He should know the position of the main towns and
> industries and farming areas of the British Isles, and have a
> general acquaintance with the main regions of the world. In
> addition he should be able to use and understand maps in his atlas.
>
> (Geographical Association, 1959, p. 5)

Junior school geography was seen to be an 'essential preliminary to a
more formal and systematic study of that subject in later years' (p. 5).

Once more, the advice offered to teachers was in general terms and
about appropriate content. There was a hint that continuity of experience was important but this was not developed. The skills required in
recording geographical facts through illustrations, models, maps,
diagrams and written work were referred to in passing. For continuity
of curricular experience to be established within any school subject,
teachers require much more than advice about appropriate content.
What is required is a developed pedagogy of the subject. By this we
mean

> a clear statement of the unique contribution of the subject to
> thinking about and understanding the environment;
>
> a recognition of important ideas, concepts and generalizations
> which are central to the subject and whether they are hierarchi-
> cally linked or not;
>
> a recognition of the skills, attitudes and values required to
> operate within the subject area;
>
> a supporting theory of learning associated with knowledge of
> how understanding and thinking develops within the subject
> area;
>
> a related theory of teaching consistent with the view of the sub-
> ject and the understandings that are to be developed in pupils.

To produce such a pedagogy is demanding. An attempt to do so, for what they call the social subjects, will be found in Derricott and Blyth (1979). From the 1960s onwards there is evidence of developments in the UK, some piecemeal, some systematic, towards this goal within the geography community.

In 1965, UNESCO produced a source book for geography teaching which, using the work of Swiss psychologist Emile Marmy, suggested three levels of geographical understanding in children and adolescents which required an unspecialized approach to geography teaching up to the age of 11, which was to be mainly descriptive, a formal approach up to the age of 15 where description begins to give way to explanation, followed by a 'genuine scientific approach' to geography from 15 to 18, where the intellectualizing approach has its origins.

In 1976, MacDonald and Walker noted that the influence of the American High School Project was being felt in the UK. They quote Ambrose who stated that changes in geography were from:

A factually based to a more concept based model of study.
A regional to a systematic approach to work.
Compartmentalized to interdisciplinary work.
Qualitative to quantitative statements.
Lesser to greater emphasis on values.

(MacDonald and Walker, 1976, p. 54)

These trends can be detected in the work of geographers amongst Her Majesty's Inspectorate who in *New Thinking in School Geography* (DES, 1972) argued for a more direct enquiry-based experience being employed by geography teachers so that secondary stage deductions, abstract ideas and broad generalizations could have a firm foundation. The booklet also emphasized the importance of continuity:

The secondary school cannot build successfully on a foundation of failure, lack of understanding, or underachievement which breeds indifference. Nor should it turn its back on what has gone before and ignore the work of the primary school. For geography as for other areas of learning, the problem of transition from primary to secondary school can be eased if the children have a sense of continuity. Teachers in primary and secondary schools have much to learn from one another, and time spent in consultation about programmes of work, resources for learning, methods of teaching and the progress

made by the children individually or in groups, will not be
wasted.   (p. 19)

What had emerged by this point was a growing consensus about the
change of direction in geography teaching in terms of the concepts,
key ideas and skills that might be included in the geography
curriculum. Indeed, the pursuit of graphicacy which had been termed
the 'fourth ace' in the pack alongside literacy, numeracy and
articulacy (Balchin and Coleman, 1965) and defined as 'the communication of relationships that cannot be successfully communicated by
words or mathematical notation alone', was seen as a set of skills
particularly appropriate to the geographer. In search of a pedagogy,
British geographers began to focus increasingly on problems of teaching and learning such concepts and skills.

Long and Roberson (1966) had asserted that the geography learned
in schools should be based on the psychological development of the
child. In the early 1970s the Schools Council's 'Middle Years of
Schooling' project based at Lancaster University (Schools Council,
1972 and 1975) explored the relationships between Piaget's ideas on
cognitive development and school learning. The Lancaster team
indicated that

> Nothing in this model [i.e. Piaget's model] of mental develop-
> ment suggests that the content of geography is in any way un-
> suitable for this age range (8–13 years). In fact our knowledge of
> children's curiosity suggests that they may be highly motivated
> towards the many aspects of geography.   (p. 90)

They conclude that

> . . . much of the teaching . . . would concentrate on concrete evi-
> dence to develop those concepts and skills that children could
> use in concrete situations, though it is expected that towards the
> end of the middle years of schooling some children would be
> able to develop abstract generalizations which would have
> meaning for them.   (p. 101)

Naish (1982) explores further the significance of Piaget's work for the
teacher planning a geography curriculum. To Naish, Piaget's work
has five major implications:

(a) It justifies Fairgreave's (1926) intuitive view that in geography

we should move from the (i) known to the unknown, (ii) particular to the general, (iii) concrete to the abstract.

(b) It allows us to think in terms of accelerated development, if we can find the appropriate teaching techniques, especially in the geographical skills area.

(c) It emphasizes the need for the teacher to ensure that the children are given thorough support in each stage of development by providing the appropriate learning experience.

(d) In the concrete operational years, about 7–12, in geography we need children to work on case studies based on real-life examples in a concrete fashion to build up the child's understanding of the world. Furthermore, stress should be laid on stimulating oral work, structuring language development and the adoption of an inquiry approach to learning.

(e) Curriculum designers in geography should ensure that the curriculum, in terms of key concepts and skills, takes note of the critical periods of mental growth.

Catling and Conner (1981) see the role of the teacher in such a scheme as being, by implication, 'one of structuring the environment and helping the child to make his own discoveries rather than the presentation of direct verbal learning'.

In an operational sense, Marsden (1976) reminds us that we cannot assume that by the time children have reached the secondary school they are at or even near the formal operational stage and that:

At the beginning of the secondary school stage at least, the geography teacher should still be thinking in terms of moving from the familiar to the unfamiliar, the near to the far, the concrete to the abstract and generally be sensitive to each pupil's stage of readiness to undertake a particular learning task.

(Marsden, 1976, p. 136)

Thus when writers such as Naish (1982) and Catling and Conner (1981) refer to the concrete operational phase of 7 to 12 or 13 years we must be extremely cautious and certainly not rigid in the interpretation of the curricular consequences. The chronological age at which individual children pass from concrete to formal operations can vary tremendously and can reach well into the mid-adolescent years and the search for an appropriate pedagogy must bear this in mind.

Bruner (1960, 1967) expresses similar ideas to Piaget's model of mental development in relation to concept attainment and logical

thinking, but in a somewhat different way. As both Graves (1975) and Hall (1976) stress, Bruner feels that the critical influences on cognitive growth are not progression through the Piagetian stages of mental development but rather that the human mind has evolved three modes of representing the environment and events in it. Bruner (1967) maintains that a child conserves past experience or internalizes in one of three ways: through action (enactive), through visual or sensory organization and the use of summarising images (iconic), and through representation in symbols, words or language (symbolic).

As Marsden (1976) observes, 'Meaningful learning is linked with the formation of concepts' (p. 136). Naish (1982) values these as the 'structural steel of thinking'. This being the case, what has been written on them in relation to geography? Graves (1975) defines a concept as being '. . . . . basically a classificatory device which enables the mind to structure reality in a simplified manner by concentrating on the essential attributes of certain experiences' (p. 154).

Having said that, though, concepts can be of many different kinds. A major attempt at classifying them was undertaken by Gagné (1966) who classified them according to 'concepts by observation', since we can relate to them by observing and contrasting concrete experiences, e.g. a port, and 'concepts by definition', which are less related to the concrete, e.g. hinterland. A more detailed example of how these can be used to classify geographical concepts is given by Graves (1975, p. 159). Another way of classifying concepts is hierarchically with the most general, an organizing concept or idea at the top, and more specific objectives lower. Examples of these being used in practice are to be found in the 'History, Geography and Social Science 8–13 Project' (Blyth *et al.*, 1976) and the 'Geography for the Young School Leaver Project' (Schools Council, 1974/5) with their advocacy of key ideas.

What concepts are most relevant to geography? Catling (1975) argues that the central ideas of geography can be reduced to three concepts. These are 'spatial location', 'spatial distribution' and 'spatial relations'. This advice would seem to be too bald and unhelpful to most geography teachers. Others have gone somewhat further. Marsden (1976) puts forward the view that a modern geography course should lie

. . . in the field of the social sciences, in which the spatial area studies and man land traditions converge; in which numeracy is as necessary a skill as literacy and graphicacy; in which inter-

disciplinary thinking is a prerequisite, and in which 'meaning' has a social as well as an intellectual relevance.   (p. 69)

The Geographical Association in 1981 was able to go further in summarizing its view of the geography curriculum from 5 to 16 as follows.

> 5–11. By the age of eleven, pupils should have been introduced to the principal aspects of the physical environment (weather and surface features), patterns of settlement, dominant occupations and forms of transport, and the leisure and recreational facilities of their home areas. They should also have been introduced to the variety of environments in which people live both at home and overseas. In these latter studies teachers will seek to avoid any stereotyping of groups and nations and their pupils should have access to accurate, reliable and up-to-date sources of information.

> 11–16. In modern geography courses pupils gain understanding of issues and problems as well as knowledge of places and people. Included in the problems studied are changes in population, industrial location, foreign trade patterns, pollution and conservation. Courses on geography, in addition to giving basic factual knowledge, emphasise the development of knowledge skills and attitudes linked to geographical concepts and generalisations which appear interesting and significant to the adolescent. By the age of sixteen a pupil should have been introduced in a systematic way to the principal inter-relationships between man's activities and the physical environment encompassing studies of population changes, farming systems, transport, industry, settlement, natural resources and landscape evaluation.

> (Geographical Association, 1981b)

It can be seen, therefore, that writers of educational geography are generally in agreement about the teaching of the subject. However, the basic problem of discontinuity in geographical experience is never tackled. It is rarely ever mentioned but in reality it is always a potential problem. There is, of course, no reason to suppose continuity of curricular experience in geography will always take place naturally and smoothly. Why should there be? As Mills (1981) points out, '. . . . . there is a tendency for geographical work to be organised in a different way in primary and middle schools than in secondary ones'.

There is also the delicate problem of which geographical topics and concepts are likely to be grasped by pupils of one age range rather than another. As Bailey (1980) wryly observes:

> We are not even sure that general advice on this . . . can be worked out because of the great variations between pupils, schools, teachers and each child's learning environment. The lack of a good breakfast patently affects a child's responses to abstract ideas.

Even if we assume that we know what, how and when to teach to whom, there still remains the problem of progression in this geography teaching, which as Bennetts (1981) points out is:

> . . . . . an element in the structure of courses which has received rather less attention than it deserves. Such neglect is understandable. Textbook writers are rarely explicit about the principles they use to select and organise content, and most teachers have probably relied more on tradition, experience and an intuitive feel for what is appropriate for each stage of a course, than on any explicit recognition of the principles concerned with the process of learning.

This view seems to be confirmed; for example, by H.M. Inspectors in their primary school survey (DES 1978a) when they found that much of the work in geography tended to be superficial and lacking in progression (p. 75).

However, we would argue that there has been increasing attention paid to this aspect of geography teaching from a variety of sources. The Schools Council's Project 'History, Geography and Social Science 8–13' in its curriculum planning handbook (Blyth *et al.*, 1976) paid special attention to sequence and progression (pp. 125–142). The DES (1978b) pamphlet *The Teaching of Ideas in Geography* has a section on progression (pp. 11–13) and emphasizes the use of progression in syllabus construction by teachers. Also writers like Bailey (1980) and Bennetts (1981) have written articles about progression and geography. The Geographical Association has this to say on the matter:

> In the past geography in school was viewed as a subject in which pupils were expected to accumulate large amounts of factual

information. The focus was more upon accumulation than progression. Increasingly, geography teachers are endeavouring to match their courses to the development of pupils' understanding. It is essential that teachers of successive age levels collaborate in their course planning.

(Geographical Association, 1981b)

Here we get to the heart of the matter: for as Tidswell (1981) rightly points out discontinuity between primary and secondary schools will impede a smooth overall progression in geographical education. He goes on to argue for urgent action if continuity and progression in the curriculum are therefore to have any true meaning.

This brings us to the embarrassing question of what assumptions are being made by secondary teachers about the knowledge and skills being acquired in the primary schools. A glance through the survey conducted by H.M. Inspectorate on primary schools (DES 1978a) would show how difficult and dangerous it would be to generalize about the teaching of geography in primary schools without knowing the actual local situation prevailing. We would argue that at primary level little thought anyway is given to what children will be doing by way of geography when they reach the secondary school, primary school teachers feeling that this is beyond their terms of reference. Does this matter? We think it does. According to Catling and Conner (1981):

Learning starts from 'where the learner is'. He brings to the situation the sum total of his experiences at the moment. Effective teaching starts at this point and builds upon its foundations.

If we are to have meaningful learning and teaching then the discontinuity between primary and secondary schools must be bridged. As Carr (1980) observes, if, for example, we view the whole idea of graphicacy as a central objective in geography teaching and:

if one accepts that a structured syllabus is necessary to allow for the acquisition of map-reading skills, then it becomes clear that this structure needs to span the divide between primary and secondary levels. If exercises on spatial awareness and mapping are to be done in the junior school then liaison can, indeed must, take place.

There are a few published examples of attempts at achieving continuity of geographical experience, for example, Bates (1978) and Freeman (1981), both of whom specifically deal with field work across the primary-secondary devide. As Rowbotham (1982) argues, this should be encouraged so that a shared understanding can develop as to what each school is trying to do in the area of visits and field work teaching. In general, though, these attempts at continuity are limited in their scope and are certainly rare. If continuity of curricular experience in geography between primary and secondary schools is to become a reality, then changes are necessary. Secondary schools will need no longer to regard their first year pupils as 'blank slates', and primary schools will need to be less insular in their approach. At present, the barriers remain and there is little evidence of any fundamental change of attitude or practice.

Curricular continuity in geography: some fieldwork

[In an attempt to assess the effects of activities within the academic community of geographers to arrive at a pedagogy of geography, Szpakowski conducted some fieldwork in four primary schools, each of which was a feeder school to a local secondary comprehensive school. When interviewing the four primary heads he was given permission to use his tape recorder. His reports on these four schools use mainly the transcribed words of the heads concerned. The secondary headteacher offered an interview which was not taped; his views are presented in an agreed summary of the interview. No claim is made about the generalizability of the findings. Readers are simply asked to relate this vignette to their own experiences. Full details of the work can be found in Szpakowksi (1983).

The fieldwork took place in a commuter suburb in NW England. Parental interest in education is high. Until the effects of the 1980 Education Act began to make an impact (helped by falling rolls) each of the primary schools in the area was tightly 'zoned' to one of the two secondary comprehensive schools. As it is now becoming possible for parents of children leaving any of the dozen primary schools to send their children to the secondary school of their choice, the simple four-into-one relationship described in Szpakowski's work is slowly breaking down with consequential complexities for those teachers pursuing curricular continuity.]

Primary school 1

Geography here is classed as part of environment studies . . . I encourage radio and television . . . Records should be kept to avoid repetition of topics . . . We are interested in stimulating children to learn . . . We don't test in this area of the curriculum as it would destroy motivation . . . Retaining and learning information is the work of the secondary school . . . We use programmes like *Near and Far* at the top and *Finding Out* for lower juniors . . . Before they go to the secondary school they do a lot of mapwork because we go to the Lakes . . . We spend a week in the Lake District and geography comes into that . . . We don't have a syllabus for these studies . . . The Inspectors who came last term were horrified at this but we weren't . . . We do have aims but we don't really need to write them down . . . If teachers are stuck they can use the Oxford Junior Project (Martin, 1980 and Elliot, 1980) of which I have got a copy of each . . . We have a Scale Two for environmental studies and drama . . . We have attempted continuity in maths, with the secondary school department . . . Sorted out methods and expectations . . . No feeling of dictation . . . It would help to know what goes on in other areas of the secondary schools' curriculum and for us to know what they want . . . This is me talking from my ivory tower.

(Headteacher)

It was difficult at this school to find out how geography was being taught as there was no syllabus. The only document passed on to me was a checklist of what this school wanted to encourage by way of investigation and research, which listed 1) developing interests, 2) research skills, 3) enquiry skills, 4) concept development of social skills and empathy. I managed to find out that in the fourth year what was covered varied from year to year depending on circumstances prevailing at the time. This year they were investigating services in their local town for one term. A further investigation of local buildings (using the building chapter out of the *Oxford New Geography* (Martin, 1980 and Elliot, 1980) series) plus a look at journeys to work and travel in general took up another term. In the summer term they followed up on the field work week in the Lake District.

Primary school 2

We have three geography specialists so we have an expertise

in this subject . . . We use geography in our English Department as well . . . Education should be from 5–16 . . . if we look at education as a continuous process it enriches everything we do . . . We have had ongoing discussions with the maths department for a long time . . . They have changed work in the light of what we have said . . . It's a sequential subject so it's easier but we should do it for all . . . Can't be anything worse than the secondary school finding pupils being sent to them that lack the necessary tools or knowledge . . . There must be no dictation though . . . We teach geography as a subject . . . However we do encourage teachers to cross the boundaries . . . Our fourths go to London every year and this is very much a geography and history visit . . . Impetus for the maths liaison came from the Teachers' Centre I think . . . We have had some meetings with the English Department and he even came here . . . Meetings have also been held with the history and geography departments at the secondary school but nothing came of these . . . Continuity programmes are held back by a lack of time, money and resources . . . I would like to see teacher exchange between the secondary school and ours so that someone could get a view of the whole curriculum . . . We have a Scale Two for humanities who looks after geography.

(Headteacher)

This school had a geography syllabus they worked from with an introduction emphasizing that 'We are anxious to create an attitude of mind to the subject rather than instil a large number of geographical facts'. There are four stated aims, five general suggestions on how to encourage 'good' geography teaching and a separate section on recording of information by pupils. In terms of content there was a triumvirate of topics taught in all four years. Each year local studies and the weather made up two of these but in year one the third was made up of children in remote parts of the world; in year two children specifically from Europe, North and South America and China; in year three a study of the British Isles and finally in year four the universe and world regions based on population density.

Primary school 3

The greater the continuity the better it is . . . We have had contact with the maths department . . . We would welcome liaison with others but there hasn't been the same enthusiasm

. . . I tried to foster this with the music department as I am interested in this but I got no response from the head of music there . . . Children want to know about the 'big school' and I always take them there when I can to look at, for example, art displays, plays, and so on . . . Even when there is good will as with the maths department it is not easy as each primary school has different ideas on how things should be done . . . In the secondary school even with a common syllabus each teacher can have a different approach. We have had meetings for maths and when we have had this contact with maths the juniors all have different syllabuses . . . Anyway even if it is on a syllabus it is difficult to ensure that it is being done . . . Primary schools also do not like being dictated to – it makes them feel threatened though I personally have never felt this with our secondary school . . . We have had a meeting with the geography department staff and this has been followed up on a personal level with their feeding materials to us and giving us use of their photocopying facilities . . . He must also have found out some kind of idea of what pupils have done here through these informal visits . . . In maths and English it is much easier to pass on records, for example, reading tests but this is not the case in environmental studies . . . In environmental studies we start with the self and here and now . . . Subjects are more appropriate at secondary level . . . Secondary schools are constrained by exam boards . . . we can adopt a far more inter-disciplinary approach . . . We have a Scale Two post for environmental education . . . Her brief was to be in geography and history for each age group using local studies as the basis for this . . . I would like to do more continuity with English but perhaps the onus might be on me doing something . . . The maths initiative was from the secondary school but there is no reason why the junior school shouldn't take the initiative . . . All of this is walking a tightrope in terms of getting cooperation and agreement . . . Also look at what happened when the head of maths left earlier this year – suddenly no meetings.

(Headteacher)

Here then geography was taught as part of an environmental studies scheme. The syllabus had no stated aims but there was a very detailed list of topics to be covered each year:

Year one: (a) Self (e.g. physical features, senses), (b) The Family (e.g. members, occupations), (c) School (e.g. classrooms, personnel), (d) Occupations, (e) Houses and Homes (e.g. types), (f) Shops, (g) Transport, (h) Farming

Year two: (a) Houses and Homes (historical), (b) The Street, (c) A Road

Year three: Detailed study of the town they live in

Year four: (a) Merseyside (e.g. Liverpool, Land Use, Neighbourhoods, Transport), (b) Work Survey, (c) Shopping in Large Towns and Cities, (d) Pollution and Conservation, (e) Lake District, based on a 5-day field work visit.

Primary school 4

We have a geography syllabus . . . We complement this old syllabus with material from the *Oxford New Geography* series which includes some physical geography, something the old syllabus hasn't . . . We think of it more as a science . . . When they get to the secondary school we believe geography will really be a new subject to them . . . We would welcome dialogue with the first year teachers of geography and history. We went to one meeting called by the geography department there which we found useful . . . They gave us a basic idea of what they teach and it allowed the primary schools to standardize terminology . . . We still do different things and there is individualism but at least the pupils won't be having to cover the same ground at secondary level . . . This is the only attempt at continuity I know of . . . There is the Authority's local religious education syllabus which we use and that follows on into the secondary school . . . The initiative in the case of maths comes from the secondary school . . . All four junior schools meet with them once a year . . . We didn't find any major stumbling blocks though I did feel there might be a threat at first . . . More could be done with other subjects . . . It would be helpful in terms of purchasing equipment . . . It would be good to see teacher exchanges between primary and secondary but teacher release time would be difficult . . . Whether primary school heads want to open doors to their domains is questionable though . . . With parental choice through the 1980 Act this will make continuity problems greater; four heads might agree with a secondary school over continuity, seventeen won't.

(Headteacher)

In this school geography was again taught as a subject. There was a syllabus but with no aims or guidance other than a list of content areas to be covered each year. In year one there were to be (a) Local Studies, (b) Children in Far Off Lands; in year two (a) Local Studies, (b) Children of Other Lands (e.g. Norway); in year three (a) Local Studies, (b) British Isles, and in year four (a) Local Studies, (b) Regions of the World based on population density.

The secondary school

Here I have tried to draw together the headteacher's feelings into a series of points.

1. He basically felt that continuity was important but more from a pastoral and social point of view than a curricular one.
2. Continuity never really surfaces as a number one priority in terms of needing attention paid to it. One can get by without it if needs be.
3. Certainly he felt that continuity was more important in subjects like maths and to a lesser extent English but of much less importance in subjects like geography and history.
4. In practice he sees continuity of curricular experience as basically a paper exercise of exchange of syllabuses between the primary and the secondary school.
5. The major benefits as he saw it were that if continuity existed there would be no need for repetition of topics and all children would be at the same place at the same time, making the secondary school's job easier.
6. In his school attempts at continuity with the primary schools had taken place with maths (still in operation), geography (now just with one primary school), history (nothing more than an initial meeting) and English (never really got off the ground).
7. In practice the greatest continuity was to be found with pupils learning individual musical instruments as the peripatetic

teacher taking them at primary level is the same person at secondary level.

8. The initiative for continuity matters always seemed to come from the secondary school.

The geography syllabus in years one–three had aims and objectives but the basic framework was traditional. Year one studied (a) local studies, (b) the North West (the region in which the school is sited), (c) The British Isles; year two, the Southern Continents; year three, the Northern Continents. Key concepts and skills to be developed were stated and topics and themes were chosen with these in mind.

What did these interviews and observations highlight in terms of continuity of curricular experience, especially in relation to geography?

(a) It seems that the schools concerned viewed continuity as a relatively simple exercise of making sure that pupils had covered common ground at primary schools so that repetition did not occur at the secondary school.

(b) It appears the primary schools were more interested in fostering continuity than was the secondary school. In practice, though, most of the initiative came from the secondary school's heads of department.

(c) The primary schools did feel threatened by the secondary school's concern regarding their curriculum and were wary of being told what to do.

(d) The secondary school saw no pressing need for continuity except in the area of mathematics. One feels they could get along without it.

(e) A temporary exchange of teachers between the primary and secondary schools would give a shared understanding of problems and might make continuity easier.

(f) The basic problems with promoting continuity seem to be a lack of time, money and effort and resources.

(g) Personalities matter greatly in that the head of maths approached the problem very carefully and was therefore trusted by the primary heads. The head of geography had established a personal friendship with the head of one of the primary schools.

(h) Continuity was felt to be more important and relevant in subjects like mathematics than in subjects like geography.

(i) The four primary schools varied very greatly in how geography was taught. It was difficult to see how their work fitted in with the secondary school's work in geography.

(j) There had been an attempt by the head of geography to come to an understanding with the primaries over continuity some years ago. One meeting was held but little had resulted from it except in relation to one primary school, with which meetings did continue but of a very informal nature.

Curriculum Coordination and Continuity in the Second and Third Years of a 9–13 Middle School

Mary Atkins

[The next contribution describes practice in a 9–13 middle school. It is written by Mary Atkins who is a very experienced middle school teacher. For statistical purposes 8–12 middle schools are deemed to be primary schools and 9–13 schools are deemed secondary. One of the educational justifications used in setting up middle schools was that such schools should act as a bridge between primary and secondary traditions. In the now famous words of the Plowden Report (p. 146, para. 383):

> If the middle school is to be a new and progressive force it must develop further the curriculum, methods and attitudes which exist at present in junior schools. It must move forward to what is now regarded as secondary school work, but it must not move so far away that it loses the best of primary education as we know it now.

From this it can be seen that the middle school was envisaged as the organization to provide a smooth transition from the education of childhood to the education of adolescence. The advocates of middle schools argued that as relatively small organizations, the schools would be able to provide pastoral care and guidance for their pupils which reflected the needs of children in this age group. They would also be able to organize curricular experiences that paced the children's development. Much effort was put into the establishment of year group teams and the coordination of curricular activities. If smallness was seen to be the desirable asset of middle schools in the late 1960s and early 1970s, with the coming of falling rolls it is now one of the grave disadvantages middle schools face as with dwindling staffs they try to continue to provide a wide and balanced curriculum.

To what extent have some of the long established middle schools delivered their promise on continuity? Mary Atkins describes the considerable energy and organization that goes into smoothing the transition from lower to upper school in one middle school. If middle schools are to achieve credibility with parents then a major task is to convince parents that the planned curriculum, especially for the second and third year pupils, represents a progression towards more challenging work which is similar to, if not superior to, the kind of work expected in traditional secondary schools. Mary Atkins gives a clear description of efforts made to communicate with both pupils and parents on this issue.]

Introduction

This paper endeavours to give a picture of the way in which a 9–13 middle school approaches the problem of coordinating the education of children in the second and third years. It will indicate the steps which have been evolved to smooth the transition from the second to the third year, and will comment on curriculum content, the acquisition of skills, teaching methods, sizes of teaching groups, record keeping and pastoral care, trying to show how the children are prepared for the demands made upon them, and how all teachers are involved in planning and discussion.

The situation described is that at the time of writing. As part of the current evaluation, some of the third year children, their parents and the teachers have been asked, by means of questionnaires, for their perceptions of the transition. It may be that, as a result of that, and as a consequence of possible changes in teacher-pupil ratio in the current round of educational cuts, some changes may occur. There are at present approximately 580 children on roll, and 30 teachers.

The School – its Ethos and Organization

When this school opened, as the county's first middle school, the town in which it is situated was a small market town whose education had previously been provided by primary schools and a secondary modern school. Children who passed the 11+ examination attended grammar schools in neighbouring towns. When the three-tier comprehensive system was set up, the new middle school was served by a number of village schools, as well as by first schools in the town, and it was established in the premises previously occupied by the secondary school, while the upper school was housed in new buildings on an adjoining site, the two schools sharing certain facilities.

From the beginning, the head and his staff worked together to evolve the school's ethos, and to establish criteria in developing its policies. They aimed to meet the needs of every individual child in all aspects of his or her development, intellectual, physical, emotional and social. Since the time when the school first opened, it has always maintained a climate in which all staff have been encouraged to contribute to its development, and changes in organization and curriculum have taken place. There is constant on-going discussion, questioning and evaluation, resulting in improvements in the opportunities offered. As the headmaster states in his notes to parents, the school aims 'to foster a desire for learning and the development of an enquiring mind, and to encourage the acquisition of knowledge and skills through interests, attitudes and aesthetic awareness.'

The school's organization in the first two years aims to provide the children with security in the shape of a form teacher who is responsible for their welfare and directs their studies, thus smoothing for them the transition from first and village schools which are much smaller entities than the middle school. To this end also, most of their work takes place in self-contained year areas, so that they do not feel 'lost' and bewildered. However, as will be seen later, they have significant contact with many other teachers, in specialist roles, and experience of working in other areas of the school, where there are specialist facilities, so that they are gradually prepared for work in the third and fourth years, which is subject-based. This in its turn prepares them for the situation in which they find themselves when they proceed to the upper school.

Teaching methods vary according to the subject and the size of the group, but throughout the school, the children have a variety of experiences, ranging from didactic methods to learning by enquiry. Staff workshops are held from time to time, in which subjects of importance to teachers throughout the school are aired, and common policies established, as for example, the teaching of spelling and handwriting, the preparation of worksheets, the introduction and development of study skills, the approach to assessing children's work, the place of homework, rewards and sanctions.

Records are kept, both for individuals and for groups, of all work covered, incorporating checklists of concepts, skills and attitudes which it is desirable for children to have acquired, and these are passed on as the children progress through the middle school, to the upper school.

The decision to change the organization at the beginning of the third year, so that the children could experience more specialist teaching in depth, was made deliberately, and was firmly based on the belief that at this stage the majority of children are ready for these changes, a belief clearly borne out by the replies to the children's questionnaires. However, a change in organization does not reflect a change in ethos or in attitude. The philosophy of treating the children as individuals prevails throughout the school, and the commitment of every member of staff to the pastoral care of the children with whom they come into contact is impressive.

Organization of the Second Year

During their second year the children work in mixed ability form groups, with a form teacher who has responsibility for their programme of studies. They are taught for much of their time by the form teacher, in their own form base, all within one compact part of the school, which includes a small library area, art and craft bay and cloakrooms.

Overall responsibility for the second year lies with one of the deputy heads, who coordinates every aspect of life in the first two years. In addition, she teaches in the third and fourth years, and liaises closely with the year leaders in the upper part of the school. She is assisted by assistant year leaders in each of the first two years.

There is a declared policy of enabling the majority of staff to have some teaching time in both the lower and upper parts of the school. Almost all the first and second year form teachers teach their 'special subject' to third or fourth year groups, and similarly, most of those who spend the majority of their time teaching third and fourth years work also with first and second year groups. This movement of staff goes a long way towards facilitating a smooth passage from the second to the third year, since the children have contact with the majority of the staff, both before and after the transfer.

The work covered during the second year is planned and evaluated by the form teachers and the year leader, as a team, in consultation with curriculum leaders, who have responsibility for their subject vertically throughout the school. This ensures that both subject specialists and form teachers are aware of the skills and concepts which need to be covered during a specific year, and of the place of the work in any year in the whole programme of studies, so that experiences can be carefully structured to meet stated aims and objectives. It also avoids a situation where, for example, work covered during the second year is repeated in the third year.

Subjects taught are mathematics; English, as a separate discipline and within the context of other work; handwriting; music; art, craft and domestic crafts; French; environmental studies, which includes science, geography and history; physical education, including swimming; religious education within the context of other subject disciplines, and in form period time. Teaching sessions are one hour in length, but the form teacher is able to use the time flexibly, offering the children variety in the demands made upon them. Homework is set during the first two years, but not on a regular basis. It is aimed at establishing the idea that it is sometimes of value to do some exploratory or follow-up work at home, in preparation for the upper part of the school where assignments are set regularly. All children are encouraged to spend time reading for pleasure, in an attempt to develop in them the reading habit.

Although the children in the lower part of the school spend most of their time in their year areas, they do become familiar with the other areas of the school, since when the subject specialists are teaching them, in form groups or in smaller groups, they are taken to the various specialist areas, such as the home economics room, art and craft rooms, music room, farm unit and science laboratories, to make use of the equipment there. In addition, they are encouraged to make use of the Central Resource Centre, and those who need extra help with literacy skills are frequently to be found making their own way to the tutorial room and working there.

Pastoral care of the children in the second year lies in the hands of the form teacher, assisted when necessary by the year leaders. Parents are involved as much as possible; for example, they assist in different areas of the school, they help supervise children when they are out on school visits. In addition, they are invited to interviews with the form teachers twice in the year, to discuss their children's progress, and should any problems arise, they are again involved in discussion with the teachers. Children are encouraged, from the beginning of their time in school, to become self-disciplined and responsible for their actions at all times, whether supervised or unsupervised. Thus, the school is open during breaks and lunchtimes, and after initial training, the children are allowed to choose whether to stay in and occupy themselves with a quiet activity, or to go out. Expectations of behaviour are therefore set, both inside and outside the classroom, which pertain throughout the school.

There are numerous extra-curricular activities in which children are invited to participate, some of which are open to every year. In addition, all children have opportunities to go away for a few days on residential courses. In the first two years these are led by the form teacher, so that the children feel secure, accompanied by another teacher who teaches mostly in third and fourth years. This prepares them for courses which are offered in the upper part of the school by subject specialists.

Organization of the Third Year

Organization in the third year is different from that in the second year, but, as has already been indicated, the children have been prepared for the changes in a variety of ways. The children are arranged in mixed ability form groups, each with one, or sometimes two, form teachers. As in the first two years, it is the form teacher who has responsibility for the child, both in pastoral matters, and in the sense of having an overall view of the child's performance in the different areas of the curriculum. The form teachers meet the children in their form twice daily, and in addition, where possible, contribute to their teaching in their own subject discipline. Overall responsibility for the year lies with year leaders, who coordinate the various aspects of life, advising on pastoral matters, and establishing links between the teachers of the various subject disciplines, with reference to specific groups or individuals.

For teaching purposes, two form groups are linked, and divided into three tutor groups, for each subject discipline. These tutor groups are mixed ability, with two exceptions. In mathematics the groups are setted at the end of the first term in the third year, the set at the lower end of the scale being a smaller one, so that children may be given additional help. In French, each form group is taught in two sets, divided according to aptitude for the language. In addition, extra help is given to children with reading and writing problems, during English sessions, by the tutorial staff. With the exception of French, which is taught in half-hour sessions, the lessons last one hour, or two in the case of practical subjects. Subjects taught are mathematics, English, French, science, humanities, (geography, history, religious education), arts and crafts (including metalwork, woodwork, domestic crafts), expressive arts (art, music, drama), physical education. Because of the way in which staff are deployed throughout the school, the children will have as tutors in many of the subject disciplines people whom they already know very well.

Work to be covered in the third year is planned and evaluated in regular meetings attended by all those who teach a particular subject discipline. The meetings are frequently attended also by the Head or one of the deputies, who can each oversee several disciplines, and act

as coordinators or consultants if required. In this way possible duplication of content (for example, a study of the Normans in French and
humanities) can be avoided.

In addition, meetings of the year leaders and the form teachers
within the year are held regularly, and when necessary subject tutors
are invited to these meetings. The latter is always the case following
interviews with parents. These are arranged in two ways. Twice a year
Curricular Evenings are held, in which parents are invited to meet all
the subject tutors who teach their children, by appointment. As a
follow-up a few weeks later, they are invited to meet the form
teachers, with whom they can discuss specific problems, or gain an
overall view of the child's development in school.

Transfer From the Second to the Third Year

At the beginning of the summer term, the coordinator and form
teachers of the second year meet to discuss matters of concern relating
to the placement of children in the third year. This generally involves
creating four administrative mixed ability groups out of five classes,
which provides scope and flexibility for movement, if necessary. Both
social and academic criteria are used, and parents' views are often
·ought. In this way, groupings which have proved socially and/or
academically successful can be maintained, whereas children who
come into difficulties in either sphere, with their peers, can be placed
in new groupings, and so given a fresh start. For the majority, *status
quo* pertains. Towards the end of the summer term, second year form
teachers spend time discussing their children with those who will be
their form teachers in the third year.

Records are brought fully up to date and passed on to the third-year
leader, form teachers and tutors. Recommendations are made regarding the children's placement in teaching groups. At the beginning of
the autumn term, a meeting is held between the new third year staff
and the previous second year staff, and important urgent information
is passed on by word of mouth, so that no problem which had been
dealt with during the second year can raise its head again without the
staff currently concerned with the child being aware of it and ready to
cope with it immediately. During this term, there is a great deal of
dialogue among the staff, involving feedback and advice. In addition,
the children are able, if they feel the need, to consult their second year
teachers about any difficulties which may arise.

Evaluation of Transfer Procedure

As was mentioned earlier, part of this evaluation took the form of questionnaires, designed in an informal manner to measure the perceptions of some third year children, parents and staff of the extent to which the systems which have been set up succeed in smoothing transfer from the second to the third year. The questionnaires were administered shortly before the end of the autumn term. The children were asked questions designed to discover the extent to which they were already familiar, at the beginning of the third year, with the teaching areas in which they received their lessons, and with the teachers by whom they were taught. In addition, there were questions aimed at measuring the success of their preparation for work in the third year, in terms of curriculum continuity and homework.

It was clear from the replies that the majority met very little difficulty in organizing themselves to bring in the necessary books and equipment, and to find their way to the appropriate rooms for lessons. Almost all of them knew well at least one of their two form teachers, and more than half of their subject teachers, and found it fairly easy to ask for help if they needed to.

There appears to have been little problem over the continuity of the work, though a number of them did have some difficulty early on in remembering to do set homework. The majority welcomed the new way of working, with different teachers for different subjects, many finding the work 'more interesting', which would indicate that they were ready for a change and an opportunity to study more specialist subjects in greater depth than previously.

The parents were asked for their observations on how their children had coped with the changes at the beginning of the third year, and about their own contact with the teachers. Unfortunately, it was not possible to ask all the parents, but of those who completed the questionnaires (a reasonable cross-section), almost all were very satisfied with the transfer, which they felt had gone smoothly, the one or two early problems being quickly sorted out by the teachers. They were also very happy with the timing of parents' interviews in early November with subject teachers, followed up a few weeks later by meetings with form teachers.

The questionnaires completed by the teachers tried to assess the usefulness of the various systems which had been set up to help them know in advance the children whom they taught in the third year. It was clear from the replies that of most value was time spent in contact with the children during their first and second years, in teaching them, running clubs and other extra-curricular activities for them, or on residential courses. Of comparable value was time spent talking with the second year form teachers during the summer term about children who would be in their third year form, recommendations made concerning the placement of children in teaching groups, and the meeting held at the beginning of the autumn term for all third year teachers.

Generally speaking, the teachers were impressed with the children's attitude to, and ability to cope with, the work at the beginning of the third year, commenting, however, that they did need help in organizing themselves to remember homework. The specialist teachers themselves took responsibility for the fact that a few problems emerged concerning curriculum continuity, and, together with the first and second year form teachers, have set to work to tackle these. Suggestions made by them for modifications to transfer arrangements and organization are forming the basis for further discussion.

Conclusion

It is hoped that this paper has given a picture of the organization of the second and third years in this 9–13 middle school, of the awareness of staff of the problems that can arise as a child progresses from one year to the next, and of the steps taken to prevent and combat these problems. The success of the systems which have been set up depend a great deal on the willingness of the staff to be fully involved in the life of the school, in planning and evaluating, in discussing current issues, in working as members of a team, and in building close relationships with the children, so as to enrich their lives in school.

Evaluation of Transfer Questionnaires

Third Year Children

We are trying to find out how easy people find it to move from the 2nd year to the 3rd year, and whether they meet any particular problems. Please could you tick the appropriate answer, or give answers, thinking back to the beginning of this term?

1 (a) Did you have any problem finding your way to your lessons in different rooms?

   (Tick one)   Not at all ____   Once ____   2–5 times ____
   More often ____

  (b) Did you have any problem remembering to bring in the correct books or equipment?

   (Tick one)   Not at all ____   Once ____   2–5 times ____
   More often ____

2 (a) How many of your subject teachers in the 3rd year did you already know *very* well? ____

  (b) How many did you know *quite* well? ____

  (c) How many were completely *new* to you? ____

  (d) Have you found it easy to ask your subject teachers for help?

   (Tick one)   Yes ____   Fairly easy ____   Not very easy ____
   I haven't needed to ____

  (e) Did you already know at least one of your form teachers?

   (Tick one)   Yes, very well ____   Yes, quite well ____
   Not very well ____   Not at all ____

  (f) Have you found it easy to talk to your form teachers or year master about problems you have met?

   (Tick one)   Yes ____   Fairly easy ____   Not very easy ____
   I haven't needed to ____
   (Give details if you wish)

(g) Have you talked to your 2nd year form teacher or year mistress about any matters that have arisen in the 3rd year?

(Tick one) Yes, several times ____ Yes, once or twice ____
No, not at all ____
(Give details if you wish)

3 (a) Have you found that the work in the 3rd year has followed on smoothly from that in the 2nd year?

(Tick one) Yes, generally ____ Not very ____
(Give details if you wish)

(b) Has it been easy to change to working for a number of different teachers, instead of mainly for one form teacher?

(Tick one) Yes ____ Fairly easy ____ No ____
(Give details if you wish)

(c) Have you had any difficulties getting homework done?

(Tick one) Yes, often ____ Yes, once or twice ____
No, not at all ____
If you ticked *Yes*, explain the sort of difficulties you have had
(e.g. not enough time, no books, work too difficult, forgot . . ?)

4 What advantages or disadvantages have you found in working with different groups of children in different subject teaching groups, as opposed to having been always with the same children in your second year form?

Parents of Third Year Children
(*There is no need to put your name on this*)

We are trying to establish whether transfer of children from the 2nd to the 3rd year is a smooth one, and would be grateful for your observations on the following:

1. As you know, in the 3rd year, the children have several different subject teachers, in contrast to the 2nd year, where they worked largely with one form teacher. Did your child find it easy to cope with this change?

2. Were there any particular problems? If so, were they sorted out by the child, with or without the help of a teacher, or by you?

3. Did you find it helpful to meet your child's *subject* teachers in November?

   Would you have preferred to have met them earlier or later in the term?

   If so, when, and why?

4. Would you have preferred to have met the *form* teachers earlier this term, or next term?

If you have any other comments, please add them here.

Thank you very much.
Please place this in the box when you leave.

Staff Involved in the 3rd Year

We are trying to establish whether the systems we operate in transferring children from the 2nd to 3rd year are achieving their objectives, and we would be grateful for your observations on the following:

1. How useful do you find the following in helping you to know the children in your *forms* and/or *tutor groups* well, with regard to their attitudes to work, potential ability and behaviour?

   Please rate (1) Very useful   (2) Fairly useful   (3) Not very useful
   (4) Other comments?

   (a) Your own time spent in the previous year, working with 2nd year children.

   (b) Time spent talking at the end of the previous (summer) term, with the 2nd year form teachers.

   (c) Records handed on from the 2nd year

   (d) Contact with children in clubs and other activities

  (e) The meeting held at the beginning of the Autumn Term for all 3rd year tutors.

2. (a) How helpful have you found the suggestions made for the placement of children in tutor groups, issued at the end of the Summer Term?

      (Please tick) Very helpful _____   Fairly helpful _____
                  Not very helpful   Other comments?

  (b) Is there any other information that you think would be useful?

3. Have you any comments to make on the composition of 3rd year groups and on their pairings?

4. How would you assess the children's attitude to work, in general, when they enter the 3rd year?

5. Are there any problems in the teaching of your subject in the 3rd year, in respect of the children's previous experience?

6. To what extent do you feel that the children are able to cope at the beginning of the 3rd year with:

   (a) movement to teaching areas
   (b) the work
   (c) homework?

Please add any other comments you may wish to make.

Thank you.

CHAPTER FIVE

A Closer Look at Curriculum Continuity: some further analysis

From Class Teacher to Specialist Teachers: curricular continuity and school organization

Les Tickle

[Les Tickle examines the organizational characteristics of schools and relates these to problems associated with the establishment of continuity. He treats continuity not as naturally desirable but as problematic. His point is that for ten to twelve-year-olds, whether transferring from primary to secondary schools or remaining within middle schools, this is a period of transition from generalist to specialist teaching. Indeed, pressures from prestigious and influential bodies, such as HMI in the Primary School Survey of 1978, indicate that the use of more specialist teachers in this age group is desirable. Tickle concludes that this movement towards specialism leads to *planned discontinuity*. A concept such as this implies that at transition children encounter specialist teaching from (say) geographers and historians or scientists that they may not have experienced before. It may also imply a more formal organization of content as reflected in the secondary school timetable, but does it also mean a necessary change in teaching style? For many children it may mean a need to adjust to a more didactic teaching style, but not necessarily so. Is it that the key to continuity lies not in how curriculum content is organized and arranged but in the elusive notion of teaching style? If this is so then the concept of curricular continuity becomes even more difficult to envisage.

I now return to the idea of *planned discontinuity*. Most of the evidence collected in the research for the present volume leads me to the view that the curricular experiences of children suffer from unplanned discontinuity. This arises from the tradition of the autonomy of the school and the individual teacher. The gate to the Secret Garden of the Curriculum has until recently been kept locked and barred. Now that parts of the Secret Garden have been opened to the public, even for limited hours, the gardeners are being asked to explain the random nature of the design and perhaps to question and to justify why things are how they are.

Planned discontinuity can be justified. There are many things that happen in schools when they do because teachers believe that these events are indicators to children that they are growing, developing or maturing. Jennifer Nias in the contribution which follows indicates some of these when she refers to country dancing being considered a lower school activity and selection for team games an upper school activity. Many other activities of this nature will come to mind such as access to certain equipment and specialist rooms which is given to older children or certain privileges of taking part in relatively unsupervised activity as a sign of maturity. The plan or purpose behind such practices is rarely made explicit.]

In the period since middle schools emerged, a number of practical innovations, expectations, demands and criticisms have concerned teachers, headteachers, parents and Local Education Authority officers as being in need of action and attention. Some of these concerns lie in the realm of curriculum coordination; record keeping and transfer; horizontal and vertical liaison between teachers in year groups or schools; the effects and effectiveness of specialist subject teachers upon non-specialist teachers; and the appraisal of schemes or programmes of learning which imply sequence or extension. The list could be longer. Each of these concerns derives from consideration of problems in, and means of improving, children's learning through better planning and coordination of curricula.

From the teachers' point of view, liaison concerning curricular matters has become an increasingly demanding part of their role. There is little doubt that liaison between teachers was not previously held to be as important as it became in middle schools and three-tier systems. It became a key word, representing what was seen by some as a key activity, deriving from a perceived need to bring closer together the decision-making process and decisions of teachers working at various points through which pupils would pass – class to class, year to year, or school to school. Where gaps or unnecessary overlaps in the experience of pupils were seen as a problem, liaison was seen as offering the way towards potential solutions. Given the extent to which consultation occurs in practice, and the conditions which make it possible, the coordination of curricular practice and communication between teachers still remains problematic. The innovation, if it has occurred, has not been monitored nor indeed has support for its rationale been measured. Recent research suggests that support for liaison activities between teachers in different schools ranges from those who believe wholeheartedly in the value of curricular coordination by these means, and work hard to make it effective, to those who consider it an inappropriate venture (Stillman and Maychell, 1984). By and large, however, liaison was seen in the emergence of three-tier school systems as a mechanism for achieving curricular continuity. In broad, crude terms it was seen as a means of avoiding two breaks where there had been only one at the point of 11+ transfer, it being assumed that one break was bad and two would be worse. Liaison and continuity simultaneously took on much greater significance in curricular preparations and as practices came to be scrutinized in three-tier systems. The scrutiny went beyond the breaks between schools and began to examine the arrangements within them. (Meyenn and Tickle, 1980).

However, I would want to question the assumption that continuity is necessarily desirable. The possibility that discontinuity, whether planned or unplanned, is inevitable or even desirable in curricular provision and in the experiences of children should not be discounted lightly. Most certainly it should not be discounted on the basis of assumptions about what continuity/discontinuity might mean.

Central to the problem of achieving a smooth transition across the point of transfer between conventional primary and secondary schools, and with it effective continuity of experience for pupils, have been two main concerns. The first is that of overcoming the conflict between primary and secondary traditions. The second is that of providing adequate teacher expertise and material provision to cater for increasingly diverse curricula as pupils progress through schooling. In considering these the Universities Council for the Education of Teachers summed up:

> . . . as was emphasised in the 1978 Primary Survey (DES, 1978) it has become more and more difficult for a class teacher in an upper primary school, still less a middle school teacher, to cater for the whole curriculum adequately. However strong the case may be for the retention until the age of eleven of the class teacher principle, according to which virtually the whole of each child's development is overseen by one teacher each year, that supervision can now be purchased only at the expense of depth of knowledge and understanding to which, across the curriculum, only a few gifted and experienced teachers can aspire. Some place must be found for teachers with more specialised knowledge and skills. At the same time, the important change of emphasis in the curriculum from content to concepts, skills and attitudes makes it easier for their colleagues if well equipped with cognitive skills at their own level, to learn from them and to collaborate with them. To this argument for a modification of the class teacher principle must be added two others; first, that if an incompatible teacher-child pair is thrown together for a

whole year it is hard for the teacher and harder for the child, and, second, that it is important in any case for children of nine or over to meet, regularly, more than one adult in school.

(UCET, 1982, p. 5.)

Herein lies an argument, albeit implicit, for change in curriculum and style of teaching at an age earlier than eleven, indeed for children of 'nine or over'. The implications of the argument in terms of school organization, and for the liaison of teachers within a school, are not spelled out. Whether considered across the transfer between conventional primary and secondary schools or within middle schools which span that age, the issues, problems and attempted solutions provide insight into the question of curricular continuity. In a small study which focused on the internal arrangements of two middle schools where a 'smooth transition' had been attempted, Meyenn and Tickle (1980) identified organizational features which showed how the relationship between generalist and specialist provision remained as a contentious feature of the schools. In the present chapter I will extend the work done in that study to consider organizational arrangements across the ten to twelve years age groups in three different types of school organizations. Although it is the intention to focus here on the period which spans that point of conventional primary-secondary transfer, the issues involved are applicable and relevant on a wider scale in the school system. The mobility of parents and their children moving from area to area in response to employment opportunities, or lack of them, needs to be taken into account. Mobility also occurs within a locality, with change of house or personal domestic relationships. School closures and amalgamations as a feature of falling rolls and economic cuts incur further possibilities of school to school transfer. The provision of the 1980 Education Act for parents to state school preferences for their children whatever their home location also increases the possibility of children moving 'horizontally' from school to school.

The structure of school organization at LEA level is one way of identifying the complexities of curricular continuity. Some arrangements are relatively neat in terms of the school-to-school transfer and intake of groups of pupils:

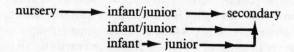

Others are more complex:

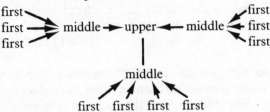

Continuity of curricular experience in such cases may depend upon agreements horizontally across each layer/tier, as well as vertically. Liaison in such cases requires external advisory coordination and support as well as considerable amounts of contact between teachers working at each of the schools. In itself such contact requires support in terms of manpower or at least a redefinition of responsibilities. Even then, given that the conditions for collective decision-making might be good, and that teachers in different schools might be willing to achieve and implement common policies within each school, the 'given' variables which affect each – the constraints – numbers of pupils, pupil-teacher ratios, allocation and distribution of scaled posts, teacher perspective and expertise, architecture and classroom provision, and other physical resources – make it likely that responses will be particular to individual schools. Factors such as teachers' perspectives, background and expertise in the curriculum are crucial in the management decisions made by headteachers when deploying staff, and mean that the likelihood of achieving common practice and common organizational patterns between schools is slim. When one imposes upon this the dynamic nature of responses at management levels to falling rolls (or in some cases to rising rolls or school amalgamations) the concepts of coping strategy and pragmatic response become of paramount importance.

In the less complex school structures which are typified in the diagram above the aspirations for agreed practices between schools may still remain. In other more complex systems, where the transfer of pupils occurs between a network of numerous different schools, the impetus amongst teachers for attempting to provide continuity of experience for pupils can be severely strained.

By identifying and documenting particular aspects of the organizational arrangements in different groups of schools, of different kinds, and provision for pupils for the two years spanning the conventional point of transfer, it is possible to define some attempts to establish continuity in terms of a gradual change in curricular arrangements, and to raise issues about the nature of continuity which these attempts, or the lack of them, illustrate.

The data below are provided from an investigation of three sets of schools: Set 1, a group of primary schools from which pupils transfer at 11+ to the same secondary comprehensive school, providing information about the organization of the curriculum for the final year in the primary school and the first year of the secondary school; Set 2, a group of middle schools catering for the 8 to 12 years age range, with information about the organization of the curriculum for third and fourth year pupils in each of these schools; Set 3, a group of middle schools catering for 9 to 13-year-old pupils, with information about the second and third year organization in each. In the case of Sets 2 and 3 the pupils normally transferred from the middle schools to the same upper school.

Following the example of the earlier study (Meyenn and Tickle 1980) it was decided to investigate specific features of organization within each school. These features were chosen as one means by which the relationship between class teacher and specialist teacher provision, as well as the nature of pupil grouping, could be described and analysed. Data were gathered within three categories. The first concerns the amount of time which pupils spend with a class teacher, and the amount which they spend with specialist teachers. Related to this is information about the number of specialist teachers pupils meet, and the subject which are taught by those teachers and by the class teacher. The second category relates to the amount of time which pupils spend in a class base, usually deemed as a non-specialist classroom or a classroom which for that period of time is used for general subject teaching. Correspondingly this category identifies the amount of time, and the specific subjects studied during that time, spent in specialist classrooms, usually deemed as classrooms in which study is devoted to one or two subjects of the curriculum. Thirdly data were gathered about the ways in which pupils are grouped into classes for teaching purposes (as distinct from sub-groups within a class).

Amongst the concerns expressed by Joan Dean (1980) was one that 'there is also discontinuity in the way the curriculum and the learning programme are built up' (p. 44). The analysis presented here will highlight features of both inter-school and intra-school transfer and continuity, and inherent conflicts between the 'typical' arrangements of conventional primary and secondary traditions. The analysis illustrates what individual pupils experience in organizational arrangements, and in changes of organization on transfer between the two years. The illustrative data are based on mean figures for each organizational feature across a year group in each of the schools. Comments on the data for Set 1 describe transfer from four 7–11 age range schools to the same 11–16 school, the type of transition which is probably the most generally familiar. Data for Sets 2 and 3 concern middle school transfer and are presented in the form of tables.

Set 1: Four primary schools transferring pupils at 11 plus to the same secondary school.

In the first year of the secondary school 4.5 per cent of teaching time was spent with a tutor or form teacher. The rest (95.5 per cent) was spent with different specialist teachers, most first year pupils, on transfer, being taught by a tutor plus eight other teachers.

By contrast, amongst the four contributing primary schools, the pupils in their last year had spent between 66 per cent and 90 per cent of their time with the same class teacher. In the case of one school, the pupils were also taught by four other teachers but the norm in this group was experience of two or three other teachers. Obviously, for these pupils there was a high correlation between the amount of time spent in specialist teaching spaces and their experience of specialist teachers. In the first year of the secondary school 85 per cent of the pupils' time was spent in specialist space. In their primary schools this ranged from 8–35 per cent of their time. In the secondary school the pupils were allocated to sets in maths, English and French but were in mixed ability groups for all other activities. In their primary schools the main experience of the pupils from all the schools was of mixed ability groups. One primary school provided remedial teaching in special groups for the basic subjects.

Sets 2 and 3: Tables 1a, 1b and 1c (Set 2) and 2a, 2b and 2c (Set 3) show comparative analysis of organization and grouping in two 8–12 middle schools and in three 9–13 middle schools.

KEY to Tables 1a–c and 2a–c			
A	Assembly	HE	Home Economics
AC	Art/Craft	H	History
B	Biology	Hu	Humanities
Cr	Craft	M	Maths
D	Drama	ML	Modern Languages
E	English	Mu	Music
ENV	Environmental Studies	N	Needlework
Gen	General Studies	PE	Physical Education
Ga	Games	R	Reading
Sw	Swimming	RE	Religious Education
		Sc	Science

Table 1a: Middle schools 8–12: pupil time allocation – teacher contact

		% Teaching Time With Form Base	Subjects or Curriculum Areas With Form Teacher	% Teaching Time With Other Teachers	Subjects or Curriculum Areas With Other Teachers	Number of Other Teachers
School 1	11+ year	70	E, M, ENV, RE, PE, Ga, Cr, Mu	30	ML, Sc, M(some), LIB, AC, D, Mu(some), Gardening	7
	10+ year	70	E, M, ENV, RE, PE, AC, D, Mu	30	Sc, M(some), Mu(some), ENV (some), LIB, Ga, Gardening	6
School 2	11+ year	40	E(some), M(some), AC, Gen.	60	Sc, Cr, PE, RE, ML, E(some), M(some), Mu, D, env.	5
	10+ year	45	E(some), M(some), AC, Gen.	55	E(some), M(some), Sc, D, PE, RE, Cr.	5

Table 1b: Middle schools 8–12: pupil time allocation – teaching spaces and resources

		% Time Spent in Home Base	Subjects or Curriculum Areas in Home Base	% Time Spent in Specialist Rooms	Subjects or Curriculum Areas in Specialist Rooms
School 1	11+ year	60	E, M, ENV, RE, Cr, Mu	40	ML, Sc, M(some), AC, PE, Ga, D, LIB, HE, Mu(some), Gardening
	10+ year	65	E, M, ENV, RE, AC	35	Sc, M(some), Ga, D, Mu(some), Gardening
School 2	11+ year	40	E(some), M(some), RE, Gen.	60	E(some), M(some), ML, AC, Mu, D, PE, ENV.
	10+ year	50	E(some), M(some), RE, AC, ENV, Gen.	50	E(some), M(some), Mu, D, Cr, PE.

Table 1c: Middle schools 8–12: pupil ability and social grouping

		MIXED ABILITY GROUPING				OTHER GROUPING		
		Individualized Learning	Grouping Within Class	Class Teaching	Divided or Regrouped	Remedial	Express	Sets	Streams
School 1	11+ year	ALL SUBJECTS EXCEPT →			Sc, D	Withdrawn 40% of week	Mu(some) M	ML(some) M	Ga(some)
	10+ year	ALL SUBJECTS EXCEPT →			AC, Gardening		Mu(some) M	M	Ga(some)
School 2	11+ year	E, Sc, Gen., M(some), AC	PE	ML, RE	MU, D, Cr			E(some)	Ga
	10+ year	E, Sc, Gen., M(some), AC + ENV	PE	RE				E(some) M(some)	Ga

Table 2a: Middle schools 9–13: pupil time allocation – teacher contact

		% Teaching Time With Form Teacher	Subjects or Curriculum Areas With Form Teacher	% Teaching Time With Other Teachers	Subjects and Curriculum With Other Teachers	Number of Other Teachers
School 1	11+ year	0	NONE (except form tutor specialism)	100	ALL SUBJECTS	11
	10+ year	57.5	ALL EXCEPT →	42.5	ML, Mu, PE, Ga, Sw, AC, HE, Sc	7
School 2	11+ year	0	(except coincidental form tutor specialism)	100	ALL SUBJECTS	14
	10+ year	0	(except coincidental form tutor specialism)	100	ALL SUBJECTS	15
School 3	11+ year	17.5	form tutor specialism and class studies and assemblies	82.5	ALL EXCEPT THOSE STATED OPPOSITE	15
	10+ year	55	ALL EXCEPT →	45	Mu, ML, PE, Ga, HU, HE, M	7

Table 2b: Middle schools 9–13: pupil time allocation – teaching spaces and resources

	% Time Spent in Home Base	Subjects or Curriculum Areas in Home Base	% Time Spent in Specialist Rooms	Subjects or Curriculum Areas in Specialist Rooms
School 1 11+ year	0	NONE (except form tutor specialism)	100	ALL
School 1 10+ year	57.5	ALL EXCEPT →	42.5	ML, Mu, PE, Ga, Sw, AC, HE, Sc
School 2 11+ year	0	(form tutor)	100	ALL
School 2 10+ year	0	(form tutor)	100	ALL
School 3 11+ year	35	E, M, Hu, RE	62.5	ML, Sc, Mu, AC, HE, PE, Ga, D
School 3 10+ year	65	ALL EXCEPT →	33.5	ML, Mu, Hu, PE, Ga, HE, M

Table 2c: Middle schools 9–13: pupil ability and social grouping

		MIXED ABILITY GROUPING				OTHER GROUPING			
		Individualized Learning	Grouping Within Class	Class Teaching	Divided or Regrouped	Remedial	Express	Sets	Streams
School 1	11+ year							ALL SUBJECTS	PE Ga
	10+ year	ALL SUBJECTS →				WITHDRAWN E, M			PE Ga
School 2	11+ year	AC, HE, PE, Ga →						ALL EXCEPT AC, RE, PE, Ga	PE Ga
	10+ year	AC, HE, PE, Ga →							PE Ga
School 3	11+ year	ALL SUBJECTS EXCEPT THOSE OPPOSITE			AC, HE, Sc, D			Ml, Mu, PE, R	PE Ga
	10+ year	ALL SUBJECTS →							PE Ga

The data in Set 2 given in Tables 1a, 1b and 1c offer a comparison between two schools which cater for the 8–12 years age range, showing a marked difference between the schools in the organization of both the 10+ year group and the 11+ year group, yet a marked similarity in the degree of change for pupils on transfer from third to fourth years in each school. In both schools the complexities of grouping arrangements and particularly the practice of 'setting' for some subjects make the contact between specialist teachers and class teachers very difficult to analyse. Similarly the time spent in a class base or a specialist room varies between pupils in the same class, so that the occurrence of 'some' in the tables indicates where the dual class/specialist teacher role occurs.

An interesting feature of these schools is that whilst in School 1 the pupils spend 70 per cent of their time with a form teacher and 60–65 per cent of it in a form base, they meet 6–7 (respectively in each year) other teachers in the remaining time for a wide range of subjects in specialist rooms. In comparison, pupils in School 2, spending only 45–40 per cent of their time with a form teacher, have contact with 5 other teachers for the larger portion of their time. There is a different kind of balance in each school between the stable class teacher provision and the short contact specialist teacher arrangements, which implies some speculative questions about the nature of 'the place which must be found for teachers with more specialized knowledge and skills' (UCET, 1982) with this age group. It also raises further questions about the nature of pragmatic responses to particular circumstances, since the data suggest differences in teaching roles and in the provision of specialist facilities in each school.

The curricular subjects which pupils in these schools experience as 'specialist' subjects include music and physical activities. Additionally these pupils have specialist provision for modern languages, science and 'practical subjects' such as art, craft, home economics and drama, together with setting provision for mathematics and, in one case, in English. These arrangements vary only slightly on transfer from one year to the next, providing continuity between the years in terms of a continued similar pattern of organization. It would only be possible here to speculate on changes which pupils might experience prior to and following these two years since it was not the brief of this work to consider the wider patterns of organization. If one assumes the 'typical' primary class teacher and secondary specialist teacher arrangements existing earlier and later, then there would be a case for seeing the arrangements in these two schools as offering a compromise amalgamation of both. On that assumption, the nature and degree of change would be greater for pupils in School 1 than those in School 2 prior to the 10+ year, and lesser after the 11+ year. In order to establish empirically the patterns of change it would require further, larger scale research.

Set 3 (Tables 2a, 2b and 2c) presents more complex information to analyse, and makes it necessary to consider each school in turn, and the differences between year groups in each, before making comparisons between the schools. In School 1 the proportion of time spent in class teacher/specialist environment is fairly equal in the 10+ year, followed by a shift to total specialization in the 11+ year. The subjects for which specialist teaching occurs in the earlier year are in the areas of music and physical activities, 'practical' subjects, and modern language and science. There is a close correspondence in this provision with the use of the physical facilities of the school, particularly the use of a 'practical block' for art, crafts, home economics and science. In School 2 total specialist teaching had been adopted as a policy, and was in operation for all age groups at the time of the research from entry at 9+. The only contact which pupils had with the class teacher was for registration. School 3 fostered a very similar arrangement to School 1 for the 10+ year group, with a fairly even 'generalist/specialist' division for a similar range of the curricular subjects. For the 11+ year group in School 3 there is evidence of retention of the stable home base, with some of that time spent with a form tutor, for subjects which use centralized resources, such as the library, or for which resources are readily duplicated and made available in several classrooms. The attempt to achieve stability and identity within a form group/home base was a stated policy of the headteacher. None of these schools could be identified as the 'hinged' school which has been said to be characteristic of many 9–13 middle schools, and which is typically represented as providing two years of general class teaching followed by two years of specialist provision. The major questions which arise concern the common experiences of the pupils all of whom eventually transfer to the same upper school. Pupils from each of the schools clearly experience the shift in organizational patterns in different ways at different times. Each school presents a different solution to the problem of just how and when the shift between class teaching and specialist teaching should occur. Comparisons between them emphasize the problematic nature of notions of 'smooth transition', and also point to the need to 'get behind' figures such as these to examine the underlying constraints and the perspectives of those responsible for organizational decisions. It may well be that such evidence would confirm the nature of pragmatic responses to particular circumstances, and at the same time identify the underlying inevitability of discontinuity in the curricular experiences of pupils which appear to be present in the data relating to the organization of curricula in these schools.

It is not easy to determine the extent to which the organization of each school represents an attempt to achieve continuity of educational experience whilst at the same time achieving the transition from the class teacher principle to the specialist teacher principle. In each case the curricular arrangements reflect the perspectives of headteachers and teachers and their responses to the circumstances in which they work, including the management of material resources such as time, staffing, buildings and equipment. There are some significant variations within each set of schools which show that the resolution of the problem of achieving continuity *and* transition has been attempted within the constraints of individual institutions. It might also be inferred that in some cases such attempts have not been made, have been abandoned, or have resulted in failure to resolve the problem.

In either case the problem is the same and the resolution is one of degree rather than kind. The conflict between primary and secondary, class teacher and specialist arrangements exists. What is more significant is the degree of similarity not only within sets of schools but across the three sets. In particular it is notable that the 10+ age group, perceived conventionally as belonging to the class teacher primary tradition, operates with varying but in many cases considerable *amounts* of contact with specialist teachers. These contacts *are important in relation to the views presented* by HMI in the Primary Survey (1978) and conveyed in the UCET report of 1982 (op. cit.). However, what is also worthy of note is that the core of this specialist contact is for curricular areas such as physical activities, music, practical subjects and modern languages. These are areas which conventionally have relied on specialist teaching and resources in some form, often requiring costly provision of instrumental teaching, workshop equipment and safety, and sports/gymnasium equipment. They are also areas where teacher shortages have been a recurrent problem. The question of specialist contact and the influence of specialists within teaching teams is a contentious one, which this study has not attempted to consider. What is clear is that without a drastic shift to a specialist teaching arrangement (such as in Set 2, School 2) with associated sudden change at some other point, the maintenance of continuity whilst achieving transition relies upon the influence of specialists with their colleagues. Here, a major contradiction is presented. At the same time that falling rolls and associated cuts are in many cases reducing the numbers of teachers available, increasing demands are being made on schools in terms of specialist provision which require the maintenance of or even an increase in staffing levels. Indeed it is interesting to speculate on what might happen as the impact of falling rolls and associated staffing cuts affects specialist curricular provision in secondary schools. Might it be that semi-specialist and even general class teaching get reborn in pragmatic responses, in the face of HMI and UCET demands? Provision for the 11+ year, perceived conventionally as belonging in the specialist secondary tradition is in some cases clearly entrenched in that position. In other cases the degree of contact with specialist teachers and facilities is widened to extensive areas of the curriculum, whilst maintaining the stability and coordination of learning associated with class teacher arrangements.

Other specific organizational factors could be considered in a case study. The features considered here reflect the curriculum perspectives in force and the pragmatic responses to the available resources. At a time of severe economic contraction associated with falling rolls a very fluid state exists with pragmatic responses dominant and inconsistencies between intentions and practices with regard to achieving continuity deeply entrenched.

The overall impression is one of schools individually and collectively responding to the perceived need for continuity not only in terms of stability and smoothness, but in terms of a managed change in the shift from 'generalist' to 'specialist' arrangements. The desirability of such change has been clearly expressed by HMI and by UCET as well as others concerned with curricular arrangements for this age group. Perhaps unwittingly this implies the desirability of discontinuity in organizational arrangements and the curricular experiences of pupils, as well as raising the question of the inevitability of discontinuity. The management of change might indeed be seen in terms of 'planned discontinuity' as pupils progress through particular stages of learning within the school system. How far such management is firmly based in policy and how far a pragmatic response to contradictory demands and expectations is a serious question, illustrated in the following headteacher's comments:

Our curriculum problem lies in the fact that since we are a growing school with a rising roll with a flexible staffing situation, we have been unable to maintain a timetable unchanged for more than a term at a time. Additionally, we have a school of hopelessly impracticable design which, in fact, prevents certain curriculum areas being covered. This arises because the 'specialist area' can accommodate approximately a half class, but we are not staffed sufficiently liberally to permit such extravagant PTR's.

The situation has been solved (or dodged) by having no specific policy regarding specialization other than that of expediency. Effectively there is no 'specialization' but children do rotate through teachers as a result. Although I could argue that there is a rationale behind the timetabling, it is mostly expedience determining the detail.

In the current climate of falling rolls and cuts in staffing the pragmatic responses to individual circumstances will be even more apparent. Data will quickly become dated, but the underlying features of discontinuity and continuity are likely to remain even though precise responses will vary.

Hinge or Bracket? Middle School Teachers' Views of Continuity at Eleven

Jennifer Nias

[Jennifer Nias returns to the theme introduced by Mary Atkins. Does the single organization of a middle school make it easier to establish curricular continuity in the education of ten to twelve-year-olds? From the literature on middle schools (Blyth and Derricott, 1977, Hargreaves and Tickle, 1980) has emerged the concept of the 'hinged' school, that is a middle school divided in ethos, teaching method and curriculum between a lower school which is primary and an upper school which is secondary in orientation.

Jennifer Nias, in a paper which is in the tradition of naturalistic enquiry, portrays, through the words of the teachers, a middle school which quite deliberately sets out to plan curricular continuity throughout the school. Despite this intention, the school emerges as 'hinged'. In part, this can be seen as one of consequences of the educational brief that guided the architect but more importantly, even though continuity exists in the planning of the curriculum and (on the evidence) in the minds of the teachers, in practice there is failure of implementation. Continuity is a long-term goal which is likely to be pushed to the back of the minds of thoughtful professionals as they deal with the hustle and bustle of day-to-day activity.]

Do middle schools (9–13) have a 'hinge' at 11? Sceptics and pessimists argue that they do; optimists that, rather, they provide a gently-graded ascent from the pre-disciplinary activities of the lower school to the disciplinary rigours of the upper school. This study presents teachers' views of children's experience as they move from the second to the third year of a 9–13 middle school, at the age of 11. It argues that, despite the clear-cut curricular aims of the head and the curriculum documents produced by the staff, the move from the second to the third year involves, for many children, a qualitative change. The reasons for this discontinuity are not so much educational as architectural, organizational and social.

The school opened in 1977 in a new, purpose-built building with one year-group (120) of children in their first middle school year. Until 1980 it took in another year-group of nine-year-olds each year. The staff increased proportionately from five to 24, and has included nine probationers. The head had experience of two previous 9–13 middle schools in two other authorities. The deputy has always worked in 9–13 middle schools, this being his third.

Using a semi-structured approach, I interviewed the head, the deputy, all the members of the second and third year teams and teachers of PE, music and French who taught throughout the school, a total of 15. Interviews ranged from twenty minutes to an hour, the norm being about thirty minutes. All except one were tape-recorded, transcribed and the transcript checked by the interviewee. With this exception, I took notes and made a summary immediately after the interview and this was then checked by the interviewee. Most interviews took place in the staffroom when it was empty though we used an office (e.g. for the head and deputy) when one was available. Being involved in other work in the school, I am a fairly familiar figure in the staffroom and everyone appeared willing to speak very freely. I tried to establish through my questions what changes teachers felt children experienced when moving into the third year, possible reasons for these changes, how important they were felt to be, both by the individual and in a larger staff setting, and the extent of the interviewee's middle school experience. In addition, I encouraged individuals to continue talking about issues which seemed of importance to them. Having written this paper, I checked it with the teachers for accuracy and to avoid possible misinterpretation of transcript material.

Curriculum continuity is a slippery and ill-defined notion, open to shared misunderstandings. I chose therefore to use, in my conversations with teachers at this school, the phrase 'continuity of educational experience'. I explained that what I was interested to discover was the extent to which, in their view, children who had left the second year in July had similar experiences of school when they returned in September for their third year. My intention in phrasing the enquiry so loosely was to discern what teachers themselves felt to be the important dimensions of this transition in the middle years of the middle school. I also wished to avoid contaminating the interview with the kinds of value judgements which are implicit in the term 'curriculum continuity'. It is not by any means clear that an education which contains no surprises, discrepancies or rites of passage is likely to stimulate development. On the other hand, schooling which requires of individual children adjustments which are too frequent, too abrupt or too great may be equally damaging to their potential growth.

To some teachers, the children's move from the second to the third year was a non-problem. 'The transition from one year to another has to be better than if it was two schools, it has to be, simply because the staff are there to talk to if there are problems . . .', said one teacher, expressing a belief which was confirmed by another, who had recently moved from an 11–18 school. Not everyone took this view, however. One teacher spoke of 'spending so much time scurrying round doing things with the children that you never have time to talk to the adults', and even those who believed the school provided the 'ideal system for transition' conceded that much of the smooth transfer was due to informal social contact between teachers (e.g. 'A lot of us know each other because we live in this area, so we find out a fair amount of what's happening in other people's classes.')

The extent of any possible discontinuity at 11 also seemed to depend on the subject under discussion. Linear subjects (e.g. mathematics and science) or those taught throughout the school by specialists (e.g. French in years 2, 3 and 4; music) tended to be perceived as a continuum. In addition, for a few of the teachers I interviewed, the children's continuity of experience was not a problem because it had not been considered. As one said:

> I'm only in my second year in the school . . . and it's not something really that you are aware of until your class has gone up into the third year . . . I'm more conscious of it this year.

Where a lack of continuity was perceived, it was not always located at 11. The first year, in particular, was seen by five teachers to be the one which created for children an educational experience different from that provided in the rest of the school. One put it this way:

> I think the children find the step from first to second year a big one. In the second year they do French, they do science in the lab. and definitely the first years feel they have taken a big step when they go into the second year . . . Yes, I think it's probably two schools; one's the first year and one's the second, third and fourth.

Some staff resented the apparent separateness of the first year. They spoke of the first year as 'a closed shop' from which 'hardly anybody comes out' and which 'the specialists haven't been able to get into'. But as others, including the head, pointed out, much depended on individual perspectives. The further a teacher was, in terms of direct experience, from the first year, the most likely he or she was to perceive the first two years as similar to one another 'in approach and teaching styles and so on'.

Moreover, not all teachers saw continuity as an unqualified blessing. The head argued:

> We are dealing with 120 individual responses and reactions to a variety of different sorts of problems and issues, so continuity matters in different ways to different people. Actually, I think for some of them it may be a positive advantage to have discontinuity. Some children do thrive on having a total change of pattern.

Others pointed out that 'it's all part of the gradual transition to the upper school – the middle school philosophy, a series of small transitions rather than a major one at 11+ . . . It's a sort of step up each year, isn't it?' while one felt that 'there'd be a split half-way through the school however long they stayed here'. As the deputy said, 'What we should be looking at is that the gap in the children's experience is not greater than you would expect in a (planned) continuum.'

Yet most of the staff whom I interviewed felt that it was. Indeed, one claimed, 'There is too much of a jump for a middle school, and I think that we're not really taking advantage of an ideal situation.' Most of the reasons advanced for this 'jump' were specific to the school and to the history of its development. In particular, a great deal could be attributed to the building. The specialist facilities are separated from two areas which lend themselves naturally to use as year bases. The head, pointing to the excellent provision for science and mathematics, said, 'There's a commonsense view which would say, "Well, you ought to put your specialist in that area" and it would be a brave man who says, "No, we won't do that at all".'

The decision to use the specialist areas for the purposes designed for them by the architect had implications both for the use of the year-bases (allotted to the first and second years) and for the positioning of the relevant subject specialists (mainly in the third and fourth years with ready access to the appropriate facilities). Once these decisions had been taken, the educational experience of the children was shaped accordingly. As the head suggested,

> The year centres do include a practical work area so that if you really wanted to, there is no reason why a first or second year child would need to move into any other part of the school, except for things like games and PE.

One of the teachers put it vividly: 'The first and second years are cut off . . . You go through that double door and the first year go one way and the second year go the other'. The head has contemplated trying to provide a third year centre in the rooms presently used as a humanities block and which a number of the third year team described as being 'spread out along a corridor'. But no one can see where a fourth year-base could be created without sacrificing the specialist rooms which are well suited to the teaching of their subjects and which would be very inconvenient as classrooms.

Thus, the first and second years are physically enclosed in their own bases and literally shut off from the rest of the school; the third and fourth years have easy access to specialist facilities but no bases of their own. Much follows from this use of a building which, in the head's words, 'celebrates the division at 11'. In the first place, children moving from the second to the third years have to become accustomed to moving from one specialist room to another, instead of remaining for much of the day in their bases. Several staff argued that 'this presents all sorts of problems in terms of a child's personal organization'. In particular, they have to learn to think ahead, select in advance the books and materials they are likely to need in another room and carry these round without losing them. Many find this difficult.

Movement also creates opportunities for individuals, relieved of the close surveillance of an adult, to transgress school norms for conduct. They have, in short, to accept more responsibility for their own behaviour. This change is reflected in the way in which teachers behave towards them. One third year teacher argued,

They are not trained (in the first and second years) to use any sort of initiative or to organize themselves, it's all done for them. They are not even asked to think for themselves . . . When they come into the third year, even in a subject area like art and design, they'll come in and every lesson they'll say, 'I want to do this piece of work, where's the paper?' It's been in the same place for the last three years but they have got to come and ask you. To me it's something that has developed through the fact that the children are looked after a bit too much.

Some second year teachers have, however, begun to prepare children for greater self-responsibility.

Just little things, like making sure they realize that they have got to get themselves to their next lesson and I'm not going to turn up and say, 'Right, off you go to your next lesson'; I give them homework two or three times a week now, and I'm very strict that they hand it in; odd things like that, things that I know if they are not ready for it they will get into trouble in the third year.

Children must also get used to a tighter timetable, as these two extracts show:

Second year teacher:

General studies in the second year covers a wide area and so when they come into a lesson they know they have got general studies but they are not sure if they are doing maths or English or topic work, whereas in the third year subject boundaries are more rigid, and they have to change between them more often.

Third year teacher:

In the second year, when they have general studies, if the kids get really lit up by something they can carry on through the whole afternoon working on it. In our situation it's one lesson-move, one lesson – move.

Organization and, in particular, grouping is often much more complex. One third year teacher saw that

One of the first things they find in the third year is that things are thrust on them all the time. Their timetable must be so alien to them. 'After this you have to go off to so and so, half the class have to go here and a third there, another third there and so on.' It's very hard on some of them.

Another teacher said,

We had 60 children in the same area with three teachers and we gave them a variety of things to do. And I said to them, 'Put your hands up if you find it difficult to make these sorts of decisions', and a good half of the class tentatively put their hands up.

Children have also to accommodate to situations which are unfamiliar rather than complex (e.g. the use of a science room as a classroom). Typically,

In maths we do three groups together (two classes and three teachers) and it takes them quite a while to get used to the situation of being with another class and in a big room, because they don't seem to experience that very much in the second year.

In particular, they have to adjust to a new relationship with their class teacher, especially if, as occasionally happens, the timetable allows the latter very few periods with him or her. The second year leader argued:

There is a degree of movement in the second year between teachers but there is always a strong pastoral class link with the class teacher and this has always been the cornerstone of evaluating a child's progress and his general social demeanour.

Seen from the perspective of a third year teacher, however, second year teachers are 'much more sort of mother figures'. One said,

I'm sure that the children don't see the class teacher in the same way they used to. I see them quite a lot so we can develop quite a good relationship but I don't see them all the time. So they talk to a lot of people besides me and I feel that we can have fairly adult conversations with them, which are quite good fun . . . The relationship I have with them when they first move up into the third year is much more business-like than friendly.

Another teacher saw this changed relationship in even more stringent terms:

I have that much more responsibility for my class because I only see them at registration, morning and afternoon, to make sure that I keep an eye on them. I give the odd good telling off then in front of a few people, because they don't see me that often. They have got to be really aware that I am the class teacher whereas in the second year they know you are because they see you every lesson.

The head and deputy both expressed fears that the lack of a 'close relationship with the class teacher means fewer opportunities to pick up the odd problem that may arise during the week and keep that monitored.' Certainly, all the third year team were aware that discipline and pastoral concern for individuals very much depended on their ability to pass information on to one another, often informally.

A final difference between the second and third years which can be attributed, albeit distantly, to the architecture is the content of the curriculum. Most of the third year teachers were agreed that they changed their 'approach to the subject' towards the teaching of 'basic ideas and concepts', when governed by a subject timetable and specialist teaching areas. Only the PE teacher suggested a developmental reason for this change (in his case from groups and teams to individual and pair work). Others referred to the constraints of single period lessons, the existence of specialist facilities, the desire to use their own specialist knowledge and perceived pressures from the upper school. Whatever the reason, they appeared much more conscious than the second year team of their identity as subject teachers.

The influence of the upper school was not however as great as might have been expected. Apart from the head, the only teachers who attributed changes in the third year in 'teaching approach' and in the content of the curriculum to upper school pressures were from the second year team. No one teaching in the third year spontaneously mentioned a sense of curricular obligation to the upper school and when questioned they did not feel it to be crucial to them.

So far, I have argued that the design of the building and the willingness of head and staff to be guided by its dictates have been largely responsible for several changes to which children have to adapt on entering the third year. A more rigid, specialized timetable, movement between different teaching areas and teachers and the resulting need that personal organization and responsibility should replace reliance on a class teacher combine to create a feeling that, as one teacher put it, 'We are getting sort of two schools within a school.'

This division is reinforced and sometimes emphasized by a number of factors which have little to do with architecture. Although, as one teacher said, 'The playground and the sporting facilities and the clubs aren't split so children do have a chance to get together', subtle divisions remain. Sporting clubs and especially teams are more readily accessible to the 'over 11s' than the 'under 11s', country dancing is for first and second years only, the third and fourth year children cooperate successfully in discos. The detention system operates for third and fourth year children, not for first and second year ones. Teachers themselves are aware that their expectations of children change between the two years. For example: 'When I was a second year teacher I stressed it to my children going into the third year, "Come on, grow up a little bit more",' and

If there's a split it's always that same one. I think the children see that difference – the children see the first and second years as the younger ones. But maybe we are treating them a lot younger . . . There does seem to be a big difference between the second and third years but I'm not sure whether that's because of how we see them and so, therefore, that's how they see it.

A similar division into 'under 11s' and 'over 11s' exists among the staff, but for different reasons. As the school grew, new staff arrived and among them, a number of probationers. Two years ago five joined the school together and for a variety of reasons, the majority of those were placed in the third and fourth years. One of them said:

A lot of us were keen to start off in a team-teaching situation with somebody else sort of carrying us along for the first few weeks. So I got used to teaching with somebody else very quickly in my career and we've sort of carried on . . . whereas there are more experienced teachers in the first and second year, teachers who have been teaching the longest and are set in the way of teaching by themselves . . . There are more teachers who would really rather shut the door and be by themselves, and not so many new teachers going in . . . .

The fact that most of the third and fourth year staff taught in both years further encouraged the growth of a team spirit among them. The head suggested, 'You can't actually identify a third year team of staff clearly.' Staff in both years knew a good deal about each other's teaching and had easy access to new ideas or syllabi emanating from those subject heads who were part of the team (as one teacher said, 'I don't ever hear about what's being introduced in the first and second year'). Formal arrangements such as duties emphasize the separation of the staff in the third and fourth year teams from those in the first and second years. Further, as friendships and mutual support systems developed among the probationers and with the rest of the third and fourth year teachers, social contact came to supplement team teaching. One team member argued:

You teach with the third and fourth year staff so it's easier to talk during the course of a lesson. And you come in direct contact with those staff more than with second year staff because it's a

different part of the school and very few staff actually spend
time in the staffroom . . . The social chat usually sparks off
following a third or fourth year meeting at which all the staff are
the same staff you teach with . . . It's very much a social discussion.

As a result of all these factors, teachers in the third and fourth years,
be they subject coordinators or relatively inexperienced newcomers,
see themselves and are seen by others as a more cohesive and cooperative group than exists in either the first or second years. It is not
surprising that some of them are reluctant to leave this team,
especially since they have invested a good deal of effort, in some
curriculum areas, in the production of resources. As the deputy
suggested,

> There is a sense in which once the package is produced, that's
> the teacher's security. To go into the first and second years,
> which are seen as being much looser in structure, is a threat –
> they've got to re-learn some skills.

One second year teacher also sensed this reluctance to move from
the upper part of the school though it was expressed in different
terms:

> If you just have one subject, and you're concerned about your
> own expertise and specialization, you may be worried about
> your own ability to keep a rapport with a particular group of
> children over an extended period of time . . . Particularly if they
> have a number of children who are difficult they may feel they
> need to spread the load and encourage the children to form
> relationships elsewhere.

Fear of teaching different age groups is not however peculiar to the
third and fourth year. Several teachers pointed out to me the existence
of a conventional wisdom which says that older children are more
difficult to teach, e.g.:

> Children of the next stage up always seem daunting . . . If you
> listen to the fourth year teachers talking you begin to think that
> there must be something different about the children in the
> fourth year and if you teach lower down the school it may make
> you afraid to tackle them in case you can't control them.

Reluctance to move from one part of the school to another may also be related to the fact that the second year teachers were widely seen as a collection of individualists – 'they shut their doors and get on with it'. One member of staff said,

'In the second year people seem to feel quite free to go off and do whatever they feel like, if they feel like it. They don't seem to feel the same sort of pressures [as the third and fourth years] to liaise and cooperate and fit in, they seem to feel more free.

If this is true, it may contribute to discontinuities in the children's experience of subject matter and teaching methods. If, as another teacher claimed, 'the third and fourth years are getting similar experiences, whereas what first and second years learn can depend a lot on the teacher's interest', some children moving from the second to the third year may find the changes more marked than others.

There is a little evidence too – though not as much as might have been expected – that the break between the two years resulted from teachers' personal histories. Two teachers, both of them with junior school experience, suggested this. One said,

It's almost as if we're afraid to adopt a sort of middle school method of working because we still feel that children between the ages of 9 and 11 are primary children and children between the ages of 12 and 13 are secondary children and should therefore be treated in a slightly different way.

On the whole, however, the teachers whom I interviewed were committed to the idea of a continuous educational experience for children in the middle years and sought to achieve it.

Their efforts were, however, sometimes hampered by ignorance of curriculum content and methods in parts of the school in which they did not teach. Several, especially in the third year, expressed feeling this ignorance. As one said, 'I don't go down to the second year, I haven't seen how any of them teach . . .' Another put it even more strongly:

When I get a new class next year I really shall not know anything about them. I shan't have ever seen them, probably (apart from one or two I might have told off around the school), I shall probably never have dealt with any of them at all. It's quite worrying really. You can't really rely on records . . .

Is there any machinery that enables first year teachers to talk to the second year teachers before first year classes move up?

Only that we probably do get together, I mean there's no sort of planned time for getting together or anything.

Moreover,

When I came here I was shown what was done in the third and fourth year but I was never shown what was done in the first and second years. It isn't anybody's fault, but [until a maths INSET programme] we haven't really been encouraged to think about what goes on in the first and second years.

This would not, however, be true for all the teachers to whom I spoke. Many, especially the subject specialists, 'would like to teach in all four years' or 'would like to know the first and second years'. Unfortunately, as they are aware, this creates acute timetabling problems, giving the need to make full use of good specialist facilities, the desire of teachers in the lower years to maintain a close link with their own classes and the expressed desire of class teachers in the third year to see more of their classes than one or two periods a week.

There is one further institutional characteristic which tends to separate first and second year teachers from those teaching mainly in the third and fourth years. When the head opened the school five years ago, he had a 'grand design in mind'.

The first year would be very much an autonomous team of staff, also very much class teacher taught with only occasional input from subject specialists and so on, but in the second year the children would meet more members of staff, the curriculum would become slightly more defined in certain areas, so you would see the boundaries slightly sharpened. In the third and fourth years this would be a continuing process, so the kind of relationship between the head of curriculum area and head of year would change according to the year in school we are talking about. So there would be a great deal of negotiation necessary between the head of first year and the head of subject department. Perhaps a little less so in areas where class teachers have the responsibility for the teaching, for example, in English and maths but in, say, the art and craft where the head of department was much more involved in actually teaching, the level of negotiation would be somewhat different. But that's a very sophisticated kind of package – maybe too sophisticated.

To the deputy it seemed like this:

> We have first and second year leaders who are pastorally and academically responsible and third and fourth year leaders who are pastoral. We have heads of department who go throughout the school. The main problem has been this very difficult and delicate relationship between heads of department and first and second year leaders, and the question of whose responsibility it is to implement, whose to innovate . . . The first and second year leaders feel that there is a need to bring things together, but ask themselves whose job it is.

The head has 'always had a hope that within the first and second year, the curriculum would be by negotiation with the head of year'. However, as I have noted above, the attention of the subject heads had been more than fully occupied during most of the school's lifetime with sorting out the curriculum in the top two years, helping new teachers to integrate into the school and, in pursuit of both aims, creating 'packages' of curriculum resources. There have been three results. Experienced teachers in the lower years, left to their own devices, have become (in the eyes of the third year teachers) 'much more powerful in what they do in their classrooms [than we are]'. At the same time ambiguity has replaced the 'negotiation' for which the head hoped. The deputy claimed:

> I've always had heads of department coming to me saying 'I want to do this in the lower part of the school but how do I go about it because, if I try, not everyone will take any notice of me?' I've had heads of first and second year come to me and say, 'I don't like this innovation that this particular head of department wants, I don't think it is the right one for my age group'. We see the first and second year leaders having – if you like – a phase expertise and obviously they sometimes feel that in their judgement something isn't particularly appropriate. So it's always an undercurrent that has been there, perhaps one that until lately has not been so talked about.

Moreover, first and second year leaders, occupied and often preoccupied with their own organizational, curricular and pastoral problems, have appeared to opt out of curriculum planning. One third year teacher put it this way: 'They don't get much contact with the maths head of department and the science head of department, but they don't seem to be worried about it . . .', while the head described how subject coordinators who begged the staff for comment on initial curricular drafts had had little feedback from them. He commented, 'It's much easier to say, "Well, there are so many other pressures on us. We have somebody who is appointed head of department, therefore let him do it".'

Predictably, this is not how the second year teachers see it. Their perspective was expressed by one teacher as: 'Heads of departments don't seem to understand that the subject is adapted by the different year groups according to teachers' perceptions of the children's different needs.'

Yet, this is not the whole story. Teachers at all levels are clear that subject coordinators and others do take an interest in the teaching of their subjects throughout the school especially now that 'we've "done" a year of third and fourth year curriculum, and they've got more time to give to the first and second year'. They recognize the practical difficulties, e.g. that discussion is easier when subject coordinators teach in a year group but that it is not always possible to adjust the timetable, and that some subjects, (such as humanities, English) are too large to allow for effective formal meetings; and they are appreciative of the subject coordinators' efforts. At the end of one interview, a teacher commented:

> Despite all this there aren't two schools because there are teachers up and down. It is a bit as if there were two schools, but the heads of departments do try and make some flow through and because it's a small school the staff all get on fairly well together. People do talk together quite a lot informally.

Arguably, none of this would matter very much if the children were not affected by it. I have not included children's views in my data and only one of my respondents (the head) had, at any point, deliberately sought the opinions of children on their move from the second to the third year. Nevertheless, several teachers mentioned the children's reactions and a fairly uniform picture emerges. Though subject specialists with no particular year affiliation tended to disagree, eight teachers from both years, the head and the deputy commented on an increase during the early months of the third year in behaviour problems. One third year teacher said,

> I definitely think the worse year to teach in school is the third year, for the first term up to Christmas, because I think they are slightly unsettled, I think they are finding their feet again. I think they know there is a change going on . . . It isn't until after Christmas that they start to grow up a little bit.

The head and deputy head also mentioned a decline in the quantity and standard of work produced by particular children. Similar checks, though, to progress in the first year following transfer to another school, have been found by Nisbet and Entwistle (1969), Youngman and Lunzer (1977) and Galton and Simon (1980).

Two main reasons were suggested for these regressive behaviours. There was widespread agreement that some children found it very hard to adjust to novel demands for personal responsibility and organization and to a more time-dominated existence. Second year teachers (but no one from the third year team) tended to feel that children who valued a strong and stable relationship with one teacher reacted adversely to the absence of an obvious 'class teacher'. The head saw both factors contributing to an undermining for some children of confidence in a stable environment:

> It's almost as if you have had the children in the first year and they have taken a while to settle into a new school situation. By the end of the first year they have started to settle down quite well; they move into the second year and that's not too dissimilar, so they can build up a confidence which is an essential part of any kind of educative process. Then just as that has been built up strongly, you move them to something, which to them, appears to be very different and you have broken that confidence.

To sum up, then, there was little consensus among the fifteen staff whom I interviewed at this 9 to 13 middle school as to whether their school had a 'hinge' at 11. Some were inclined to see the qualitative change taking place when children moved out of the first year into the second. Others felt that the school was characterized by a series of incremental transitions, each cushioned by the ease with which individual teachers could contact and talk to one another.

Yet a substantial number, and especially those teaching predomin-antly in the second and third years, thought that the children's experi-ence of school altered radically at the start of the third year. The design of the building led logically to year-group teaching in enclosed bases in the first two years with, in the third and fourth years, move-ment around a number of specialist facilities (and therefore specialist teachers), in accordance with a fixed timetable. Unfamiliar and some-times complex groupings and modes of behaviour were coupled with changed relationships with teachers, and especially with class teachers. Children had suddenly to assume much greater responsibil-ity for themselves, their belongings, and their learning. Moreover, divisions in extra-curricular activities and subtle changes in staff expectations and disciplinary procedures stressed for them the fact that during two months' summer holiday they had ceased to be 'the younger ones'. Not all of them were able to adjust easily to these changes; the behaviour and work of some regressed.

The architectural division of the school into two year-bases and a specialist 'wing' was mirrored by staff groupings which coalesced as the school grew. A number of historical factors combined to fuse the third and fourth year teachers into a social and working group with a greater degree of cohesion than either of the other year groups. The presence of most of the subject coordinators in the third and fourth year and the reluctance of many members of staff to teach older or younger children tended to restrict vertical curriculum planning and the provision of related resources to the top two years, and to confirm teachers in their ignorance of the content or methods used in other parts of the school. The negotiation on curriculum matters between subject coordinators and the leaders of the first and second years, which the head saw as the 'bracket' ensuring gradual transition throughout the school, does not take place.

However, the staff as a whole are committed to the notion of a school which provides a coherent and continuous education for children in the middle years. Certain teachers continue to teach across the age groups, many more would like to do so if timetabling made this possible and the overall commitment and friendliness of the staff facilitate informal contact at all levels. Moreover, a mathematics INSET programme during the current academic year has made teachers of all age groups much more aware of one another's aims, methods and activities. It would not be true to suggest that the school is split, despite its building, into two halves, nor that the staff deliber-ately connive at radical changes in the education of children moving from the second to the third year. As one teacher said, 'It's not intended to be like that. It's just sort of grown . . .'

It would, however, be fair to leave the last word with the teacher who said, 'I'm not sure about this continuity. It's planned and it has been built into the syllabus, but it's not built into the staff's knowledge at the same time.'

Out of the Mouths . . . Pupils' Perceptions of Continuity

Ray Derricott

As part of this work on continuity I thought it appropriate to obtain some consumer opinion by talking to children. The group I report on were all just beginning their third term in a secondary comprehensive school. I chose the school on no other grounds than the fact that I was known by many of the staff, I knew that I would be welcome and that I could almost guarantee a relaxed atmosphere in which to talk to children. The deputy head set aside her room for the interviews. The children were chosen from three different first year classes that happened to be timetabled for humanities on each of my three visits. I talked to each group for around 25 minutes with a tape recorder operating. Inevitably, much of the early talk in each of the groups was intended to settle and reassure the children that they were not being 'tested' but that I and their teachers were interested in how they had settled into the school.

One group consisted of ten, five boys and five girls. Having played back the discussion I found it impossible to distinguish some of the individual contributors. This group also tended to be dominated by two children. On my other two visits to the school I chose to talk to two groups of four. One group was equally divided by sex but the other contained three girls and one boy.

The school served a mixed owner-occupier and council estate area. The area could be classified as outer suburban but, in Merseyside terms, not 'commuter-belt'.

I tried not to structure the discussion too much but found that the children did not naturally talk about their curricular or classroom activities unless prompted. Quite a lot of other talk was about 'school' in general. I do not claim any generalizability from this small scale 'research'. Any links with their own situations or any reflections on continuity that emerge from this portrayal, I will leave to the readers. I let the children's own words speak for themselves.

Settling in

Q: You all came to this school last September – about six months ago – can you tell me, looking back, how you felt in the first few days here?

B: We'd come here before with Mr. H. [junior school teacher] when I was at — school. We saw the sports and the gym hall and some classrooms and the metalwork . . .

B: I didn't . . . we were on us [our] holidays . . . my sister's been here . . . told me some things . . .

G: It's good here . . . yes even at first. I was with P. [her friend] . . . there were a lot of us from our school. We came over to this block for science and HE and over there for PE. Games are good, the netball's better and badminton and . . . volley ball.

G: We didn't see much of the older school . . . the sixth formers and the older ones . . . some are a bit er . . . bossy . . . the ones who showed us round were nice.

G: No we can find all the classrooms . . . except M1 and M2 . . . we know they're the huts . . . we were there for English and for religion.

B: I couldn't remember week 1 and week 2 [the timetabling arrangement].

B: That's easy.

B: I used to carry all my books and kit and things . . . I got a detention for physics . . . not having my book.

G: I liked it at — [primary school] . . . I'd rather be here now.

B: I don't like the dinners – it's all right when you're first but last dinners is worse.

B: The dinners are good sometimes – you can choose . . . it's noisy . . . the pizzas are . . . ugh!

G: Assembly's worst . . . I don't know . . . everybody [inaudible] and looking when you're at the front.

B: That's what I don't like, assemblies.

B: Tutors is best [reference to the Tutor Group System]. It's good fun – we go skating and things.

G: Our tutor group is boring.

G: I'd like Miss X as our tutor.

B: I've made good friends with Andrew and John . . . they were from — [primary school]. I still have mates same as before at — [his ex-primary school].

G: I wanted to be with Pam [her friend from primary school] but I've got some new ones as well as Pam. Me mum wrote to — [the head] for Pam and me to be in the same group but he said no I have to make new friends . . . I was upset but it's OK . . .

B: The homework's all right. Some teachers are good but some of 'em think you've got hours to spend on it.

G: She's [the deputy] strict about skirts and socks and the right
coloured shoes. It's better than our old uniform [primary school].

B: We didn't have one then [primary school]. It's OK but we can't
wear jeans – me mother's always going on about me trousers . . .
it's better with jeans.

The curriculum

Q: Can I ask you now to think about what you do in lessons. Is it the
same or different compared with your primary schools?

B: The assessment's the worst. We have assessments and they don't
tell you. You think – oh a nice English lesson now and then PE
but in comes Mrs — [teacher of English] and gives us assessment
test for our grades, for your reports, for your parents and the class
you're going to be in. They should tell us, that's best. Too many
assessments.

B: I've been moved out the maths set . . . the assessment decided.
The maths is worst, not like at — [primary school]. They're mad
on maths here.

Q: Can you tell me what the difference is between maths here and at
—? [primary school]

B: It's SMP here and it's not the same.

Q: How is it not the same?

B: It's different . . . it's hard . . . it's like . . . mapping and sets and
different graphs . . . [long pause] . . . it's different sums . . . and
the teachers think you can do it . . . you're stupid if you can't and
you can't catch up . . . some can do it but I haven't . . .

Q: Can somebody else tell me – yes – what do you think about maths
– here?

G: I've got — [teacher's name] for maths . . . she's nice, she explains
it and comes round and talks to you . . . but we've got some brainy
ones in ours and they're always showing off but I don't think Miss
likes him very much . . . Miss sends him to the computer.

G: Maths is OK . . . here . . . it's like at — [primary school] but some
of us are doing Book B now . . . we've all changed classes and
teachers . . .

Q: Since September? You've changed . . .?

G: Not all of us but for maths.

B: Only in maths.

Q: Which primary schools did you come from? [In this group of 4
children, 3 primary schools were named].

G: — [primary school) is the best school.

Q: How do you know that?

B: My dad says and it's been in the paper.

G: It's the best with — [another primary school]. Everybody knows, you can tell from what the teachers say.

Q: What do you mean? The teachers?

G: Mr — [maths teacher – head of dept. I think] says which school do you come from and then says we haven't done that – whatever it is – work.

Q: So some of the primary schools did different kinds of maths than you do here? What do you think . . .?

B: It should be the same – for everybody in junior schools the same.

G: I think it is the same . . .

B: Yes for you but we haven't done SMP . . .

G: We haven't but it's like what we did . . . in some ways but . . . It's the same really. Sir, the bell's gone we've got science.

Continuing exploration of similarities and differences between primary and secondary school curricula with another group

G: We had some geography [at primary school]. We did about the docks and containers. We had a film about oil from the sea . . .

Q: Can you remember what kind of books you used in geography . . . did you all have the same text book?

G: We had atlases and I think we had all the same geography books, we had history books. When we did topics we used the library in the school.

B: We went to this old house . . . a big place . . . something Hall . . . we went to the Wildfowl Trust place . . . We went to Alton Towers and a big park place . . . we went on lots of trips . . . sometimes we had questions . . . these sheets . . . and checked them when we got back.

Q: Do you do geography now . . . here?

B: Yes . . . we have notes and sheets for working off . . . we have slides.

B: We do map references and about contours.

Q: But you said you were having humanities?

G: Yes . . . we did about ancient people . . . how they lived. They were hunters – hunter gatherers and what different kinds of things men did and women and the girls. Now we're doing some geography about maps and different landscapes. I like it, all these different things.

G: Miss — goes mad if you draw blue outlines round your maps for the sea. We always did that before.
Q: What is the difference between what you are doing now in humanities and what you did in your primary schools?
B: We did mostly topics.
B: We did topics and we did history and environmental studies.
G: Yes, topics, we did, mostly by ourselves but sometimes in a group.

The conversations with children seem to indicate that for these individuals at least, settling into the secondary school held no particular traumas. Also indicated is that children of this age are capable of making shrewd judgements about the organizational rules and constraints to which they are being subject and that at times they are conscious of not being kept informed of the intentions behind some of the decisions being made about them on issues such as assessment and grouping.

Techniques of assessment experienced by pupils as they cross the primary-secondary transition probably represent one of the most obvious, but taken for granted, discontinuities. Tests, assessments and examinations are not unknown in primary schools but they often do not assume great importance. Sometimes standardized tests of attainment or general or verbal intelligence are used to provide 'an external' measure of individual progress. Some local authorities apply these as a matter of policy, but during my work I came across numerous examples of schools within the same secondary catchment area using unknowingly different and incompatible tests. In general, much of the assessment throughout the primary years is in the form of *a global appraisal* by teachers of their pupils' cognitive and affective behaviour. An example of this form of appraisal is as follows:

John is an able lad. His reading is fluent and above average. He likes books and uses the library often. His number work has improved recently and he is now able to cope with most of the work in his group. He needs to try to concentrate on his work for longer periods. He often prefers to chat rather than get on with his work. I think this should improve as he matures. He is a popular lad and has many friends.

As indicated in my conversations with children, assessment can take on a much more formal characteristic in the secondary school. Assessment at this stage is used to support grouping and setting systems and decisions can begin to be made which have a serious effect on future option choices and possible career patterns.

The continuity which smooths the transition from the practice of appraisal to assessment appears to be neglected in the literature. Cooper (1976) provides the beginning of a framework for assessment and record keeping which spans the 8 to 13 age group. Currently, Blyth at the University of Liverpool is working on appraisal, diagnostic and assessment techniques across the primary-secondary divide.

CHAPTER SIX

Curricular Continuity: frameworks and guidelines

Ray Derricott

My intention in this chapter is to review some of the suggested frameworks for planning and guidelines for curriculum construction that are available to teachers interested in curricular continuity. The examples I have chosen are ones which I judge to be worthy of wider dissemination than they have hitherto enjoyed. Most are the results of individual local authority initiatives and are well-known within those boundaries but less so nationwide. The limitations of space and time available have made it necessary for the schemes reviewed to remain few in number. I have chosen to concentrate on examples from the social subjects area because there is clear evidence both from 'Place, Time and Society' and from the HMI Primary Survey of 1978 that work in this area is random and repetitive and unsystematic. The social subjects area is often afforded low priority in curricular appraisal and the notion of what might constitute continuity and progression is unclear, to say the least.

The social subjects

Under this label I include history, geography, the social sciences and the many labels used in schools to describe this area of the curriculum such as humanities and social studies. My choice of this area also reflects my own involvement in the major project 'Place, Time and Society' for more than a decade. 'Place, Time and Society' provides teachers with a planning framework of objectives and key concepts. I do not intend to elaborate on this framework as it is adequately covered in the various project publications. However, one of the more rewarding aspects of working with PTS has been the way in which the project's planning framework has been used, adapted and referred to in a number of local authority initiatives. All these initiatives have taken much further the general ideas of PTS and put a considerable amount of meat on the basic skeleton.

A scheme for the humanities 9–13: history, geography, social science.
Oxon County Council, Communications Centre, 1978.

This slim, attractive and very readable document produced by a team of Oxfordshire advisers and teachers is a development from their own discussion paper produced in 1977 and entitled *The Child at 13 – expectations in the field of humanities.* Both documents are a fruitful source of ideas for interested teachers.

The scheme for the humanities includes a *model programme* of units or modules of equal length. It is suggested that these may be taught more effectively over a period of about half a term. The modules are related to subject areas, some mainly historical, some geographical but it is suggested that 'some on human themes are . . . essentially interdisciplinary in structure.' The scheme also uses key concepts. The programme has this to say about continuity:

Continuity and development are achieved by a broad concentric approach over the middle years (local, regional, national) and by a scheme which introduces important concepts, skills and topics at a succession of levels. The scheme also indicates a broad progression in terms of man's development and suggests certain lead lessons or courses in this context.

The general aim is expressed thus:

We are educating for humanity – those inherent virtues of tolerance, concern and brotherhood without which Man himself, with science and technology, may destroy all that makes human life noble and fulfilling. Such an aim is not easily translated into objectives. Men are sometimes inhumane, sometimes driven by greed or by a grinding sense of injustice. But men are also capable of higher things, of seeking something beyond personal gain and immediate reward. It is part of our role to show the heights to which men can aspire, the range of human potential. The child should begin to recognise the choices, and the constraints, that lie ahead in terms of our communities and our environment.

The general study skills involved in the model programme are:

GENERAL STUDY SKILLS
Finding appropriate sources of information.
Using a library efficiently.

Observing and recognizing helpful evidence.

Using instruments to measure.

Reading with understanding.

Exploring the human body's ability to communicate ideas and feelings.

Recording evidence in a suitable way.

Sifting evidence for what is relevant.

Distinguishing between fact and fiction.

Interpreting and analysing documents, maps, statistics, statements, graphs, buildings, sites, photographs and pictures.

Keeping an open mind in the face of incomplete evidence.

Organizing information on a suitable conceptual basis.

All humanities schemes involve the negotiations of meanings and procedures amongst the collaborating specialists. It is not unusual for those representing a subject interest to feel that essential skills and ideas in their discipline are being neglected in a coalition. I recognize an element of this in the Oxfordshire model programme because it includes a separate section on *mapwork skills*.

The Oxfordshire scheme provides an agenda for continuity across the 11+ divide whether the children concerned are being educated in middle schools or are in transition from primary to secondary schools. The brevity of the document (about 16 pages) and its attractive 'semi-professional' layout make it very accessible to busy teachers.

Humanities: A curriculum guideline for the middle years (8–14)
Northamptonshire Education Committee, 1979.

This quite substantial document is mainly the work of Keith Driscoll, Senior Inspector for the Humanities in Northamptonshire, although the writer acknowledges the contributions of many other teachers and workers. On first acquaintance this document with its approximately 200 pages of closely written text seems formidable and perhaps only for the specialist/enthusiast humanities teacher. However, no one has to read the report in its entirety to get the message. Chapter One is a well written introduction to curriculum design for all those teachers whose initial training courses were not burdened with Curriculum Studies. Even for more recently trained teachers, this chapter serves as a reminder of things past and perhaps forgotten.

Chapter Two which concentrates on the humanities is one of the most accessible introductions to what has been described as a jungle. Chapter Six on the social sciences and the humanities tackles a potential area of misunderstanding if not conflict in a sensible and readable manner. A useful distinction is made between introducing the social sciences into the school curriculum and introducing ideas or concepts from the social sciences into the curriculum. The latter approach is favoured. An extensive list of units divided into phases is provided with a view to establishing consistency and continuity of treatment over the five years between 8 and 14.

Although this book is less immediately helpful to teachers seeking advice and guidance on providing continuity of curricular experience, it will certainly repay careful study.

The new approach to the social studies: continuity and development in children's learning through first, middle and high school.
Schools Council, 1981.

This is a report of a local project sponsored by the Schools Council and located in the London Borough of Merton. The report has seven authors who at the time of writing were all teachers except for the late Eileen Harries who was a member of the authority's advisory staff. The Merton Project was a response to an assessment of needs in the area

for prepared teaching materials on the local environment, and clarification of the nature and objectives of social studies and of how children at different stages of development best learn social subjects so that the largely integrated work of the first and middle school and the predominantly single-subject work of the high school could be better related and an overall improvement achieved.

This was clearly an ambitious purpose and within the limits of its resources (money, time and energy) the report provides a clear set of guidelines to work in a difficult and messy area as far as the selection, organization and sequencing of content is concerned.

At the outset the report makes clear a value position about social studies. Social studies is not seen as soft-centred escapism but should be the area of the curriculum in which sensitive social issues and values are confronted.

The social studies are the social and political education which schools provide.

Their purpose is:
to develop children's interest in human affairs and their ability to think about them; to help children understand the attitudes and values of other people, and to develop their own value system.

The writers acknowledge that progress is hard to identify and to measure. The Merton Project is committed to what the writers call the Brunerian philosophy of a spiral curriculum,

to discovering the nature of each of the disciplines and simplifying them to meet the children's stage of development, so that at an appropriate level children may learn something of the concerns, concepts and procedures of the geographer, historian and the social scientist.

The project then outlines an approach to social studies using its contributory disciplines for the ages 7 to 9, 9 to 13 and 13 to 16. With continuity across the 11+ divide in mind, I have selected two examples from the report which indicate the suggested approach for nine year olds and that for twelve year olds.

Example 1. FIRST SCHOOL
Extract from inter-disciplinary topic work on 'The Neighbourhood', which also included an economic component on commercial competition from the supermarket and a historical account from life in the thirties (when the estate was built) and during the war years.
Age of pupils: nine years.

The local shops
Aims: (1) Key idea: There is a hierarchical pattern of shopping in cities.
(2) Skills: Basic fieldwork and mapping skills, for example, classification, questionnaire, interpretation of large-scale plan.

Suggested exercises:
(1) Map/plan of local parade of shops with some shops named – children to identify all the shops and note type.

(2) Shopping lists containing a variety of items including food and consumer durables (cornflakes, carrots, milk, nails, dress, carpet).
Which shops sell which?
Which products can't be obtained from the local parade?
Where would your parents buy these?

(3) Questionnaire: ask shoppers in the local parade
– Where do you live?
– What goods are you buying?
– Where do you buy furniture/clothes?

(4) Discuss other shopping centres, for example, local town centre (Mitcham) or regional centre (Croydon).
How are they different from the local parade?

Example 2. MIDDLE SCHOOL
Extract from a regional study of India.
Age of pupils: twelve years.

Growth of cities in India – Calcutta
Aims: (1) Key idea: (a) An increasing percentage of India's population lives in towns and cities.
(b) People migrate to towns and cities for various reasons, relating to both the sending and receiving areas.
(c) Very great and rapid immigration can lead to severe pressure on resources which may result in unemployment, homelessness, etc.
(d) Certain areas of cities attract concentrations of new immigrant groups.

(2) Skills: Atlas work.
Analysis of text/maps/photos.
Analysis of statistical data transferable into graphical form.

Content
(1) Growth of cities in India; for example, Calcutta.
Location of major cities. Distribution pattern.

(2) Reasons for movement to cities:
(a) Attractions (real and perceived) of city life.
(b) Disadvantages of life in country areas
– sample study of West Bengal village life.

(3) Distribution pattern of migrant settlements (shanty towns or 'bustees') in Calcutta. Explanation.
(4) The problems of shanty town inhabitants.
(5) Possible solutions to the problems of shanty towns.

Resources
e.g. 'Oxford Geography Project' Book 3, p. 79–81.
16mm. film 'Calcutta' (Christian Aid).
Slide set: 'Shanty Towns'.

The report also provides an outline syllabus which spans the years nine to thirteen. The syllabus concentrates entirely upon suggested appropriate content. Apart from the development of map use skills there is little detailed help in how other skills such as the ability to evaluate information might be incorporated into a scheme. The Merton Report is of course not alone in this omission. Map skills and graphicacy have received special attention from geographers because these skills are highly valued in the community of geographers. A disproportionate amount of help would seem to be available here compared to that available in other areas of skill development. The publication of the Schools Council Geography Committee's *Understanding Maps* (1979) is an example of the clear guidance available to teachers in this particular area of skill.

The study of places in the primary school
ILEA Curriculum Guidelines, 1981.

This is one of an increasing number of beautifully produced guidelines for teachers emanating from the ILEA learning materials service. There is a companion booklet available on the study of the past in the primary school. I include it here because of its emphasis on the importance of continuity in 'developing a wide range of basic communication skills, from talking to map making.'

Continuity is vital on two counts. It enables the teacher to build logically on concepts that the children already have, and offers the children opportunities to use their skills. This logical progression will then avoid the repetition and duplication (oh, no, we did dinosaurs in the infants!) that inevitably leads to boredom. The topics studied may recur but the ways in which they are treated should vary according to the ages of the children. The need for continuity is especially evident at the primary/secondary transfer stage. For some first year secondary pupils, the geographical/environmental component in their work may be, at best, repetitive and, at worst, considerably less demanding than studies carried out in the primary school. For other children, unrealistic expectations by the secondary specialist teacher (for example, the inability to use an atlas) may induce feelings of bewilderment and/or hostility.

The *Study of Places* goes on to make the point that it is the skills and concepts employed, rather than the content area, which should be geared closely to the pupil's age and ability. As with the Merton Project, a spiral curriculum is advocated. The diagram from the ILEA document (Fig. 1), reproduced with kind permission of the ILEA, illustrates this point.

The ILEA scheme, then, is an attempt to plan for system and continuity in the geographical experiences of primary school children as a platform upon which secondary school geographers can build.

At this point I am including an example of a scheme in the social subjects from another country. It provides points of comparison with the British work already considered and begins with a recognition of important skills but goes much further in listing key ideas or concepts.

Social studies syllabus guidelines
Department of Education, Wellington, New Zealand, 1977.

The guidelines provide a framework for a four-year course. The course contains suggested themes which it is stressed should be adapted by teachers to their local circumstances. The framework includes a statement of general objectives, a statement of specific objectives, the basic themes for each of the four years, suggestions on the planning of a theme, and more detail about the way in which a theme might be organized, containing important ideas and basic questions. I am indebted to the School Publications Branch of the Department of Education in Wellington, New Zealand, for permission to give this extract here (Fig. 2).

Figure 1: The Spiral Approach

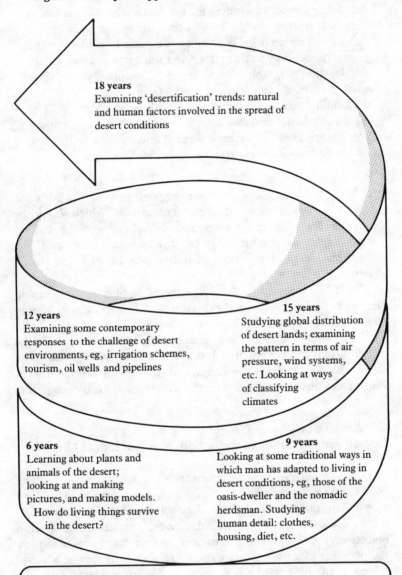

18 years
Examining 'desertification' trends: natural and human factors involved in the spread of desert conditions

12 years
Examining some contemporary responses to the challenge of desert environments, eg, irrigation schemes, tourism, oil wells and pipelines

15 years
Studying global distribution of desert lands; examining the pattern in terms of air pressure, wind systems, etc. Looking at ways of classifying climates

6 years
Learning about plants and animals of the desert; looking at and making pictures, and making models. How do living things survive in the desert?

9 years
Looking at some traditional ways in which man has adapted to living in desert conditions, eg, those of the oasis-dweller and the nomadic herdsman. Studying human detail: clothes, housing, diet, etc.

The study of any topic, for example, deserts, is not especially appropriate for any specific age level. Rather, the age level helps to determine which aspect of the topic is considered.

18 years
Examining recent and proposed legislation
relating to housing: rehabilitation or replacement?
private or public? Consultation with local planners

12 years
Investigation of the evolution
of the local landscape: what was
there before the houses? Use of old
maps and pictures

15 years
Looking at
contemporary change in
the locality, eg, population
trends and movements.
Use of census data to
calculate densities

6 years
Drawing individual
and imaginary houses:
labelling *roof, door,
chimney, window*, etc.

9 years
Simple classifying of houses according
to type: terrace, detached,
semi-detached, etc. Use of symbols
and colours on maps and
sections. Designing the
ideal house

Study of the locality should be present at all levels of environmental work.
This diagram suggests how an element of local study (housing) can be investigated
in appropriate ways at all levels. Of course, the effectiveness of each 'stage' would
be enhanced by the preceding treatment.

Figure 2: Guidelines for 'The Study of Places': Extract

The study of places in the

	Experience	
	Direct	**Indirect**
lower primary	Direct observation of the environment will be centred on the immediately accessible (ie, that area normally reached without the aid of transport). The school grounds and the neighbourhood are ideal and sufficient. Such observation will be the basis for much 'labelling' activity, involving the acquisition of vocabulary. Specific destinations or features (eg, the park, the library, the church) will be more appropriate than more general 'surveys'. Clearly identifiable people in the immediate locality (eg, lollipop lady, policeman, postman, milkman, bus driver) will provide a basis for discussion, and could also be invited to talk with the children. Recognition and discussion of broad weather categories (eg, rainy, windy, frosty weather) and seasonal changes can lead to simple scientific investigation and creative work. The children will be indiscriminate 'collectors', both privately and when on class excursions. Some of these collections (eg, of pebbles, postcards, matchbox labels) may be used as a basis for discussions about places, and provide opportunities for sorting and classifying in various ways.	Stories can be particularly important in extending children's range of imagining. Whether stories are set in unfamiliar contexts (eg, the countryside, distant lands, imaginary places) or familiar environments, they will be a major stimulus to thought and discussion about places. (The stories selected must, of course, be good as stores; ideally they might feature children of the same age range.) Traditional folk-tales from other countries might also be employed. Stories will often provide a basis for discussion, drama, and other creative activities. Topic work based upon animals (eg, polar bears, camels, lions) and their habitats can be a very appropriate way of fostering children's early awareness of broad global contrasts. There will be opportunities to 'share' the direct experience of others in the class (eg, journeys, holidays).
middle primary	Observations in the immediate environment will increasingly take the form of simple 'surveys' of small areas. Such surveys will often involve various methods of classification (eg, of types of buildings, open spaces, traffic). The children's interest in individual environmental detail can be used in the investigation of changes in the locality. Visual 'clues' (eg, the conversion of houses to offices or shops) can be identified, indicating past and current changes. Simple weather records may be kept over short periods (eg, two to three weeks); these would not necessarily involve standard measuring units. Organised visits may extend to whole-day explorations beyond the immediate locality but not normally beyond an hour's travelling time. Typical destinations would be a farm, a major open space (eg, woodland, common, heath), a zoo or a museum. A major objective for such visits is to provide a stimulus for the use of communication skills.	Stories will increasingly be supplemented by documentary material about other environments. This should normally be in the form of sample studies of specific locations (eg, a farm, a village, a mine, a factory, a port). An emphasis upon families and individuals, preferably names, will add a sense of reality. Such investigations should attempt to bring out the universal nature of human needs and activities (eg, food, housing, clothing, work, trade, travel) and to establish that all localities contain elements of change. Personal linkages with the wider world (eg, through travel, relatives in other countries) will also provide opportunities for extending the children's range of imagining. Publicised journeys (eg, a round-the-world yacht race, international sports, royal visits) that have already captured the children's attention may form a starting point for investigations of other countries. The natural interest in spectacular environmental events (eg, volcanoes, earthquakes, hurricanes, floods) affords another appropriate 'way in' to wider world studies. The emphasis should be upon the impact on people and their responses, rather than on causation. The children's growing awareness of basic global contrasts might be sustained through the discussion of selected stories of exploration. A useful teaching strategy is to invite the children to imagine themselves in another environment, as travellers or inhabitants.
upper primary	The area used for local study will expand to include locations and networks familiar to the children, involving investigations of journeys and destinations for shopping, recreation and work. The awareness and consideration of live local issues (education for the environment) will emerge as an increasingly important element. This will complement the use of the locality for the development of skills (education *through* the environment) and collecting information (education *about* the environment). At this stage there will be more concern for the neighbourhood and townscape as a whole. In weather studies, standard measuring devices may be introduced (eg, the rain-gauge, the thermometer), with a greater emphasis upon averages and generalisations (eg, seasonal patterns). In addition to day visits, a residential school journey may facilitate elementary comparative studies of different environments. Coast and countryside, river and village all provide opportunities for consolidating map skills in the field. Simple relationships between rock types and scenery (eg, chalk downland, clay vale) may be introduced.	Several topics or projects of a geographical nature may be undertaken. These might often be selected for their topicality (eg, the Soviet Union during the 1980 Olympics) or personal relevance (eg, areas with which children or teachers have links). Geographical topics may be organised around a theme (eg, mountains), an area (eg, Canada) or a product (eg, petroleum). Such topics may include selected contrasting environments within Britain (eg, a hill farm, a mining town, a fishing port). There will be increasing opportunities for reference to non-school sources of environmental information, such as television and the press. An emphasis upon global linkages in trade, tourism and migration will be appropriate. Some systematic support should be provided for the children's early attempts to sort out the nature of the 'building blocks' of the political map (ie, district, county or state or province, country and continent) and the physical map (ie, mountain ranges, plateaux, plains, estuaries, peninsulas and broad climatic types). Simulations and role-play (eg, the selection of holiday destinations, the routing of a motorway) can be very effective at this stage. Well-chosen stories set in other environments will continue to be the basis for much environmental imagining.

primary school: the matrix

Graphicacy	
Maps	**Other aspects**
There will normally be little or no formal, systematic 'mapwork': printed maps of any kind will rarely be appropriate. A large scale map of the local area may be displayed as an element in the room decor, reinforcing the small child's sense of territory. Most representations of place, whether provided by the teacher or produced by the children, will be essentially pictorial, though some will incorporate a 'map' element. Such early spontaneous picture-maps (eg, 'my house', 'my visit to Granny') should be encouraged. Early 'map' activities will often be based upon imaginative experiences. Stories may contain picture-maps or be the basis for individual or collective pictorial map making. Such map making may also follow on from the discussion of pictures. Many simple games involve the representation of routes, destinations and the location of hazards, and provide further opportunities to explore this mode of communication.	Pictures will be a particularly important stimulus for developing ideas about places, and for acquiring vocabulary. Pictures of local places will be as useful as pictures of environments unfamiliar to children (eg, mountain scenes, seaside scenes). Aerial photographs of the immediate locality can be a stimulating part of the decor. Films or slide sequences should be very brief. As well as being a source of environmental information, pictures can be employed by the children to communicate their own ideas; they can be encouraged to make pictures of the locality, possibly using cheap cameras. Recording will commonly take the form of simple pictograms (eg, of weather, jobs, modes of transport) which will start to establish the notion of 'standard symbols' to represent real-world experiences or features. Modelling (eg, of a farm, a street, a zoo, a village) will also be an important way of communicating about places. Scale is unimportant, but the recording of the layout of a model can be a useful early approach to the concept of the map.
Maps should increasingly complement, but not replace, the pictorial representation of places. Free-hand maps (eg, of the journey to school) should be encouraged; however, by the age of nine there should be a greater use of provided maps. These will normally be in the form of simple duplicated base-maps (eg, street maps, a farm plan) to which the children can add labels, colours and other information. Map skills appropriate for this age group include the use of colours and symbols, together with keys to explain them. The map languages or codes, however, should preferably not be imposed, but should be devised by the children themselves. The use of simple grids to assist in locating places ('My house is in square B3, the school is in square D5') may be introduced, possibly through games (eg, battleships, treasure hunts). 'Imaginative' maps based on stories or ideal layouts for a school, park, zoo, etc, will continue to be important. The study of local and distant places should involve large scale maps and plans (eg, the local shops rather than the British Isles, an Indian village rather than India). Grasp of scale should not be a major objective at this stage; a 'subjective' approach to scale (ie, features regarded by the child as significant being recorded on a larger scale) is likely to persist for most children. Early practice in map using should be integrated with local work, relating map shapes and symbols to features observed in the field. A wide range of types of maps of the locality (eg, old maps, estate agents' maps, A-Z maps, maps from local newspapers) can be involved, whilst for wider world topics the globe is a most useful adjunct at this stage.	Pictures will continue to be very important. Discussion of a picture will often continue the process of categorising environments (eg, a city centre, a village, a port, a harbour, a resort) and the annotation of pictures (eg, postcards, posters, duplicated sketches) can consolidate vocabulary. A set of slides and/or photographs of the local area is an invaluable resource at this stage, as are large scale vertical aerial photographs of the area. The children should be encouraged to make as well as to examine pictures of places, both local and distant. Other graphical devices that can be introduced include the histogram (eg, showing the results of traffic count), the compound bar (eg, showing activities during a day, week or year), the flow diagram (eg, milk from cow to classroom) and the section (eg, upper floor uses of a shopping street). Models continue to be useful and can now be more closely related to actual places.
Spontaneous free-hand 'map' making will continue to be encouraged, complemented by an increasing emphasis upon basic map skills. Some children are able to grasp the notion of scale at this stage, but much systematic practice in the measuring of distances and areas is necessary. It is important to explore the ways in which the scale adopted imposes constraints on (i) the area covered by the map and (ii) the degree of detail shown. There will be a greater emphasis upon understanding and using standardised map language (eg, Ordnance Survey symbols and atlas conventions such as layer tinting). These skills will be most purposefully consolidated if used in the field (eg, a school journey programme could include an introduction to the use of the compass). Large scales will continue to be dominant in both local and global studies (eg, a plan of a dairy farm, a plan of a Jamaican plantation, an airport layout), but there will be increasing use of smaller scale atlas maps in work on journeys and distant locations. Regular use of the atlas will develop familiarity with 'thematic' maps which show one dimension (eg, relief, political units, rainfall, population). Conventional map grids (eg, Ordnance Survey four-figure references, latitude and longitude on atlas maps) may be introduced. The design of ideal layouts, possibly linked to the discussion of a local issue, will continue, as will the mapping of stories.	Work will involve much collecting, making and studying of pictures of all kinds, with emergent emphasis upon the selecting of appropriate pictures to represent a local or distant environment. The school journey may provide an opportunity to develop simple transects and cross sections, whilst the comparative study of places may establish the matrix as a useful way of recording information. The use of relief, rainfall and population maps will afford an opportunity to introduce the isoline concept, which can be employed in local studies (eg, linking locations 5, 10 or 15 minutes away from school). Children could also be introduced to 'topologically transformed' maps in which the scale used relates not to distance but to some other factor such as travelling time or population size. Work on broad climatic regions (eg, tundra, desert, rain-forest) can involve simple climatic graphs. Conversion graphs (eg, kilometres, miles, degrees centigrade/Fahrenheit) may continue to be required. Studies of farming, trade and so on may involve the use of pie diagrams to represent proportions. Other devices include the balance sheet as a way of arranging information (eg, the costs and benefits of an environmental decision) or for assessments of environmental quality and the design of publicity materials (eg, posters, leaflets, newspapers) for real or imagined locations. Vertical and oblique photographs continue to be an important resource and will help the children's understanding of map and townscape. Model making will become increasingly sophisticated and will be linked to specific purposes (eg, developing an understanding of scale, or designing a redevelopment for the locality).

SOCIAL STUDIES SYLLABUS GUIDELINES, DEPARTMENT OF
EDUCATION, WELLINGTON, NEW ZEALAND: EXTRACT

General Objectives

Social studies should help students:
To develop those ideas and skills that will
contribute to their understanding of themselves
and their society.

To think clearly and critically about human
behaviour and values so that they may make
reasoned choices.

To apply their knowledge and abilities to the
welfare of mankind.

Specific Objectives

The syllabus is designed to help students:

To move towards an understanding of some of the important ideas about human behaviour that are presented in the yearly programmes.

To identify and formulate an appropriate inquiry.

To locate and gather relevant information.

To interpret information.

To make inferences from information.

To make tentative generalisations.

To form and express new ideas.

To relate ideas to personal experiences.

To identify the value positions likely to influence the outcome of the inquiry.

To identify their own values.

To recognise how values affect the way they think and act.

To recognise the influences that have shaped their values.

To identify values in their own and other societies.

To examine their own and others' values in terms of their consequences.

To recognise that values change, and to be able to identify some of the causes of change.

To accept that people strive to maintain their values.

To accept that value conflicts exist.

To attempt to resolve conflicts by applying rational procedures.

To show by their actions that they are sensitive to the needs and interests of others and that they respect and accept the idea of individual and cultural difference.

These objectives are the basis for selecting and organising content, and for deciding the kinds of learning experiences that should be provided. They also indicate the criteria for continuing evaluation.

Basic Themes

A basic theme has been suggested as an *emphasis* for each year, e.g., "Form I. The basic theme is Cultural Difference." Each theme focuses on a major aspect of human behaviour, and this provides cohesion for a year's programme. *Other ideas, including some from other themes, may also emerge from studies made in any one year.*

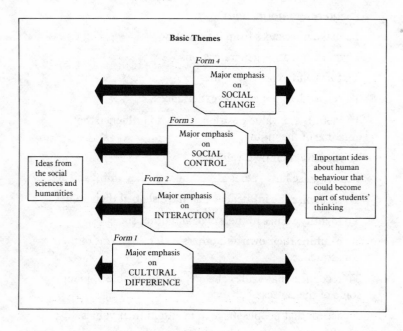

Each year one theme is emphasised, but some aspects of the others could be developed.

Important Ideas

For each theme, some important ideas are provided for teachers. They are drawn from the social sciences and humanities, and in most cases have the support of more than one discipline.

These ideas are stated in adult terms. They are guides to the selection of content and learning experiences, not statements towards which students are to be directed. The ideas students might state will reflect the quality of their experiences, the variation in their abilities, and the resources available to them.

Planning the School Scheme

The THEME provides an emphasis and cohesion for the year's study.

The BASIC QUESTION is a means of organising approaches to the theme.

The IMPORTANT IDEAS are the teachers' guides to the selection of appropriate content and learning experiences.

Sections A, B, and C give a general framework of study and set out the minimum range of cultural and social settings appropriate to the questions and themes.

Important aspects of the study are numbered 1, 2 and 3. All these important aspects of human behaviour should be considered with any of the recommended studies.

Recommended studies are printed in italics.

Some examples are listed alongside each recommended study. Teachers may choose one of those listed or they may choose another one that illustrates the recommended study and can be supported by available resources.

FORM I. The Basic Theme is Cultural Difference

The INTENTION is that a study of cultural differences will lead to a better understanding of some aspects of human behaviour.

The IMPORTANT IDEAS about human behaviour that follow could become part of students' thinking during the year's work. They are guides to the selection of content and learning experiences, not statements towards which students are to be directed. Other ideas, including some from other themes, may also emerge from studies made during the year.

As well as all the differences among individuals and groups, there are certain common characteristics and needs.

People living in groups develop a common way of life. It is known as their culture, and shows in shared patterns of behaviour, material products, forms of expression, institutions, beliefs, attitudes and values.

Differences in the patterns of behaviour, values and attitudes of different groups arise from differences in their backgrounds, environment, experiences and ways of looking at the world.

Present patterns of behaviour include elements derived from past patterns.

Each person acquires the culture of his group as he lives and learns within it. By his conscious and unconscious choices, he helps to maintain and modify it.

There are differences within as well as between cultures. Not all people in one culture share the same value system.

Each person in a society fills several roles which are influenced by the expectations of some or most members of that society.

All societies rank individuals on some scale of values.

People tend to view their own way of life as the most reasonable and natural.

People in different cultures perceive individual freedom in different ways.

As people seek to meet their material and non-material needs, they may co-operate, as well as come into conflict. The patterns of co-operation and conflict vary within and between cultures.

Each group develops its own way of producing, distributing and exchanging goods and services.

As specialisation increases, the need for interdependence becomes greater.

Every culture is continuously changing.

A BASIC QUESTION that should help guide student inquiry is: How do ways of life differ, and what can be discovered about human behaviour (including our own) through studying these differences?

It is recommended that STUDIES be selected from each of the areas printed in italics. Examples other than those listed should also be considered. The examples selected will provide settings for students

A.
1. To investigate such aspects of contemporary life as work, order, security, health, the arts, customs, beliefs and aspirations, in:
   A nomadic community, e.g., Australian Aboriginal, Bedouin, etc.
   A village community, e.g., in Africa or Asia.
2. To compare the aspects of life studied and to relate the findings to our own lives.
3. To discover what significant cultural differences emerge from these studies, and what can be learned from them.

B.

1. To investigate aspects of the life of individuals and selected groups in:

   A town or city in nineteenth-century Britain; e.g., London, Birmingham, etc.

   A New Zealand settlement in the nineteenth century.

   An Asian city of traditional importance, e.g., Kyoto, Bangkok, Mecca, Peking, etc.

   A large Western city, e.g., New York, Rome, Rio de Janeiro, Sydney, etc.

2. To compare the aspects of life studied and to relate the findings to our own lives.

3. To consider what significant cultural differences emerge from these studies, and what can be learned from them.

C.

1. To investigate and compare:

   Selected aspects of the life of individuals and groups in our own and other communities, e.g.,

   practising religion
   ranking members
   choosing leaders
   caring for the needy
   nurturing and educating children
   spending leisure time
   welcoming visitors
   talking things over
   regarding possessions
   mourning the dead

2. To consider what significant cultural differences and similarities emerge from these studies, and what can be learned from them.

Although I have quite deliberately confined this brief review of guidelines for continuity to the social subjects area I feel that I cannot ignore what is in my opinion an excellent example of a local authority initiative. It is in the related area of Religious Education.

*Paths to Understanding. A handbook to religious education in
Hampshire schools.*
General Editor: Warren Laxton, County Adviser: David Naylor
Hampshire Education Authority, 1980, Basingstoke,
Globe Education.

The format of this handbook is attractive. It is loosely bound. Pages
can be taken out or added to the book. It is well illustrated but not over
illustrated in black and white with photographs from Hampshire
schools. It is rich in suggested syllabuses, practical ideas, useful
resources and mini-case studies of work with 4 to 18-year-olds. The
handbook is the product of advisers and teachers working together.
The writers are well aware of the limitations of such guidelines.

In print, even the liveliest ideas can seem cold and analytical,
although an attempt has been made to retain the flavour of origi-
nality and personality . . . The value of the material offered
depends not only on careful reading, but on the reader's
sympathetic, imaginative and constructive response.

Curriculum guidelines are difficult to write but by its rich portray-
als of specific situations, the Hampshire handbook overcomes many
of the difficulties. Examples of syllabuses and work are taken (an
infants' school in a village, an infants' school in a town, a junior school
in a new town, a middle school in a housing estate, a comprehensive
school (mixed 12–16, multi-racial) in an urban area, a sixth form
college. There are useful sections on assemblies and on teachers'
expressed anxieties about teaching religious education. Arid lists of
concepts provide no points of contact with potential users but the
strong situational references in terms of children, environments and
ideas encourage and should engage teachers to consider the message.

Other local authority initiatives

There are many more local initiatives in providing guidelines for
curricular continuity of which I am aware but which I cannot do
justice to in the present work. There must also be many excellent
schemes of which I am totally unaware. Globe Education has provided
a useful format in which to present these local initiatives. For West
Glamorgan County Council, Globe Education has published:

Flow and Control in Mathematics 5–13, edited by Derek Gray,
County Adviser in Mathematics.

This is a mathematics scheme which gives 'a county view' of continuity. The scheme is in four phases and within these, nine stages, and is linked where appropriate with Nuffield Mathematics and the Schools Mathematics Project. A printed progress chart for an individual child is also provided.

The same publisher has also produced:

Science Horizons: The West Sussex Science 5–14 Scheme

The course is 'a complete structured science programme . . . designed particularly for use by non-specialist teachers.' It consists of a teachers' background handbook and separate teaching materials on such topics as 'Ourselves', 'Floating and Sinking', 'The Home – from Rain to Tap', 'Materials in the Home' and 'Light and Colour'. The West Sussex Scheme is a good example of materials written and edited by an adviser and groups working through a teachers' centre.

How helpful are guidelines?

The writers of curriculum guidelines assume that their efforts are helpful to teachers. They assume that an outline plan for teaching can be readily translated into an action programme. Teaching is a practical activity. Teachers make hundreds of practical decisions about what to do, what not to do and how to approach situations every day during their lives in classrooms. How one writes to help and encourage this activity is I believe a great deal more problematic than many guide writers would admit. Are some guidelines more useful than others? If so, what makes them useful?

Most of the guidelines we have considered in this chapter assume that the appropriate structure for writing about curriculum is what is called the rational curriculum planning model. References in the above works to aims and objectives abound. How far do written objectives relate to what happens in classrooms? There is, of course, no necessary relationship between written statements of intent about a course and the teaching that takes place. Written curricula may be *ex post facto* descriptions and more related to past events than to future ones. The use of the language of rational curriculum planning also assumes shared meanings and a common technical language. Some objectives are written in such general terms that they are open to infinite varieties of interpretation. The use of written objectives is no guarantee that the related teaching is more systematic, more structured or more effective in providing continuity of curricular experience.

When teachers, within the same school and in different schools, agree to be guided by a common statement of objectives, a common set of skills, concepts and content, they lose some of their autonomy. Meetings of primary and secondary school teachers to consider a common curriculum plan often result in initiatives being taken by subject specialists who are expected to give a lead to their generalist colleagues. All these factors make curriculum guides difficult to write. Is it possible to identify some of the key features of an effective guide? The following would be my tentative list of criteria:

1. Guides are more likely to be effective if they identify and are written for a specific target readership. Groups of teachers involved in cooperative planning for continuity in their own situation and producing their own scheme are likely to encounter fewer problems of communication than groups that have a scheme imposed on them by another school or an authority.

2. If attempts are being made to implement guidelines for continuity over the area of a local authority as in the Oxfordshire or Hampshire schemes described above, then communication is probably helped by identifying and describing critical situations, such as those of the inner-urban area with multi-racial mix of population, or schools serving an inner-suburban area. Other examples might include primary schools and secondary schools with different curricular patterns. These may include primary schools working in the social subjects area mainly through topics feeding a secondary school that teaches history and geography separately from the first year.

3. When concepts or key ideas are being advocated as a basis for continuity, examples need to be provided of their organization and sequence.

4. Similarly, examples of skill development will be required. I have discovered few examples of this kind outside the detailed treatment given to mapping skills in geography. 'Place, Time and Society' provides examples of the development of the interpretation and evaluation of information and also of the development of empathic understanding through its published materials (see Derricott and Blyth, 1979, 'Cognitive development: the social dimension' in Floyd, A. (Ed) *Cognitive Development in the School Years*, Croom Helm in association with Open University Press.)

5. Teachers are likely to find written guidelines helpful if they include full and up to date lists of available resources for teaching.

CHAPTER SEVEN
Establishing Curricular Continuity

Ray Derricott

I now come to the difficult part of this work. Having dissected the process of transition and identified many of its key concepts and having presented examples of continuity in practice, I will now set up, quite deliberately, an Aunt Sally. From my experiences and from the work of my colleagues as represented in the foregoing chapters, I find that insufficient attention is paid to *process* in attempts to establish what is in effect a complex innovation – namely curricular continuity. The agenda for establishing continuity needs to be given considerable thought and carefully set up.

Clearly, the degree of implementation of any innovation depends to some extent on the *clarity of the message*. A high degree of explicitness about the nature and intent of an innovation may lead to a high degree of implementation and vice-versa. See, for example, the work of Fullan and Pomfret (1977) on this. However, clarity of communication is not the only issue. A message can be expressed loudly and clearly but be on the wrong wave band for the potential receivers or a potential receiver may know and understand the nature of the message but refuse to tune in to listen to it.

There are other crucial factors which influence the implementation of an innovation such as a system of curricular continuity.

(a) *Resources* are needed to support the innovation; in our case, possible help from the outside in the shape of an adviser or consultant; financial backing from a local authority in order to support teachers in travelling to meetings in other schools; help in providing supporting supply staff to underpin teacher release that may be necessary.

(b) *Competencies and inservice support.* An ambitious innovation such as curricular continuity is likely to fail if the teachers involved are being asked to use skills which they do not possess at all or which they possess at an inadequate level. The kinds of competencies demanded of teachers in an innovation of this nature are many, namely:

(i) social and interpersonal skills,
(ii) administrative and procedural skills, especially in the organization and running of meetings,
(iii) political skills in being sensitive to existing traditions, hierarchies and power positions (i.e. teachers' actual or perceived relationships to each other within and between schools),
(iv) subject knowledge and skill,
(v) skills and knowledge in curriculum planning.

Many of these skills can be trained and will therefore need the backing of an inservice programme, either school based or inservice course based at, for example, a Teachers' Centre.

(c) *Values.* The values implicit in an innovation or made explicit through it will affect the way it is received. Assumptions and value positions about how schools should operate, about primary and secondary education, about structure, systematization and teaching and learning may be challenged when considering curricular continuity. As Stillman and Maychell (1984) put it:

> This positive attitude (towards collaboration) is not helped by the inherent problems set up by an education system which exacerbates teacher and school isolation. Teachers are not encouraged to be open about their work, and knowledge of what happens in other's classrooms within their own school is relatively poor. Knowledge of what happens in other schools is even weaker. If discussing about one's teaching method is perceived as being threatening then progress will be limited.

Clearly then, at some early stage of attempting to set up a process of continuity some exploration of individual value positions needs to be on the agenda. These issues become multi-layered when one contemplates the complexities of values between stages and amongst teachers whose whole training and socialisation process has led them to very different value positions. John Stephenson in Chapter Four refers to some of these.

(d) *Motivation*. Finally, commitment to and involvement in an innovation can greatly affect the degree of implementation. At a base level the question 'What is in it for me?' is rarely, if ever, brought into the open from the hidden agenda. Teachers' motivations for active involvement in time consuming innovation have to be coped with. Highly motivated teachers find time where they do not think they have it for involvement in innovation, others may use the problem of time as a 'flight mechanism' and reject innovation on that basis.

Keeping the above factors in mind, I now put up my Aunt Sally as a basis for discussion and possible action. It assumes school based activity in the main with the possibility of support at appropriate times from more conventional, perhaps Teachers' Centre based, inservice education. It is tentative and taxonomic in that it is programmed with suggested steps or stages. I am well aware in using this approach that it has behind it a strong ideological belief in client-centred or, as the Americans call it, 'user-driven' innovation. I am also well aware that it is devised by me well away from the front line (wherever that is in educational terms) and that it is devoid of context. I believe quite firmly that meaning is situation specific and I know that a general framework such as the one I express will prove meaningless to many teachers. In this sense it fits neatly into a recent analysis of school centred innovation (SCI) conducted by Andy Hargreaves (1982). He says:

> Taxonomic accounts are programmatic, but more elaborately so. In meticulous detail, they outline many different kinds of SCI that might, in theory, be developed. The language in which such schemes are described is a hypothetical and conditional language of the possible. The authors of taxonomic accounts take it for granted that SCI *should* take place: their more precise purpose is to specify the different conceivable ways in which it *could* be organised, and their repetitive use of 'could', 'might' and 'may' reflects this nicely.   (p. 355)

Therefore, with my gum shield out and my guard down I deliberately walk into Andy Hargreaves' straight left. I present the suggested framework for those in the thick of everyday practice, to test against their own realities. Those teachers who believe that continuity of curricular experience has meaning at more than the rhetorical level will perhaps try this test. Others may have been convinced by some of the accounts in Chapters 3–5 that continuity is not a goal worth pursuing.

Establishing Continuity: A suggested framework

STEP 1

Does *liaison* exist with primary schools?

INFORMATION

What *information* does the secondary school receive from the primary schools?
  (a) Official Report Card
  (b) Official Profile
  (c) Specially designed card or profile
  (d) Special reports, e.g., from the remedial service
  (e) Special health reports
  (f) Folders of children's work.

PEOPLE
AND
ROLES

Which personnel are involved in liaison with primary/secondary school?
  (a) Primary head, deputy, class teachers
  (b) Secondary head, head of lower school, special post teacher, Heads of Departments, others
Are staff visits specially arranged? Do they happen when the need arises or only once a year?
Do the teachers (at all levels) involved in liaison have clear job specifications? Are these job specifications communicated clearly to all teaching staff?

PUPILS

Do all primary children make at least one visit to the secondary school in their last term of primary education?
Do primary pupils host the secondary school on any other occasions?
Are any special/specialist facilities offered by the secondary school for occasional or regular use by primary children? (e.g. swimming pool, sports hall, computers, science facilities)

STEP 2

CURRICULUM

FROM THE PRIMARY VIEWPOINT

What do primary school teachers *know* about the curriculum and organization of the secondary school to which their children transfer?

What would the primary school teachers *like to know* about the curriculum and organization of the secondary school?

Is there a set scheme (such as SMP) in mathematics?

How is English taught?

What attitude does the secondary school have to spelling, grammar, punctuation, handwriting, presentation of work, creative writing?

What kind of literature does the secondary school introduce to the children?

Is drama included in the curriculum?

What is the secondary school's approach to lower school science?

What grouping system is used immediately on tranfer to secondary school?

If setting is used, what attention is paid to primary school records?

Does the secondary school use any standardized tests to aid grouping practice?

Is any part of the first year in the secondary school used as a diagnostic period?

What attitude does the secondary school have to remedial provision? How and when is this provided?

What continuity is there in the provision of reading materials for children with learning difficulties?

What kind of pastoral, house, tutorial system does the secondary school operate?

At transfer, does the secondary school have a policy of maintaining, wherever possible, existing friendship groupings? Or is an attempt made to form new social groupings?

Does the secondary school provide the primary schools with feedback about ex-pupils? What kind of feedback?

FROM THE SECONDARY VIEWPOINT
What do secondary school teachers *know* about the curriculum and organization of the primary schools?
What would the secondary school teachers *like to know* about the curriculum and organization of the primary schools?

MATHEMATICS
What is the school's approach to mathematics?
Are the children encouraged to use calculators?
Do the primary schools have computers?
How are these used?
What view does the primary school take on the learning of tables and number bonds?

READING, LANGUAGE AND LITERATURE
How is reading taught in the primary school?
Is there a remedial scheme or remedial provision?
Does the primary school have a policy on extending reading skills?
Are library and reference skills taught?
What does the primary school do about spelling, language, grammar, handwriting, creative working?
What experience is offered the children in literature and poetry? Is drama encouraged?
Does the primary school have a policy for the development of language skills?
How is oral communication encouraged?

SCIENCE
What scientific experiences have the children had?
Has the approach to science been systematic through the use of a scheme such as Science 5/13?
Have the children been encouraged to handle

animals? Have they been encouraged to conduct their own simple experiments?

HISTORY AND GEOGRAPHY

What has been the approach to history and geography in the primary school?
Has a topic approach been used?
Have the children been encouraged to read or listen to historical fiction?
Does the primary school use a history or a geography text book?
Have the children been introduced to maps, atlases?
Have the children experienced any historical/geographical field-trips?

ARTS

What kinds of aesthetic, creative, musical experiences does the primary school provide?
What kinds of media (clay, paint etc.) have the children experienced?

STEP 3

STARTING DISCUSSIONS
A suggested programme:

| CURRICULUM |

1. Informal social/professional meetings of heads. The place of the meeting should be chosen carefully and not automatically assumed to be in the secondary school.
2. Informal meetings of individuals (e.g. head of lower school and primary class teachers) on each others' territory.
3. The exchange of any written documentation of a general nature such as school brochures or handbooks.
4. The exchange of any available documents about aspects of the curriculum, e.g: a primary school language or maths scheme, a secondary school statement on the teaching of English.
5. Meetings to plan more formal developments. Possibilities:
   (a) Regular meetings of departmental

staff from secondary schools and primary staff.

Perhaps making a start with one department – maths or English.

(b) A whole day conference involving the closing of schools and the bringing together of primary and secondary staffs. [This is the kind of activity described by John Stephenson in Chapter Four.]

For such a conference what will be the format?

Is there a need for key lectures?

If a major objective is beginning systematic professional discussions between stages should this activity predominate?

STEP 4

PLANNING GROUPS

There is considerable evidence from my own work and that of Stillman and Maychell (1984) that the planning and handling of teachers' meetings is a vital element in the 'success' of the outcome. At this stage of the proceedings teachers are coming together to plan (with a view to implementation) for curricular continuity. These kinds of meetings can appear threatening. Not only are the teachers involved subjecting themselves to *professional exposure* but also to *intellectual exposure*. Not only will they be expected to talk about their own approaches but they will also be exposing their abilities to use the language of curricular planning.

TASK ONE: CLARIFICATION

At the planning meetings is the *task* of the group clear?

Is there a clearly laid out time-scale for discussion?

Are the tasks too vacuous or all-consuming or are they manageable in the time available?

How are the agenda of meetings arrived at?

Who is in the chair? Why?
What kinds of outcomes are envisaged?
What kind of priority is the activity being given?
Is time available being used effectively?

TASK TWO: THE LANGUAGE OF PLANNING	What assumptions are being made about the technical language in which planning is being discussed?

Do the members have the necessary competencies in this activity?
Is the language of Rational Curriculum Planning – aims, objectives, learning experiences, evaluation – the most appropriate language in which to conduct the planning discussion?
Are there alternatives?
Is it possible to begin with a critique of existing practice and ask
What are we doing?
What can be improved in what we are doing?
How do we improve?

TASK THREE: NATURE OF AGREEMENT	Is agreement on *aims* and *objectives* being sought? Is agreement on the range of *skills* encouraged within a curriculum being sought?

Is agreement being sought on the *selection* and *sequencing* of content?
Is agreement being sought on *methods* of *teaching* and *learning*? (pedagogy)
Is agreement being sought on methods of assessment?

STEP 5

COOPERATION IN TEACHING	Is possible cooperation by junior and secondary staff in actual teaching and assessment a distant goal?

What form will this be in?

STEP 6

Is the process of attempting to establish continuity of curricular experience being subject to

| EVALUATION | *evaluation?* |

By whom? How? When?
Who will receive the evaluation feedback?
What action will be taken on it?

| OUTSIDE HELP | Can the process described above be self-generating and self-maintaining? In other words, do you have the resources (time, competencies, |

etc.) to do it yourself? Or is the help of an outside agent thought desirable or essential? How far can local advisers be expected to do more than legitimate such detailed and intensive activity?
How far can *consultants* be used?
Who should they be?

Some concluding remarks on continuity

I have argued in this book that continuity of curricular experience is an idea that is more prevalent at the level of rhetoric than at the level of practice. When we examine practice we still find continuity to be a slippery concept, difficult to define and to identify. The contributions in Chapters 3–5 are illustrations of attempts by teachers to implement the idea. The guidelines reviewed in Chapter Six represent efforts at a more general level to plan, encourage and implement continuity. All are presented in a positive light. Perhaps the most poignant comment on continuity is that by the teacher in the study by Jennifer Nias when she pleads that although she very much supports continuity it is not an idea that is 'built into the staff's knowledge . . .'. She seems to be saying that it is the *process of implementation* that is most difficult to understand and to master. It is with this in mind that I produced the preceding section which is intended as a guideline to the process.

The diagram on p. 156 is an attempt to summarize the arguments put forward. This is meant to illustrate that the process of transition involves liaison which has three facets:

(a) *administrative*, the goal of which is the efficient passing on (in both directions) of information about pupils, teaching methods, curriculum between schools;

(b) *social/pastoral*, a part of the process which has as its goals the smooth adjustment of pupils to a new system and is manifest in visits by teachers and pupils to each other's schools and in discussions amongst staff of children with special needs;

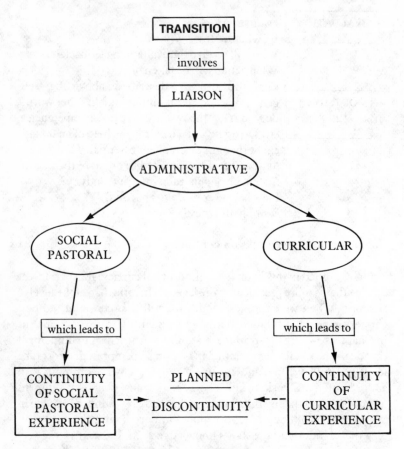

(c) *curricular*, which has as its goal the establishment of curricular continuity. It is manifest in meetings of teachers from different schools to discuss, plan and implement related courses and approaches to teaching.

Sitting uneasily in this diagram about continuity is the idea of planned discontinuity. In Chapter Five we raised the issue of the natural desirability of continuity and wondered whether it is a taken-for-granted notion. Planned discontinuity, as opposed to unplanned discontinuity which is the *drift* into random, unrelated activities, would seem to have a clear purpose and is worthy of further consideration. Planned discontinuity is a deliberate change in practice with the intention of stimulating growth and development. It is manifest in the practice of breaking up primary school friendship groups on entry to secondary school in order to foster the development of new friendship patterns. It could be manifest in a deliberate and abrupt change in teaching or content as a symbol of the process of maturity or growing older. The disequilibrium caused by such an experience challenges children to accommodate to it and to develop new ways of learning. Such an idea, of course, needs careful handling. It is not as extreme as the 'clean break' or 'second birth' theory. The challenge is to provide continuity of experience as a general goal but to recognize those areas in which discontinuity is likely to be fruitful.

The idea of continuity of curricular experience has been shown to be complex and multi-dimensional. The contents of this volume are intended to contribute to a continuing debate amongst teachers.

Bibliography

BAILEY, P. (1980). 'Editorial: progression', *Teaching Geography*, 5, 4, 146.

BALCHIN, W. G. V. and COLEMAN, A. D. (1965). 'Graphicacy should be the fourth ace in the pack', *Times Educational Supplement*, 5 November 1965.

BATES, P. (1978). 'The transition of children at eleven-plus', *Journal of Applied Educational Studies*, 7, 2, 7–13.

BENNETTS, T. (1981). 'Progress in the geography curriculum'. In: WALFORD, R. (Ed) *Signposts for Geography Teaching*. Harlow, Essex: Longman.

BLYTH, W. A. L. (1967). *English Primary Education: a Sociological Description*. 2 vols. London: Routledge and Kegan Paul.

BLYTH, W. A. L., COOPER, K. R., DERRICOTT, R., ELLIOTT, G., SUMNER, H. and WAPLINGTON, A. (1976). *Curriculum Planning in History, Geography and Social Science*. London: Collins-ESL/Bristol.

BLYTH, W. A. L. and DERRICOTT, R. (1977). *The Social Significance of Middle Schools*. London: Batsford.

BRIAULT, E. and SHAVE, D. (1952). *Geography in the Secondary School*. A report prepared for the Geographical Association. Sheffield: Geographical Association.

BRIERLY, J. (1980). *Children's Well-being: Growth Development and Learning From Conception to Adolescence*. Windsor: NFER.

BROWN, J. M. and ARMSTRONG, R. (1982). 'The structure of pupils' worries during transition from junior to secondary school', *British Educational Research Journal*, 8, 2, 123–31.

BRUNER, J. S. (1960). *The Process of Education*. Cambridge, Mass: Harvard University Press (Vintage Books, 1963).

BRUNER, J. S. (1967). *Towards a Theory of Instruction*. Cambridge, Mass.: Belknap Press.

BULLOCK REPORT. GREAT BRITAIN. DEPARTMENT OF EDUCATION AND SCIENCE. (1975). *A Language for Life*. London: HMSO.

CAMPBELL, R. J. (1971). Anxiety about school amongst pupils moving from primary to secondary schools. Unpublished M.Sc. dissertation, School of Research in Education, University of Bradford.

CARR, B. (1980). 'Is there liaison between primary and secondary schools?', *Teaching Geography*, 6, 1, 39.

CATLING, S. J. (1976). 'Cognitive mapping: judgements and responsibilities', *Architectural Psychology Newsletter*, 6, 4, New York.

CATLING, S. J. and CONNER, C. (1981). 'The influence of learning theory on the teaching of geography'. In: MILLS, D. (Ed) *Geographical Work in Primary and Middle Schools*. Sheffield: Geographical Association.

CHANDLER, S. *et al.* (1981). *The New Approach to the Social Studies: Continuity and Development in Children's Learning Through First, Middle and High School*. London: Schools Council.

COOPER, K. R. (1976). *Evaluation, Assessment and Record-keeping in History, Geography and Social Science*. London: Collins-ESL/Bristol.

COTTERELL, J. L. (1982). 'Student experiences following entry into secondary school', *Educational Research*, 24, 4, pp. 296–302.

DEAN, J. (1980). 'Continuity'. In: RICHARDS, C. (Ed) *Primary Education Issues for the Eighties*. London: Charles Black Ltd.

DERRICOTT, R. (1977). *Themes in Outline*. London: Collins-ESL/Bristol.

DERRICOTT, R. and BLYTH, W. A. L. (1979). 'Cognitive development: the social dimension'. In: FLOYD, A. (Ed) *Cognitive Development in the School Years*. London: Croom Helm and Open University Press, pp. 284–316.

DERRICOTT, R. and RICHARDS, C. (1980). 'The middle school curriculum: some uncharted territory'. In: HARGREAVES, A. and TICKLE, D. (Eds) *Middle Schools: Origins, Ideology and Practice*. London: Harper Row.

DODDS, P. and LAWRENCE, I. (Eds) (1984). *Curricular Continuity: Fact or Fiction?* West London Institute of Higher Education.

DOWLING, J. R. (1979). The prediction of children's adjustment after transfer to secondary school. Unpublished M. Ed. thesis, Cardiff University.

ELDER, R. and HEWITT, G. (1981). 'Liaisons not so dangerous', *Teaching English*, **14**, 3, pp. 24–7.

ELLIOTT, G. (1980). *Oxford New Geography: A Course for Juniors.* Books 1–3. Oxford: OUP.

EWING, B. T. (1983). Continuity and assessment of curriculum from middle schools into a secondary school: a case study. Unpublished M. Ed. thesis, University of Liverpool.

FLOYD, A. (Ed) (1979). *Cognitive Development in the School Years.* London: Croom Helm and Open University Press.

FREEMAN, B. (1981). 'Primary-secondary liaison: a positive beginning', *Teaching Geography*, **6**, 4, 175.

FULLAN, M. and POMFRET, A. (1977). 'Research in curriculum and instruction implementation', *Review of Educational Research*, **47**, 2, 335–97.

GAGNÉ, R. M. (1966). 'The learning of principles'. In: KLAUS-MEIER, H. J. and HARRIS, C. W. (Eds) *Analysis of Concept Learning.* New York: Academic Press, 1966.

GALTON, M. and SIMON, B. (Eds) (1980). *Progress and Performance in the Primary Classroom.* London: Routledge and Kegan Paul.

GALTON, M., SIMON, B. and CROLL, P. (1980). *Inside the Primary Classroom.* London: Routledge and Kegan Paul.

GALTON, M. and WILLCOCKS, J. (Eds) (1983). *Moving from the Primary Classroom.* London: Routledge and Kegan Paul.

GEOGRAPHICAL ASSOCIATION (1953). *Geography in the Primary School* (2nd Edn.) Sheffield: Geographical Association.

GEOGRAPHICAL ASSOCIATION (1959). *Teaching Geography in the Junior Schools.* Sheffield: Geographical Association.

GEOGRAPHICAL ASSOCIATION (1981). *Geography in the School Curriculum.* Sheffield: Geographical Association.

GILLESPIE, M. (1978). The transition from primary to secondary mathematics. Unpublished M. A. (Ed.) thesis, Queen's University, Belfast.

GRAVES, N. (1972). 'First we must understand how children think', *Times Educational Supplement*, 28 April 1972.

GRAVES, N. (1975). *Geography in Education*. London: Heinemann Educational Books.

GRAVES, N. (1979). *Curriculum Planning in Geography*. London: Heinemann Educational Books.

GRAVES, N. (Ed) (1982). *New UNESCO Source Book for Geography Teaching*. Harlow, Essex: Longmans.

GREAT BRITAIN. DEPARTMENT OF EDUCATION AND SCIENCE (1972). *New thinking in school geography*. Educ. pamphlet no. 59. London: HMSO.

GREAT BRITAIN. DEPARTMENT OF EDUCATION AND SCIENCE (1974). *School geography in the changing curriculum*. Education Survey 19. London: HMSO.

GREAT BRITAIN. DEPARTMENT OF EDUCATION AND SCIENCE (1978a). *Primary Education in England – a Survey by HM Inspectors of Schools*. London: HMSO.

GREAT BRITAIN. DEPARTMENT OF EDUCATION AND SCIENCE (1978b). *The teaching of ideas in geography*. HMI series: Matters for Discussion 5. London: HMSO.

GREAT BRITAIN. DEPARTMENT OF EDUCATION AND SCIENCE (1979a). *Local Authority Arrangements for the School Curriculum – Report on Circular 14/77*. London: HMSO.

GREAT BRITAIN. DEPARTMENT OF EDUCATION AND SCIENCE (1979b). *Aspects of Secondary Education in England*. London: HMSO.

GREAT BRITAIN. DEPARTMENT OF EDUCATION AND SCIENCE (1981a). *A View of the Curriculum*. HMI series: Matters for Discussion 11. London: HMSO.

GREAT BRITAIN. DEPARTMENT OF EDUCATION AND SCIENCE (1981b). *A Framework for the School Curriculum*. London: HMSO.

GREAT BRITAIN. MINISTRY OF EDUCATION (1959). *Primary Education*. London: HMSO.

GREAT BRITAIN. MINISTRY OF EDUCATION (1960). *Geography and Education*. Pamphlet No. 39. London: HMSO.

HADOW REPORT. GREAT BRITAIN. BOARD OF EDUCA-
TION. CONSULTATIVE COMMITTEE (1926). *The Education
of the Adolescent*. London: HMSO.

HADOW REPORT. GREAT BRITAIN. BOARD OF EDUCA-
TION. CONSULTATIVE COMMITTEE (1931). *The Primary
School*. London: HMSO.

HALL, D. (1976). *Geography and the Geography Teacher*. London:
Unwin Educational Books.

HAMPSHIRE EDUCATION AUTHORITY (1980). *Paths to
Understanding. A Handbook of Religious Education in Hampshire
Schools*. Basingstoke: Globe Education.

HARGREAVES, A. (1982). 'The rhetoric of school-centred evaluation', *Journal of Curriculum Studies*, **14**, 3, 251–66.

HARGREAVES, A. and TICKLE, L. (Eds) (1980). *Middle Schools:
Origins Ideology and Practice*. London: Harper and Row.

INNER LONDON EDUCATION AUTHORITY (1981). *The
Study of Places in the School*. ILEA Curriculum Guides. London:
ILEA.

JENNINGS, K. and HARGREAVES, D. J. (1981). 'Children's
attitudes to secondary school transfer', *Journal of Educational
Studies*, 35–9.

LONG, M. and ROBERSON, B. (1966). *Teaching Geography*.
London: Heinemann Educational Books.

MacDONALD, B. and WALKER, R. (1976). *Changing the
Curriculum*. London: Open Books.

MARLAND, M. (1977). *Language Across the Curriculum*. London:
Heinemann.

MARSDEN, W. E. (1976). *Evaluating the Geography Curriculum*.
Edinburgh: Oliver and Boyd.

MARTIN, K. (1980). *Oxford New Geography: A Course for Juniors,
Book 4*. Oxford: OUP.

MEYENN, R. and TICKLE, L. (1980). 'The transition model of
middle schools. Two case studies'. In: HARGREAVES, A. and
TICKLE, L. (Eds). *Middle Schools: Origins, Ideology and
Practice*. London: Harper and Row, pp. 139–58.

MILLS, D. (Ed) (1981). *Geographical Work in Primary and Middle
Schools*. Sheffield: Geographical Association.

MURDOCH, W. M. (1966). The effect of transfer on the level of children's adjustment to school. Unpublished M. Ed. thesis, University of Aberdeen.

NAISH, M. (1982). 'Mental development and the learning of geography'. In: GRAVES, N. (Ed) *New UNESCO Source Book for Geography Teaching*. Harlow, Essex: Longmans.

NEAL, P. D. (1975). *Project 5 – Continuity in Education*. Educational Development Centre, Birmingham: City of Birmingham Education Department.

NEW ZEALAND. DEPARTMENT OF EDUCATION (1977). *Social Studies Syllabus Guidelines*. Wellington, New Zealand: Department of Education.

NISBET, J. D. and ENTWISTLE, N. J. (1969). *The Transition to Secondary Education*. London: University of London Press.

NOLAN, M. B. (1979). Analysis of pupils' self-reports of adaption to the transition to secondary school. Unpublished M.A.(Ed.) thesis abstract, Queen's University, Belfast.

NORTHAMPTONSHIRE EDUCATION COMMITTEE (1979). *Humanities: A Curriculum Guideline for the Middle Years (8–14)*. Northamptonshire Education Committee.

OLIVER, D. (1982). 'The Primary Curriculum: A Proper Basis for Planning'. In: RICHARDS, C. (Ed) *New Directions in Primary Education*, pp. 111–34. Lewes: Falmer Press.

OWEN, J. T. (1981). Curriculum continuity: relations between middle and third tier schools. Unpublished M.Ed. thesis, Liverpool University.

OXFORDSHIRE COUNTY COUNCIL (1978). *A Scheme for the Humanities 9–13: History, Geography, Social Science*. Oxford, Communications Centre.

OXFORDSHIRE DEVELOPMENT EDUCATION UNIT (1981). Curriculum Continuity in Development Education: a 'strategy grid'. Research Project, Oxford Polytechnic, Department of Education.

PETERS, R. S. (Ed) (1969). *Perspectives on Plowden*. London: Routledge and Kegan Paul.

PIGGOTT, C. A. (1977). Transfer from primary to secondary education – from selection to continuity. Unpublished M.A. thesis, University of Southampton.

PLOWDEN REPORT. GREAT BRITAIN. DEPARTMENT OF EDUCATION AND SCIENCE. CENTRAL ADVISORY COUNCIL FOR EDUCATION (ENGLAND) (1967). *Children and their Primary Schools*. London: HMSO.

RICHARDS, C. (Ed) (1982). *New Directions in Primary Education*. Lewes: Falmer Press.

ROSS, A. M., RAZZELL, A. G. and BADCOCK, E. M. (1975). *The Curriculum in the Middle Years*. Schools Council Working Paper, No. 55. London: Evans/Methuen Educational.

ROUSSEAU, J. J. (First published 1780). *Emile*. Everyman's Library Edn. (1911). Trans. B. Foxley.

ROWBOTHAM, D. (1982). 'Can we do fieldwork in primary schools?', *Teaching Geography*, 8, 2, 75–7.

SCHOOLS COUNCIL (1972). *Education in the Middle years*. Working Paper no. 42. London: Evans/Methuen Educational for the Schools Council.

SCHOOLS COUNCIL (1975). *The Curriculum in the Middle Years*. Working Paper no. 55. London: Evans/Methuen Educational for the Schools Council.

SCHOOLS COUNCIL (1981). *The Practical Curriculum*. Working Paper no. 70. London: Methuen Educational.

SCHOOLS COUNCIL (1983). *Primary Practice. A sequel to the Practical Curriculum*. Working Paper 75. London: Methuen Educational.

SIMON, A. and WARD, L. O. (1980). 'A comparison of grammar and secondary modern school pupil anxiety prior to comprehensive re-organisation', *Counsellor*, 3, 1, 42–6.

SIMON, A. and WARD, L. O. (1981). 'A comparison of former grammar and secondary modern school pupil anxiety subsequent to comprehensive re-organisation', *Counsellor*, 3, 3, 34–9.

SLIM, S. (1980). A study of the first year transition programme in a North Wales secondary school. Unpublished M.Ed. thesis, University College of North Wales, Bangor.

SMITH, D. J. (1981). 'Opinions of school, academic motivation and school adjustment in the first year of secondary education: a pilot study in West Yorkshire', *Educational Studies*, 7, 177–83.

SPELMAN, B. (1979). *Pupil Adaption to Secondary School: a study of transition from primary to secondary education and subsequent pattern of adjustment among 3050 pupils who first entered secondary school in September 1978*. Belfast: NICER.

STILLMAN, A. and MAYCHELL, K. (1984). *School to School: Local Authority and Teacher Involvement in Educational Continuity.* Windsor: NFER-Nelson.

STURGESS, D. (1979). 'Primary–secondary school liaison on mathematics teaching', *Maths in School*, **8**, 1, 26–7.

SZPAKOWSKI, Z. J. (1983). Continuity in curricular experience between primary and secondary schools with particular reference to the teaching of geography. Unpublished M.Ed. thesis, University of Liverpool.

TIDSWELL, V. (1981). 'The overlap between school and university geography'. In: WALFORD, R. (Ed) *Signposts for Geography Teaching*, pp. 106–12. Harlow, Essex: Longman.

UNESCO (1965). *Source Book for Geography Teaching.* London: Longmans.

UNIVERSITIES COUNCIL FOR THE EDUCATION OF TEACHERS (1982). *Postgraduate Certificate in Education Courses for Teachers in Primary and Middle Schools.* A further consultative report. London: UCET.

WALFORD, R. (Ed) (1981). *Signposts for Geography Teaching.* Harlow: Longman.

WARBURTON, S. J. (1981). The effects of different ages of transfer between pre-secondary and secondary schools on the nature and effectiveness of the sciences provision for children aged 10–14. Unpublished Ph.D. thesis, Wolverhampton Polytechnic.

WEST SUSSEX EDUCATION AUTHORITY (1980). *Science Horizons: The West Sussex Science 5–14 scheme.* Basingstoke: Globe Education.

WILSON, D. J. (1978). Patterns of co-operation between schools in East Cleveland. Unpublished M.Ed. thesis, Newcastle on Tyne University.

YOUNGMAN, M. B. and LUNZER, E. A. (1977). *Adjustment to Secondary Schooling.* Nottingham: Nottinghamshire County Council.

YOUNGMAN, M. B. (1980). 'Some determinants of early secondary school performance', *British Journal of Educational Psychology*, **50**, 43–52.